"A fine, unsettling work. Through Guy's heroine, Jonnie Dash, the novel is a chorus in praise of being."
——John A. Williams, author of
The Man Who Cried I Am and *Click Song*

"Lush . . . robust . . . multilayered."   ——*Hudson Valley Black Press*

"Interesting . . . thought-provoking. . . . Guy's descriptions of Haiti, its history, and its people are generous and sincere."
——*Virginian-Pilot*

"A psychologically harrowing and culturally acute tale. . . . As Guy adroitly meshes historical fact with emotional truths, she plumbs the depths of our collective suffering but, ultimately, holds out hope for redemption."   ——*Booklist*

"Intriguing . . . a story of resurrection and renewal."
——*Publishers Weekly*

"A powerful novel that takes us to the edge and over . . . a bold book, sexually explosive and peopled with unique characters."
——Louise Merriwether, author of
Daddy Was a Numbers Runner

"A multilayered landscape of colorful, robust characters that pull the reader into their web of deceit, love, and lustful urges."
——*Wilmington Journal*

"A highly compelling story."   ——*Multicultural Review*

ROSA GUY was born in Trinidad and emigrated to the United States at the age of seven. The prize-winning author of many books for young adults, including *Ruby and Friends*, and of the acclaimed novel *A Measure of Time*, she now lives in New York City.

ROSA GUY

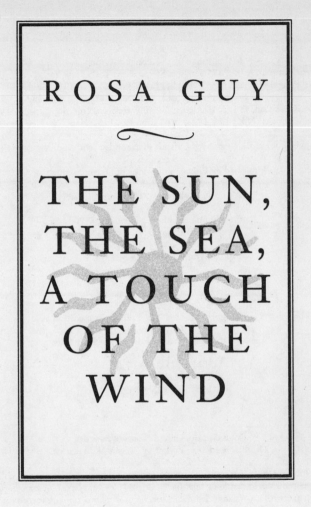

THE SUN, THE SEA, A TOUCH OF THE WIND

A PLUME BOOK

PLUME
Published by the Penguin Group
Penguin Books USA Inc., 375 Hudson Street, New York, New York 10014, U.S.A.
Penguin Books Ltd, 27 Wrights Lane, London W8 5TZ, England
Penguin Books Australia Ltd, Ringwood, Victoria, Australia
Penguin Books Canada Ltd, 10 Alcorn Avenue, Toronto, Ontario, Canada M4V 3B2
Penguin Books (N.Z.) Ltd, 182–190 Wairau Road, Auckland 10, New Zealand

Penguin Books Ltd, Registered Offices: Harmondsworth, Middlesex, England

Published by Plume, an imprint of Dutton Signet,
a division of Penguin Books USA Inc.
Previously published in a Dutton edition.

First Plume Printing, November, 1996
10 9 8 7 6 5 4 3 2 1

Ⓟ REGISTERED TRADEMARK—MARCA REGISTRADA

The Library of Congress has catalogued the Dutton edition as follows:
Guy, Rosa.
The sun, the sea, a touch of the wind / Rosa Guy.
p.   cm.
ISBN 0-525-24780-7 (hc.)
ISBN 0-452-27551-2 (pbk.)
PS3557.U93S86   1995
813'.54—dc20   95–7745
                                                  CIP

Printed in the United States of America
Original hardcover design by Steven N. Stathakis

PUBLISHER'S NOTE
This is a work of fiction. Names, characters, places, and incidents either are the product
of the author's imagination or are used fictitiously, and any resemblance to actual
persons, living or dead, events, or locales is entirely coincidental.

ALSO BY ROSA GUY

A Measure of Time
Bird at My Window
The Friends
Ruby
Edith Jackson
The Disappearance
Mother Crocodile
Mirror of Her Own

Dedicated to my sister Ameze, my niece Jean,
my son Warner, my nephew Kwsei Onwubuemeli,
and all those who walk the path of shadows
and dreams, protected only by a touch of madness.

—R.G.

ACKNOWLEDGMENTS

I am forever grateful for the Harlem Writers Guild, the organization that I helped found and in which I spent many years perfecting my gift as a writer, and to those other founding members: John Oliver Killins, John Hendrick Clark, Bill Ford, Audre Lord, Lonnie Elder, Sarah Wright, all searching for perfection, who, through those years, tirelessly encouraged other gifted artists, attempting to bring them to the forefront of the American literary scene. A special recognition to author William Banks, who, as its president today, is keeping the Harlem Writers Guild an active and a vital place for all aspiring writers.

And at this time, April 1995, at the death of Warner Guy, my son who was the anchor of my life, I do deeply thank: Marcia Gillispie; Louise Meriwether; Carol Faulkner; Brenda Joyce; my godchildren, Kathe and Eve Sandler; Joan Sandler; and Jean Genoud—for forming a wall of love and friendship on which I could lean in my despair. And to my sister-friend Maya Angelou, whose relentless presence, from afar, assured me that I had the strength—I had the strength.

Rosa Guy

BOOK
ONE

1

DRUMS. DISTANT DRUMS. The woman heard them. Leaving her bed she moved to the window to stare out. Hedges, trees, flaming poinsettias, shadows—shadows within shadows twisting into one solid wall of darkness. Night.

Drumbeats rising, rising, climbing over thickly woven shadows, spreading out, forging denseness. Denseness of the dark, earth, sky . . . Drums pounding, pounding on her ears, the cavities of her heart, pounding her, crushing her formless, merging her into the pulsing night. A nightmare . . . ?

"Gérard, Gérard!"

Had she called out? Had she screamed? Had her screams caused this trembling of the earth, the crumbling of the walls, unraveling shadows, uprooting trees? Had her screams turned the world upside down? Had she caused the deafening, splitting, splintering of the earth, opening the deep gorge into which she fell?

"Gé—rard! Gé—rard!"

A tomb! Dark, dark tomb! The stultifying darkness of the

tomb; the dust-filled darkness, ash-filled imprisoning darkness of the grave. Yet the drums beat. The drums beat. . . .

Or was it he who descended? Drifting down, his bright-as-the-sun phallus streaking the dark, his hard-as-a-rock phallus, to-his-knees phallus, sharp-as-a-scythe phallus slashing through the bones of her head, spilling her brains into her eyes, cleaving the wall of her chest, separating one part of her from the other. Still her heart beat. Still the drums.

Golden phallus slashing the flesh of her stomach. Guts, hot, gushing over her thighs. Womb flaccid, empty, falling to her feet. Blood. Blood filling her throat. Blood gagging, gagging, pushing through her mouth, oozing from nostrils, flowing through her eyes like tears.

Now he ascended. Bright-as-the-sun body soaring, hard-as-gold phallus burning. Christ-like he ascended, streaking up out of the dark earth leaving her charred, mutilated in the silent earth. Yet her heart pulsed, yet the drums beat. . . .

Silence.

Silence. Such silence. The drums had stopped. Yet her heart pounded, kept pounding. Her arms moved. Kept moving in time with her legs beating through water . . . dark, swirling water . . . two-three-four. A wall, turn, two-three-four.

Sweet water. Good water. Ash-melting water, dust-melting water . . . two-three-four, two-three-four. Saved? Truly saved? Oh, the magic of it. The pure magic of it.

She raised her head and saw the sky. Stars. Dark, dark sky, hundreds of stars. Pinpricks of stars dotting a blue-black sky. Two-three-four. A wall. The pool. The pool! Turn two-three-four. Keep the rhythm going, baby. Keep the rhythm going. . . .

Shadows. Winged shadows, hovering overhead. Wide-winged shadows. Diving. Wide-winged shadows, diving, hitting water, taking off. Shadows, silhouettes against the sky. Diving? Taking off? Bats? Bats!!! Keep the rhythm going. Thirsty bats! Keep the rhythm—what else? Laughter gurgled in her throat. Humor hadn't deserted her. Laughter in that silence. Tropical silence, the never-silent silence: loud, constant cacophony of night creatures creating a din too loud to be heard.

Swim. Swim. One end of the pool to the other, one end to the other. Alone. Yet not alone. Beyond the pool, behind the wall, the high wall carpeted with bougainvillea—behind the "separating us from them" wall—they slept: peasants, vendors, the homeless. They leaned on it for support, crouched beside it, desperation palpable, beating against the dark, slow, passing night, impatient for the day with its demands—begging, selling, scrounging for food. Waiting to walk on sunlit roads, searching out spots to piss and shit, to do all things that living things do.

She, too, yearned for night to pass. She, too, needed the sun to give form to things, to ease the pounding of her heart, the frantic quivering of her stomach.

Floating on her back, she lifted her arms to the air. They disappeared into the dark! She spread wide her fingers. They, too, blended into the night! She had seen shadows of bats! Why not her arms? Why not her hands?

A nightmare! Still a nightmare? The night swallowing orphans, spitting them in the sky as stars. Her fluttering heart threatening her rhythm. Panic. "Wake up, world! Wake up, all you mother's children! I'm here! Come touch me! Feel me! Fondle me! Certify my reality! Where's that goddamn son of a bitch of a moon?"

A star fell, hung low over the water. A low-hanging star. Her lucky star? Swimming, swimming . . . two-three-four.

Like the peasants, she dreaded eternal night. Dreaded the seal of debilitating darkness, dreaded the blotting out of things. Swim until movement mattered. Swim until sunrise, until thinking made her whole again. Oh, to piece together the tale of how and why she found herself swimming in the hotel pool with bats as companions on the darkest side of night? Coaxing herself to keep the rhythm going, baby, keep the rhythm going.

Her invisibility terrified her, made of her a thing suspended between earth and sky. But she had a star, a lucky star. She gazed at the star, saw it flicker, flicker again, travel through darkness, drop. A new flame erupted. A new star glowed—no, not a star—a cigarette. Someone out there smoking in the dark, looking at bats? At her?

She swam to the shallows, stood staring. A sudden breeze fanned her body. Shivering, she climbed out, moved toward the glow. Laughter. Then: "Thank God it's not attempted suicide."

"You see me?" she asked into the warm breath of laughter.

"After a fashion. It's bloody dark out here."

"Did you see me swimming?"

"Someone was out there swimming. If you say it was you, I'll go with that."

"You were waiting to see me drown!" she cried out, accusing. "You wanted to see me die!"

"Whatever for? Of course, if you wanted to . . . but if you didn't, God forbid. All you had to do was cry out, and I promise you I would have come to your rescue."

"So you did see me?"

"I did not. I felt you. First dashing by, then I heard the splash. The thought occurred that it might be someone fed up with life. Then your strokes, rather frantic at first, but you soon settled in. Good rhythm. Still I waited around, to be sure. You were at it for quite a while, a long while. Doing quite well indeed."

So someone had been watching over her—her lucky star. "I don't want to die," she said. "I never want to die!"

"My sentiment exactly." Teasing. "So I was damned pleased, I can assure you, when you didn't need my assistance, which very well might have brought me down to a watery grave."

"I often swim at night," she spoke in her defense. "It relieves my tension."

"One shouldn't have tension in paradise." Again his laughter, soft, teasing.

"Paradise?"

"Yes. Haiti. It's paradise to me."

Paradise—the word—released an eerie laughter in her head. "Why in paradise would one wait to come to the rescue of shadows?"

"For restless souls, driven out of their beds by all sorts of un-natural influences."

"Zombies?"

"Fellow sufferers." He laughed again.

His laughter, loud in the silent night, pleased. Standing shadow to shadow, watching the glow of his cigarette, pleased. The smell of him delighted her. The cigarette and whiskey smell of him. She liked the smell of whiskey on a man's breath. Inhaling the unfamiliar scent of his cologne excited her, forced her to react to a sudden need.

He moved. To go? She reached out to hold him there and touched instead his hand reaching out to her. His fingers touched her face, searching it like someone blind. Fingers moved over her eyes, her nose, her mouth, her hair.

"I haven't seen you around," he said.

"You don't see me now."

"I spent the last few weeks at the bar with Dominique—hours at times—and I haven't seen one Negro guest," he said, squeezing water from the thickness of her matted hair.

"Black," she corrected him.

"Black—girl or woman—or whatever."

"I've been staying at a cottage in the mountains," she said.

"Oh, an artist."

"How did you know?"

"I know Haiti. American artists are terribly attracted to its mountains. They are quite lovely."

"How did you know I'm American?" she asked.

"Your 'credentials.' Your hair—revolutionary vintage. Your accent—Yankee for sure—and the fact that you chose the mountains."

She wished he didn't know so much. It lessened the romance, the mystery, the force holding them in the realm of shadows, hovering outside of being. Nevertheless, she needed his acknowledgment, his living presence to certify her existence.

"And my loneliness?" she asked.

"That I can't speak of . . . but then perhaps that, too."

She shivered, leaned toward him. The silk of his robe touching her bare skin sent a terrible heat washing through her. She pushed against him, moved her legs, trying to walk through him, to merge with him.

Pushed off balance, he encircled her with his silk-clad arm to stabilize himself. "Hel-lo, what have we here?" he whispered at the feel of her naked body. His whisper made everything private, mysterious. Awareness flared around them, changing a chance encounter to one charged with intentions.

A bat flew overhead, dived into the water, squeaked, flew out into the distance. She forced him to lean against her, his weight to carry her down, down, down until her back pressed to the hard tiles of the floor.

Solid muscular thighs against hers. A firm, strong body. His broad back a bulwark against breezes. She opened her thighs to him. He entered her. One quick movement—hips went to meet his downward thrust. Anxiety, terror exorcised in one massive orgasm to his rapid ejaculation. A nameless union.

"Ahh—breaking the monotony?" he joked. Standing, wrapping himself in silk to protect his sudden fragility. She clutched at him. "Look here, my girl, I have earned my sleep. Let me get to it before this precious tranquillity evaporates." Sensing her desperation, he added, "Sleep is needed to replenish the reservoir."

Still she clutched his thighs, his hips, her lips searching past the silk of his robe to his shriveled penis. She pulled it into her mouth, and as it hardened she forced him down, pulling him ever deeper into her mouth. He threw off his robe, thrust his head between her thighs, nibbled her clitoris, pushed his tongue into the passage of her vagina. They gave themselves over to minutes of mind-emptying passion. After orgasm, they lay side by side wrapped around each other.

There they remained until the skies streaked pink, sending a band of color across the pool. Outside the bougainvillea-covered wall, the first sounds of those awakening reached them, and from the distance a clanging of the outside gates of the hotel warned of the imminent arrival of early morning workers. "This is the way lovemaking should always be," he whispered. "Spontaneous, natural, without guilt."

Slowly she stood, stretched her body, her arms up toward the sky. She looked up at her fingers spread out, and at the sight of them outlined in the pink light of dawn, she murmured, "What pleasure. What pleasure."

"The only way one can feel alive," he said.

"It makes one never want to die." A hardly heard whisper.

"Then let's not. Let's not ever die."

Quickly she knelt again. Their bodies brushed, silk against silk. Again he entered her. Now, free from anxiety, from desperation, her pleasure contained, a flow of tenderness.

"Perfect." He stood up as workers could be heard coming nearer. "Absolutely perfect."

"Thank you." An overwhelming rush of gratitude brought those words. Gratitude toward this stranger, this shadow, who had guided her through a most agonizing time . . . of danger? "Thank you so very much," she repeated.

"Perhaps we'll see you later," he said. "Breakfast? Lunch?"

Did it matter? Did anything matter except the pure joy of being alive, well, and knowing she had been saved—from what? She didn't know. "Perhaps," she said. "Perhaps."

2

SHE OPENED HER EYES to the pressure of sunlight against her eyelids, squinted at the sun-sparkled windows over which someone had forgotten to draw the curtains, then pulled her head beneath the sheet, waiting for sleep to claim her once again. Instead, bells of alarm resounded through her, forcing her to uncoil, to sit up, to look around the depersonalized yet familiar room: the paintings of European scenery on the walls, the dresser with its oversize mirror, the stuffed chair with the floor lamp beside it, the desk, the long mirror on the bathroom door.

Her naked reflection in the mirror stared back. She slumped against the pillows, pulling the sheet up to her chin, closed her eyes. "Jonnie Dash," she murmured, "what are you doing back in this room at Old Hotel, when you went to sleep in your cottage in the mountain?" Why? How?

No answers appeared beneath her closed lids, so she opened her eyes to stare up at the ceiling. What had brought her back here when she had definitely decided that the hotel did not suit her particular needs?

Forcing her mind, she remembered supper—the *petit pain* and confiture which the maids, Marie and Damzel, had prepared before readying her bed. Before eating she had cleaned her brushes, putting them in their respective jars, preparing them for the next morning's work. She had eaten and had dressed for bed. She remembered getting into bed, happy at the thought that in the morning with a touch here, a touch there, her painting of old M'sieur Ambroise would be finished.

Had she? She tried opening up her mind further, to force away the curtain of darkness that hung over her movement when she awakened that morning. What morning? Yesterday's? Today's? What time was it now? She closed her eyes, straining. No, she didn't see the painting finished. That she would remember. Incredible then to find herself here, in this bed, when her work had been going so well.

M'sieur Ambroise? Had the old man gone to sit on the rock at the side of the road at sunrise? Was he sitting there still? She had to get back. Poor old man sitting on that hard stone, smiling, exposing black gums between his two remaining incisors, dried legs pushing out of ragged pants, elbows jutting out of ragged shirt, bare feet slapping the ground to circulate the flow of blood suspended from hours of sitting, posing. Did the dear man believe that she had deserted him?

Jonnie Dash gazed over her head at the bright windows. They winked back, giving no clues. "Hell, maybe I flew in through the window on a broomstick." She tried to laugh, grimaced instead. Still, that image might not have been too far off. She had hoped that her voyage from New York, over the ocean, to Haiti might put an end to her years of unexplained blackouts. Obviously not so. Still, she hadn't had one since her arrival—and that had been six months ago. Disappointment, chagrin spread through her, forcing her out of bed.

Standing in the center of the room, she made a note of its absolute neatness. Clothes had not been flung around as per her habitual disorder. No telltale signs of her occupancy. Nothing! The room was utterly lacking in intimacy. Things she had not taken to the mountains had obviously been packed away by Cécile, the girl Gérard had given to her as a personal maid—and guardian—a gift after thirty years of separation?

Thirty years . . . Jonnie studied her reflection in the mirror, the body of a stranger: small breasts, still-muscular legs, stomach stretched to flatness. A stranger. She dove back in bed and beneath the covers, pulling the sheet up to her chin.

Gérard, Gérard, Gérard! Did he know yet that she had left? What to say if he didn't know? She had made life a misery, forcing him to ask his old friend Madame Raymond to move her tenants out of his cottage, so that Jonnie Dash might have her *"petite maison dans les montagnes."* She had had to work. And then to leave! Why had she come back here?

Sounds at the door drew her attention as the girl Cécile came in. She went directly to the closet, opened it, and began taking down Jonnie's valises. Next she went to the dresser, opened the drawers, and began pulling out Jonnie's remaining garments.

Jonnie studied the seventeen-year-old. Claire had made her part of the hotel staff—to please Gérard—when Jonnie had gone to her mountain retreat. She had on the black cotton dress with starched white apron worn by the other maids. It emphasized her fragility: tiny bones, copper-toned skin, thin arms and legs. Good-looking, except when she spoke or smiled, exposing her rotten front teeth, which she self-consciously tried to hide with her hand.

Sensing Jonnie's scrutiny, Cécile raised her eyes. They met Jonnie's through the mirror. Immediately her hand went to cover her mouth. *"Mais madame—vous êtes là?"*

"Oui, Cécile, je suis ici."

"Mais non, madame," Cécile protested. *"Je croyais que vous êtiez à Fermath."*

"Non, Cécile, I'm not in the village of Fermath, as you see. Here I am back at Old Hotel, Port-au-Prince, *n'est-ce pas?"*

"Mais non-oui." Cécile gazed at Jonnie confounded. As well she might be. Fermath was a long way up the mountains—past Pétionville, past La Boule, almost to the approach to Kenscoff, the town highest on the mountain range. What if the girl asked her how she had come? Who had brought her? She had no answers.

"Madame, what I must do? Madame Claire, she tell me pack your *vêtements.* She say M'sieur Gérard—he come today to take them."

So now it was definite; Gérard didn't know she was here. It hadn't been he at any rate who had brought her down. Which narrowed things somewhat, but it also made them more confusing.

"Faire la valise, madame?" Cécile asked.

"Non! Don't touch my things!" Cécile jumped at her sharp response. Jonnie softened her tone. "I'll explain to Madame Claire." Her sharpness had surprised her as much as it had Cécile.

Relieved of that responsibility, Cécile walked toward the

door. On her way she picked up something from the floor and puzzled over it before putting it at the foot of the bed. Jonnie waited for the door to close behind the girl before reaching for it.

She had recognized the floral design on her long-sleeved flannel nightgown that she remembered having put on for bed. The garment, now tattered beyond recognition, held clumps of dirt and dried leaves. Jonnie examined her body. No cuts, no bruises. The soles of her feet were perfectly clean. Unreal . . .

"If Cécile hadn't talked to me, I'd swear that I'm a fucking ghost."

Wrapping the sheet around her, she went to stand at the window, grateful that hers was the last of the row of cabinlike rooms, an annex built to enlarge Old Hotel while preserving its elegance. A corner room, it offered an uncluttered view of the back gardens. The back gardens, too, became a natural barrier against interlopers. Thick, lovely, they rolled back to meet the impenetrable forest— lovely in its own right but disquieting in its density and the sounds of its myriad occupants that defied category.

With a sigh, Jonnie raised her eyes to the distant mountains: remote, picture-postcard perfect, presiding over all—the gardens, forests, the entire island.

Indescribable the pleasure she found living up there, in those mountains, awakening with the peasants, listening to their calls, in Creole, as they made ready for work. Donkeys brayed, roosters crowed, every animal alert at the first hint of day.

She, too, joined the workforce, painting from the side of her cottage, watching women bearing baskets heavy with provisions on their heads, making their daily trek down the mountainside; men astride their mules forcing obedience from those stubborn beasts with a kick of bare heels; *camionettes* coming down from Kenscoff, bulging with market women—loud, arguing, laughing— bags and boxes strapped to the tops and the backs of the vehicles braving the precarious narrow slopes down to the small markets in Pétionville and the larger Iron Market in Port-au-Prince.

Evenings, her day's work done, she waited on the porch for the procession: the return trip—women walking more slowly, empty baskets and trays on their heads; *camionettes* packed with women, now silent, the measure of a burdened day. Yet as darkness fell, the drums sounding through the night from some unknown village, voices raised in song, told of laborers throwing off weariness, drawing on some inexhaustible source of strength, to join neighbors and other villagers at places of worship.

Haiti. The Pearl of the Antilles, Christopher Columbus had called it. Or had it been Jamaica? Or Cuba? Whichever. Each island claimed the praise of that explorer as their own even as the United States claimed him as its discoverer. Just as they all laid claim to the song "Yellow Bird," sung in English in former British possessions, in French on French-speaking islands, in Spanish in former Spanish colonies. Each island claiming to be unique while fighting passionately over flimsy memorabilia from a past that underlined their sameness: beautiful islands in the sun, a lifestyle of ingrained poverty for blacks, middle-class pretensions or wealth generally determined by the amount of European blood inherited. All legacy of a colonial, imperial slave past, the shackles from which the Western Hemisphere kept struggling to be free.

She, Jonnie Dash, had chosen Haiti to continue her own struggle. Because of its history? Because of Gérard? Perhaps because she had found it impossible to work in New York?

Nor had she found it easy to work here—until she went to the mountains. So why? How did she find herself back here?

In the shower she let hot water beat down on her head, then cold sprays tingle her, shocking her memory alert. It had never worked before. But she was no longer completely alone with only herself to answer to. There were people around, people she dared to consider friends. Did she tell them that she had come down from the mountains in good form, and indeed remained so, although her nightgown was in tatters while she remained unscratched. That she had danced over the treetops, flown like a bird through forests, charged about the countryside on a pitchfork before entering her old room to rest?

Jonnie laughed, enjoying the possibility, yet denying herself the wish to melt into fantasy in a world where fantasies abound. She grew serious. No, she didn't believe in fairy tales. Life had not allowed that.

Slowly she began her morning routine, preparing for the day: oiling her smooth, dark brown skin, massaging muscular thighs, torso, arms, face. Gazing into the mirror, she slapped her stomach, caressed her breasts, massaged the taut muscles of her shoulders, her neck.

Her skin held her together beautifully. She now worked hard to maintain it—a bulwark against years of shattered vanity. She loved her body. She loved bodies. She painted them well. Never did she remember a time when the human anatomy had not evoked her passionate interest.

Yet, all during her growing-up years—right into her thirties, she had completely overlooked her own body, never seeing herself through her body, only through her work. In the first few decades of her life she refused to accept that women used beautiful bodies and clothes as weapons. She had preferred to believe the man of the cloth: the way through the gates of Paradise is through purity of the soul. By the time she had understood that lie, she had gone into many a battle with some damned shabby weapons, losing every one. "Goddamn sons of bitches, liars," she blurted in a flash of anger. In her thirties she began to care about clothes, makeup, things like that. Not to compete. Never to compete. One never competed with the Deloreses and Friedas—the Black bourgeoisie. Intellectuals born with the knowledge of clothes, a knowledge that they never taught, preferring instead to preach the gospel of Black Liberation, pointing to their less fortunate sisters as examples of oppression while offering themselves as proof of the limitless possibilities of a free and progressive society.

Style. She had had to develop her own. White on black had been her decision. White simplified her life, released her from the terror of having to consider what color went with what color, what went with her complexion. Work had not allowed her the time.

White on black was high drama for all occasions. White in all materials. For the pool she chose a white latex bikini. Over it she slipped her white batiste coverall—easy, attractive, and, she hoped, sexy. Yes, sexy.

Cécile had come into the room with flowers while Jonnie was dressing and pretended to arrange them while covertly studying Jonnie. And Jonnie, aware of the attention, exaggerated making up: drops to brighten the whites of her eyes, a dusting of powder, protection against the sun. She searched in the drawer for her Afro pick. In the mirror she caught Cécile's exasperation as she picked through her hair's thickness.

"*Mais, madame,*" the girl pouted, "*pourquoi vois ne faites vous pas vos cheveux comme toutes les blanches?*"

"*Parce que je ne suis pas blanche,*" Jonnie snapped with the habitual rush of anger. It made no difference. The Haitian poor, the peasants, insisted on calling her *la blanche,* meaning, of course, American.

Her first—and only—time alone in the commercial center of Port-au-Prince, peasants had pointed at her, laughing at "*la blanche aux cheveux frisés.*" The white woman with the kinky hair. First two, then three, then dozens. Drivers had stopped to see what was so amusing, creating a traffic jam for blocks. With half of Port-au-Prince following at her heels, laughing and jeering, Jonnie had appealed to the drivers with her eyes, expecting help from the more enlightened. They all had turned their heads, waited for the traffic light, then taken off. She had quickened her steps. So had her pursuers. She walked fast, faster, then started to run. They ran, too. The hecklers became abrasive with their humor. Finally she had ducked into a government building along the corniche and waited for guards to disperse her tormentors. Even so, she had waited hours before having the courage to slink out of the building, then had hidden in shadows until hailing a taxi back to the hotel.

She had wanted to pretend she didn't understand their laughter. But she did. It had happened to her in the States every time she stepped into a subway train, her hair not straight. Black women used to turn from her or stick their heads into newspapers to read until they or she left the train—ashamed or angered by her betrayal. Until the Black Revolution. Yet it had been easier for her to understand Americans. But here, in Haiti? Was she betraying Haitians? All of them?

Jonnie kept lifting her hair, constantly aware of Cécile's disapproving stare. Slowly she brushed her eyebrows, wiped her teeth dry with a towel to bring out a dull shine, applied colorless lipstick to gloss her lips. Finished, she posed in the mirror, then winked at Cécile. Automatically Cécile's hand went to her mouth. She giggled.

"*Madame est toujours belle,*" she said. "So beautiful."

"*Merci, merci.*" Jonnie rewarded the girl with a smirk. "But why do I always have to work so goddamn hard for such a little compliment?"

Jonnie stepped out in the sun and adjusted her sunglasses to its glare before strolling across the grassy island that separated the annex from the main building. Habit forced her to pause and turn to look over the winding traffic lanes toward the guarded gates, where vendors hawked their wares to incoming or outgoing tourists and where the poor and homeless kept their hands pushed through the bars in supplication, while gatekeepers used their batons with vicious abandon, keeping the would-be intruders at the other side of the restraining barriers.

With great effort Jonnie pulled herself away and continued her passage to Old Hotel. The charming structure had once been the palace of one of Haiti's presidents. The floors above remained steeped in old-world charm and elegance, French provincial furnishings, reminiscent of colonial days. The main floor, however, had been completely transformed, modernized by the use of sliding glass panels, easily moved to form rooms or to separate them from one another. Panels that when all rolled back created one massive room, called the grand ballroom, used every Monday for Gala Night—an affair that each of the island's hotels held on a different night to share in the bounty of the limited tourists visiting the island.

Walking up the steps into the corridor, Jonnie stopped and closed her eyes as familiar smells rushed to surround her. So she had missed the place after all. She turned right to enter the long, narrow barroom through which she strolled, looking out of its glass walls, searching the well-landscaped pool area for Claire.

Tables had already been set for drinks and snacks, enticing those on the terrace who might have lingered after breakfast. A few people were swimming. But Jonnie did not see Claire, or Sam. She walked to the place she usually occupied at the end of the bar and waited for Dominique bent over behind chipping ice.

"*Bonjour*, Dominique," she finally said, not expecting him to stop until he had finished. He straightened up, and seeing who had greeted him, cried, surprised, "*Mais, c'est toi?*"

"*Oui, c'est moi.*" She gazed into his eyes, tiny beneath his thick framed silver-rimmed glasses. She had missed him, too.

"What you do? You come back? You stay? You go back?"

Jonnie shrugged. She didn't know. She kept studying his black, round cherub face, the skin beneath his eyes magnified by the thick lenses. His surprise seemed genuine. No, he hadn't seen her last night—or the night before or whenever she had made her mysterious return.

"So, you quit me," he said, half joking. "Now you want that I take you back? You hurt me here, you know." He placed both hands over his heart.

"I gave you a rest, Dominique," she teased. "But you have had it. You got me to watch over again."

"Okay. Okay. So now I make you my rum punch?"

"Not now, Dominique. I'm looking for Claire—or Sam. Have you seen them?"

"They around." He waved his hand. "Maybe in the office. Maybe the pool."

A customer approached the bar. But after Jonnie's long absence Dominique seemed reluctant to leave her. "You look in their room?" She shook her head no. Dominique also knew that the last place to find the proprietors of the hotel would be their rooms. Finally he moved from her, but as she started toward the door, he called out, "Jonnie Dash, you know M'sieur Charles?" He indicated the newcomer who sat on the stool near the entrance. "Come. You must meet him." Dominique beckoned to her. "M'sieur Charles is your new American attaché, or counselor—something like that—at your embassy. M'sieur Charles McCellen, you must meet our Jonnie Dash."

Dominique enjoyed introducing his customers. Sensitive to others' needs, he liked to think that he created for them a home away from home. Jonnie looked over at the young redheaded man, smiling. He, too, looked at her, ready with his smile. Then he raised his green eyes, saw her hair, and his smile vanished. His eyes assumed a total blankness, his nostrils flared, just perceptibly.

"Scotch and soda, Dominique," he demanded. Hostile, hostile, hostile. Jonnie wanted to joke. Instead, anxiety threatened. Her heart quickened, the hairs at the back of her neck bristled.

If before the 1960s she had suffered the scorn of Black Americans because she wore her hair in an Afro, after the sixties it had been the suspicions and downright animosity of white American officialdom—police, and one supposed the CIA or FBI—with whom she and the thousands of young Blacks who had decided to wear their hair "au naturel" had to contend.

Jonnie stared over Dominique's head at the liquor bottles lining the shelves behind him, sorry for him, that his customers' American paranoia had shattered his good intentions.

What threat did this young redhead, with his character, already screwed up behind his plastic diplomat mask, imagine that she posed to him and his country because she wore her hair natural? Did he really see her as a rebel? A terrorist? An enemy of the system? Terrifying to think that those in control of gunboats offshore, those who covertly represented the power on this tiny island and the surrounding islands saw a Black American woman's hair, worn natural, as a threat.

Whirling fans overhead sounded loud in the unbearable silence. Shouts from the pool as from a distant planet invaded the bar. To put Dominique at ease as well as to prove to herself she could speak without a stutter Jonnie said, "Dominique, what's with the Black Rose—dear André. I missed him, too."

"André?" Dominique cried, delighted to have a subject with which to break the strange silence. "Hey Jonnie, *toujours* André? But why you want him? Look at me. I'm here, *non?*"

"You're here, yes, you fine thing, you," Jonnie teased the round, short bartender. "And you got to know that we'll give it a try—at least one time, *n'est-ce pas?*"

They laughed, enjoying the games they played. And as they laughed Jonnie sensed the young man studying her, going through those mental handbooks in which the myth persisted that Black women who believed "Black and beautiful" were un-American. No one had stopped to tell the assholes that that fad had gone out of fashion. Real shit. To be in a totalitarian country and unable to call on one's representative if one needed help? Where did one go? Old anxieties, the familiar twisting of her stomach. Did it ever stop? She kept laughing with Dominique to cover her uneasiness.

Jonnie found Claire in the alcove crammed with fifteen years of old newspapers and magazines that she and Sam called their office. "Hey," she called. But Claire's head stayed bent over a *Newsweek.* Jonnie removed a stack of magazines from the other chair in the room and sat down, waiting.

"Now," Claire looked up finally, two red spots of anger burning her cheeks, "they're accusing Nixon of stonewalling. They are actually talking of appointing a special prosecutor to investigate our president! How dare they!"

Relief flooded Jonnie. Thank God she hadn't done a Rip Van Winkle. Watergate had been headline news when she went up to the mountains. Watergate was still in the headlines.

"A sitting president is entitled to executive privileges," Claire said, anger expanding. "Don't you agree?"

Jonnie picked up an old *Newsweek* and pretended to read. Nixon and Watergate were the farthest things from her mind. Watergate had been and still was a clear case of miscalculation, an accident bound to happen anywhere men exchanged their souls for power and money. Nixon's personality dictated that at the pinnacle of power he would abuse power. Whatever the talk of democracy, millions of dollars exchanged hands behind the waving flags, the handshakes, the deafening screams of patriots.

"After all," Claire said, nettled by Jonnie's unresponsiveness, "he is the leader of the free world!"

At that moment a big, Black, uniformed Haitian general appeared in the doorway. Hearing Claire's pronouncement, he grinned, exposing a mouthful of gold crowned teeth. "Madame Levine, please, I am looking for your husband."

The general's arrival rendered them silent. There was so much about him to see—his decorations, the big guns strapped around his waist with accompanying ammunition. A startling presence, he filled the room and beyond to the portals of the hotel—a reminder that even subjects of the free world, with their plastic-faced diplomats and the gunships outside the harbor, had to tread carefully.

"Have you looked down by the pool, General? He might be there. It's time for his massage." The general bowed to her, withdrew. Seeing mockery reflected in Jonnie's eyes, Claire's cheeks flamed.

Jonnie grinned. She liked to see Claire angry. Without the ordinary conflicts of prejudice, dishonesty, cowardice, or arrogance that etched character on the faces of others, Claire's little-girl chinless face remained remarkably uninteresting—except in anger. Indeed, Claire reminded Jonnie of the old-fashioned long-legged dolls popular in the 1930s: blond hair, round, expressionless blue eyes, clear porcelain skin that refused to tan.

Claire and Sam lived simple lives in their rambling mansion. They had two preteen boys staying with Sam's retired parents, going to school in Florida. They ran Old Hotel with their underpaid staff, absolving their guilt by comparing the salaries they paid with the lower salaries paid by the Haitian elite who owned plush mountaintop hotels. Jonnie liked Claire for one simple reason. Claire liked her.

"For God's sake, Jonnie, what are you doing back here?" Claire asked.

"Have you any plans for my room?" Jonnie countered.

"No. God, haven't you noticed how slack things are around here? Tourists have been attacked in Jamaica, so the tourist trade has gone to Europe. You know how it is. Jamaica catches the flu, and Haiti gets put to bed.

"But what happened? Gérard told me he was sending someone to pick up the rest of your things today. I sent Cécile to pack them. She tells me you're back. To stay, Jonnie? What's happened between you and Gérard?"

"Nothing happened," Jonnie answered. Nothing had.

"Not that you would tell." Claire pouted. "Jonnie Dash, you are the most secretive person. At any rate, I'm glad to see you. And of course your room is there—for as long as you want." Then, to show Jonnie she had not been let off the hook she mimicked, "Oh, this is the dream for which I have been waiting. The most perfect spot in the most perfect setting. I'm going to work, work, work. I shall be happy, happy, happy." Then added: "And in six weeks, Jonnie? Six weeks! Here you are. Something had to have happened."

Six weeks? Had it only been six weeks? All that work in only six weeks. She had been happy. Still, if one had said six months, even six years, that would not have surprised her. But six weeks! God, how slowly time moved in Haiti.

"I wish you weren't so secretive, Jonnie."

That was it! Secrets! Secrets she had not told. Secrets she didn't know how to tell. All those lives lived. All those decisions carelessly made, never thought out. . . .

"Anyway, I'm glad you're back. I missed you. If you can't afford . . ."

"I can afford," Jonnie spoke sharply. She had money, damn it.

Granted, one rarely saw single Black American women paying for lengthy stays in luxury hotels, but she had told Claire that she had money—and certainly she was rich by anybody's standard. So why did Claire feel it necessary to treat her like a poor relation?

Outside the alcove waiters moved in slow motion, taking trays to and from the terrace. She wondered, suddenly, at an entire island in slow motion. Why? Because people had nowhere to go? Nothing to do? One of her first and most lasting impressions was of a peasant, a man sitting at the front of his shack at sunrise, shifting only to follow the shade, eventually finding himself sitting again at the front of his shack at sunset.

Perhaps the slow movement had something to do with the awesome reality of complete lack of roads, keeping other cities, other towns just outside the bounds and impulses of Port-au-Prince. The absence of roads making all things just out of reach, supporting sensations of places yet to be discovered—tomorrow.

Yes, the pace of life in the mountains suited her. "M'sieur Ambroise appearing mornings, day after day. Painting throughout those long sunny days touched by breezes. So, so restful. M'sieur Ambroise, patient, gaunt, unmoved by peasants standing around, admiring his likeness springing to form on the canvas. Nor had his patience fled when the admiration had changed to something else—murmurs, protests. Suddenly, their plush surroundings had changed into an unremitting bleakness, the bleakness she had seen in M'sieur Ambroise's toothless smile. The peasants had laughed. Why did they always have to laugh?

Aware that Claire had been attempting to read her thoughts and finding that impossible, Jonnie said, "It's my work, Claire. I think I must put distance between me and it before I make a final decision."

"Final decision?" Claire scoffed. "Isn't that why you left? Gérard thought you had made a final decision when he told Madame Raymond to get rid of her tenant for you. He thought you had made a final decision when he turned out his long-time friend . . ."

Of course that's not what she had meant. But then, what had she meant? Exhausted by her thoughts, their talk, and the cramped quarters, Jonnie stood up suddenly, walked from the room, and out onto the terrace. She refused to accept guilt, which

Claire appeared to be insisting on. In her relationship with Gérard, nothing had ever been fair: not her expectations nor his responses to them.

Claire followed Jonnie out to the terrace, and together they walked its length, Claire greeting the late breakfast guests. At the end of the terrace, they walked down the steps to the pool area, where beneath the shading palms waiters, with their white shirts and black bow ties, moved restlessly in preservice boredom. Swimmers splashed around in the pool. The general stood over Sam, his head thrown back in gold-toothed laughter, while Sam, flat on his back on the massage table, his flabby belly being kneaded by the hotel masseuse, kept giving out the jokes.

"Hey, Sam, howya doin'?" Jonnie stopped to speak as Claire walked on to sit at a table.

"You gotta see how I'm doing," Sam said, indicating his big stomach.

"Oh, man, you got to do something about that," Jonnie joked, "or we'll be using it as a welcome mat."

"What can I tell yah," Sam groaned. "Got a greed and a need. So I pay the price." Jonnie laughed. The general laughed louder, his tone indicating a friendship. And Jonnie asked herself, what war did he fight in to earn all those medals. And why come visiting with so much ammunition? Intimidation? Style? Both? Jonnie didn't really want to know. She walked on, joining Claire at the table.

Jonnie liked Sam. Liked that they spoke New Yorkese together. It told of the rigid structure governing lives lived in the States. She and Sam had lived in overlapping neighborhoods, yet had never met. They had been poor. They shared the language of poverty, having experienced ten-cent Saturday movies, nickel hot dogs with sauerkraut and free root beer. Depression kids who had known no other president before Roosevelt. No governor before Herbert Lehman. No mayor before Fiorello La Guardia. Kids out on cold street corners, hanging around grown men who made fires in the snow and stamped their feet to keep blood circulating. Kids out of Depression and right into War.

Sam had gone into the merchant marine. It was there he had met and made friends with Dominique—a friendship that became the reason he had come to Haiti. Young and carefree, he had gambled all his savings buying the house of a former president and leasing its land for ninety-nine years: this house that he had transformed into Old Hotel. Before that he had lived with and loved, it was said, a Haitian woman. But then he met and fell in love with the clear-eyed "Quaker girl" who had come to Haiti, a volunteer nurse at the Albert Einstein Hospital. Scandal! He hadn't cared then. He didn't care now. He had fallen in love.

Jonnie forgave them—the five-foot-five Jewish man and his six-foot Quaker wife—their fairy-tale existence, living happily ever after on their enchanted island, healthy, wealthy, and wisely enjoying life.

They sat across from each other, Jonnie and Claire, legs stretched out to the heat of the sun. Jonnie had recognized one of the swimmers: André Bienaimé. And with a thrill of pleasure she gazed out at him doing laps. Long graceful strokes, cutting cleanly through the water.

"I'm sorry that things are in a slump," she said. "How many guests do you have?"

"About forty couples—the annex is not close to full. But then we're used to it, Haiti is the Caribbean's stepchild. At any rate we can always depend on the Haitianophiles. Jessica Winthrop's here—with her companion," she added suggestively.

Old Hotel was the stop-off place for those who fell in love with the island. Its air of simplicity pleased them. Such visitors favored it over the more plush palaces of the Haitian elite.

"Who's Jessica Winthrop?" Jonnie asked.

"I told you about her," Claire said with an air of irritation. "She's the British aristocrat. She helps out at the hospital. She is a wonder. Tireless. She really makes a difference."

"I don't suppose you missed me, then," Jonnie teased. "Not with Her Ladyship around."

"Stop that, Jonnie. I really missed you. Jessica is up to her old tricks. I hear she's taken up with a young captain—Gilbert. I don't see much of her. This place has been a morgue. There's no one to gossip with."

"Since when do I earn high marks for gossip?"

"For listening. You are the perfect listener. Oh, and Jonathan Anderson's here, too."

"He's been here for a while, hasn't he? He was here before I left."

"That's right. Well, he's been to Santo Domingo since then, and back. But you said you didn't like him."

"I never said that," Jonnie protested. "I said he reminds me of a type I find distasteful. I haven't exchanged more than two words with the man."

"He's charming—and handsome," Claire said. "I'm glad he makes Old Hotel his home between islands. He's got a going concern in Santo Domingo. Now I hear he's about to set up something in Haiti. Lord knows why. He's got millions. I hear his wife's coming today. He left to pick her up at the airport while I was having breakfast. That I don't understand. The wife of Jonathan Anderson visiting Haiti. From what I hear she usually takes her vacation in the Swiss Alps. Why bring her here?"

"Why not? Even snobs can find something to like in Haiti."

"Gee, thanks." Claire resorted to sarcasm but immediately snapped her fingers, bringing Maurice to the table. "*Eau de coco pour moi,*" she said. Jonnie placed her order by putting up two fingers, without taking her eyes from the swimmer.

"Jonathan's a special breed of man. Oh, I always knew he had a family—kids. I understand his daughter just married his cousin—a man twice her age. But he's never mixed family life with business. He is . . . quite discreet. Know what I mean?" Jonnie shook her head no, she didn't. "At any rate his wife being here is bound to make things . . . interesting."

Jonnie grinned. "Lucky for me I came down. By next week this time you'll be so involved in intrigue you would have forgotten I existed."

"Nothing is interesting without someone to tell it to," Claire said. Maurice placed their coconut water on the table, and for the next few minutes they drank without stopping, then indicated that they wanted another.

"Coconut water must have been the nectar of the gods," Jonnie said. Coconut water was the thing she had missed the most in the mountains.

"The most refreshing drink in the world," Claire agreed.

Guests were appearing at the tables around them, and waiters moved briskly. André Bienaimé kept cutting through the water—strong, graceful, so very beautiful.

The sun moved to twelve o'clock high. Breezes stopped. The air dried the softness from voices, making them fall flat on the ears. A general movement of guests into the pool, swimming, playing, shouting to overcome the languor imposed by the heat. Fronds of the coconut palms hung still, listless. Claire and Jonnie simply sat while Jonnie looked at André Bienaimé. They roused themselves occasionally to sip the water or call for more.

Finally Claire roused herself to plead, "It's so romantic the way you two found each other, Jonnie. I don't want anything to happen. . . ." Irritated, Jonnie focused her eyes on André, allowing her admiration for him to be reflected on her face.

"Gérard's been unhappy for so long, Jonnie. Now that you have found each other—don't spoil things."

"We didn't find each other." Jonnie wanted to shout, I found Gérard. After thirty years I came to Haiti and I found Gérard. But her words had the habit of getting trapped between her intentions and her tongue. So she kept her gaze on André.

Claire reached for Jonnie's sunglasses and removed them. "Look at me, Jonnie Dash. I'm serious. Gérard comes from one of the best Haitian families. That means a lot—if you intend to stay here. Besides, he's handsome and crazy about you."

What a delight to listen to Claire's romantic illusions. Gérard, too, was a romantic. What was it about this little island that made illusion pour from the air—thick, heavy in the sultry movement of its slowly passing time? Illusions moved with the languid pace of cold molasses, spreading out effusive, sticky, rolling out to its shores where, pushed back by the sea, it gained in thickness, coyness, as it turned upon itself.

Since awakening to find herself in her hotel room, Jonnie had been suppressing sighs. Now one escaped. She smiled: a sigh, a draft between an empty mind and ancient fears. "Claire, I guess I need time."

Claire looked skeptical. She picked up her glass, finished her water, then said, "I do agree with you, Jonnie. This is the greatest nectar in the entire world."

Having reached a topic on which they agreed, they sat back

looking out at the swimmer until the Black Adonis rose from the
water, his body sparkling from the drops encasing him as though
in crystal.

"Jonnie Dash, Jonnie Dash." He walked directly to their
table, glad to see her. *"Mais,* you're here. Back with us. How
happy you make me." The handsomest man in the world smiled
down at her from atop his six feet three inches. He had broad
shoulders, a slim waist, and long white teeth that slashed across a
black face. Water dripping from his curly jet-black hair joined the
crystal droplets on his shoulders. How did one help loving him for
so much beauty?

"André, how could I stay away knowing you were down here
thinking of me?"

High and loud, his laughter rang out, demanding attention
from all. Even up on the terrace, diners looked down. A true nar-
cissist. André saw his beauty reflected in everyone's eyes. And this,
too, she loved. Certainly she allowed it to reflect brightly in her
eyes, flattering him as they moved to his muscled thighs, the soft
hairs beginning at his navel, disappearing into his white bikini, his
bulging crotch. . . .

"Your painting, *mon amie.* It's coming good?" he asked.

"It's coming good," she replied.

"Ahh, my fabulous friend." Pride in her sounded in his loud
voice. He wanted all around to hear about this artist—his friend.
His Black American friend. This pleased her. As did his eyes, ex-
amining her see-through coverall, then up into her eyes, flirting.
"You are too beautiful," he said.

Jonnie, too, exposed her white teeth broadly. He didn't think
her beautiful. He wanted to see her as beautiful. He needed to find
a deeper meaning of himself through her, her dark skin, almost as
dark as his; the way she wore her hair; her art. His need to be
more like her, when in reality he felt so different. "I love you, too,
André," she said.

"May I come to you, Jonnie Dash? Will you take time out
from your work to make a painting of me?"

"You don't have to travel so far, André. I'm back in my old
cabin, six-F."

They shrieked with laughter. Seeing Claire's scowl of disapproval, Jonnie said, "Sit, André. Let me buy you a drink and let's talk about it."

"You forget. I don't drink, Jonnie."

"A Coke?"

"If you insist."

"I insist."

"Then of course I accept." Again their loud laughter.

Laughter came easily between them, as did their meaningless flirtation. Yet beneath the banter there rested an undertow of seriousness—an attraction, one to the other, which neither wanted to examine. The time to examine had not yet come. Might never come. It remained unfocused, puzzling, unarticulated. To articulate it might give it a shameful connotation, which their sensibilities could not endure.

"*Voilà*, André," Maurice called to him. "Dominique."

Indeed, Dominique stood on the top step beckoning André. With him were two girls, both white—one blond, the other a redhead—both bubbling with the unsuppressed gaiety of the young and free.

"Ahh," he said, trying to sound disappointed. "Jonnie Dash, I must go. You must owe me this one."

"I'll hound you until I pay." Again they laughed, a laughter that forced every eye to follow André as he walked away, up the steps to his giggling teenagers. All were still watching when, putting an arm around each, André disappeared with the girls through the bar door.

"Close your mouth, Jonnie," Claire said. "Your disappointment is showing."

Jonnie smiled at her friend. Claire didn't know, had no way of understanding the intimate language their laughter concealed. "One supposes that being a proprietor of hotels gives one easy access into minds and intentions," she said, then regretted her sarcasm, which at any rate passed Claire's notice.

"It improves knowledge of P and P—people and pocketbooks. You can't afford André. Besides, he's too young for you."

Anger flashed through Jonnie. What right did she have to make such an assessment about someone or something of which she knew nothing? But again her anger passed. She did like Claire. "Hit me over the head so I can see," she quipped.

"What does an intelligent woman like you want with an André Bienaimé? Or is it that you are actually thinking of painting him?"

"To the second question, I doubt that I can capture the true André on canvas at this time. But to the first . . ," Jonnie gave a wicked grin. "I can do with a bit of his youth and beauty. Ahh, to see that young flesh against mine—not just see it hanging on my wall, okay?"

"I'm afraid you have to settle for friendship," Claire spoke in a superior tone. "I have never seen André with a girl over eighteen."

"But dear Claire, I am not a girl. And being his girl is not exactly what I have in mind," Jonnie said, then she sat back to watch the red spread to the roots of Claire's hair.

"Do stop!" Claire cried. "You make the myth of women thinking between their legs sound like gospel."

"Do I? That ought to make an interesting difference. I've spent my life trying to use my head for that purpose and I haven't been all that successful. Time for a change—know what I mean?" She winked.

"How old are you anyway?" Claire asked in exasperation.

"Why?"

"Because you never say."

"What's there to say, Claire?"

"I always tell. I'm forty."

"Ancient," Jonnie said, looking over the pool to the quilt of bougainvilleas draping the wall, petals drooping from the noonday heat. By evening they would revive, be young and fresh again. Bees buzzed around the petals, colorful butterflies floated in slow motion, following the tempo of the day.

"You look younger than me," Claire said.

"Do you have a problem with that?"

"You're much older."

"How did you ever reach that conclusion?" Jonnie asked.

"The way you talk. Sometimes you sound as old as those mountains."

"My, you are perceptive."

"Then of course—if you and Gérard had this famous love affair thirty years ago. Do you know how old I was then?"

"But I was only five, Claire," Jonnie teased, grinning.

"Thirty years ago I was only ten. That means you met . . ."

Jonnie wanted to explain to Claire that she had last seen Gérard thirty years ago. "Does it really make a difference, Claire?" She didn't want it to make a difference. If it was forty or fifty years ago, the end result would have been the same. "I am an artist of a certain reputation, a woman of means—now. A woman. My work is my life. What's more to know?" In an inexplicable shift of mood, she reached out, caught Claire's hand, and said, "Claire, I don't know why I came back here. Perhaps something happened with my work. Perhaps I just can't paint anymore. Perhaps my talent is all used up. . . ."

Of the dozens of *perhaps*es that flooded her mind since awakening, this was the most terrifying. To lose the one constant of life—all that she had. All that she was. The one thing she had had to cling to through all times—good and bad. What devastation. Then the thought came: Was that the reason for the bleakness in M'sieur Ambroise's face . . . ? She shuddered.

Sensing her panic, Claire reached out to her, held her hands, squeezed them. "Jonnie, you have artist's block, that's all. I meet many artists—painters, writers, musicians—passing through. They go up to the mountains to work. Some get blocked. At first they panic. Some give up and leave. Others stick it out and get over it. Darling, that's all that's the matter. You have artist's block."

Jonnie found Claire's simplistic explanation charming, her aura of innocence irresistible. It kept her in the shallows—just outside the depth of understanding. Nevertheless, as she listened to Claire's attempt to soothe her, she'd already come to an irreversible decision: she had no intention of going back to the mountains!

The revelation stunned her. She tried to push it aside, change it, shake it out of her mind. Thinking it out now might make that probability a fait accompli, something that she might regret.

"You think so, Claire. Maybe you're right. Maybe that's all it is—artist's block. We shall have to see."

3

Volé volé
Ou volé tè
Ou volé fruit boi'm
Ou volé toute mon fôce
Main, jamè, jamè
Map kité ou volé
L'air nan zantrail
Petit moin

IN HER SLEEP SHE HEARD IT, the Creole chant that she knew yet understood not at all. She opened her eyes and through the fronds of coconut trees, beneath which she lay, saw colored balloons floating in the bright gold of the sky. She knew the chanter to be on the other side of the wall and she struggled for full awakening. But sleep held her strapped to the chaise, staring up at the balloons.

Volé volé
Ou volé tè
Ou volé fruit boi'm
Ou volé toute mon fòce
Main, jamè, jamè
Map kité ou volé
L'air nan zantrail
Petit moin

The chant rose over the wall and all the way up to the terrace where guests and waiters stood seemingly motionless—a watercolor painting wilting in the hot unmoving air. Drumbeats seemed to accompany the chant but there were no drums. Music seemed to accompany the chant but no music played.

Jonnie's body shook; sweat rushed through her pores, wet her hair, dripped from the sides of her face, her neck, in the valley between her breasts. Sweat soaked the cloth of her bikini, washing her body. Had she really opened her eyes? Sleep still held her fast. Struggling, struggling—a nightmare, this straining, this being trapped between sleep and a terrible awareness. Those balloons, red balloons, green balloons, yellow balloons, were real. As were the paper bags, brown air-filled paper bags, tied with strings; balloons and paper bags, floating over her head, along with the chant. . . .

Volé volé
Ou volé te
Ou volé frits soupie boi'm

Laughter. Mocking laughter. Those on the other side of the bougainvillea-covered walls—they mocked the chanter. Their laughter seeped through the stones of the wall, ringing in her ears. *"Fou, fou, fou,"* they taunted, shouting at his madness. They threw stones. She heard the stones hitting the wall. *"Fou, fou, fou."* They laughed. Why were they always laughing? Jonnie shivered. Shivered, then wept.

"So there you are. . . ." Her eyes snapped open. Wildly they looked around, then focused. The eyes looking down into hers were blue, blue eyes staring, laughing.

"Did Boysie make it?" She wanted to know. "Did Boysie make it?"

"I really have no idea," Blue Eyes smiled. "But I have torn this place apart searching for you."

Struggling for control, Jonnie licked her lips. Boysie? Had she been dreaming? A nightmare? She twisted her shoulders. Relief. She had moved. She shook her hands, exercised her fingers. No, no longer entrapped. She still heard the chant. It haunted the air, growing fainter, fainter. The balloons floating in the distance grew smaller and smaller.

"Of course, you didn't promise." The man standing over her said, an I-know-you smile lighting up his face. "But neither did you refuse. So I took it upon myself to tell Jessica you'd join us."

His face had been tanned by the sun and many storms—or so it seemed. Light brown hair, streaked blond, tousled, framed his face, lending it a youthfulness. She tried to sit up. Her limbs ached. They told her that the sleep from which she had awakened she needed still. "I had supposed you were a bit tired from your late-night swim," the man said. "I thought it likely that you might have decided to sleep all day. I searched everywhere else. But of course this is where I should have started, isn't it?"

The suggestiveness of his tone jerked her to attention. Her head snapped around to search the tiles at the far end of the pool for telltale remains of spent passion. Remembrance. Her face burned. But at the same moment the cavity of her stomach opened, painfully. She smiled. "So now you found me. Good. I'm as hungry as that proverbial Haitian dog."

AGE HAD BROUGHT TO JESSICA WINTHROP what youth had obviously denied her: handsomeness. Tall, broad-shouldered, a long nose—the nose of an aristocrat. Gray hair thickened by waves and stylishly cut gave her head a massive lionlike quality. The rosy complexion for which English women are famous exerted a formidable attraction.

The regal head turned slowly when Jonnie walked up to the table. Gray eyes impaled her from beneath shaggy, black eyebrows, forcing Jonnie to blink behind her sunglasses attempting to return the stare.

Hunger and desire had guided her willingly to their table.

She could have walked away, refuse to submit to the woman's scrutiny. But hunger and desire held her—and curiosity. So she stood, as the gray eyes moved from her head to the see-through coverall to the skimpy bathing suit beneath.

"Stephan told me about the American girl he had met," Jessica Winthrop said. "But he didn't say she was a Black woman, nor that she was pretty."

Aha, Stephan was his name. Jonnie removed her sunglasses to match the steady gray stare. "Then Stephan is obviously a gentleman," she said, adding, "or does it matter."

Startled, Jessica raised shaggy eyebrows, and bared long, discolored teeth in a smile—a leer. "I really can't say. However, here you are. So what about lunch?" She raised her hand to bring the waiter.

"Vous êtes prête, Madame Winthrop?"

"Oui, Jacques. Perrier pour moi. Whiskey soda pour M'sieur Stephan. Et pour mademoiselle—madame or *mademoiselle?"* she asked.

Annoyed by the woman's overbearing manner, Jonnie looked around for someone with whom she might share a look or a sign of criticism or contempt, letting the silence hang on and on. Then, "Madame," she answered.

"What will madame be drinking?" Jessica demanded.

"Martini," Jonnie said from habit.

"French or American?"

"French," she heard herself answer, annoyed with herself. She hated French martinis.

"Good show," Jessica Winthrop said, approving. "Americans have the ghastly habit of drinking strong spirits in the heat of the day."

"And you don't approve?" Jonnie asked.

"My dear, whatever Americans do or don't is quite their affair. I don't drink," she bragged. *"Jacques, martini français pour madame."*

Pretentious bitch, Jonnie fumed. She's got to know that Claire's waiters all get along in English, and everyone in the world knows about English drinking habits.

"What will you have for starters?" Jessica Winthrop asked.

"I haven't had breakfast," Jonnie answered, "so I would like scrambled eggs and tons of bacon."

"Splendid," Jessica Winthrop nodded. "Neither have we eaten. I'll go along with that. Do you agree, Stephan?"

"Perfect," Stephan agreed. And Jonnie, annoyed by the woman's proprietary attitude and fearing that her admirer would soon be eclipsed by their budding hostility, gave her full attention to him.

His good looks amazed her. A slightly built yet well-developed man, around five-eleven, with so much grace. His demeanor—an arrogance in style, movement, and speech—gave Stephan and Jessica a resemblance to each other. "Are you related?" she asked.

"Cousins," Stephan answered.

"Perfect," Jonnie said, mimicking Stephan's tone. She allowed herself a smile of relief. Perhaps he was Jessica's paid companion and the "we" suggested in the early morning hours was not a "we" she was bound to respect.

The woman had quick eyes, and she kept them going from Stephan to Jonnie, but obviously they could not see Stephan's knees touching hers beneath the table. Their secret.

She liked him. Liked his silky tan cotton shirt, the brown slacks, the silk ascot worn loosely, exposing a sunburned neck. Glancing down and seeing his bare feet thrust into brown moccasins sent a thrill of remembrance charging through her. He crossed an ankle over hers, forcing Jonnie to reach for her sunglasses as shield against shrewd, probing gray eyes. She looked around the terrace studying the other brunch guests.

Americans. Most had arrived after she had gone to the mountains. All things considered, Jonnie preferred sitting at a table with the daunting Englishwoman. Americans were polite enough, increasingly so when they learned of her success as an artist. But the fabric of the society by which they had been formed—guilt, avarice tempered by fear—in one way or another affected them all.

Jonnie searched the tables for the "ugly one," the fat elderly woman with the double chin and thick saliva-dripping lips, who when she had first met Jonnie at the pool asked, "How is it you happened to be here? How can you afford it?" shaking her head in disbelief.

Still here. There she sat—uglier than ever—eating, chins still shaking, lips still drooling, probably still waiting for an answer.

Farther down the terrace Jonathan Anderson sat reading a

newspaper. Jonathan Anderson, a figure so familiar. A type. Thick white hair, a strong frame, thick neck, well preserved for whatever age. The benefit of great wealth and power—he reeked of it.

Jessica Winthrop refused to accept inattention. She kept probing, her eyes attempting to bore through Jonnie's head, intending to read her mind. The intensity of her gaze drew Jonnie's eyes to the table in search of another target. But as her eyes brushed Jessica's they were immediately trapped. "What do you do, my dear?" the woman asked.

"Name is Jonnie," she snapped, an unreasoning rage shaking her. "Jonnie Dash." She struggled against the urge to strike, to swear, but barring that, simply to leave. Still the question once posed demanded an answer. Outside of screwing handsome men in the dark of night or flirting with them in broad daylight, what had she been dashing around doing? Was she doomed to roam, to fly around the countryside, mindless? Mindless in search of her soul? Lost talent? She who'd had everything done to her humanly possible—what next? What the hell next?

Jonnie glanced again at Jonathan Anderson and remembered. Her first employer, the one who had controlled life and the lives of many, a boss against whom she had fought, had been fighting against when Gérard Auguste came into her life and convinced her to turn her energy from the no-win situation to her own talents.

She had struggled for the rights of workers—Black workers, Puerto Rican workers, Italian workers—in their demands for decent wages. A union organizer before learning that unions were not against big business. They were big business: controlled by the Jonathan Andersons of the world conspiring to deprive the American poor of work that they sent to Santo Domingo, Korea, Taiwan. Keeping the poor poor, faceless, and fighting each other while their children . . . their children . . . Emmanuel. Oh God, Emmanuel! Gasping for air in the sudden heat, sweat oozing from her pores. Yes, she had been many thing in this life—factory worker, housewife, parent—she had been every goddamn thing. Battling shadows. The thing was one always lost when battling shadows.

"I'm an artist, goddamn it," she hissed, spittle flying over to the imperial, smiling face. "I'm a goddamn great artist."

Unimpressed, Jessica nodded. "Hear, hear. I'm sure you will give us an exhibition of your work . . . in time?"

"That can be arranged," Stephan said, unaware of the battle of wills taking place. "Just tell us when, and we'll see to it."

Jessica's smile faded. Majestic, her head turned slowly to direct a glare at Stephan. Surprised at her disapproval, Stephan reached over and took her hand to reassure her he intended no challenge to her authority.

The sight of their interlocked fingers further agitated Jonnie. She waited for the unexpected upsurge of jealousy. Do I give a damn? she wondered. Do I really give one good goddamn . . . ?

Jacques came up and set their glasses on the table. Jonnie decided that what she really wanted was a drink. She snatched up her glass. But Stephan, to deflect the antagonism at the table, raised his glass for a toast. "To us," he said.

Jessica fingered her glass of water, reluctant to surrender the upper hand hostility gave her. Jonnie lowered her glass to the table. Then Stephan, looking around, exclaimed, "My God, who is that stunner?"

Indeed, the slender woman who had just made an appearance on the terrace had brought with her an aura of excitement. Golden hair hung to her shoulders. Her skin, a unique tinge of gold, carried through to her clothes—overblouse and scarf fading into light tans and browns, worn over tan slacks through which gold threads were woven.

Slowly she walked between the two rows of tables along the terrace. The sunlight caught and heightened glints of amber in her eyes. The golden lady. She must have worked a lifetime to perfect that image.

Every eye on the terrace followed her progress down the aisle. She walked toward Jonathan Anderson, and upon seeing her he put aside his newspaper, went to meet her, and escorted her back to his table.

"Roxanne Anderson," Jessica murmured. "Claire did say she would be arriving. A remarkable-looking woman, wouldn't you say, Stephan?"

"Riveting," Stephan said. "Anderson's wife, did you say? Then, by all means . . ." He stood up quickly, making his escape from the escalating tension over to the Anderson table.

For a time Jonnie stared at him, resentful, disappointed that he laughed, talked, looked down in admiration at the golden woman. Charm. So much charm. She gazed into the vermouth.

Why had she been sitting there at war, within and without herself, since accepting their invitation? By what right? Because they had made love? How had that happened? Jonnie knew as little about that as she knew how she happened to be back at the hotel . . . "To us," she said, raising her glass, thinking: Hear! Hear! To an advanced state of Alzheimer's.

Jessica's eyes kept trying to probe through hers and Jonnie widened them for Jessica to get a better look. Welcome to the club, lady. Go ahead and look. Tell me about me. Psych me out with those all-seeing gray eyes. Maybe together we can work out this puzzle.

"Stephan Henshaw's a bit of a rake," Jessica said, misreading Jonnie's intention. "Nevertheless, he is a dear." Jonnie's eyes went blank with disappointment. All that looking and she had seen nothing? All that posing and all she had to offer was jealousy?

"How long do you intend to stay in Haiti, Jonnie?" she asked.

"Forever," Jonnie snapped.

"It is a wonderful island," Jessica said. "Stephan finds it most fascinating, and he's been all over the world. You do know that he was a sailor?" She exposed crooked discolored teeth—a leer? A wicked woman. A very wicked woman.

"I know nothing about Stephan," Jonnie said. "I thought him your companion. Interesting to know you're related." Then, after a short silence, "How long do you intend to stay in Haiti?"

"That depends. I love Haiti. It's my second home. I love its people, its climate, its religion."

"Its poverty," Jonnie said, attacking again.

"I'm used to poverty," Jessica shrugged. "I have lived in Africa. As a matter of fact, most of my adult life was spent in Africa."

"Really?" Once again Jonnie's anger stirred. "I suppose poverty can be useful. I'm sure if you didn't find it, you would find ways of creating it." Sinful, her joy at Jessica's blank expression.

Then: "Oh you mean India, Rhodesia, and what your doctor Du Bois calls the islands of the sea. The happy native sort of thing." Jessica nodded, understanding. "Quite. I am heir to all the stolen wealth. Imperialism. But one supposes those things occurred before my time, don't you see? The situation there, and here, are very much the way things are. I must confess that I haven't an inkling as to how to turn things around. One tries to do what one can—which is never very much, is it?

"Nevertheless, I love Africa and I love Haiti. Still one must wonder at the difference it would have made for them—for the world—if we hadn't squeezed them of all their wealth. Don't you agree?"

Straightforward, clear, uncluttered. Seeing one's self in relation to one's history, and all that that now meant. Accepting guilt. Bravo. Damage had been done. Yet Jessica had the arrogance of the victor and none of the humility of the victim. Never the victim.

A sudden restlessness swept through Jonnie. What the hell was she doing here, in Haiti? Had she come thinking that love and marriage would wipe away her victimization? Marriage to Gérard? What security had she expected? How fragile an assumption. Meaningless. But had there ever been such a thing as security for her, for her friends: Boysie, Sylvie? Whatever her reason for coming, it had to be worlds away from Jessica Winthrop's.

"I came to Haiti because of its history," Jonnie cried in defiance. "Because of its great revolution."

Once again, Jessica's face assumed blankness. "Oh, yes, I see what you mean. Black Power—that sort of thing?"

"No, you don't see what I mean!" The woman's presumed knowledge of Black people, the downtrodden of the hemisphere, infuriated her. "Obviously you're not interested in the historical fact that Haiti is the only nation on earth where slaves fought for their freedom and won."

"Good heavens, no," Jessica said. "I hardly think of it. I'm here to gain my own freedom."

"England is a free nation."

"Civilized, my dear. We are the most civilized of nations. But that's quite the reverse of freedom, isn't it? That's conformity. We send our young to schools and let them conform. You see, in England it's a matter of language." She raised both hands to restrain argument. "The upper classes in our colonies have understood this—and have adapted remarkably. We're not at all like the States, where one talks freedom but the notion of wealth prevails."

"Oh, come on. You British in the States do damn well in terms of wealth—a damn lot better than we—"

"Ahh, but in the States it's our accent. We might have lost the war but your veneration—never!"

Jacques put an end to that conversation by placing one large platter of scrambled eggs and another of bacon on the table. At the same moment a butterfly floated down to set on the table near Jonnie. Remembering that in Haiti papillons came calling to signal the arrival of a lover, Jonnie glanced over to the Anderson table at the same moment that Stephan looked over the head of the golden lady. Their eyes met. He smiled.

"He is lovely, isn't he?" Jessica said, reclaiming Jonnie's attention. "Dear Stephan, he is so self-indulgent. I find myself instrumental in the happiness of many young women."

"Mighty big of you." Jonnie reached over and took two strips of bacon with her fingers.

"Grand, really," Jessica said, correcting her. "Quite grand."

"I thought such fucking nobility went out with the Round Table." Touché. Jonnie enjoyed bringing down sanctimony with a touch of the street. She reached over, took a few more strips of bacon. Jessica watched the bacon going from hand to mouth.

"Well," she said finally. "It's obvious you're not Muslim."

"I was—briefly." Jonnie remembered that moment in time when she had given up freedom.

"That must have been confining," Jessica said.

"That's the kind of life I lived," Jonnie answered. "First I was Catholic."

"By choice."

"By birth. Married a Baptist."

"I take it that was by choice. But my dear—a Muslim?"

"That, too, was by choice."

Jessica picked up her napkin, shook it out, and smoothed it carefully over her lap. "I dare say you hardly deserve freedom."

Startled, Jonnie stared, angered by the impertinence. Then she laughed.

"What pretty teeth," Jessica said. "You should do that more often."

Jonnie closed her mouth, tried to keep it closed. But Jessica's observation had been so relevant, so to the point after their mean-

ingless sparring. She laughed again and suddenly found herself
bent over the table, her body shaking with laughter. She tried to
close her mouth, to hold her breath, but irrepressible laughter
kept her bent over.

Jessica's heavy black eyebrows came together in a frown. Seeing the frown sent Jonnie into another paroxysm of laughter.
Tears came. She removed her sunglasses, wiped her eyes, noticed
Jessica's lips drawn tight in displeasure, and that caused another
peal of laughter. Jessica looked around at the tables, looked back
at Jonnie, smiled. Then laughed. Another second and she, too,
was convulsed by laughter. Jonnie, hearing her, tried to be still.
She did not want to laugh with the woman. That thought brought
another peal of laughter. Soon they were both holding their stomachs, gasping for air. Then, for no apparent reason, laughter
stopped. They sat tall, pulled their chairs to the table, looked up,
and saw Stephan staring down at them, concerned. Once again
they broke into gales of outrageous belly-splitting laughter.

"Don't go," she said. He sighed, fanning hot breath against her
navel, which further aggravated her need for him to stay.

"Almost dawn, my love. M'lady's work day often starts
at dawn."

"I can't bear you leaving."

"There's always tomorrow and days after. . . ."

"Is there, Stephan? Is there always tomorrow?" He laughed,
his breathing on her stomach stoking the demands within.

"If not for us—for others. . . ."

For others. Always for others. The dread sensation of a time
passing. She placed her hand against his chest and worked it upward, touching his head, pushing fingers through his damp hair.
"Put your legs around me, Stephan. Hold me. Hold me."

Lips found the base of her neck, arms went around her, holding her tight, tighter. Once again he entered her. Once again they
moved in unison. Oh, this need—this need.

"Now, my love, let me have my honor. I must flee."

The terrifying screech of a bird outside the window startled
them, forced them to hold on to one another. An owl? A hawk?
An omen?

Jonnie shuddered, remembering awakening in the room

and treading the maddening edge of superstition. She laughed sarcastically.

"Flee to your cousin?" she said, then regretted it. She hadn't meant to mock the relationship. He hesitated, and his hesitation audible in the dark ricocheted around the room louder than the screech of the unknown bird.

"Would it matter?" He pulled from her to sit at the edge of the bed.

She reached for him. He evaded her searching hands. In the dark she heard him fumbling.

"Why must you go?"

"I'm a working man—and you a lady of leisure. How does one keep up? You're insatiable. Jonnie, have you always been so—overwhelming—so passionate?"

Jonnie's nostrils distended. She hated that he made her passion sound pathological. "We orphans are inclined to be overwhelming in our demands," she said.

"Orphan?" he said, pausing. "One would not take you for an orphan. You're so . . . so bold. So in charge. The complete woman." The darkness outside invaded the room, obliterating its soft shadows. Did he understand nothing then? Did her frailness, her vulnerability on that first meeting make her appear a nymphomaniac? Like most men, did he mistake a woman's real need for wantonness—or proof of his own virility? She struggled against anger. Why anger? She had long accepted that her disquieting need for affection sprang directly from her orphaned childhood.

"I am an orphan." She spoke simply, pushing out the darkness, welcoming back the shadows to which their eyes had grown accustomed. "It is the whole fabric of my being, Stephan."

"Were you very young at the time?" he asked.

"Eighteen months young. But I remember the day."

"Imagination," he scoffed.

"I live through it still. My mother? Her image never enters my mind. I don't dream. I have willed myself never to dream. My mind cannot support the terror of my dreams.

"Yet I am here because my mother once lived. I had already taken my first steps when they perished—she and my father.

"My father is the constant of my life. I see his face—black, lit by amber eyes—or perhaps the flames of fire reflecting in his eyes.

His body: big, black. I feel him scooping me up in muscular arms. I lean against his bare chest while he knots the sheet around me.

"I am safe. Protected. He lowers me out of the window—a third-floor window. I look up at him and scream. I stretch my arms up to him but he keeps lowering me and I am no longer safe. Never again shall I be safe. Never.

"I see him now, his broad chest filling the window, his long hard cock jutting out over my head. He lowers me into the arms of others, then turns from me—never looking back. I scream, I scream, calling out to him—and he goes back into the flaming room to her, my mother. . . .

"Can you imagine, Stephan? A New York tenement blaze. An entire building gutted. It remained so for years. Often I went back to that street to look up at that burned-out building, to the third-floor window—a constant reminder of my orphaning. A man lowers his eighteen-month-old baby out of that window and goes back into a flaming room. . . .

"Yes, yes. I remember. I never dream. But that's the stuff from which dreams are woven—nightmares. That's the stuff from which art springs. My art. I know that to be a fact. A big Black man, a caring man saves his child from a blazing building, then goes back to die in the arms of the woman he's fucking."

"An exaggeration, Jonnie. They had to be overcome by smoke."

"No! Overcome by love. So much love for each other they had none left over for me."

"Most illogical, Jonnie. Absolutely illogical. You are seeing all this through the mind of a child."

"Perhaps. Will you be my confessor?"

"Yes, but another time. I must go."

Gone. Just like that, gone—leaving her, going to Jessica, the woman with the leonine head and the crooked teeth.

They had laughed together and enjoyed each other's laughter. She hated that they had laughter together. Hated that they had dined as friends, that the romance born of her needs had to be burdened with guilt.

Why guilt? If the cousin-employer-employee relationship was a farce, then the guilt had to be theirs—not hers. Never hers. Jonnie lay back on the pillow gazing through the darkness at the ceiling, dreading the fog of descending loneliness. Each night she saw her life as it had been lived, apparitions through the screen of her eyelashes, among the pictures on the walls, the shadows on the ceiling, until her eyes finally closed in sleep. Each night she lived again the loneliness begun the day she had been turned over to Aunt Olga, her mother's sister.

She was only eighteen months old, yet her aunt never let her forget that she bore no guilt for her sister's death, had accepted no responsibility for her sister's marriage, and had accepted her sister's child as a charge, reluctantly.

Never did she learn what had caused such hatred between the sisters. A romantic, she had made up her own scenes—of her Aunt Olga being in love with her handsome father, and her mother stealing his affections. How else to explain?

Her aunt had never shown her one moment's tenderness. Nor did she have one picture of her sister. And so Jonnie imagined her mother as beautiful—as fair as her aunt, with hair as soft, but with full, soft lips instead of Aunt Olga's ugly, tight, mean mouth. Aunt Olga was considered a good woman by her friends. Never gracious. She had planned her life well. And like all who painstakingly follow a pattern to guarantee bits and pieces of success, she had nothing left over for greatness.

Daphne, Aunt Olga's daughter, two years older than Jonnie, was considered a genius by her mother. She got every advantage. The orphan intruder became one such advantage—the Cinderella syndrome pushed to the limits within the framework of Black lower-middle-class striving. There was Jonnie, from age five, scrubbing and waxing floors, cleaning the toilet bowl by hand, setting the table for dinner, washing, wiping, putting away dishes before being forced to her room, where she closed the door from behind which she listened to Cousin Daphne playing the piano. She could still hear the strains of Chopin's Polonaise, Paderewski's Minuet in G—the metronome marking time like a clock.

Never had she been kissed by any member of that family, never tucked into bed at night nor shown how to wash herself. Once a week she was told: "Go bathe." Off she'd go to sit in the bathtub in her petticoat—she never saw herself naked—where she hummed along to Chopin while hitting the water to hear it splash. Never did she wash behind her neck, in her ears, beneath her arms, or between her legs. She stank! And thought it natural to stink!

Her street friends thought it natural, too. Boysie, her best friend in the world, used to say, "I don't like girls. They smell like fish."

Jonnie dug her face into the pillow, still writhing in embarrassment thinking back. Sylvie, another child of the streets, read pornographic magazines. In one magazine she read an article describing how women ought to wash: pull back the vulva, wash around the clitoris . . .

Oh, the problems of being a girl, a child, and unloved. From the day she read that article, every department store or cafeteria she passed, she dashed into the ladies room to wash. What a blessing, that magazine! What a joy to be clean! No more burning. No more itching and getting sores. What happiness—to be rid of that fishy smell.

Jonnie studied the remembered image of her aunt. She was not short, not tall, not fat, not thin—an ordinary woman. Being with her had taught Jonnie that ordinary people are the worst abusers of power. Aunt Olga created and controlled the atmosphere of hatred in her house, to which husband and daughter bowed. Her husband worked days and went to school nights. He studied languages. Cousin Daphne played and studied hard to become the genius Aunt Olga insisted on. Jonnie had nothing and so they found pleasure in denying her everything. Ordinary, ordinary, ordinary. Her Aunt Olga might have remained the most ordinary of women if Jonnie hadn't entered her life and so stretched her to her limits.

Jonnie saw her now: plain, mouth pursed, beady eyes glittering, darting around, searching for the most degrading work for a poor, helpless child to do. She saw herself looking up into her aunt's face, a stupid, begging grin spreading on her little face. Wanting—indeed, anticipating—the one stroke of terrifying wickedness or brilliance with which she would banish Jonnie once and for all from the face of the earth. A horror never achieved. Aunt Olga was a most ordinary woman.

Cousin Daphne played with her one day. Aunt Olga had gone out. Jonnie saw Daphne taking out toys from the back of a closet, a hiding place. They played together. Then the key turned in the lock. Daphne snatched a doll from her, rushed and pushed the toys back into the closet, closed the door, ran to greet her mother—looking away from Jonnie. They never talked again.

Like a death sentence, hearing them laughing, talking, playing parlor games, and she listening at the door, never to be invited. She used to pray then—fall to her knees and pray to a mother she had never seen and a father who had saved her life but hadn't loved her enough to save his own.

They were Catholics. Aunt Olga did right by her on that score. She made her take catechism lessons, then Confession, then first Communion. For this Aunt Olga earned great praise: "God will surely reward you for showing such compassion on this poor, motherless child. . . ."

Church became her salvation. Dutifully she went to Confession on Saturdays and Communion on Sundays. Whenever she found the chance she went to church to pray. Aunt Olga, unable to logically stop her, hurled an accusation: "You're a zealot!" And indeed that's what she was. Jonnie again saw herself in the long line of children waiting outside Father McDermott's confessional. To confess her sins to that priest, beloved by all the young parishioners, became her raison d'être.

Kneeling in the confessional, listening to his somber tones, waiting for his long sighs, which washed his clean antiseptic-from-whiskey breath over her face. What ecstasy.

Making up lies to confess: "I curse," she said. "I don't pray." How else could a poor, lonely, Black orphan with limited knowledge of sin get attention?

For months she kept repeating the same confessions and getting the same penance, until one day she decided to tell him her real sin. "Bless me, Father, for I have sinned. It's been a week since my last Confession. I accuse myself of masturbating. Is that a sin, Father?" She knew she had caught his attention. The long deep sigh, his bourbon-smelling breath washing over her face: "No, my child," he said. "It's not a sin—but it's wrong."

She drew her longest penance for that confession, which she never did in order to have another sin to confess. "I accuse myself of not doing penance. The devil stopped me. He took my hand and moved it between my legs, Father. He forced me to masturbate every time I tried to pray."

She hounded that man. In the corner of her little mind, she might have known what she was doing. It became a game between them—an exciting game which took weeks, months? She didn't know. But one day he did say, "My child, come to me in the vestry, and let us pray together."

How old had she been? Eight? Nine? Years somehow run together, just as the memories of the actual experience ran together. She remembered ringing the bell of the rectory that day, of being admitted by an old white woman, her face chalk white, dressed in white, her features indistinct except for black eyes and eyebrows.

She waited in a high-ceilinged room, darkened by heavy wine-colored drapes, which were closed. She remembered her surprise when he appeared: tall, big-bellied, wheezing—an old man. She had not expected him to be old. But she recognized his heavy breathing, the smell of whiskey. So she followed him down the hall into another darkened room. There he made her kneel. "Let us pray together," he said. She kneeled before him, his hand heavy on her head.

He prayed. Muttered, thick-tongued. Prayed about heaven, hell, the devil, purgatory. She didn't pray. Just knelt, leaning her head against his thighs, his penis hard against her forehead.

Did she know what she was doing? Conflicting thoughts. Perhaps. Secrets seeping from behind closed doors, in a house where nothing was discussed. Secrets of her father, and then that last memory, him lowering her from the window as she looked up at his long hard penis jutting out over her head, and then she had always masturbated.

She did know why Father McDermott had asked her to join him in prayers, in a darkened room. All her instincts were attuned, alert. She felt him fumbling with his robe, saw him bring out his swollen penis. What she hadn't expected was for him to push her head back, put his penis to her lips, force her mouth open to receive his benediction.

From that moment it became a secret, their secret. Never would she confess to anyone—nor would he. Partners in sin. Sin bound them and bound her forever to secretiveness.

Criminal? He? She? No. She believed in God then. She also believed in Father McDermott. God's Messenger—and Son.

She, a child of loneliness, had responded to the well of loneliness in him.

She left him praying that day, exulting in the corner of her yet-to-be-developed mind that he, the Son of God, had a secret: Her.

Three times she went to him. Twice she received his benediction through her mouth. The third time, he laid her on the carpeted floor, lifted her skirt, took off her bloomers.

Jonnie experienced again his spreading wide her thighs. She smelled again his breath, always asthmatic, always reeking of bourbon, blowing over her face. She heard his prayers. The Act of Contrition: "Never have I meant to offend thee my Lord, who art all good and deserving of all my love. . . ." He pierced her then, and in a whispered shout cried, "All my love. My love. My love." Pain. She still experienced the pain. What pain! What bravery! What strength! Proving her love of God, of him, the Son. Her lips held a most pious smile. What a great pride! She, a little Black orphan girl to be so blessed as to be the proud possessor of His most precious semen on earth, through this most holy Messenger. . . .

He grabbed her by her arm then, pulled her to the door, pushed her outside, pushed something in her hands, then closed the door. On her way home she saw what he had given her: her bloomers.

The next time she went looking for him he was gone.

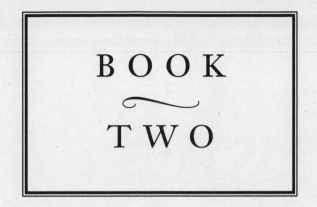

BOOK

TWO

1

S HE HEARD THE VOICES, the laughter of children, and seeing groups of them walking toward her added to the relief of escaping the sterile atmosphere of Old Hotel. It didn't matter that the day was hot, the sun burning. The road she had to travel to meet Gérard at Le Restaurant was narrow, dusty, and the chances of her finding the place with the directions given—unlikely. Cross the (no name) road, turn left at the big twisted tree, then straight to the big flat rock, and right to Exposition. Across from Exposition, *voilà:* Le Restaurant.

She had resisted seeing Gérard until she learned that Cécile had begun nursing resentment against her—preferring to protect the rights of her Haitian patron over the privacy of *"la femme américaine."* And Cécile was right. Whatever Jonnie's reason for having gone from the cottage, Gérard did deserve an explanation. What to tell him?

Jonnie stood aside on the narrow road, letting the children go by. Lovely children. Girls with long thick hair braided and tied with ribbons, faces dusted with talcum powder, protection against the sun; boys with closely cropped hair, shining anxious faces. Robust children, healthy, well cared for.

She liked the look of them, the sound of their laughter, their polite, intelligent-sounding conversation, their voices polished with precise French. They were so unlike the children in the mountains, whose clear bell-like laughter and poetic Creole carried on the breezes, adding pleasure to her workday. Children playing in pants too ragged to hide their bare behinds, or no pants at all. Grubby children, ashen faces, red hair, and bellies swollen from malnourishment.

Oh, that they all could be like those who wore white blouses or shirts, who wore shoes and socks—regardless of what color their skirts and trousers. Jonnie knew the color mattered. It told their religion: dark blue, Catholics; dark green, Methodists; gray, Seventh Day Adventists or Jehovah's Witnesses or Bahai's and other religions she had never before heard about—all struggling for their souls. Yet ninety-five percent of Haitian children never went to school.

The hot sun beamed down on Jonnie's head as she walked on, wishing her meeting with Gérard were already over and the weight of her guilt lifted. Whatever her expectation when she first arrived, Gérard Auguste had been most gracious. He had helped her to see Haiti through his eyes. His Haiti. Its beauty, which he described in full; its history, which he had praised and eulogized in New York when they had first been together. He had taken her for short trips through the countryside, looked down at waterfalls where lovely girls bathed, naked, and naked little boys romped, carefree in the waterfalls—waterfalls that became the streams and rivers where women washed clothes and bleached them by beating them against rocks on riverbeds. He had shown her the places of poverty over which he had anguished, like Les Salines, then he had taken her to Jacmel, the quaint, lovely town steeped in eighteenth-century French culture, down to the very chamber pots used in its hotels. The trip had been tiring, driving over dried riverbeds. But the town was well worth investigating. Its church bells, the town's middle class, dressed in their Sunday best for church—and coming back from church to hand out food to the poor standing in lines. He had taken her to beaches, driving her past miles of devastation: plantations destroyed by the failed

American experiment, the planting of the shrub erypotosegia in an attempt to develop synthetic rubber for use during World War II. And of course he had discussed Haitian history—the way he used to, back in New York.

Eight weeks. Eight weeks, and with the exception of that one weekend in Jacmel, he left her every evening at six o'clock to go home. Still, she had held firm to her belief that he intended her stay at Old Hotel to be temporary. That any day he might come and swoop her away to be with him. Forever? The dream. Her life had been made up of dreams—buying dreams, selling dreams, believing in dreams—one after the other, after the other, after the other. Only when she worked was she free of dreams. But now she could no longer work.

The road seemed long as the sun beamed down on her head. Its dirt raised a fine dust that settled over her low-heeled pumps. Yet she found the walk pleasing. No one had crossed her path with the exception of the school kids—a difficulty in this overcrowded island. There was always someone within sight or sound of her thoughts, down the road, across a field. But despite Jonnie's being alone, her thoughts went around and around, and still she came up with no explanation she could reasonably give to Gérard that he would believe. Worse, she could now see the restaurant— the restaurant, which he had picked himself, breaking his self-imposed exile to suffer the cautious greetings of old friends, the curiosity of strangers, in order to speak to her. He deserved an explanation. Not the truth. Truth is only truth when the mind can accept. Why expect Gérard to accept what she hadn't expected Claire or Stephan or even superstitious Cécile to accept: that she had gone to bed in the mountains and awakened at Old Hotel— by magic?

They were almost upon her when she saw them. Two women, peasants, walking the same narrow road, trays on their heads. A rush of sweat stuck Jonnie's blouse to her back; the fine dust turned her damp ankles clammy, itchy. Her face burned in a rush of rage. No, she wasn't going to run from them—not even walk fast. She was going to face them, goddamnit. Yes, she wore her hair natural. So did they. But she had overcome. Best proof, she walked with her hair nappy and exposed to the sun, not hidden beneath a bandanna.

Hell, she had style. If they laughed—haha, she'd laugh right back. She squared her shoulders and marched toward them.

They came toward her swaying like reeds, graceful in the way of women accustomed to carrying baskets on their heads. Tall, young, talking, giggling in the way of girls sharing secrets—intimate secrets.

Stiff-backed, squinting in the glare of the sun, Jonnie marched toward them, determined to confront them at the least word, a snicker, a suggestive look.

They approached appearing not to have seen her, yet when they neared, they stepped from the narrow path, letting her pass. Jonnie kept on marching. A few steps farther, she stopped, turned, and on an impulse, called out, *"Bonjour, mesdemoiselles."* They turned, and smiles like sun through clouds lit their faces.

"Bonjour, madame." Lilting voices, eyes bright with admiration touched her. Jonnie floated on their glow.

"God, I love Haitian peasants," she murmured, pleased with her discovery, so very pleased, so very happy. "They're the most wonderful, most graceful, most gentle people in all the world."

Still glowing, she arrived across the street from Le Restaurant, her destination. Reluctant now to dim her glow she decided instead to visit Exposition only to find the traffic of the boulevard backed up. A truckload of soldiers being held up by an old woman on an overburdened donkey. Behind the truck a procession of luxurious cars waited: Mercedes-Benzes, Jaguars, Porsches, Citroëns, Fords. Gay, laughing beautiful women resplendent in glittering dresses and men formally dressed, going to or coming from a wedding. They were creating a sensation, smiling and laughing, drawing the attention of onlookers. Horns blasted, soldiers cursed. Some left their cars to move the beast from the road. Resisting their brutal tactics, the donkey stopped walking altogether while the woman, her face shaded by a wide-brimmed straw hat beneath which she wore a red bandanna, puffed her corncob pipe calmly, indifferent to the soldiers or the commotion behind her. The scene continued and might have gone on until sundown, with onlookers gathering at the curb enjoying it. Then an old man, a peasant, went up to the woman, whispered in the donkey's ear, and led it to the side of the road. In minutes the boulevard cleared.

Jonnie crossed over to Exposition, soberly reflecting on the cross section of Haitian life—the poor, the rich, the loud and powerful.

Gérard had brought her to Exposition during her first week in Haiti, and she had never ceased being amazed at how well the paintings had withstood the elements. The paintings had been a part of the Haitian Exposition at the Haitian World's Fair of 1949.

Reds, greens, yellows—portraits of Haitian life—as vivid as if they had been painted that day or the day before. A miracle.

Jonnie stood studying the paintings, thinking how different they were from her works: roosters running from outstretched hands, people washing clothes at river's edge, faceless figures, which nevertheless gave the sense of a people—a life force.

Jonnie thought of the peasants laughing at her work. Perhaps they preferred that which they knew, things they had in common. Her paintings were indeed individual, personal objects and scenes—the way she saw them. Every stroke she had ever drawn in her life was made with an unshakable inner conviction, even when at times she worked in utter confusion.

She had never drawn a portrait before M'sieur Ambroise. She had never wanted to, preferring only nudes. She had always felt that people were at their best without camouflage—naked. In a sense her painting of M'sieur Ambroise had been that of a nude.

Indeed her life in art had begun in confusion—after she had lost her Father McDermott. She had searched for him. Had she ever stopped searching?

She had begun by drawing his penis, the penis of her Holy Father, then the penis of her own father. In detail. Penises—called cocks or pricks in her early days, phalluses as she got older—had permeated her imagination. Apparitions on her walls, her ceiling at nights. They had given new dimensions to her lonely life. She had never heard the word mentioned in her home, yet she had known that if Aunt Olga ever saw her drawings, she would drop dead.

That thought had given her pleasure. And so she drew and drew and kept on drawing—first with pencils, then with charcoal—hiding her work behind the brown paper that lined the back of her closet. The more she worked, the more her work developed, and the more she ceased being a victim—and became a person.

Even now Jonnie remembered her sense of exultation when Aunt Olga had recognized the change. Her eyes no longer begged. They had ceased to reveal a yearning to be loved. Her shoulders no longer drooped, asking for pity or goodness or justice or mercy. If dear Aunty had asked her to wash shit and separate the undigested parts she would have done it—with alacrity—in order to get back to her room and her drawing. Soon Aunt Olga's scorn had changed to hate and Jonnie hadn't cared.

Revolution. The family no longer took pleasure in their privileges. Instead of a room where they laughed and played games, their living room became a brooding room. Hostility grew, thickened, and Jonnie kept on drawing more cocks.

They were forever listening, whispering about what might be going on. Aunt Olga's footsteps outside her door, walking back and forth, back and forth, became a way of life.

Then one day while she was wiping the dinner dishes, she heard a loud "Eeeeeek" from her room. Jonnie laughed, remembering the never-to-be-forgotten sight: Aunt Olga standing there tearing up her drawings into tiny bits, pieces so small they stuck to her fingers, as though they had been spread with honey, screeching, "Ewwwk, eeech, eeek . . . If I see anything like that in this house again, out you go." The next day after school, Jonnie granted her her wish—she didn't go home, she never went back.

"Madame speak English? You give me money?" Jonnie's broad smile changed to a frown, which she leveled at the boy standing before her. Turning from him, she walked away to stand at the seawall, staring out at the sea.

Already late, a few steps from Le Restaurant, and still not one suitable explanation to give Gérard. "Madame, you American?" The boy had followed her to the seawall.

"*Non, je ne suis pas américaine,*" she answered. And because she knew that Haitian beggars seldom begged Haitians, added, "*Je suis haïtienne.*" A mistake. Haitians spoke only in Creole to their poor.

She walked away from him to stand at the curb, waiting for the traffic light to change. "*¿Habla español?*" The boy had followed her. "*Necesito dinero.*"

Jonnie prevented herself from smiling at his change to Spanish. She glanced over the sidewalk awash in sunlight that ran the

length of the corniche—the most well-kept sidewalk she had ever
seen in or near the town. Yet so very few people walked there.
Only one man, well dressed, carrying an important-looking brief-
case, stood a short distance from her, also waiting for the light.
Yet the boy ignored him to address her.

"*Sprechen Sie Deutsch?*" the boy asked. German, too! Jonnie
laughed. She looked down at the ragged child who spoke so many
languages. A beauty. Wide eyes—black, their blackness overwhelmed the whites of their pupils—a round head with tightly
curled hair, uncombed; lovely smooth dark-brown skin, ashen
from lack of care. A lovely child.

She hated that he begged—that he had begged her. Boysie
had never begged. Sylvie had never begged—and she—no, she had
never begged, although they had been out on the streets for years,
or so it seemed.

They had met one another—she, Boysie, and Sylvie—out
there between the breasts and torsos and thighs of the adult world.
They had been close, living together in an abandoned old synagogue. Never stole. Never begged. Never hanging with the gangs
whose members were living with parents. They had picked over
discarded fruits and vegetables evenings under Park Avenue
Bridge, cooking over Sterno stoves. And they hustled—she and
Boysie did. Boysie blowing the golden flute, which his uncle
in France had sent him, and she selling her drawings. No, they
never begged. . . .

"Madame?" Jonnie had been looking down into his wide
eyes—and beyond their whites to a gleam so familiar it pierced
her. Seduced? Still, she hesitated as she reached for her purse. She
had been warned. But shrugging, she opened her purse, took out a
dollar. The boy snatched it from her hand and ran.

Then, as though by magic, all around her ragged boys converged: "American, American, give money, give money . . ."

Dumb, dumb, dumb. Angered at his betrayal, at herself for
being gullible, she waited for the light to change. Damn lights,
change! The boys kept coming, one endless stream. Other pedestrians had come to the curb to await the light: well-dressed
women, in sleeveless colorful sheaths and classic pumps; men in
two-piece suits, white shirts, and ties. The boys ignored them, sin-
gled her out—only her.

Heat pushed up through her, drenched her in sweat; sweat pushed through her pores, sticking her clothes to her—a second skin. Her scalp moved in a sensation close to rage, almost to hate, against the black-eyed boy, even more than his begging friends. Then the light changed.

Quickly she started across the boulevard, the boys following. Jonnie kept looking into cars that had stopped for the light, hoping that someone seeing her being followed by so many ragged boys might get out to help. The faces of the drivers were blank. Somehow, they never saw their poor.

Jonnie quickened her pace. So did the boys. "American, give money. American, give money . . ."

From the corners of her eyes Jonnie glimpsed peasants grouping across the street from Le Restaurant—whispering, pointing, giggling. No help. No help.

Wanting to run, she forced herself to walk. Panic mounted. She kept telling herself, "If I fall, I'll be trampled. The boys will snatch my purse. They'll stomp me. Instead of beggars, they'll become a mob. And while they feed on my dying flesh, those goddamn peasants will kill themselves laughing."

Someone touched her back. Someone had actually touched her! She ran. They ran, too. And as they ran, their bantering tones changed to anger. She had become their enemy—responsible for their ills.

She raced to the restaurant. But the boys were already there, standing at the door to bar her entry. She stifled the urge to scream. She wanted to beg—but not in an American accent. She wanted to square her shoulders, stand tall, but her quivering body sent out the signal that she was a victim—their victim.

Then, from the doorway of Le Restaurant she heard an indignant shout: *"Mais qu'est-ce que c'est. Petits cochons! Sales nègres! Allez! Allez! Attendez! Allez!"* The boys vanished—like vapor—and she stood alone, in front of the restaurant. The handsome mulatto opened the door of the restaurant and stood aside inviting her in.

From the blistering heat of the street into the cold, conditioned air of another world, an explosion of staring faces, white-clothed tables, flowers in vases—all swirling around her. She shivered.

"Chérie, chérie . . ." She heard his voice, saw him coming toward her, the handsome man on whom she depended. The man

whom she had traveled over an ocean to see, to be with. She fell against his chest. "Gérard, Gérard, Gérard."

"*Mais Philippe, qu'est-ce qui s'est passé?*" Gérard asked the tall mulatto—the proprietor.

"*Pas grand chose. Il y avait des petits mendiants . . .*"

"*Eh bien!*" Gérard laughed. "From your face, *chérie*, I thought something had happened."

Something had happened! Something terrible. She had been scared damn near out of her mind. How dare these two sons of bitches look at her calmly and say, "*Pas grand chose . . .*" Still shivering from fear and the cold of the room, Jonnie snapped, "Bring me a scotch. A double."

"*Mais non.*" Gérard shook his head. "*Chérie*, it's too hot—a Pernod perhaps?"

"I want scotch," Jonnie rasped. "Right now!"

"Perhaps madame does need a stiff one, as they say in the States." The proprietor's eyes twinkled. He stood a moment, then walked away.

"You didn't come by car, *chérie?*" Gérard scolded. "That wasn't too intelligent. The sun doesn't act too kindly to those who are not *habitué.*"

"I walked." Jonnie teetered on the brink of tears. "I wanted to walk. I needed to walk." Did she have to defend her right to walk through the streets of Haiti? "I wasn't the only one out there!" she cried.

"Peasants," Gérard shrugged. "They are used to the sun."

"The sun didn't upset me. Those urchins did," Jonnie said. Those black eyes looking into hers had started the entire incident.

"And it is so you shake?" He laughed.

"They terrified me!"

"Terrified?" *Chérie*—no. They do not terrify."

"It's me they chased," she shouted. "It's me they touched. They might have killed me!"

"Those little boys?" He tried to force her voice lower by keeping his soft and pressing his hands downward. What infuriating nonsense. He and his little island and their poor, doing their Haitian thing—against her! We'll talk about ours, you talk about yours. They didn't care about her being savaged out there—because she happened to be American?

"*Non, non.*" Gérard kept shaking his head. "*Chérie,* you're not
in the States, where everybody has everything and always wants
more. Where children go snatching purses and putting knives to
the throat. Our boys—they do not put the knife to the throat.
They beg because they are poor. They do not kill."

A great wave of rage rose within Jonnie, threatening to con-
sume her and everything in the room. How dare he sit in this
place of gentle blank-eyed bastards trying to destroy the linkage
between poor and poor—the link he had established in her mind
when she had been his student? That had been his claim to fame
in the good old USA. Fighting to unite the world's poor. What
had reduced him into a bourgeois bigot?

Seeing those wedding guests on the boulevard, she had
thought them of another generation. But he, too, was a man from
that generation: undiluted colonials. Then she noticed for the first
time how he had aged. His light tan skin had darkened. What did
the Haitians consider him now? Mulatto? *Griffon?* In the States he
had been a Black man, pure and simple, and he had been proud.
But the French had left so many crumbled categories of skin col-
ors as their legacy that Haitians had to do research to find their
identities. No wonder he sounded so fucking screwed up.

The waiter came with her drink and set it before her. Jonnie
snatched it up, drank down the scotch, then banged the glass hard
on the table. "That's goddamn good to know," she said, waiting
for pain caused by her vulgarity to register on his face. No small
thing, sounding off and gulping down a shot of straight whiskey
surrounded by all those staring bourgeois curious about the
woman who had pulled Gérard Auguste out of seclusion. Why not
take him back to the time when he had accepted her, street talk
and all—so confident he was in himself that he could smooth out
her raw edges, remake her into the image he chose.

They had had a ball. Drinking straight whiskey in New York
City. The big-time proletariat. He had laughed loud, embraced
life with a freedom intended to shock—all to gain her confidence.

There was no need. She had loved him, this first French-
speaking Black man she had ever seen. She had been willing to do
anything to please him.

The banging of her glass on the table had shifted the attention of the curious discreetly away from them. Now she waited for

his anger. Instead, he reached out and, taking her hands, gently squeezed them. Her anger scuttled away. She regretted its departure—her only weapon against her guilt.

Since her arrival he had been kind, though not in the way she had wanted or expected. She had not expected him to meet her at the airport and deposit her at Old Hotel, leaving the turbulent years they had spent together politely buried. But as Claire had said, thirty years is a long time. If not to her, certainly to him.

"What are we having for lunch?" Gérard asked, playing with her fingers. Jonnie looked around the plush restaurant, at the casually dressed older customers, the brightly dressed tourists; handsome young men in office-perfect clothes, lovely brown-skinned girls with rounded arms, thick, well-groomed hair—the working young in the privileged luxury of the air-conditioned restaurant.

"Guinea fowl," she said on impulse and with a wicked grin.

"Ah, you haven't asked for that since you came. I thought you had forgotten."

How could she forget their constant border-to-border search for the sweet-tasting hen with the delicious flesh that most Americans didn't know. He smiled and Jonnie noticed for the first time since she came that his eyes no longer shone as they had back then.

Back then those eyes had given to his face its force, tantalizing, giving off an energy that made all endeavors seem possible. Their lights had now dimmed. Around the edges of dark brown, the pupils had been lightened as though burned out by the sun. They appeared now to be questioning instead of demanding. The corners of his mouth had also changed. Now they turned down in perpetual sadness—a memorial to dreams once dreamed? Ideals crushed during those years spent in prison? The death blows given by his onetime idol, François Duvalier? Why hadn't she noticed before?

Suddenly she thought of him sitting in the wing back chair in the center of Miss Ilma's living room, worshiping students sitting at his feet listening to him while he expounded Négritude, the antiracist racism philosophy brought forth by the French-speaking West Indian Islands—long before "Black Is Beautiful" as a theme had gained prominence in the United States. Doctor François Duvalier had been one of its chief exponents.

"How can I forget, Gérard?" She spoke softly, wanting to hold on to that time now past. He squeezed her fingers.

"Ah, Jonnie Dash, what a beautiful woman you have become. *C'est fantastique.*"

"You always thought me beautiful, Gérard." Jonnie laughed, heard mockery in her laughter, stopped. She didn't intend to mock him.

He had been the first person to tell her she was beautiful. The first to say he admired her hair worn natural—again before the Black Revolution of the sixties. "You are just like a Haitian girl," he used to say in a way that made her believe that all Haitian girls were beautiful.

"Beautiful then?" he mused, pausing to recall. "Perhaps. But now you are magnificent—so accomplished."

Jonnie studied Gérard as he studied the menu. No, he had been the beauty back then: tall, tan, lean, intelligent. She had not known before him that such intelligence existed. The zeal with which he had approached his students in Miss Ilma's living room had broadened all their lives. Hers most of all. She had been the most ignorant.

Knowing they were thinking the same thoughts, they turned away from each other, Gérard to order their lunch, Jonnie to stare out the window, over the corniche, at a lone woman who had walked up to stand leaning against the seawall, gazing out—Jessica Winthrop.

She wore a two-piece light-tan cotton suit and a wide-brimmed straw hat with bright yellow ribbon. Taller than Jonnie remembered her, with her long stride and strange walking shoes, a stranger from another planet. Nevertheless looking so relaxed.

Despite the chill in the room, sweat broke out on Jonnie's neck, her back, hatred, jealousy for this woman whom she had no desire to hate. Jonnie put her hands to her face to soothe its burning. What had caused such emotion? Surely not Stephan.

No. Jessica Winthrop dared to walk the streets of this island as though she belonged. Where were the beggars to follow her? Where were the peasants waiting to point, whisper, giggle at the gawky woman with the floppy hat? This was how she must have walked through Africa. Walking, walking, owning the goddamn place, going wherever she chose with no one to challenge her.

Something was wrong. Something had to be wrong with the whole goddamn picture.

"... she said you were gone—that she looked all over but didn't find you ..." Jonnie fought to hear Gérard, but the roaring in her head prevented her. She forced concentration, knowing she had to control her quick emotional changes. Turning her head, she stared hard at Gérard's mouth, attempting to read his lips. Slowly blood receded from her face—her head.

"What? Who?" she asked. Her temples still throbbed, keeping her eyes unfocused.

"Damzel ..."

"Damzel?" Jonnie blinked. She had heard that name before. Where? She turned her gaze back to the seawall. The woman had gone.

"Marie, too," Gérard said.

"Oh—the maids. Yes. What did they say, Gérard?"

"I did tell them to look after you, Jonnie. I told them to take good care of you. They say they did. Then you just leave? Like that? Why did you not say something?"

"I'm at Old Hotel, Gérard," Jonnie said. But he knew that already, so she added, "To stay."

"*Mais, c'est pas possible!*" Gérard cried. "How is it possible? How can you do this thing? How you can make those poor girls so unhappy? Jonnie, it is me, *n'est-ce pas?* There is something I didn't do? Something more that you want of me?"

He asked. But he knew! Impossible for him not to know. Yes, there was something he didn't do, hadn't done, possibly couldn't do. Why then didn't he tell her? Explain.

She shook her head. "No, Gérard. You did everything possible."

"*Non,*" he insisted. "I left you too much alone. But you said that's what you want—to be alone—to create."

Had she said that? Then she had lied. She had not wanted to be alone. If she had wanted that she would have stayed at home in her loft in New York painting, visiting Harry, who lived in his loft, pretending to admire his painting of bicycle tires. She had not come all this way after years of loneliness—friends gone, acquaintances coming, going, like smoke. All she had left were ghosts. Ghosts stifling her will to create—ghosts occupying her troubled mind. She needed to be free of them, and so she had come to him, then ended up in the mountains. . . .

Still, she had worked well up there. She had wanted to stay there with her work. If she had stayed, she would be working still. Why, then, didn't she? In all her life, had she ever had a choice?

Women's soft bell-like laughter, exquisitely polite, eased into her consciousness; voices of men, exaggeratedly charming, a pure distillation of highly palpable sameness, a monotonous absence of culture—or perhaps a too-perfect blending of cultures. Did it matter? Did any of it matter?

She gazed at Gérard, his stooping shoulders, his lined face, and remembered Claire's title for him: the old rebel. Wonderful. That title suited him, clung to him like his clothes—slightly out of date, but nevertheless elegant.

"Marie—she said to me that old man Ambroise, he sits on the rock from early morning. She says in the evening he goes, but then he comes back always in the morning. . . ."

"Don't." Jonnie writhed in anguish. She loved that old man. Loved his face, its toothless smile, its lines so deeply etched into his soul—the hopelessness to which he refused to admit. A father's face when it had given all he knew—and knew that hadn't been much. That's why they had laughed? She had painted it well. But they, the people, his people, had rejected her final insight.

Jonnie crossed her arms over her chest and rocked to still the moaning sounds she felt rising from deep within her. Who was she? How dare she? A woman coming all the way from *les Etats-Unis* to paint so hopeless a portrait of an old man, who—if the truth be told—might well be younger than she. His son was a lifetime younger than Emmanuel. . . .

"I'll send money to him for his time. To them. I'll give it to Cécile to take it." Yet, the money had to be the smallest part. She wanted to go back, she wanted to want to, desperately—to resume her life up there in the mountains as though she had never left. She ached to be away from the hotel, from town. She yearned for the calm, her head, her heart when she worked. She longed for the atmosphere, the thrill of seeing the big red ball of the setting sun, the anticipation of simply sitting still, waiting.

Oh, the pain of it. The pain. She pressed her fingers to the sides of her head, still staring at Gérard's mouth. What was he saying now?

"What shall I tell them?"

"Tell who?"

"Marie, Damzel."

"Oh . . ."

"It's important, *chérie.*"

"Whatever you want, Gérard. Tell them what you want. I'm staying on at the hotel."

"But your work, *chérie?*"

"I'll send for the paintings before I leave."

"But you're not leaving. You cannot. I shall never let you go from me again—not again."

But it had been he who had done the leaving. It had been she who came in search of him. They had not talked—deeply. Not of permanence—hardly of love. Not in the weeks since she had come had they reached for each other in a way that anticipated passion—a tenderness that might have sustained hope. It would not have mattered if, in his time away from women, he might have become impotent. She didn't care—had not cared. She knew she would make things right again—if only he had reached out aggressively. They had allowed all presumption of her coming to hover—waiting—too fragile to be rushed, too precious to be revealed.

The waiter came with the guinea hen, the rice, the black-bean sauce. As Gérard served their plates, Jonnie, wanting to ease Gérard's concern, said, "You don't have to worry, Gérard. I'll pay up the lease. . . ."

She had no idea how he maintained himself or his family. His wife had long since died. His sons, with the exception of one, were in exile. He had vaguely spoken of family property that produced coffee among other things. But he had never spoken to her about payment for the house, from which he had asked a good tenant to vacate.

"Nonsense." He dismissed her offer with a wave of his hand. "I cannot let you go back to the States—not now. Not ever." His face had paled. His lips trembled.

"I'm not going back to the States, Gérard."

"Where to, then?"

"I don't know. I have no idea—I still have to think it through."

True. Where to go in all the world? For the first time in her life she had money. A half million dollars for one painting bought by a European man, a friend of Miss Ilma's. After years of struggle, first as an oppressed ignorant, then as a hard-working artist, suddenly she had been freed from the limitation of poverty. Now where to go?

"I'll be at Old Hotel until I decide."

"Then we have time, Jonnie." He reached over to intertwine his fingers with hers. "I know you're trying to punish me," he said. "You're here to make me ashamed. Isn't that why you came to Haiti?"

Jonnie disengaged her fingers, took up her fork, and tasted a bit of the hen. So he had thought so little of her that he had not been able to pull any deeper meaning from the letters she had written or from the very fact of her visit. How small had been his interest that he could not conceive of a woman who had kept love for him as a motivation of her life.

"Yes, yes, that's why you're here. You want to make me pay. . . ." Jonnie took another forkful of the hen.

"This hen is better than any I tasted in the States, Gérard. You ought to have suggested this place sooner."

She had to get his conversation off that track. She hated that now when she had decided to leave, his eyes had acquired a permanent plea—a plea for which she no longer had an answer—a plea that would certainly not soften the long lines of despair etched on his face.

"I know you did suffer, *chérie,*" he said. "But I, too, have suffered." Jonnie put another piece of guinea fowl into her mouth.

They both had suffered in ways not to be compared. Who had suffered more? In the end their suffering had to be determined by the amount of trust betrayed. But this high drama? This querulous tone of self-pity? That jarred.

Did confession serve his ego? How did it make him feel that he too had had the power to commit the ultimate sin against another—in this case her? And he had expected her to forget.

Jonnie took a deep breath, served herself more rice and beans. Still he sat, elbows on the table, his mouth—which had always been soft, sensitive—on the verge of a tremble, his brown eyes anguished, the brows still thick but mixed with gray now, raised, beseeching.

Thirty years, and now he agonized? Why? Because he had assumed that she ought to have been devastated, finished by his leaving? Yet, here she sat: this beautiful, magnificent, accomplished once-upon-a-time grimy factory worker whom he had re-created like some modern-day Pygmalion. And yet . . .

Impossible to forget Miss Ilma taking out her old charcoal drawings, preserved in frames, and how he, after looking for a time at cocks and breasts, unable to hide his distaste, had nevertheless said, "Good, good. And can you draw legs and arms and feet the way you draw these?"

Because he had asked, she had drawn them—had brought him pages and pages of limbs in all shapes and sizes, forcing him to take her to Madame Colette, his French artist friend, telling her, "You must work with her." Madame Colette had informed him: "She's already a genius. But I'll do whatever I can."

And he had been quite serious about getting her the right books to read—books on biography, history, geography. And he had talked with her for hours, explaining all manner of things. Had there ever been a poor homely Black girl with more done for her? Never. Would reliving those years take the pain from his mouth or put the shine back into his eyes?

Had she traveled these miles to play games? No! If she had deceived herself in coming, she had not done so intentionally. If she permitted that lie to continue she would be entrapped by it.

"Your lunch is getting cold, Gérard." She was no longer angry. Her tolerance for anger had diminished. She did not want to hate Gérard Auguste. He had done all things to her. But she had been his accomplice. Whatever sins he had committed against her, she had anxiously bowed to his demands. He had robbed her of ignorance—and so she forgave him all. He had insisted on that robbery; for that she loved him still.

What if when he had come to collect her at the airport he had closed the thirty-year gap by holding her in his arms, squeezing her loneliness away, or by dashing away with her—to his home or a room or some unknown place where they might have been together, twisted into each other, holding, kissing, with all their old passion, repeating exhaustive promises of everlasting love? Might she have been caught up in the game?

Or was she now too old? What if when flimsy passion ceased, that nebulous forever-after love on which young couples placed their faith might prove instead of steel to be ash, easily disappearing into the earth? Then might she not be preparing—just as now—to take her leave?

Placing her fork on her plate, Jonnie looked into Gérard's eyes. "Gérard, why is it that since I came you haven't invited me to your home?"

His lips dried. His hands shook. After a long pause he finally said, "But you must come. Today. After lunch I shall take you. . . ."

2

A S THEY DROVE THROUGH TOWN and into the hills of Pétionville, Jonnie kept glancing at Gérard's hand steering the wheel of his Peugeot—long, expressive fingers. Fingers that expressed, as did his eyes, his disillusions. François Duvalier had to be in part responsible, having changed during his time as president of Haiti from liberator of his people, as Gérard had so passionately lectured, to the tyrant securing their oppression. Still Père Duvalier had been dead—years. His son, Baby Doc, now head of the government, didn't have the intelligence to last. Why, then, did Gérard's natural optimism seem to have failed him? For her part, she had carried his beauty, his intelligence, as part of her drive. She had held on to his image, the way he had looked the first time she had met him at Miss Ilma's. . . .

Miss Ilma had introduced them.

Miss Ilma—God, that woman had a greater influence in her life than she had ever cared to admit. A European woman. Scandinavian? Swiss? She had not cared about nationalities back then. Hadn't known to care.

She had first met Miss Ilma when, as a little girl hustling drawings at the Mount Morris Park entrance, a long limousine had pulled up and a white woman looked out its window and ordered one. Jonnie had been selling the drawings for ten cents apiece. The woman had bought one for a dollar. The next week she had come again, bought ten, and paid twenty dollars. Then she brought friends to point out "the little girl who drew the most delightful pricks," and all through the time of knowing her, Miss Ilma always introduced her as "the little girl who draws the most fantastic cocks—the little girl I told you about who really knows about dicks."

The money she gave had made a difference in their lives—hers, Sylvie's, and Boysie's. They began to eat real food: cans of Vienna sausage, sardines with their day-old bread. Instead of eating discarded vegetables and fruits, they bought fresh produce.

Up to that time she had gone to school every day. They left the synagogue every morning, went to a cafeteria, ordered coffee, took turns going into the lavatory to wash up. Then she went to school, Boysie went to the Wall Street district to play his flute, Sylvie went back to the synagogue to read her pornographic magazines. Jonnie had gone to school every day expecting her aunt to come for her—perhaps even with the police. She didn't understand how a child could just walk out of her home and no one would come looking for her. She sat in classes, eyes staring at the door stretched wide, brows touching her hairline, waiting. . . .

She did work in her art class. Her art teacher had given her a spray of flowers to draw and she had done it so well, she had been selected to draw something for a mural.

Around that time, Miss Ilma had invited her to her home—a white stone town house on the east side, its elevator opening into a living room furnished with the softest white sofa—and pillows.

Miss Ilma walked into the room kicking off her shoes, stripping off stockings and clothes, then stood rubbing circulation back into her body while her maid picked up her clothing. While instructing the maid to bring Jonnie cookies and soda, she read her mail. Jonnie had never seen a naked woman before. She had never even seen herself without a petticoat. Yet, here was a woman who sat in her living room as though it was perfectly normal to be naked!

Miss Ilma was fat but firm, with full breasts high on her chest. She had a small waist and immense hips and thighs.

After Jonnie saw Miss Ilma naked, Jonnie decided to draw Venus de Milo for her mural. Her teachers liked the idea, liked the first sketch she did. But Jonnie had not achieved her desire. She had wanted the breasts to look exactly like Miss Ilma's. In her zeal she kept drawing, erasing, drawing, erasing, to attain her idea of perfection.

Slowly the teacher's attitude changed—from admiration to concern, then to suspicion. One day she simply took Jonnie's drawing, tore it, threw it into the wastepaper basket, saying, "We're not going to have such goings-on in this class."

The insinuation in the teacher's voice, the snickering of the students forced Jonnie to her feet. She walked out of the classroom knowing that she had given up her one chance of ever seeing her family again. She never looked back.

Years later walking down Miss Ilma's street as she had developed the habit of doing, she had seen Miss Ilma getting out of her car. Miss Ilma had not recognized her until she smiled. Then she had said, "No. It can't be. You're the little girl who used to draw those glorious cocks." When Jonnie nodded, Miss Ilma said, "Look, we're having a meeting upstairs. And there are some wonderful people I would like you to meet." And so, once again, she had walked from the elevator into Miss Ilma's living room. This time into the life of the handsome Gérard Auguste, French-speaking lecturer, bright-eyed and smiling, ready to transform the entire world. He was thirty-six, she twenty-three, and Emmanuel six.

GÉRARD'S HOME WAS ONE OF A FEW old French gingerbread-type houses ringed by wrought-iron terraces, separated one from another by wide lawns and intense growth of vegetation. His house possessed the same air of aloofness affected by its owner. Even the stone steps leading from road to door were shaded by an arbor, deepening its sense of isolation.

The young man who opened the door as they approached had obviously heard the car drive up and had been waiting. He stood aside, letting them enter the foyer. Before Gérard went upstairs to alert his son of their arrival, he led Jonnie into a spacious dining room, a room furnished with heavy mahogany furniture: tables, chairs, china closets, sideboards, all elaborately carved—the unquestionable stamp of the Haitian worker. Hardwood floors gleamed beneath scattered goatskin rugs. A heavy chandelier sparkled over the dining table, and poised on other tables around the room were antiques created to endure an eternity. The room had a stuffy elegance lacking the charm and creativity needed to blend the old with the new. Yet all was well preserved with care, no doubt supplied by the three parlor maids who kept peering in at Jonnie from behind the door of the library, pulling back and giggling when she turned to them.

"*Madame, qu'est-ce que je peux vous servir?*" the servant asked. Jonnie shook her head to indicate she wanted nothing. Then Gérard came in. "As you can see, it's an old house," he said. "It belonged to my father and to his father and the father before him." Removing his jacket, he handed it to the hovering young man, then led her into the adjoining room—the parlor. "And soon you shall meet its next master."

Nervous at the thought of meeting Gérard's son, claustrophobic at being in the overfurnished rooms, so foreign after years spent in her partially empty loft, Jonnie walked out onto the terrace.

"Is all this your land?" Jonnie asked, indicating the wide expanse rolling out from the side of the house.

"Yes—all mine."

"And whose land is that over there?" She pointed to a field in the distance, stretching out at the back where sunlight reflected on the sweaty black bodies and on swinging machetes of workers bending and slashing in the fields.

"We grow many things," Gérard explained. "Bananas, carrots, aubergine, sweet potatoes. . . ."

"Then, this is the family land you used to speak of?"

"No, this is all mine. The family has land in the mountains. We grow coffee, cocoa. That land belonged to my great-grandfather—and he had three sons. His sons have sons, and their sons have sons, and so on and so on. That's family land."

Jonnie stared out at the workers bending over in the field. Sweat-soaked black skin, swinging machetes, and in the bright sunlight, she had a sudden vision of herself, Boysie, and Sylvie standing beside them, outside the old synagogue that had been their home.

In anger she remembered Gérard Auguste—young, handsome—in Miss Ilma's living room arguing about the poor, their struggle. His defense of the poor made her a part of the great world movement. Important. It had rid her of the shame of her childhood, had released her from guilt of the tragedies built into poverty.

Had he seen her as one of these workers? Despite his lofty-sounding words, this luxurious retreat had been where he spent Christmas and New Year, away from her, from Emmanuel. In this house built to last forever, on this land, his land—happy with his wife, his children of whom she had known nothing, and these truly poor workers of whom he never spoke. In this place where he had needed nothing—certainly not her.

A darkening rage consumed her. She had waited for his return. She and Emmanuel had waited and longed and prayed for his return. Waited with their meager little gifts—a tie, a scarf, cheap cologne—never dreaming that in reality he had escaped from them, from their little apartment, their dingy lives.

Frieda and Delores had waited, too. As had the students who sat at his feet worshiping him, eager to welcome back their god, a new leader. Waited for him to ascend his throne in the center of Miss Ilma's living room, waited for his eloquence condemning the injustice done to the working poor, the impoverished Blacks of the world, eloquence celebrating brotherhood—all that brotherhood of which he spoke a lifetime ago.

Why quake now at the magnitude of his betrayal? Why, after all the things that had happened to him just as they had happened to her. Did anything cause him shame, guilt? Still, the ringing in her ears, warning, threatening . . . "I must get back to the hotel." She spoke hurriedly, moving toward the door. At that moment two people appeared in the doorway: a light-skinned middle-aged woman leading a young man by his hand.

"My sister-in-law, Emilie," Gérard said. "She is the nurse to my son. And this is Petit Gérard, my son."

"What a lovely child!" Her words came spontaneously, for he was lovely, although not a child, but a young man—tall, thin, the image of Gérard when she had first met him. Except that Gérard's face had never been so clear, so innocent.

"My youngest." There was sorrow buried in the smile at the corners of Gérard's mouth. "My other two sons are in exile. But Petit Gérard was small; he stayed with me. When the soldiers came, he tried to fight them. They beat him on his head—with guns. Part of his brain is dead. He kept growing—but in his mind he's still only eight years old."

Had Petit Gérard been conceived during one of Gérard's Christmas trips back to Haiti? Or after he had left her, never intending to come back!

"Four years I stayed in prison," Gérard continued. "I gave to that man my heart. I who had never said one word against him. I who had believed in him. Yet he listened to the lies of others and sent the soldiers to this house, my house, and he jailed me. Four long years."

Jonnie remembered the hell that she had lived through.

"Only after my wife died—cancer—did he let me go. But where could I go and take Gérard? Where would he have somebody to care for him? You see yourself? The States? *Ce n'était pas possible.* So I had to stay."

Or what? Or go into exile like his other sons? Like the army of Haitian historians, poets, artists, intellectuals one found the world over—the States, Africa, Europe? Obviously he felt he could not go. . . .

"Gérard," Jonnie said, understanding what she had missed since coming, missed in him, in Haiti. He had not been the Gérard she had once known and loved. "Where are all your bright young people, the thinkers and artists? Why are they not here? Haiti is lost without its intellectuals."

"Intellectuals," Gérard scoffed. "What do we need with intellectuals? Was Toussaint an intellectual? Was Dessalines an intellectual? Christophe? Pétion? They were slaves and sons of slaves! Slaves built this country! Slaves freed this country! Slaves it was that defeated Napoléon's army. A slave it was who duped Leclerc, ravaged the forces of Rochambeau, and drove them into the sea! Slaves gave Haiti independence—not intellectuals.

"See them?" he cried, pointing to the men bending over, swinging machetes in the hot sun. Long fingers jabbed the air.

"See them? They are working for this country. As long as they live, Haiti will not die! Never will they let Haiti die!"

And there he was again as he had been in Miss Ilma's living room—bright eyes flashing, a pure intelligence, overpowering, rousing them all to passion. And seeing him so, she loved him again.

"When the French kidnapped Toussaint and took him away to die in the dungeons of France, Toussaint said to them, 'In overthrowing me, you have cut down only the trunk of the tree of liberty. It will spring up again for its roots are numerous.' "

Transfixed, Jonnie gazed out at the men—knights thrashing the fields in search of life-giving seeds or gold, muscled bodies shining like armor in the glare of the sun. What else? What else is there for the heirs of slaves: dreams, hopes, lies. . . .

"That is why I am so happy that you have come, Jonnie, *chérie*. You and me. We shall go among the people. We shall talk to them. Look at you—you can inspire—when I tell them that you were poor just like them." He clasped her to him, held her against his chest—and broke the spell.

She pulled away from his arms, the feel of his flaccid flesh. Then watched his face in fascination. One moment it was flushed with the spirit of youth, revived, the next its flesh had fallen into its folds of weary resignation.

Dreams and lies. Dreams and lies. For him the dreams went on and on. For her the dream had ended—and so the lie. Why then had she, the betrayed, remained young? While he, the betrayer, had grown incredibly old?

Later, resting across her bed, Jonnie remembered the workers in the field and thought of herself, of Boysie, of Sylvie—ghosts emerging from the past.

Never would she have become a painter if she had not met Gérard Auguste. His conquering style, the brightness of his eyes, his confidence had resurrected them—their childhood—in her eyes. His grand vision, his eloquence, had elevated their childhood to special importance.

Jonnie, Boysie, Sylvie—waifs clinging to each other out there to survive. Only they had not called it survival but adventure, love. Boysie, Black and ugly in a family of beautiful people, so hated for his ugliness that his mother had put him out at age nine; Sylvie, tiny, dainty, fragile, Puerto Rican—accused by her mother of being a whore when her uncle had raped her. The mother believed her younger brother, and so he had continued to rape her until she had run away. And Jonnie Dash, the true orphan among them, who had run away to be free.

Meeting in a world that had no place for them, in a life already burdened by depression, living in an old synagogue that Boysie had discovered and to which he brought them—first Jonnie, then Sylvie—like kittens needing shelter. And in that shelter they had huddled together to keep warm in winter, spreading out like royalty in summer on the huge white marble floor. Locked in, a hole in the surrounding wire fence their only exit—a secret they kept because Boysie had to secure a hiding place for his golden flute, which his uncle, a jazz musician, had sent him from Paris.

Would she have remembered them with love—in a life which had turned so ugly—if Gérard's eloquence hadn't placed their lives beside the Haitians and Africans, the exploited of the world? Would she have looked back at them, their life, with scorn, if she had not met Gérard in Miss Ilma's living room, and had heard him expound on *Négritude*, the clarion call of his then mentor, François Duvalier, the doctor whose praises he used to sing? Would she have forever kept her past a secret—a stone in the deep recesses of her brain—seeing their lives only through the warped consciousness of "decent" society as mounds of ash and bits of turd?

And school? What if she had kept on in school? What if she had gone from junior high to high school, had graduated? Might she have if she had not met Miss Ilma? She had wanted to. Even now, she often wondered—dreamed.

Drums in the distance forced Jonnie's eyes open. She lay waiting for her thoughts to readjust before getting up to dress for evening. Her throbbing head told her that she hovered on the brink of blackout. She needed rest. But she needed more the flow of people around her to rid her of the stupidity of holding on to a dream for thirty years: no, he had not been thinking of her while he sat in jail, knowing his wife was dying of cancer and his child had been rendered brainless. Who the fuck did she think she was?

She had survived a lifetime only now to sleep nights knowing that tomorrow and tomorrow and tomorrow and the day after held no expectation.

Jonnie stepped out of her room surprised to find it only twilight. From dawn to dark had taken an eternity. Had she known a place existed where time moved so slowly, she might have come a lifetime ago. She stood looking out at the multicolored sky, listening to the drumming from the distance. A soft breeze blew the silk of her dress against her skin, moved invisible hairs along her arms and shoulders, nestled in her armpits—a lover's breath, a wave of nostalgia, stirring up those remembered pleasures so ardently clung to—their young years, their gay years, their never-to-be-relived wild years. Never again to curl into his sleeping back, nor to smell the funkiness of their dawn-to-dusk activities or the stink of liquor and cigarettes oozing from their pores, the smell of garlic or sex breathed into equally offensive faces. Forever doomed now to the purity of grit-free bodies, the dulling of the senses with commercial soaps, designer perfumes—his and hers—one fart and perfection goes down the drain, the end of an illusion.

The last rays of the sun slipped from the sky. Night had come. In the darkness Jonnie joined tourists and guests from the other hotels around the city, arriving for the Monday night tourists' gala at Old Hotel. Going into the ballroom, she stood watching the musicians, lavish in their bright green brocade jackets and black cummerbunds, tuning their electrical instruments. Restless, she moved away and went into the bar. Dominique was giving final instructions to his Monday-evening helper, Nicholas. Finally he turned to her.

"Jonnie Dash, what can I get for you? My rum punch?"

Jonnie shook her head no. "Dominique, have you seen André?" she asked. She hadn't intended to ask, didn't know if she wanted to see André. But then, why not André?

Dominique reacted with uncharacteristic annoyance. He pulled the towel from his waistband, wiped the bar with angry, wide, circular strokes. "Hey, but Jonnie—I sell drinks. I can get for you what you want . . . to drink."

"Sam." The woman who called to him softened the edge of his anger. She walked up to stand beside Jonnie.

"Madame?" he answered her.

"Mrs. Anderson," the woman said. Jonnie looked around. Roxanne Anderson. The woman had not spoken since they had first met. Each time they passed each other, their eyes slid one from the other in the way of people who had no desire to communicate, no wish to know the other better.

"Madame Anderson," Dominique said. "What can I get for you?"

"Mrs. Jonathan Anderson." Roxanne insisted on full recognition.

"Ah *oui*, yes. M'sieur Anderson, he is my friend. He stay here all the time when he come to Haiti."

"It's a handsome hotel," Roxanne said, turning her head peacock fashion so that her hair hit her shoulders, spinning off golden glints.

"*Oui*—Madame Anderson. I think so, too," Dominique nodded. "And Madame Anderson, I make the most handsome rum punch in all Haiti. Can I make for you a rum punch, Madame Jonathan Anderson?"

Roxanne tilted her head higher. "Sam, I saw the most incredible sunset this evening."

"*Oui*, Madame Anderson, in Haiti we have the most beautiful sunsets."

"It does give one an entirely different sense of the tropics. When I first saw the poverty on my way here from the airport, I thought I had made a most horrible mistake. Then those beggars at the gate . . . Thank God for the security, or I might have had to leave—immediately. But that sunset . . . and this evening I saw a most handsome young man swimming in the pool."

"*Oui, madame?*" Dominique's cherub smile turned sour. Once again he wiped the bar with wide vigorous strokes.

"A very black but very handsome man."

"*Oui, madame.*"

"I'd like to know his name."

"But, madame, you are in Haiti. There are many Black, many handsome men around this hotel."

"This young man had three young American girls with him. They were . . . swimming." She nodded significantly to the window overlooking the pool. "For a very, very long time."

"Jonnie Dash, what can I get for you?" Dominique turned from Roxanne, then turned back. "You know Madame Dash?" he asked.

"I am asking you about the young man, Sam." Roxanne's voice hardened; her eyes bore into Dominique's, her attitude suggesting she was not one to be trifled with. Strangely enough,

Dominique's annoyance disappeared as angry brown eyes stared into his. He responded, gently.

"Maybe you talk about André—André Bienaimé?" he said.

"André? André ..." The name rolled around Roxanne Anderson's mouth. "Yes, that would be his name. Has he come down yet?"

"Madame Anderson, André—he don't live in this hotel. Now can I make you a rum punch?"

"Does he come here often?" Roxanne demanded.

"Who?" Dominique asked. "Oh, M'sieur Anderson? When he come to Haiti he come in here all the time."

Now the eyes burned, turned into shimmering balls of amber. "I am talking to you about this André Bienaimé."

"I don't know about André, Madame Jonathan Anderson. What I know is—I make good rum punch. I promise I make you the best."

"Does one have to stand on line?"

"For my rum punch, Madame Jonathan Anderson?"

"For the beach boy," Roxanne snapped. "I want to leave him a message."

"For M'sieur Anderson?" The usually sweet, cherubic Dominique had to be angry. Yet there appeared a glimmer of humor in those eyes beneath the thick silver-rimmed glasses. Supposing this to be a test of wills that might go on forever, Jonnie interrupted.

"Dominique, will you let me have a scotch and soda, please."

The woman next to her stiffened. "Why didn't you tell me that your name wasn't Sam?"

The smile behind the thick lenses brightened. "Americans they like that name—Sam. They like to say, 'Fill 'er up, Sam,' or 'Play it again, Sam.' "

"Is that supposed to be funny?" Roxanne fumed.

"I think so." Dominique spoke in a voice cushioned with innocence. "I tell 'em okay, but I don't know to play the piano. All I know is I make the best rum punch in all Haiti. Madame Jonathan Anderson, you want that I make you one very good rum punch?"

"No—give me bourbon."

Beaming with satisfaction, Dominique set their drinks gently down on the counter.

Taking her glass, Jonnie sauntered back into the ballroom,

where, standing with her back to the bandstand, she let the loud Haitian merengue beat at her head, around her ears. She searched the room for Claire. With everyone looking for André, better to be satisfied with Claire.

But Claire sat across the room in the back, portioned out as the dining section, with the American expatriates—retired army officers and their wives. Jonnie detested them. The men were loud, pretentious, and often rude. Nonetheless, as a group they functioned as the social arbiters of the island, relishing crimes of passion and gossiping over petty grievances. The women were depressingly ordinary—not rude, just remarkably indiscreet. Their attitude toward Jonnie implied "How strange seeing an American Black in places she would never be seen back home." Of their Haitian maids they complained, "You can't trust them; the minute you bat an eye, they'll just get on to stealing. They'll steal you blind."

Most had stumbled into the middle class thanks to the army, their exact status depending on the rank of their husband. In Haiti they lived in luxurious homes in Pétionville. Most had pools, although few knew how to swim. They had maids, two, sometimes three, and spent their spare time playing cards, being invited to luncheons, getting fat, and complaining about it. Indeed, in Haiti they were living lives of which they had never dreamed. Yet only after Claire had shown them clippings of Jonnie's exhibition in New York did they acknowledge her as American.

The merengue ended. The band struck up a tango. Haitians adored the tango. Carole Lombard and George Raft had tangoed on screen, and Gérard had taught her in her living room, moving to its beat with fluid grace. Blood rushed to Jonnie's head, a scream strained to push out of her throat. It didn't matter. Her feelings for him were dead. They would never live again. But God, what part of her life had he *not* touched? They had shared everything at one time—even Emmanuel. . . . "Would you like me to be your father?"

She had to get out of Haiti now, to put thirty years of dreams behind her. In desperation she looked around the ballroom as though expecting to find a path opening up for her to start running, running, and never stop.

Their eyes met. She fought to regain her calm, to rid her

head of its heaviness. His eyes cool, smiling. She breathed in relief, set her glass down on a nearby table, and waited for him to weave his way through the dancers to where she waited, still tense, her desperation reaching out to him.

It was the best in lovemaking. Necessity pulling them through their eyes, distending their nostrils. Their bodies touched, melded. They moved onto the dance floor. Her loneliness had demanded this. The night with its aches, its pains, its whispers of times gone by, its sweet breezes stirring up unnamed demands.

The heat from their bodies mingled, binding them one to the other. His thickening penis against her thighs, forcing her to walk into him, through him. . . . Stephan, Stephan, Stephan. The flurry of movements around them, the dipping, swirling, the exaggerated display of expertise, the last strains of music—the end of the tango.

Their bodies parted. A sense of displacement forced her to respond to the pressure of his hand on her back guiding her. They stopped at the doorway. Eyes staring at them had forced them to turn. Now the pressure of his hand against her resisting back moved them to where Roxanne sat. Roxanne staring, mocking them with amber-colored eyes. At the table sitting across from her, Jessica. Ahh, the master's voice.

Jessica, enraptured by the young man with whom she spoke, paused only briefly to say, as Jonnie and Stephan walked up, "Jonnie, won't you join us?" then turned her full attention back to the tall, handsome young man without waiting for an answer. Jonnie hesitated, Stephan pleaded.

"Please, Jonnie?"

This is not what I want. Not where I want to be, she shouted to herself, looking around the crowded room. Guests squeezed around the buffet table. A blast of music. Again the merengue. More guests crowding in; Americans throwing themselves into the music with abandon—exaggerated movements, missteps, twisted hips, determined not to miss a beat of the good times. The Haitian sisters, Germaine and Colette, looking around for a place to fit themselves, smiling, being charming to American guests. She could almost hear them: "We come because we like the music. But we are poor, haha, you know that in Haiti, even the well-bred are poor."

She didn't want to be in this room, listening to the merengue. She wanted to be with Stephan, lying next to him, body against body, his cheeks soft against her thighs. And yet, she sat, not wanting to be alone and having to give in to dizziness and the throbbing over her eyes.

Jessica kept up her conversation with the young man. "Now that I'm assured, Captain Lavel, that you haven't abandoned me, shall I go on with our arrangements?"

"Abandon you? What a thought, Lady Jessica." He laughed, holding on to her hand. "I would have called to tell you I was held up—but these damn telephones . . ."

Jessica smiled, acknowledging the culpability of unreliable phones. "Now, shall I ask Sam to draw up the necessary papers?"

"By all means," the handsome Robert Taylor look-alike said with a hint of tenderness. "How could you have believed differently?"

He laughed softly—a lover's laugh—soft, intimate, compromising. And Jonnie saw the young woman standing just behind him, waiting. A woman of indescribable beauty—a *métisse*, tall, young, slim, her skin dark brown, wearing a white Grecian-style dress, black wavy hair hanging down past her hips in one thick braid. Standing tall, she assumed a posture that suggested anger. Impossible not to see her. Her beauty caught and held attention. Certainly in the case of Jonnie and Roxanne. Not so Jessica. She kept her back deliberately turned from the woman while holding on firmly to the young man.

Jessica looked at Stephan and said in a businesslike tone, "I shall leave it to you to make arrangements with Sam."

Stephan nodded. Jonnie looked away. Claire, at a table in the back, was deep in an argument. The two sisters, Colette and Germaine, had found patrons—wealthy Americans at a table near the band. Aging women of light tan complexion, bobbed and straightened hair. They affected the manner of the anxious petite bourgeoisie in search of . . . what? Money? Happiness? A job? Germaine, the eldest, might. But Colette was surely searching for an invitation to be a star. Each dream equally difficult to achieve, and in Colette's case, impossible.

Two young men, Americans, at the table next to theirs, were shouting, trying to hear each other above the music, which was getting hotter and louder. More and more guests kept pushing into the ballroom. Jonnie once again turned her attention to the regal beauty standing tall, straight, and motionless with anger.

"Then Gilbert—Gil—shall we say tomorrow, lunch?" Jessica said, exposing her long crooked teeth in a flirtatious smile.

"Lunch it is, milady." He bent to kiss her hand. Just as the waiter, Jacques, passed, his tray heavy with food and drinks. The lovely *métisse* moved abruptly into his path. He swerved to avoid her, the tray tipped over, fell. Food and drinks crashed to the floor.

"*Salaud!*" the young woman cried, hitting Jacques on his shoulder. "*Tu ne vois pas? Regarde ce que tu as fais . . .*"

"*Je m'excuse, mademoiselle,*" said Jacques, his head bowed in supplication. "*C'est ma faute. Pardon, pardon . . .*"

Waiters from around rushed to help Jacques. "*Il faut pardonner Jacques, mademoiselle,*" they said on behalf of their abused comrade.

"*Tu es un cochon,*" she spat, vicious, mean, angry. "*Un idiot.*" She showed her dress, which had not been touched. "*Imbécile, imbécile!*" she shouted, and reached out to strike Jacques again.

Hurriedly, the captain kissed Jessica's hand, grabbed his beautiful companion, and hustled her to the back of the room.

"But," Roxanne protested as the waiters went about cleaning up the mess, humbled, nevertheless enjoying the scene. "It was her fault. Didn't you see? She did it deliberately."

"My dear Roxanne," Jessica said, her voice lofty. "I have made it one of my never-to-be-broken laws never to interfere in any relationship between Haitians.

"Now, Roxanne, where were we? Ahh yes, as I was saying, I can't see why Jonathan would be considering doing business in Haiti. In the five years since he's been coming . . ."

Jonnie watched the young couple walk away, their steps matched like dancers locked in a tango, both so tall and graceful, moving in a way that brought sex to mind. She kept watching them until they were seated at the table with Claire and the American contingent.

"Jonathan?" Roxanne's surprise caught her attention. "Has been coming here—for five years?"

"Since I first met him," Jessica answered. "He's been stopping off on his way to and from Santo Domingo. But to actually go into business here? Tell me, will he be into commodities?"

"I have no idea. . . ." Roxanne, forced to admit to ignorance of her husband's affairs, looked suddenly confused, vulnerable. "Jonathan never discusses anything with me. And as you can see, he's so angry that I came here—he's decided to abandon me."

"Abandon you? No, my dear, Jonathan would never do a thing like that," Jessica rushed to reassure her. "Certainly not on your first trip to Haiti."

"What else? Since I came I have been in my room alone."

"Jonathan is the epitome of the American businessman. He eats, sleeps, breathes business. He might be forgetful, but that's not abandonment. Never mind; I'll see to it that you are well taken care of while you're here. Staying alone in a hotel room can be most depressing."

"I'm perfectly capable of taking care of myself, thank you, Mrs. Winthrop," Roxanne said, assuming a resentful air.

"The name is Jessica. Not to worry. I have a wonderful chauffeur who would be delighted— As I was saying, if I were you, I'd caution Jonathan to go slow. One can start out doing quite well in Haiti, but American enterprises manage to fall apart in the shortest time. Some call it the curse of Dessalines."

"Curse?" Roxanne scoffed. "An intelligent woman like you . . . believes in curses?"

"It doesn't matter what I do or don't believe, Roxanne. It is a fact of history that Dessalines . . ." She smiled. "You do know about Dessalines?"

"No, I don't," Roxanne said, bristling in anger at Jessica's manner.

"Dessalines, my dear, was the first emperor of Haiti. A slave. So tortured from birth that he carried the deep scars all over his body to his grave. His education was the cruelty taught by the French. Yet, he became the greatest general in Haiti—and was responsible for the defeat of Napoléon's army and the British forces on this island. His battle cry was *Coupe tet blanc, brûle caille!*

"And he did cut off the heads and burn the houses of those Frenchmen who had joined forces with Napoléon."

"No cruelty of the French can justify that kind of brutality," Roxanne snapped.

"No one ever can justify cruelty, my dear." Jessica smiled. "But compare the actions of the French General Rochambeau. He imported dogs that we trained to attack Blacks. He then built a vast amphitheater where French officers led Black youths into the arena, slit their stomachs, then let loose the dogs. Seeing dogs eating the entrails of those unfortunate youths drove the French into such overwhelming ecstasy that men and women grabbed each other and fornicated in the aisles and in their seats."

"Obscene!" Disgust seamed Roxanne's face. "I don't believe it."

"What don't you believe, my dear? The cruelty of Rochambeau or the greed of the dogs?" Jessica's eyebrows arched in surprise.

"French women would never so demean themselves."

"I have always heard that French women are the most passionate of women," Jessica said. "Isn't that so, Stephan?"

"Oh, I don't know," Stephan said, with a smirk. "When I think of passionate women I think of the Japanese geisha women. Better still, those lovely women of Thailand."

In the silence all eyes turned on Stephan's animated face until it darkened, then Jessica continued, "The Haitians all love Dessalines—the peasants praise him as their leader, while the mulattoes accept him as their liberator. After independence, Dessalines promised amnesty to the French. They had gone into hiding. They came out and he had them all killed.

"Unhappily, in killing off the French, he eliminated the one group who might have cushioned the hatred of the ex-slaves. Left to themselves, Blacks and mulattoes—who are, after all, family—fell on each other and have been going at it ever since. Impeding progress. *Voilà*—his curse."

Overhearing, one of the young men at the next table turned his chair to face theirs. "I was told there was no violence on this island; that's why we came here." Eyes round and wide with terror, veins wiggled at his temples like worms.

"There is no violence here." Jessica hastened to reassure him. "Except the violence used against Haitians by the Haitian government."

"But we heard you, didn't we?" He asked support from his companion—a thin, aesthetic-looking individual with a tight face—sitting across from him.

"I heard you say they kill whites. . . ."

"I was speaking of another time. . . ."

"I'm from Utah," the plump, round-faced man said, pulling his chair closer. "I had to leave my home state because of its violence."

"Are you joking?" Roxanne protested. "I come from Utah. It has one of the lowest crime rates in the States."

"My father was killed in Utah," the young man shouted loud enough to be heard over the blasting strains of the merengue. "In his home. In our house. Thieves broke in and robbed us. They killed him—bashed his head in with a hammer. . . . I found him."

Jessica clucked her tongue in sympathy, the young man spoke directly to her. "We went to Puerto Rico. We found the most adorable little village. We lived there for three years. Then one day we came home and our house had been broken into. Everything gone! What if we had been at home?" He shuddered at the thought. "Of course we had to leave. We went next to Jamaica. What an impossible, violent island. Then someone told us about Haiti. They said it was nonviolent. What if something were to happen?"

"What is your name?" Jessica asked.

"Stanley. My friend's name is Bernard." He indicated the disdainful young man who obviously preferred privacy.

"Stanley—Bernard, I suggest that you let your imaginary horrors catch up with you. That's the only way to have them exorcised."

"Is that all you can say?" Stanley said, turning away from her, from them, in anger.

"What else," Bernard said in precise, cutting tones, and twisted his head, satisfied with himself that he, at least, had ignored them.

"If you don't," Jessica said, teasing, "you're bound to go on living with them forever."

Roxanne said to her, "One can hardly be a friend to advise them to come here—this island is absolutely wretched."

"Haitians are poor, not violent," Jessica informed her.

"Living in such abject poverty naturally leads to violence," Roxanne answered.

"But Stanley's father was killed in Utah," Jessica pointed out, adding, "Poverty is a crime. But poor people are not criminals."

Despite Jessica's smile, her relentless tone kept Roxanne on the defensive. She looked around, and finding no one to support her, settled on being malicious. "Miss Winthrop . . ."

"The name is Jessica."

"Jessica, I'm so glad you invited me to sit with you—and your son. Stephan is one of the most charming young men I have ever met."

Still smiling, Jessica leveled intelligent gray eyes on Roxanne's. "Stephan is my companion, Roxanne." She smiled—leered? "One shouldn't be deceived by his appearance. Stephan's about our age, give or take a few years."

Roxanne's face flamed, angered by the fifteen or more years between them that Jessica preferred to ignore. "A deception that can hardly be accomplished with Captain Lavel," she retorted. Jessica grinned.

"Noooo—ab-so-lutely not, not . . ."

Stephan laughed, attempting to dispel the animosity growing at the table. But his laughter sounded insincere, strained. Thankfully, at that moment Jonathan Anderson came up, thundering with excessive hilarity. "Jess, how grateful I am to see that you're taking such good care of my wife."

3

JONNIE AWOKE TO THE SOUND OF THUNDER, and reaching to caress the head beside her, touched the pillow instead. She stretched out her leg to the other side of the bed, then lay still, hearing the thunder fade in the distance. No, he had not come with her. She had come back to her room alone.

A loud boom as from an explosion forced her eyes open. Lightning flashed across the ceiling, and in the brightness she saw an apparition: herself, Sylvie, and Boysie huddled together alongside the workers in Gérard's fields. She lay still, petrified as she saw the image of a woman taking form—an old woman with gray hair stumbling along a long, twisting road, following the fading rumble of thunder. The lightning went out. The thunder faded. In the dark, she searched for the way back. But the road had been too long, too twisted; the weight she carried too heavy. Then she heard that familiar voice.

"She's dead," the nurse said. "TB." Looking into their blank, staring eyes—Jonnie's and Boysie's—she said, "There's nothing that you can do now. Where is her family?" Boysie took her hand, pulled. She ran with him—away. Why? Where were they going? Away. Away from the hospital that might keep them, examine them for TB. Ask questions they didn't know how to answer.

They'd had to take her. She had a fever, talked out of her mind. So they had brought her to Harlem Hospital. But who was she? What was her name, other than Sylvie? Who were her parents? They only knew that her uncle had raped her, and her mother had let him.

For three years they had lived together. She was their sister. They were family. How little they knew of her, of each other, after having talked for all those hours about the hurt done them. They had no other background, no history. How were they to know the reason for Sylvie's fragility? Small bones, small face, tiny hands and feet—a wicked grin that would always haunt them.

Days they sat at the entrance of the hospital—ragged children with big eyes, staring and afraid. They had gone in to see her, twice, but she had not regained consciousness. She never looked at them again. They had loved her so very much. They had cared for her. Boysie had bought alcohol, and every night had rubbed her back, her arms, her little feet. Jonnie had tried to force soup down her throat, until the day she had begun to talk out of her mind, crazily, and then lost consciousness. They'd had to take her! And they had waited for her. Holding on to one another, they had waited until the nurse said, "She's dead."

Later, Sylvie haunted them for giving her over to the dark. She blew the fire out from the Sterno cans, knocked over their Vienna sausages, their sardines, giggling in the dark, casting big shadows over them where they slept huddled together now in fright. She kept reminding them that they had been responsible for her going.

Born to die. Jonnie sighed, looking up in the predawn darkness. All the kids out there were born to die. Certainly they were—lying in the damp unheated synagogue winters, hugging worn clothes to shivering bodies, standing on corners or sheltering down in the subways away from the wind, away from the gangs, who didn't mind fighting, to the death, over turf. They were all marked for death—and never knew it.

Wise guys, toughening it out winters, to smile their victory come spring. Laughing, playing the way ordinary children did in summer, hanging out in the park, breathing the full-blown ripeness of an exhilarating autumn, praying that winter would not come again. It always did. Then, shivering beneath blankets and on top of the cardboard placed on the cold marble floors, lying back to back instead of curved into each other, to protect themselves from the hand of death hovering over them in the form of Sylvie's ghost. They came to accept the fact that poor, fragile Sylvie had had to die.

And they? Thinking of the father and mother she never knew, Jonnie cried, "Boysie, everyone who's supposed to love me and who I love always dies." And he had answered, "I love you and I ain't about to die. I might go off sometimes but I'll be back." She believed him.

Another rumble of thunder, this time from the distance, forced Jonnie back to herself, forced her to resist the downward pull of her failed life.

Failed? Why failed? She had sold a painting for half a million dollars! She had indeed become a rich woman—nigger rich—but a grand success nevertheless. If so rich, why then had she come here—needing Gérard?

Restless, impatient, she dressed and left her room. She had to have a swim, had to get back to where she had been before yesterday. . . .

But as early as she had come, Jessica had preceded her. Jessica, sitting calmly on the terrace, working by candlelight. The woman's calm made her fully aware of her own highly emotional state.

"What are you doing here so early?" Her voice sounded ugly, angry, rude.

"Oh, is that you, Jonnie? Good morning. Join me. Coffee will be coming. I'm working on a list for our grand weekend."

"Weekend?"

"Yes, a weekend cruise—on Captain Lavel's yacht. You do remember Gilbert?"

"The guy from the other night?"

"Yes. We're planning a cruise to Jamaica. I expect it will be a smashing affair."

"Have you ordered coffee?" Jonnie asked, suddenly needing that first cup of Haitian coffee.

"Yes, I awakened Ti Boy and had him put on a pot. What about you, Jonnie? Have you given up on sleep? Or are your demons driving you from bed?"

Startled, Jonnie looked at the woman's bowed head. But the rumble of thunder provided her with a grace period before she answered. "What demons are you talking about, Jessica?"

"They abound in Haiti, my dear. Only the sun can drive them away." Their hushed tones respected the early morning silence, although a human stirring from the other side of the bougainvillea-covered wall alerted them that the day had begun.

"Ahh, the sun . . . ," Jonnie murmured, gazing out at the rapidly pinking sky. Then, in a voice remarkable for its audacity she demanded, "Where's Stephan?"

Startled, Jessica's head jerked up. She stared at Jonnie from beneath raised eyebrows. "In bed sleeping, I suppose," she said, adding, "Stephan's been sleeping quite a bit lately. Dear Stephan forgets he's not as young as he once was."

Jonnie studied the woman in the brightening day—her face still in the shadows, her gray hair touched by the rising sun, forming a halo around her head. "Are any of us?" Jonnie replied. Then remembering Jessica's young captain, she added, "But we like to believe what makes us happy."

Jessica smiled. "Still one can't live forever and remain as young as Stephan obviously wants to remain. Something must give. Wasn't it your American general who spoke of the old soldier just fading away—or something to that effect? So it is with sailors, my dear, who insist on bucking the tide."

"Bucking—and grinding—weld people together." Jonnie leered back. "Wouldn't you say?"

She hated vulgarity, and yet at this moment she wanted to be vulgar. "My husband quit me because I couldn't buck and grind."

"The Catholic?" Jessica asked, assuming a mild interest. And Jonnie, sensing the angry past cloud her mind, fought for control.

"Hardly. I was never married to a Catholic. I married a Baptist." She saw Jessica's smile, the attempt at being polite. Jonnie decided to preempt it.

"I loved the motherfucker," she spat out, and Jessica jumped. "He married me, you see, because he couldn't get into my pants and was scared somebody else might beat him to it. The war—dig? He proposed the day after Pearl Harbor so he could keep it sealed up until he got back. He didn't have to. But then I never told him that he had been chosen for me by the Holy Father to germinate his seed—the second Immaculate Conception."

Nerves beat over Jonnie's face. Her body twitched, her eyes blinked. "Ignorant, right?" she laughed. "All those years of guarding that seed in the cleanest pussy ever. Ignorant! Ignorant!"

"I'd rather say quite a lovely imagination." Jessica spoke in cautious tones. "Ignorance comes in different packets, don't you see? One of them is called innocence . . ."

"But you don't forget the pain," she whispered. "The pain lives on, you know. It accumulates. What a beautiful child—Emmanuel, the Second Immaculate Conception. Ted Dash was off to save the world for him. Normandy—he was invading Normandy when Emmanuel was born.

"War changed Ted Dash. Europe changed him. Not true. You don't train a man to kill. Men are born killers. They have wars so they can have their jollies shitting over people on battlefields, then go back home bragging about what killers they are, and how they got screwed for not winning medals and Purple Hearts.

"Dash was a son of a bitch before he went to war. A street stud, half-educated, a mother's child who screwed around and bragged about it—bragging's what boosts the egos of street cats."

Suddenly, Jonnie's tone changed. She smiled, her face calm. "You know, there is nothing bad that happens to women anywhere in this world that doesn't happen to poor Black women in the States."

The calm lasted but a second. Then the nerves twitched in her face. "We had so much going for us. Emmanuel was so beautiful and I worked hard for him—for us. Then one day I heard Ted talking to his friend on the phone. 'Man,' he says to this stud. 'I don't be needing no broad who thinks she's too good to fuck. My old lady's like a board in bed. I needs me a woman who can get to bucking and grinding.'" Jonnie threw her head back and screamed with laughter.

Jessica searched nervously around the terrace. "Where is Ti Boy?" she asked, then started carefully stacking her envelopes, wanting to get up, to leave.

"Passivity," Jonnie said, still laughing. "I thought passivity was purity. Ted had loved me because he thought me pure—but what he really wanted was a bucker and grinder."

And then Ti Boy arrived with the pot of coffee. Jessica tried to catch his eyes, signal him to stay. He must have thought her grimaces, her raised brows meant they wanted to be alone. He left.

"I didn't masturbate!" Again Jessica jumped. "The Holy Father said it was wrong!" Jonnie's body shook, her teeth chattered. Jessica saw a movement at the other end of the terrace. She breathed a sigh of relief, put up a hand, but it had been a waiter checking the terrace. He had already gone.

"Three in the morning this bitch calls. He snatched the phone from my hand. Still I can hear her. 'Baby,' she said. 'If you don't get up out of that bed and bring your Black ass to spread over this one—right now—don't you never bother to come back no more.' Five minutes later he was up, dressed, and gone."

Jonnie stared into space, brooding; her body rocked back and forth, back and forth. Helpless, Jessica waited, trying to find the right moment to leave. She hated the intrusion on her early morning peace. She had come to work, to meditate, not to listen to true confessions. Still she hesitated.

Suddenly balloons appeared in the sky. Blown-up paper bags skimmed the top of the carpeted wall. A chant rose from its far side:

> *Volé volé*
> *Volé tè*
> *Ou Volé fruit boi'm*
> *Ou volé tote mon foce*
> *Main, jamè, jamè*
> *Map kité ou volé*
> *L'air nan zantrail*

Thankful for the distraction, Jessica translated: "Thief, thief. You have stolen my land. You have stolen the fruit from my woods. You have stolen all my force. But never, never shall I let you steal the air meant for the lungs of my children." She laughed, pointing to the balloons. "So he hoards air in those balloons and brown paper bags."

Jonnie refused to join her in laughter. She seemed not to have heard.

"It's a lie!"

"What's a lie, Jonnie?"

"A damn lie. I went to church, the big church on Fifth Avenue. I sat on the steps outside and watched them. I watched them go in and I watched them come out. Piety!" Her voice rose. "Piety on every face. Lips curled up, eyes turned down, so they couldn't see. They're not chaste, you know. They are liars! But I didn't know . . ."

"What didn't you know, Jonnie?" Jessica spoke with compassion. Reaching out, she laid a hand over Jonnie's. Jonnie snatched hers away.

"He . . . is . . . a . . . liar! A thief! He's in jail, you know. He stole from me—from us—our work, my work, my life's best. No, he's no Immaculate Conception, just a fucking thief! Those drugs, you know?

"That's how he destroyed me! From my womb into the drugs! Stealing my life! He joined in the conspiracy against me." Seizing the handle of the coffee pot, Jonnie glared at Jessica. Jessica eased her chair back.

"I breathed life into the holier-than-thou little shit, and there he sits, in jail. Dreams and promises. Dreams and promises. All lies."

Jessica stared at the smoking coffee pot. "Jonnie," she said softly. "Why don't we finish this discussion another time?"

"It bruised my mind," Jonnie muttered.

"My dear, let's not exaggerate," Jessica said, easing her chair even farther back.

"It bruised my mind!" Jonnie shouted, her hand on the coffee pot tightening.

"I'm sure it did. I'm sure it did," Jessica said soothingly, staring at the smoking pot, at the same time pushing herself to her feet. Then, from out of nowhere she heard a big, booming voice that traveled over the terrace.

"Hey, Jess, whatcha know?"

"Maxie!" Jessica cried, and collapsed in her chair. For a moment, too weak to speak, she sat breathing hard, hand against her chest, then: "I say, jolly good to see you." Wide-eyed, she looked up at the big brown-skinned man who had appeared, standing over them, as though by magic.

"All that much?" He grinned, pushed a soiled captain's cap back on his head, and hooked his thumbs through the belt of his dirty ragged shorts. He looked down at Jonnie. "Well, looka here," he said. "Hey, baby, what's happening?"

"I—beg—your—pardon." Jonnie spoke, jumping to her feet. With poise she pushed by the heavy-set young man, and walked away.

Maxie watched her go. He watched as she walked down the steps to the swimming pool, then went to the rail of the terrace to look down at her. "What's with her?" he asked when she had disappeared in the water.

"I really can't say," Jessica answered, still weak, still unsure of what she had just witnessed. 'Her' happens to be Jonnie Dash— artist from the States. And between you and me, I think she's a bit of a snob."

They laughed long and hard.

4

MAXWELL GARDENER THEY CALLED HIM. Jonnie hated him. Hated his crudeness, his loud know-it-all attitude, his overstuffed ego that allowed him to go around the hotel and the island barefoot, pretending he had to account to no one.

But despite his fatness, his heavy legs, his fat feet with toenails packed with dirt, the Haitianophiles loved him. Waiters fawned over his jokes. They brought him tidbits from the kitchen. Claire adored him, happy to have someone with whom to argue, as she was now doing.

Jonnie resented the fact that he had claimed her customary side of the pool, forcing her over to the other side. Unable to relax, she could not shut out their conversation, particularly since Claire insisted on raising her voice.

"I don't believe this, Maxie Gardener. The president of the United States has a slimy counselor who has agreed to implicate him in the Watergate mess, and all you can do is lie there and say '*et alors* . . .'?"

"Believe it, believe it." Maxie wiggled his hips to settle better into the chaise. He rubbed his fat stomach, reached for something from the table to put into his mouth. Then: "Look, your president turned loose his goons to snare his victims and got caught. What else to say? *Et alors* . . ."

"Do you hear what you're saying?" Claire's voice raised to a squeal. "You're saying that our president's dishonest."

"He got it down better than that, baby. He says, 'I'm no crook.' Like hell he ain't. It ain't for nothing that he's called Tricky Dick. How you think he got into politics or got to be president? By praying?" He grinned at Claire as the waiters nudged each other. They might not have understood everything being said, but they always knew when Maxie Gardener had scored a point.

"It seems to me, Maxie Gardener," Claire protested, her long porcelain body in a bikini curved over him, her fists clenched, "you're always pleased when something tragic happens at home. Have you no pride in your country?"

"Which part? The air? The sea? The soil? The people? Man, everything is going to hell—contaminated—just like on this island." He spread his arms wide. A rumble of thunder sounded in the distance, although not even a hint of cloud marred the clarity of the sky.

"Claire, dirty things, shitty things, immoral things, decadent things, crimes against man, against human decency—have been happening long before I came on the scene. Hundreds of books been written on that theme and it's still happening in every backroom of your so-called democracy. So what do you want from me?

"Look around. Take a good look. This island needs help to survive. Your government supplies it. How? By giving arms to this bloodsucking dictator?"

"You're mixing your arguments." Claire lowered her voice, looking around to see who might have heard. "Do you mean to imply that because you consider Duvalier a dictator, the island has no need to defend itself?"

"From whom? The peasants?" Again waiters nudged each other, grinning. Again Max reached for the snacks they had brought him.

"Traitor!" Claire hissed. "At a time when our country needs its citizens abroad to stand by her, there you go villifying her. . . ."

"Do I need to listen to this shit?" Maxie roared, and the waiters wisely busied themselves, rearranging the table as Sam came out on the terrace. "Hey, you guys, give the guests a break. They're not here to listen to the battle of the States. They came to get away from it."

André Bienaimé, coming down the steps to the pool, a girl on each arm, called out, *"La Révolution, la Révolution, toujours la Révolution, n'est-ce pas, Maxie?"* Maxie looked at him, smirking with admiration. "Man, I just talk about it. You're into it."

"A man must choose his life. *C'est la vie, n'est-ce pas?*"

She heard them, André and his girls, as they hit the water, splashing and squealing, acting like children. She buried her head in her arms and listened. She liked the sound of it, loved the sound of the uncaring carefree young. She, Jonnie Dash, had never been like that. She had always cared, carried the pain of caring. About what? Did she want to think about it? No.

Instead, her thoughts turned to Jessica. She sensed a new shading of gentleness when they spoke. Was it understanding? Or patronizing?

Some time later, Jonnie awakened to the sound of Jessica's voice cutting through the droning stillness. "Maxie, my God, what have you been doing since I saw you last, apart from adding to your girth?"

Maxie stretched, looked around the area, emptied except for Jonnie. He caressed his round fat stomach. "This is from staying too long in Jamaica. When I got there, folks were calling me 'pretty boy'; when I left, they were calling me 'big man.' But never you mind. All this grease will be gone when I set out again."

"I hope you're not planning on leaving soon," Jessica said. "I think I'll be needing your help."

"I'm leaving soon. Lucked up on beds of scallops off the Cuban coast. Been unloading them at hotels all up and down the Caribbean. Good money in scallops, Jess."

"You were gone too long. I'm glad you're back."

"It's good to be back. I sailed without sleep night after night just to see a Haitian sunrise. I miss the hell out of this island when I'm away. Then when I'm here for a time, I can't wait to get the fuck out."

Again silence settled over the pool, intensified by sounds from the other side of the thick, flower-carpeted wall: laughter, voices calling out one to another as though from another world.

"Haiti always misses you, Maxie. And you will be doing me a favor if you stay."

"I'm a hustling man, milady. Got to make lots of loot. Loot that stretches and stretches, like elastic."

"I think I'll need your help with the cruise I'm planning. I'm willing to pay."

"How much? Like I say—there's money to be made in scallops. I want to be rich. Not as rich as you, but I'm striving."

"At least you're consistent," Jessica said. "Are you still planning on settling in Brazil?"

"That's where I'm heading."

"What makes you think you'll like it better in Brazil any more than Haiti—or the States? What makes you think that in the shortest time you won't be bored and ready to dash off again?"

"Brazil's the place for me. Haiti's the place I most want to be. . . ."

"Most want to be?"

"Yeah, this is the island where Dessalines kicked the shit out of the French, established the first independent Black state in the hemisphere, and where Charlemagne fought the U.S. Marines to a standstill—until he was sold out."

"But he was sold out," Jessica reminded him. "And nailed to a cross just like your Jesus. What if you don't like Brazil? That would be the end of a dream."

"That's why I'm taking my time to get there. Holding on to a dream. The scavengers are there. It might all be pillaged by the time I get there. But I'm still young."

"Youth lasts such a short time."

"Have boat will travel."

"And leave your youth behind."

"Naw. Ain't about to leave my youth nowhere."

"Whatever. . . . I will be needing your help with this cruise, Maxie, no more than a week."

"What 'bout cuz?"

"Stephan? Sleeping, I presume."

"Why can't he help?"

"Stephan exhausts easily."

Jonnie came to full attention. Until Stephan's name was mentioned she wasn't aware that she was eavesdropping. Now everything said concerned her.

"Besides," Jessica went on, "Stephan doesn't have your understanding nor your broad shoulders."

"Shoulder," Maxie corrected. "The other one melted from the salt of your tears the last time around. By the way—how is your protégé, Jean-Pierre, was it?"

"Maxwell Gardener, you have the ability to make whatever you say sound ugly."

"Now, tell me something new. What's that bastard been up to?"

"Being Stephan, what else? He's a dear—as tolerant of me as I am of him."

"A sleep-in companion who works full time instead of a work-in companion who sleeps full-time," Maxie chanted, and they both laughed.

"Maxie the beachcomber, may you never die."

"Not before you, Jess."

"Then you are courting the possibility that you may never die."

"So what's this cruise about?"

"A weekend in Jamaica."

"Well, I'll be damned. The lady doth find my tub worthy. But I'll have to give her a good scrub down to make her presentable."

"The name of the yacht is *White Swan*, not *Bessie Smith*. The name of its captain is Gilbert Lavel, not Maxwell Gardener."

"Snob."

"Definitely not your boat."

"Yacht, Jess, my yacht."

"It would hardly accommodate a hundred people, Maxie. Captain Lavel's can. Besides, he's a most intriguing young man."

"Yeah, so intriguing that that boat's all he's got left from the millions his father left him. If I live three lifetimes, I couldn't expect to make half as much."

"You won't," Jessica agreed. "But then your worth comes from your abilities."

"Thank you so much. I deserve admiration. But just tell me—how much is your weekend extravaganza gonna set you back?"

Jessica hesitated, then: "We agreed on thirty thousand."

"Thirty thousand?" Maxie sat up, and Jonnie fought against the desire to sit up as well. Having always been poor, the thought of spending that much on anything . . . Thirty thousand for a cruise?

"Jessica, you didn't tell me you were putting a down payment on that tub or that you were ready to jump the fuck out of your simple mind."

"Please, Maxie, there are times when I adore your vulgarity, but this is not one of them."

"Christ, you should be drawing up a contract to buy the fucker—or rent the *QE2*. I'll take you the hell on to Tahiti and back for half that."

"The kitchen staff alone would sink your boat . . ."

"Yacht, Jessica, yacht. I'll give you two cruises for the price of one."

"And host them in your bare feet, with dirt one inch thick around your toenails, while you poke around in your navel and smoke stinking cigars?"

"And she claims she loves me? By the way, you're talking about my cubanos."

"And your teeth," Jessica kept on. "Those lovely teeth can do with a bit of cleaning."

"Baking soda and salt will take care of that. But you, Jess, are you craving adventure or courting senility? If you have to do crazy things, why not just kill yourself and get it over with? That dude is into a lot of things."

"Like what?"

"For one, a beautiful Syrian-Haitian Creole named Monique. Anyone with eyes got to have seen that chick. Folks say she's worked a voodoo spell on him. . . ."

"Shhh." Jessica looked to the terrace, putting a finger to her lips. The object of their conversation had appeared and was looking over at them. "Look at him. Isn't he the most lovely . . . ," Jessica said, and went to the steps.

"Have fun," Maxie called after her.

"Thank you." She laughed. "That is so sweet of you that I'll buy you lunch."

"And that's the most sensible thing you have said all day." "Hey, Maurice," he called to the waiter. "*Apportez-moi, grillio, du riz au poire*—and throw in a bottle of champagne." Then he shouted to Jonnie, "Hey, baby, I know you ain't asleep over there. So get up and come on over—old Jess is buying."

Jonnie stood up, and she, too, walked to the steps. Maxie kept calling out to her, "Ain't no sense in your acting all hincty, baby. It's written in the stars: you and me, we gonna make us some love!"

BOOK

THREE

1

"HATE TO INCONVENIENCE YOU, old man," Jonathan Anderson said, getting into the back of their rented car when they had stopped to merge into ongoing traffic. "But I need a lift to Chez Le Renard. I have business to finish before I catch a plane out before noon."

"Jonathan, I'm sorry," Stephan apologized. "We're off to the beach and late getting started."

"A nuisance not to be able to conduct business by phone. But what can I do?" Jonathan said, not hearing, or preferring not to. "Damn shame. Still, it's better than a few years ago after Hurricane Inez had devastated the island and the entire telephone system. For eternity, it seemed. At least now there are a few lines operating. Not that that helps me out."

Stephan lacked the will to resist. Jonnie resented this giant of a man, who had power, magnetism, and the assumption that whatever he did or said had to be accepted—which proved to be the case. Stephan turned the car around.

"Why are telephones so important when over ninety percent of the people live without toilets, plumbing, or electricity?"

"So true," Jonathan agreed. "But the government needs investments, so they ought to provide the convenience of telephones."

"Which begs the question, doesn't it," Stephan said. "Why are you interested in starting a business here? You're wealthy—and if you permit me, sir, long past the age of retirement."

"Ego," came the prompt reply. "I can make a great contribution, turn this little island around. Adam—you have read of him in the Bible, yes? He was my great-great-grandfather, don't you know. God took a bit of clay to make him, blew breath into him, and said, 'Let there be life.' Then God turned around and gave Adam the power to name all he saw. Since then, we Andersons have been creating situations, building working classes."

"And so now Haiti?" Stephan laughed. "But doesn't a country reflect in equal parts the capabilities of its people? Ninety percent of Haitians are uneducated. Wouldn't it make more sense to build schools first, hire teachers . . . ?"

"Schools?" Jonathan shrugged. "That would be fomenting revolution. I'd rather stick to putting people to work. That brings me joy."

"And a bit of profit, too," Jonnie suggested.

"Possibly . . ."

"A fifedom?" Stephan asked.

"Always possible, but not likely."

"Your friend, Le Renard, why doesn't he have a telephone installed?" Stephan fretted. "Hotels around the island do. And he certainly has the means."

"What? And render Anton Le Renard Dumas a mere mortal? His ego would never support that. His very existence depends on his—and Haiti's—uniqueness, or what rhyme or reason for either?"

"Except perhaps to help out the ugly Americans?" Jonnie guessed. "In one way or the other you must need the man."

"Politics, politics," Jonathan Anderson chided. "What joy would there be in Haiti if one only saw her politically? Le Renard belongs to one of Haiti's most influential families. He's a renegade who sits—"

"Waiting for you to come and breathe life into him?"

"Hostile, hostile," Jonathan chided playfully. "But Miss Dash, I take it you have never met Le Renard?"

Jonnie turned around in her seat to look at him. It surprised her that he remembered her name. "No, I haven't," she admitted.

"Then Stephan, my boy, I suggest that you stop off for a minute so they can meet. You may never have such an opportunity again. Le Renard never leaves his home. You'll find him charming."

"Oh, yes, quite charming," Stephan agreed as their car burrowed through the noise, the mayhem of rue Jean-Jacques Dessalines—its dense crowd standing, talking in the streets; vendors shouting, selling their wares; laughing buyers; people meeting, embracing, exchanging gossip.

Cars maneuvered for space, loudly painted tap-taps—the light trucks used by workers—taxis, and passenger cars; children screamed and cried, dangling around the legs and torsos of adults; mothers sat at the sides of the road, nursing babies from breasts jutting out of ragged dresses while, all around, pigs oinked, brushing past legs, pushing through thick crowds; emaciated dogs shivered, tails fearfully tucked between their legs maneuvering around hostile villagers. At roadside, bleating goats nibbled at vegetation and anything else to be found along the way. Jonnie understood the irate driver of a tap-tap who shouted at a woman in his way, "Your ass is not made of bricks; one tap with this car will start a shit storm from here to eternity."

"Eh," the woman stood her ground. "The man desecrates me and my resting place." A movement toward the driver halted as he stepped on the gas, forcing the woman to jump out of his way.

Determined vendors defied the intention of slow-moving cars displaying wares and produce, only to be forced to scramble to safety, menaced by equally determined drivers.

Closing windows against the brouhaha did not shut out noise. It did keep Jonnie and her companions out of reach of angry chickens, pressed up to windows by anxious vendors.

Miracles sometimes happen in Haiti. One did when they finally turned off the dense, noisy thoroughfare and onto a narrow dirt road—a silent jungle. A deafening calm in contrast to the noisy turbulence left behind. Giant butterflies floated over the hood of the car; birds of brilliant color darted this way and that.

The silence and the vision before them left the sense that, however far they drove, they were nonetheless trapped within a texture of the exotic, giving to each a loneliness, a vulnerability, a sense of helplessness against some great unknown.

Finally they came to a highly varnished hardwood fence, and Stephan honked the horn with the abandon of a newly released prisoner. The barrier parted with automated precision but was in fact pushed by two barefoot men, one on each side. They drove through, and the heavy fence closed behind them with the same studied precision. They found themselves in a vast clearing, desertlike, surrounded on all sides by the same lovely, expertly crafted hardwood barrier.

The first thing that captured their attention: the house with its gold roof, brilliant in the sun—a roof that resembled a Japanese temple. It had been built at the far end of the clearing. Happy dogs rushed up to greet them as they stepped from the car. The happiest and best-cared-for dogs Jonnie had seen since arriving on the island—eyes bright, fur shining.

Jonathan took time out to rub their ears, grateful for the welcome. But Jonnie turned her attention to the monkeys—about seven of them—chained to a wooden cross planted in the yard. They, too, were moved to see visitors. They paced the bars of the cross, jabbering, pointing to the jungle like old men puzzled at being chained so near to the freedom they desired. And standing there gazing from monkeys to woods it became apparent what great, indeed herculean, effort had been required to make so vast a clearing in so dense a jungle.

Nor had the jungle given up. Its plush vegetation crowded the restraining fence that had been made strong, damned near impregnable, to hold it back. Here and there over its top, large plants had unfurled their leaves, branches had tested its seam, forcing bulges in the finely finished planks. Vines had sent tendrils through microscopic openings, which having twisted and turned, found a way to run down the forbidden side, to take root at its base and send other tendrils searching for space. Thick branches that had succeeded in pushing over its top had been cut, and now held out twisted leperlike stumps—threatening.

A feeling of evil, of danger, of entrapment, surrounded the entire area, born of the tension, the ceaseless struggle being waged around the seemingly bare yard. One had to choose sides. And the side Jonnie had chosen was not on the side of M'sieur Le Renard.

On their way to the house, Jonathan diverted them. "Before we enter, permit me . . . ," he said, leading the way to the farthest corner of the opposite wall. There, women were sitting on stools or squatting on heels, working, silently setting stones in cloth by hand, using tiny instruments to tighten the prongs in the casings.

"These women are setting diamonds and pearls in silk," Jonathan informed them, a waiting look in his eyes. "The most exquisite work in the world is being done on these grounds, the pieces to be sent to France for the completion of dresses."

Jonnie stood gazing down at the bent shoulders of the women, knowing they were afraid to look up. Afraid they might damage the cloth or the stones or both. She knew the feeling well. She had done just this sort of work by machine in New York sweatshops—on rhinestones. The diamonds and pearls had been done by higher-paid workers in other factories. Even so, there had been abuse. Loss of jobs for workers—women like her, who had children to support—if one stone broke, one piece of cloth was torn, even by a faulty machine. The threat had kept them glued to their machines from bell to bell.

She realized suddenly who and what Jonathan Anderson reminded her of—a type of employer she had fought against when she had thought her union would back her. Until she had learned that union and boss were both about business, big business; that she and those she had led were but commodities, easily replaced. She had never met her boss, had only looked at him once from across a factory, and his eyes—light gray, almost white eyes—had that same waiting-to-laugh quality.

Yes, she had fought hard for such back-breaking work not to be sent overseas. And for her efforts on the part of the workers she had been fired. She had spent weeks, months, locked out of her job and any other job in that line by her union, not knowing where to go, what to do next. But then she had met Gérard.

A feeling of hopelessness descended over her. Why had she fought so hard to keep these women, as poor as she or poorer, from working? The poor fighting the poor. She sighed, then noticed with satisfaction that around these stalls the forest was succeeding. Vines thick and luxurious had spread out over the stalls, providing a shield for the women against the sun that beamed down on the galvanized tin roofs. The vines wrapped around the supports and down to the ground—a victory of sorts.

There's always a time when one senses the next step shouldn't be taken. She didn't want to move toward the house. "Let's not go in, Stephan," she said. "We have to get back early."

"What for?" Stephan asked.

"I promised Jessica we would be back in time for dinner."

"Never mind Jessica," Stephan said. "She's so taken with her Captain Lavel, I doubt if she'll have time for dinner."

"I don't know . . . ," Jonnie said. "I promised."

"Haven't you noticed how ravishing she's been looking? She's happy."

Still watching the monkeys chained to the cross, she hesitated, and Stephan, not understanding the reason for her hesitation, said, "I told you you'd find him interesting."

"The word used was charming," she corrected.

Jonathan led them, and they followed him to the templelike house, up marble steps to the wooden front door, decorated on both sides by Japanese lanterns. The bell, when pulled, sent a riotous clanging throughout the house.

A cheerful Haitian youth, dressed in Indian Kafir trousers, opened the door, but when he saw Jonathan, the bright smile with which he had greeted them dimmed. Jonathan, too, started when he saw the boy. But only for an instant. He smiled—that smile that never lit his eyes. *"Dis à M'sieur Le Renard que je suis là."*

They followed the boy through a curved foyer and into a spacious parlor where they were greeted by the tumultuous screeching of a world hovering on the edge of madness.

More monkeys. Pastel-colored monkeys in cages along a wall, shrieking, jumping up and down, shaking the bars of their golden cages in outrage. Then, from another part of the room, came the greeting: *"Bonjour, bienvenue. Bonjour, bienvenue."* This greeting from parrots, also caged along another wall, brightly plumed parrots—red and blue, green and black—all with large curved beaks, all staring out at the visitors with dignified curiosity as they intoned, *"Bonjour, bienvenue. Bonjour, bienvenue."*

A nightmare—walls covered with skins, tigers, giraffes, leopards, zebras. Elephant tusks, crossed over one wall, added to the sense of the unreal.

"*S'il vous plaît,*" Jonnie heard the boy say. She came out of her trance to see him smiling at her, knew he had offered her something.

"*Non merci,*" she said, looking around the strange room—its high-backed Indonesian chairs, hardwood floors covered by goat carpets, windows permitting a clear view of the combatant forest.

Heavy red velvet drapes hung over the entrance of a side room or enclosure from which the pungent aroma of hashish and incense and the sounds of voices emanated.

"Come, don't be naughty," one voice said. "One must practice patience in Haiti."

A murmured response brought an impatient "Why must you have just that one? There are so many others—equally handsome. But then you are the romantic, *n'est-ce pas?*"

The murmured response brought another jaded remark: "Cold water, my love. Cold water is known to check one's urges." Then, "Silly boy, who'll hear? Who dares enter my house who would even wish to cause you ennui—and who cares."

Jonnie knew the type well: a man cruel to the point of inhumanity. Arrogant, corrupt, a son of Lucifer; knowing all human weaknesses, he had infinite power to exploit them—for the pure joy it gave him.

It seemed they waited for hours, staring at the monkeys, quieting down now and staring out at them. Actually it had only been minutes when the heavy red curtain lifted and M'sieur Le Renard stepped out, looking very much the fox that Jonnie had imagined. A mulatto with tan skin and kinky red hair, an ageless face creased only by corruption, green eyes young with mischief, old with cynicism—a magnificent decadence.

He floated into the room on a cloud of hashish, still burning in a long ivory cigarette holder held in long, skinny, yellowed-from-nicotine fingers. "Jonathan, *mon cher.*" He walked over to kiss Jonathan on his cheeks. "I thought you had gone off to Santo Domingo by now."

Jonathan glanced at his watch to put meaning to time in that timeless room. "I expect to be leaving by noon. But before I leave I want to clear up some minor details on that real-estate deal." He glanced at the boy standing near the doorway. "I see you have yourself in control." He spoke with the smile that never left his lips, but his nostrils flared gently.

"Oh that," Le Renard said with a wave of his hand at the Kafir-dressed youth, then took a puff on his holder. "Trivia, trivia, trivia. Don't worry, my love, I have the—"

"Stephan dropped me off," Jonathan interceded quickly. "He thought that Jonnie Dash might be pleased to meet you."

"And Jessica?" Le Reynard said to Stephan. "I see you have succeeded in forcing her to abandon me. The time was, Jess always called on me first when she came to the island."

"Jess is quite well," Stephan said, "but busy."

"With the young captain no doubt," Le Renard tittered. Stephan's face darkened.

"For a caterpillar who never leaves his cocoon, you're remarkably well informed."

"*Comme toujours,*" the mulatto shrugged. "I am a very rich man. The world beats paths to the doors of the very rich—to buy, to sell—*n'est-ce pas*, Jonathan?"

Jonathan looked at his watch. "I have a plane to catch, my friend. I came to find out about the contract. Or is there something that might prevent it from happening—the curse of Dessalines?"

"Curse of Dessalines?" Le Reynard's green eyes crystallized in anger. "Of what curse do you speak? You people . . . When you want to talk about the poverty of my people, it's greed and corruption that brought it about. We Haitians don't suffer the curse of Dessalines, my friend. We suffer the curse of Europeans."

Jonathan laughed. "Scratch a Haitian and he bleeds history."

"It's a glorious history from which we bleed," Le Renard snapped. Then he slipped from anger to charm. "*Cher* Jonathan, Haiti's a tiny island compared with your United States. But here too we have a minister of the interior who must be consulted."

"How much?" Jonathan asked. "Anybody can consult, but I'm the man with the money, remember?"

"Oh, vulgar," Le Renard tittered. "You Americans—*mais j'adore la vulgarité, n'est-ce pas?*"

Thinking of the person behind the red curtain, obviously hiding, Jonnie felt a touch of pity. Whatever he wanted had to mean a great deal to him, to have him in league with such a monster.

"M'lord," Le Renard smirked. "So happy to know that you haven't cut my humble abode out of your port of call." Then he looked at Jonnie. Pure wickedness glittered joyfully in his eyes.

"Charles, come. Come see who we have with us."

His bright eyes searched through Jonnie's, making her a part of a conspiracy. His sadism, so pure, so much a part of his personality, deepened her pity for his unseen victim.

Seconds passed, and Le Renard, unable to contain his pleasure, winked at them, then went behind the red drapes and came back dragging his companion out.

"Will you ever believe this," he said as the room exploded into silence. "Jonnie Dash. Isn't that a wonderful name?" The kinky-haired man, with his bright green eyes boring into her, expected her to share his moment of bliss. "It's not often we have the honor of entertaining a Black American sister in our trysting place, is it, Charles?"

Jonnie's heart contracted, then hammered against her chest. Charles McCellen. He stood staring at her, red flooding his face, then receding, leaving it white, its freckles standing out like measles. Speechless, his silence sounded louder than words. Then his green eyes iced over; the plastic diplomatic mask fell, disguising his confusion. If he had hated her before without reason, now he had reason. She had seen him in this house, which if she wanted to joke about it, she would designate a den of iniquity. And what means did he have of silencing her?

Jonnie stifled the urge to plead: "I didn't mean to be here. They made me come. I'll forget that I saw you, I swear. Let's just go on as before—natural enemies, without cause." Their eyes met, fear fused into fear. Le Renard, the man who never missed a blink, never a single beat, laughed joyously.

"We must celebrate this occasion, *n'est-ce pas*, Charles? Champagne!" he called to his boy.

"We have to go," Stephan said. "We're on our way to the beach and it's getting late. Sorry, old man," he said to Charles. "But we'll make it up the next time around."

Le Renard sank into a high-backed chair, crossed his legs, and dangled a slipper from the tip of a well-manicured toe. "Oh sit, sit, sit; what's the hurry?"

Like the images that played over the ceilings and walls before she drifted off to sleep nights, Jonnie saw the end of this king of depravity: he sat in that very chair, while outside the leperlike stumps of arms pushed down the fence, growing, growing as they reached the walls of the house; tendrils of vines, having wormed across to surround the house, slid up its walls, entering through the window, wrapping around his neck, down his arms to his feet, binding him, fastening him to that chair, while the forest went about its work, reclaiming what rightfully belonged to it.

In years to come, children stumbling upon the old house with its golden dome in the center of the dense forest, where monkeys swung from limb to limb, crisscrossing the rooms, would report the discovery and set off a stampede of historians and researchers determined to decide the period when the house had been built and the manner of creature belonging to its skeletal remains.

They were almost out of the room, Stephan and Jonnie, when the clanging of the bell outside the house once again set the monkeys running up and down, screeching in their cages. Once again the bright-colored parrots in their cracked voices chanted their monotonous *"Bonjour, bienvenue. Bonjour, bienvenue."*

The bare-chested servant boy entered, followed by a middle-aged man who came into the parlor pushing a child before him. The child, a boy, stumbled, and in an attempt to break his fall, caught and held on to a golden cage. This sent the terrified monkeys into an even greater panic.

The man, portly and brown, with a gentle face and kind eyes, wore a brown cotton suit. The belt around his waist and the holster that held his gun were brown. The brown man.

"Voilà, M'sieur Le Renard." He spoke in a loud hearty voice to be understood over the din of screeching monkeys. *"Il était bien caché, mais moi—je l'ai trouvé."*

"You see, Charles"—Le Renard's smile took on the aspect of a wolf—"patience always pays. If anyone could find your *petit amour*, it's M'sieur Constant. It takes time, but in Haiti, no matter how one tries to hide, someone always sees, and someone always tells. . . . *Voilà le beau Lucknair. Lucknair, dis bonjour à M'sieur Charles,"* he instructed.

The child mumbled. *"Bonjour*, M'sieur Charles." In an instant, embarrassment, anger, hatred, the plastic formality had fled

Charles McCellen's face. Happiness sparkled in his eyes. He stood mesmerized, softened by passion and tenderness.

"I say, McCellen," Jonathan Anderson joked. "You do have stunning good taste."

What to do? What was expected of her? Who was the boy so precious that he had to be dragged from his hiding place to please Charles McCellen? Resentment beat at her head, blood rushed over her eyes. She hated them—these men with money and power that gave them the right to track down little boys, dragging them to this devil's manor on command. Frightened, she remained silent—and so powerless.

She looked toward the boy, the object of so much activity, this child, who made diplomat Charles McCellen smile. She looked into black eyes, black, black eyes, bright black, which had haunted her, kept haunting her. There he stood, the child of many languages . . .

Where is your mother, child? Where is your father—you with those black, black eyes that have drunk in their whiteness? Little Black boy with your skin stretched over fine bones, black skin stretched over carved stone.

An artist must have fashioned that face. A sculptor must have chiseled its perfection. A poem. A poet is needed to juxtapose words to describe such beauty, to give it meaning. So much beauty, such absolute degradation.

All stared at the child. He stared back, hate and fear clouding his eyes. He stared from face to face, seeking compassion, a way out—the mulatto who had requested him to be brought, the white who desired him, and all who conspired to make of him a thing, their thing. Then he looked at Jonnie. Seeing her, he shrank back, cringing, trying to lose himself in the shadow of cages.

Jonnie, too, cringed into herself from shame and fear. Shame she could do nothing. Fear making her helpless, when she wanted so much to be brave. She cringed from the stare of those wide, black eyes that demanded nothing of her except that she not see him.

And the monkeys, maddened because he had disturbed their cages, screeched. Shrieked in terror. They beat against the bars of their cages and the parrots chanted, *"Bonjour, bienvenue. Bonjour, bienvenue. Bonjour, bienvenue."*

SOMETHING KEPT PULLING AND PULLING her from where she wanted to stay, where giant trees grew, their branches interlocking, allowing tiny streaks of sun to beam through; where children's voices tinkled in her ears. Eyes closed, she imagined little beings running, laughing through fields of green, disappearing behind great trees, reappearing in the bountiful fields, their laughter pure. She wanted to stay, to hide behind trees, to be brave, strong to defy power—to be as precious as the poem of a boy with black, black eyes.

The wind on her face kept pulling at her, cutting her breath; hot sun forced her eyelids to remain closed. She struggled against returning consciousness, struggled to remain in the darkness behind her closed eyes.

Gulping snatches of tangy, pungent, sulfur-laden air, she waited: black eyes fading; trees, plantations, moving back; stilled laughter dropping from the ledge of her mind.

"Did Boysie make it?" she asked in panic. "Did Boysie make it?"

"I have no idea, but I'm certainly glad you're back."

Jonnie raised her eyelids, looked into the too-bright sun. Then she sat up, bowing her head to escape its glare. The top of the car had been rolled back. She looked out at the passing landscape. Gérard had driven her along this road, past the bare mountains, the barren earth, unyielding scrubby mountains—dead mother earth, breastless mother, nippleless mother, bosomless mother, turned-to-silt mother earth.

"Are we near?" she asked.

"Jonnie, what was that all about? Thank God, you're back."

Back? From where? She stared at the road rushing up to them only to disappear beneath the wheels of the racing car. The hands on the wheel held steady. Strong hands, aristocrat-turned-sailor hands, with their sunburned hairs. Stephan's hands. Yes, Stephan's hands.

They had decided to go to the beach. No, Jessica had decided that they go to the beach. Jessica had decided that she, Jonnie

Dash, needed a rest, and should go to the beach. And here they were—on the way to the beach.

"Why did you start running?" Stephan asked.

"I . . . running?" She closed her eyes, closed them to summon darkness. But she remembered and kept remembering.

"Yes, you. You ran out of that house as though demons were chasing you. I took off after you. I supposed the others thought us quite mad."

Ahh, Le Renard. Anton Le Renard Dumas, the fox with the wolf's smile. Then with a sinking stomach she thought of Charles McCellen, his face with its rapidly changing sentiments—fear, hate, love—the passion and all that that meant.

"How is your neck?" Stephan asked. "I had to apply a bit of pressure. Sorry about that."

"Pressure—on my neck?"

"Yes, love. Had to subdue you. You did get a bit violent." Stephan laughed, loud and hearty. He kept laughing.

"I? Violent . . . ?"

"Oh, Jonnie, you are strong. I had no idea. And you are also a damn good sprinter. You must have broken every track record. Even with the car, I had great difficulty catching up. But I refused to let you run loose around the countryside."

There were scratches on his hands and neck and, despite his cheerful manner, concern in his voice when he said, "Talk to me, Jonnie. What is it all about? There we were in that God-awful place—and then there you went . . ."

The screeching monkeys, the chanting parrots—the little boy, the black, black eyes. Jonnie closed her eyes, attempting to close her mind. Pushed those eyes away. His shame. The shame that burned her from her head to her feet now.

How much farther to Jessica's shack anyhow? She needed the water. Needed her body, her head, submerged—complete submersion.

She stared out over the bleak landscape, the barren miles of scrub grass spreading out, making her think once again of Gérard—the tales he told of once-upon-a-time, when these were plantations, the richest in the world. Cocoa plants and the richest coffee in the world. Mountains, thick with mahogany, teak, as far as sight stretched. All devastated by the United States government's futile attempt to produce substitute rubber for World War II that instead had added another layer of poverty to this, the poorest island in the hemisphere.

Gérard had told her tales—and so had forever linked up their memories—of children during the War of Independence bringing messages to the rebels about the movements of the French, from one end of the island to the other.

"Did you ever put up a struggle," Stephan said, calling her back with his laughter. "But what fun! Whatever pumped up your adrenaline, my darling, it took more than a chase to catch up with you. I'd rather take my chances with a claw-snapping lobster in boiling water. The peasants had a great time. They were howling."

"At me?" Jonnie cried, her temples throbbing. "Why are they always laughing? What the hell do they have to laugh about?"

"We were funny," Stephan said. "Damn funny." He laughed louder. "At one time I managed to catch up to you, grabbed you, shoved you in the car. By the time I ran to get behind the wheel, there you were—in front of me doing sixty down the road." Stephan bent over the wheel, almost hysterical.

Jonnie massaged her throbbing temples. She wanted him silent. Still. She needed his silence, his sympathy, not his laughter. How was she supposed to think! Her head ached. She kept rubbing her temples. Stephan attempted to restrain himself. But each time he did, he exploded again with laughter. He was still laughing when he turned off the asphalt road, drove through scrub grass, and pulled up at the side of a dilapidated shack.

"*Voilà*, Jessica's shack!" he said, reaching across her to open the door. Jonnie jumped over the side and ran. As she ran she kicked off her shoes, tore at her clothes, rushing over the sand and into the sea, swimming out in the tepid water, unhappy that it wasn't cold enough to ease her anger.

Agitated, she nevertheless realized that Stephan's laughter had been with, not at, her. At another time she might even look back at this as experience shared—a moment to be enjoyed. Now she needed quiet, needed to collect thoughts. Thoughts that collided with other thoughts, creating an incredible din almost impossible to think through.

Swimming. Swimming, waiting for the return of calm, the easing away of tensions, of anxiety. She swam out until when she looked around, she saw only water. Then she turned on her back floating, her head in her hands, ankles crossed, letting the tepid water cradle her, suspend her between the questionable reality of the sky and the supporting calm of the deep. Only by its absence did she become aware: the roaring in her head had ceased.

So she had run and she and Stephan had struggled. Why had she run? To get away from fear? In her life had she ever left fear behind? Never. Never when it came to law, to authority and power.

Better not to think of it now. Nothing mattered out here on the sea. Pushing all thoughts away, she opened herself to the calm of the sea—and to temptation.

Cradled in the lap of temptation, never to think again or try to; never to care again or care to. Free from noises—the ever-churning machinery of the mind, its agitation, its silent screams—the pain, the constant pain forcing her brows to furrow, the struggle to keep its lines from being forever stamped on her face. Unacceptable.

And in that silence of the sea, Jonnie Dash turned her thoughts inward and looked into the deepest part of her where Emmanuel lay curled up in perpetuity. Into the darkest corner of her mind. She was mad, of course. She had been mad—for how long? Since childhood? Her heart shuddered at the thought. Surely not that far back. She willed her heart still.

And Boysie? Had he made it? Had he, like her, gone back to the synagogue to find that it had become a Father Divine church, where people buzzed around, like angels, and ate food for fifteen cents a plate, and sang songs that had nothing to do with her or him or Sylvie? And had he been forced to adopt a life in which the tunes he played no longer had true meaning? Had he known, as she had, that that part of their lives had been doomed? And had he retreated into that strange inner life to carry the burden of poverty into middle age and beyond? Did she care? And if so, why? Better not to care. . . .

Better to give in to this temptation and be one with the sea—part of its stillness like the seagulls flying overhead—loud, noisy, yet a part of its peace.

"Ahoy!"

She heard his call but remained still. She had joined the spirit of the sea, and she no longer wanted to be touched—not by man nor tree—nor ever put her foot again on sand or earth and so alter her peaceful state and once again start the churning of her stomach, put the furrows back on her brow. All that fear and all that pain. She could not bear that. She didn't want to.

"Ahoy. . . ."

A speck in the distance—and she, another speck floating. Simply by lifting her arms over her head she would sink—out of life, out of his life—without leaving a ripple.

A school of fish swam about her feet. Some nipped at her heels, and suddenly her body tingled! She had begun to feel again. An unreasoning impatience seized her. The fish had disturbed her peace, agitated it, churned up a need, a desperate need. Stupid. Stupid. She tried to relax, to sink back to near stupor. Desperately she tried to summon the will to raise her arms, to sink, sink down out of reach—forever out of reach.

"Where else in the world can you enjoy such delightful water?" Stephan said, swimming up, shattering peace and calm with meaningless talk. How to bring it back? He looked too alive, too vital. "I know," he kept on. "I have tasted the waters of the world, and I promise you this is the best of all waters. I love it. Jessica loves it. And you must love it, too. I insist. This water eases tensions—cures madness." Startled brown eyes searched his blue eyes. Did he know? Had he guessed? "And promotes sex."

Jonnie's body screamed. Desire leaped through her. He put his arms around her, cementing her to him. She wrapped her legs around his hips. Her demands sprang to life—all peace had fled.

They clung together, bodies hard against each other, pulling each other down, down. Wrapped around each other, his prick hard against her stomach, tight, tighter he wrapped his legs, weighing her down into the deep, which moments before she had decided was to be her grave. He crushed her to him, and legs intertwined, they surfaced.

Diving beneath her, he moved between her thighs, nipped at her clitoris even as the fish, moments before, had nipped her feet. Surfacing, he crushed her to him, then in desperation entered her, forcing her to join the noisy seagulls with her screams.

Moving together, into each other, fantasy gone wild, an endless no-beginning-and-no-ending world. Their bodies strove for fulfillment denied to them, even as desire mounted. Each layer of desire becoming more and more poignant, each movement more painful, exquisite. Their bodies melded, forcing them to cling in silent desperation. Tears ... hot tears flowed, wetting one another's cheeks. Without will the tide moved them closer, closer to shore.

Beached, Jonnie dug her toes into packed sand, anchored herself deep in the sand, letting his thrusts reach to the center of her, her stomach, her heart. The agony of it, the absolute agony flowing like blood from head to stomach, peaking, exploding, and in relief they fell from each other, sobbing.

JONNIE AWAKENED FROM A SOUND SLEEP—because of the rumble of thunder? She opened her eyes to the bright cloudless sky. The strident tones of seagulls, the constant sounds of the tide. Perhaps because the water had moved up to their thighs? Perhaps the shifting sands beneath had alerted her to the rapid movement of tide. Stephan still slept.

An imperceptible movement—perhaps a sigh—forced her to look back over her head. A tall, gaunt Black man, his dark gums exposed in a toothless smile, stood looking down at them. Jonnie pushed up to Stephan. He held her close, closer, then becoming aware of her rigidity, opened his eyes. He, too, looked up, then he stretched.

"*Bon soir, bon soir, Afrique.*" He scratched his pubic hairs. Then: "*Mais quelle belle langouste.* Jonnie, have you ever seen a lobster so beautiful?"

The man held a giant lobster up for inspection. "A godsend," Stephan said. He got up and brushed sand from his genitals. "Jonnie, I promise you that you have never tasted the like of lobsters from these waters or those prepared by Afrique." He kissed the tips of his fingers. "*Magnifique. Le feu! Le feu!*" he shouted.

Jonnie sat up, knees drawn to her chest. Stephan's Adam-and-Eve response to the man upset her. His assumption that the man had a right to be there violated her sense of decency, of privacy. Stephan had obviously taken another view. Why not? She had been bathing naked in the hotel pool the night they met. Her official garb around the hotel was the bikini beneath see-through overdresses, which revealed her body. Their perceptions had been spun from different circumstances—and defied logic.

She understood Stephan's thinking. How did a piece of cloth elevate her morals, and how, in this country, did a man walking on an open beach violate her privacy? The contradiction was hers, of course. But this did not prevent shame from spreading through her when he pulled her to her feet.

"Come, love," he sang out in obvious high spirits, satisfied with the way their entire day had turned out. "Let Afrique prepare our supper while we prepare to dine."

They walked toward the shower, with Stephan extolling the virtues of the man.

"Jessica named him Afrique. He reminded her of someone she had known in Gabon. She fell for him because of his uncanny instincts—he is sort of a magician, you see. There are no pipes, no huts, no telephones for miles around, yet whenever we come, *voilà* Afrique, with all the luxuries: water, lobster, sometimes turtles."

While Afrique went to start the fire at one side of the shack, they went to the other to take their shower, which turned out to be a big can punctured with holes, tied to a pole next to a barrel full of fresh water on which a big calabash floated. They bathed each other. First Stephan kept pouring the calabash filled with water over her, then it was her turn. Shame forgotten, they laughed, giggled, and squealed with an energy reminding her of André's teenagers. Had it been Shakespeare who said: All's well if the end illusion makes one happy? She delighted in the illusion.

The shack was remarkable in its humbleness. Boards nailed together made up the long room; the galvanized roof had been covered with banana leaves, and it was furnished with one long table with two long narrow benches on each side, one unvarnished chest used to store swimming apparel, and one long mirror leaning against a wall awaiting someone's good intentions to hang it. Tiny lizards scurried out of their way and around their feet and were, it seemed, the only occupants.

Stephan took two towels, gave her one, then went to supervise the cooking of the lobster. Drying herself, Jonnie looked around for her clothes and not seeing them called out, "Stephan, where are my clothes?"

"Where did you leave them?" he called back.

Jonnie vaguely saw herself running toward the water, undressing as she ran. Hadn't Stephan collected her things? She looked out the door. The tide had risen, almost approaching the shack. The entire beach had become the sea, even the spot where they had recently been sleeping. Her clothes were gone—swept away by the tide.

"They're gone!" she wailed. Stephan came to the corner, eyes twinkling, attaching no more importance to her lost clothes than he had to Afrique standing over them, staring at them as they slept, or to the peasants laughing at them on the road. To what did this man attach importance, this laughing man-child? How vast the difference in their way of seeing things. As vast as the sea.

"Never you mind," he said, still laughing. "We'll think of something." Then he went back to the side of the shack to watch Afrique cooking over the charcoal grill.

Jonnie stood leaning against the doorjamb, gazing out at the approaching sea. All her tensions, her anxieties had returned. In desperation, she fought against depression, fought to hold on to the euphoria she had felt while taking the shower, fought to fit into Stephan's mood, hearing him laughing and joking with Afrique.

Oh, to be like Stephan Henshaw—to walk around naked, unfettered, free from all the contradictions that bound her. Stephan Henshaw, a free man, so free that he never had to think of the word freedom. For one moment out at sea she had known freedom—but only for a moment.

"What am I to do?" she asked Stephan as he came toward her, holding the grilled lobster on a banana leaf.

"Eat," he said putting it on the table.

And the lobster justified Stephan's faith in the man. Never before had Jonnie tasted one better prepared or more succulent. They shoved fistfuls of the fleshy meat into their mouths, sucked the tiny claws, chewed them until shells grew into mountains.

Eating quieted her down, yet when Afrique came to scrub the table, she gazed at his back and wondered how many naked bodies he had seen stretched out on the beach in front of Jessica's shack. Had he ever seen Jessica sleeping naked? And had he stood looking down at her, perhaps admiring her full breasts?

What nonsense. Who had a better right to sleep on the sand

in front of the shack than Jessica herself? "I promised Jessica I'd be back for dinner," Jonnie confessed, to assuage her guilt.

"Never mind; we'll be forgiven," Stephan said in his uncaring way. "By the way, Afrique promised to bring back something for you to wear."

The sun had almost set when Afrique left. With his going, a sense of contentment prevailed. Sheer joy to be alone, unobserved, and still have a small part of their day left.

Darkness came sneaking in. Stephan lit the gas lantern and placed it near the door. Stretching out on the table, they looked out of the door, watching the sea approach, until sea and sky joined. Darkness deepened, and they watched moths fluttering around the lantern, heard beetles hit against its glass with musical clicks.

Silence extended from them to the sea, a serenity made profound by good food eaten, good sex, and the determination to enjoy all.

"Stephan," Jonnie whispered, "if you were asked to make a wish and it could be granted, what would you wish for?"

"Now? This minute?"

"Yes."

"To keep this moment going forever."

Was he being glib or had he thought she wanted just that answer? Had she? That would mean, then, that they were both dishonest.

But the day had been a revelation for her. The full awareness of her madness, her willingness to let go, and then the complete sexual experience—an experience that had touched the core of her. That had never happened before. Why today? Because of the man? Her constantly shifting attitude toward life—and death? Her desperation? Or did she love him? Did it matter?

"Have you ever thought of leaving Jessica?" she asked without intending to. That question, once asked, placed a burden on their relationship—one she wasn't ready for.

"No, I haven't," Stephan said. His hands, as they caressed her body, never faltered.

"Do you love her?" Jonnie asked. She didn't want answers. She had been pleased with their established pattern of morality. It had been satisfying. Their calculated deceit. Infidelity, if that's what it was, committed by willing adults, companions, cousins, lovers—an uncommitted commitment.

"Yes, I love Jessica," he answered. That simple answer sent a violent wave of jealousy through Jonnie. "I have always loved Jessica, really. She is an extension of me, and I her. We are tied by something called culture—background, family.

"Tales of Jessica, the brave, headstrong Jessica, were a part of my childhood, as much as the Knights of the Round Table. It was she who made it easy for me to break with tradition and go off, an ordinary sailor. She had broken with tradition first.

"I met her when I was already grown—in Africa."

"You met Jessica in Africa?"

"Gabon. I was a lad when she left England—after the Great War. She never went home again, that is, until I went to bring her back. She'd been quite ill, you see. The bottle. Quite broken up over an African chap. They were to marry—then an accident—a terrible blow to her.

"She had been creating quite an uproar, which eventually called for governmental intervention. The French government got in touch with the British government, and they thought it best that she come home. She had absolutely refused to leave, and so they sent me. I was the only one who didn't know her, since she had left home when I was a child.

"So off I went to Gabon to confess my undying love. And so, because I was young, and comely, she decided to go home with me to get much-needed care—in a sanitarium."

"Drinking?"

"Yes. Jess is frightfully allergic—can't touch the stuff. We have been together ever since."

"But you're so much younger," Jonnie said, and her face burned from the shame of betrayal.

"Absolutely not," Stephan protested. "Jessica might have been born some twelve years before me, but in temperament she's far younger."

"Do you love her enough to go on like this forever?"

"Yes—and no. At first I thought I might. Recently I'm not so sure. I'm not getting any younger. Now I think of children—heirs, that sort of thing. But I do love her."

Jonnie pulled away from him, and feeling her withdraw, he

cried, "But, Jonnie, I love you, too! I have loved you since you brushed by me in the dark on your way to jump into the swimming pool. Exciting. Wild. An untamed woman out there swimming with bats. Never have I been so excited. You excite me now." He pushed against her, his penis hard against her thigh. "And today—our struggle on the road—until the peasants laughed?"

Once again Jonnie was struck by the difference in their perceptions. How differently they saw her, the woman. To him, indeed, she was an illusion—a Black, exotic woman. His idea of her drawn up from his need for excitement, his love of the flesh.

But she, too, had a love of the flesh. She had thrived on hard dicks and firm behinds, and long fingers and sensuous mouths. Never had she drawn a clothed figure—only nudes. She had made a living drawing soft breasts, soft stomachs, and the swollen veins of throbbing pricks—the pulsing need behind stone faces, the consuming need of sinners, the greater need to delve beyond sin to art.

And Jessica—how noble to be loved beyond need. She, Jonnie Dash, had never been so loved. That one time—Gérard—it had been an experiment, one that had succeeded. *Hélas!* No, never loved, not in her entire life—not with love that never died, tied as that was to culture, background, family. That love remained beyond the reach of orphans. "You love women!"

"Yes."

So simple an answer to an accusation meant to be harsh confounded her. She had expected a lie—indeed, wanted a lie. She had needed him repeating the details of his love, his excitement the night of the swimming pool, the tidal passions felt today at sea.

"Like this?" she asked, pushing against him. "You love all women like this?"

"Never like this," Stephan whispered.

"Never like today?" Jonnie insisted.

"Jonnie, I swear to you—never!"

"I want you, Stephan!" she cried in desperation, and his answering cry also reflected desperation.

"Jonnie, give me a child!" Barter? A promise. A pact? The impossible?

"Stephan, I have no child to give."

Silence spread out to touch the sea, the moving tide. It came back and hovered over them, waiting.

"Then, Jonnie, we can only share pleasure—never pain. But let's always have this pleasure to share."

And in that orgasm, with those words sounding, resounding through her, with the sound of lapping waves and the constant sighs that came with the tide, Jonnie heard the truth and gained knowledge of a life already spent.

THROUGH THE SOLID WALL OF DARKNESS Afrique miraculously returned. Wedged between the sliver of sand near the shack, he handed Stephan the dress.

"Afrique says it's his daughter's best." Stephan laughed. "I have given him my word that we'll take the best of care with it."

Jonnie slipped into the dress and stood staring into the mirror at her image reflected in the flickering light of the lantern. Gone were the years of determined sensuality. Instead she saw a childlike figure in a shapeless dress torn at its armpits, its material frayed from too many beatings against too many rocks at riverbanks. A lonely girl whose face merged into the insignificance of the surrounding gloom.

"Love!" Stephan cried, laughing, teasing. "You make an adorable orphan." Jonnie grabbed the dress at its neckline, ripped the fragile fabric down to the waist, then kicked it as it dropped to her feet. "I'll drive through the streets of Port-au-Prince naked before I'll have that dress against my skin. My days as an orphan are over. Do you hear me! Over!"

2

AFRIQUE, AFRIQUE, HOW ASHAMED I AM. I am so ashamed. Unmoving, Jonnie lay staring up at the ceiling, her thoughts going around and around. I am not like them. Like Frieda. Like Delores. I have fought—hard—to be their opposite. How, then, did it happen that I have become them?

She remembered the last time she had seen them standing at the door of Delores's apartment. She had not been invited. Miss Ilma had, and had sent her with regrets. They had both come to the door: Delores and Frieda. "We didn't invite you," Delores had said, adding: "Just because Gérard has accepted you, did you think we had? He's gone—back to his wife. I guess you didn't know he had a wife, did you?" The door had slammed in her face, shutting her out. She had stood there, not knowing what had happened, hearing only their laughter—Frieda's and Delores's. She heard their laughter high over the music, the background voices of invited guests. Then Frieda had said, "Talk about a sow's ear. Did Gérard really think he could make out of *that* the proverbial silk purse?"

"If she wants to see us again," Delores had added, "she had better look around for another French-speaking professor—or an African diplomat." Their laughter had been loud, hilarious to be heard on the other side of the door.

But she had loved them. She had sat side by side with them at Gérard Auguste's feet in Miss Ilma's living room. She had worshiped them as they had worshiped him. She had fallen in love with them as she had fallen in love with him. Never had she seen the likes of them—Black intellectuals—sitting alongside white intellectuals, listening to the brilliant, philosophical pronouncements of the West Indian scholar.

One did not see them on the streets, nor were they ever portrayed in the hundreds of motion pictures, shown in the dozens of cinemas around the city. Only in the privacy of the salon did one chance to meet these young, attractive, educated women.

How could she not love them—their expensive clothes, their well-dressed hair, their fingernails never showing the chipping or peeling of ordinary people's. Their faces made up, the clean smell of them. Their conversation. Words that revealed how empty her world—hers and Sylvie's and Boysie's—had been.

They had oohed and aahed but raised their eyebrows when Miss Ilma had pulled out her drawings and said, "Just take a look at these pricks our Jonnie drew when she was little." Then had looked away and promptly forgotten them.

Yet each time they met, a new word was added to her vocabulary. A word, which she ran home to look up and repeat and repeat and repeat until it became a part of her vocabulary.

Words used to describe the plight of the poor Black children, the crimes done against them by the Establishment, the constant struggle needed to elevate them from poverty. Beautiful words that located the potential in every poor person, if only they were given a chance. Had Gérard Auguste used her as an example to prove their hypothesis?

She played her part perfectly. Dark girl with kinky hair. So intelligent, so beautiful. She, a mere factory worker, had only tales to tell of sweat and tears? While they had futures—the professions—in which to disappear and take refuge? Why had he chosen her, when they loved him, too. Ahh, Afrique . . . Afrique.

She lived once again through the blinding, deafening pain that only they could have caused her. She had walked the streets for hours, for miles before she heard what they had said: "He's gone back to his wife."

He had gone home for Christmas, she had thought. He was coming back as he always did. But they had said, "He's gone back to his wife."

She didn't believe them. Didn't believe he had a wife. She didn't believe that he who had helped her to draw again and had been at her side at her first showing, who had helped her find a loft and thus the space to work and nurture her talents, had gone.

There was no one to talk to. Behind their big words, their brave talk, their intelligence, there was a blank wall—and she hit it. A wall of crushed hopes.

Had she intended to end her life that day? She stood staring into the water, Hudson River, and then she heard a voice from behind. "Ma?"

Miracles. How had he known where to find her? Love. Love had guided him. Love for Gérard—they had spent many never-to-be-forgotten summer days at the pier, the three of them. They had been there the day Gérard had asked him, "Would you like me to be your father, Emmanuel?" And Emmanuel had answered, "Yes."

How dare he! How dare he!

"Ma, let's go home," Emmanuel had said. Little boy that he was, he had opened up his arms for her to crawl into. Young, sweet, yet never to have a man to call Dad or Pa or Father. Neither of them to have a man to claim as their own. Yet he had stood up under it better than she . . . or had he?

"Ah, Afrique, Afrique, Afrique . . ."

"HEAR, HEAR, WHAT'S GOING ON IN HERE?" The door of the room flew open and Jessica strode into the darkness. "What nonsense. You refuse to eat? To talk? To see anyone? Cécile told me you are still alive. She claims you want to be alone to write. What? Your obituary? How dare you shut yourself away when I have so much work to do."

She stood over Jonnie, her gray eyes pretending anger. Reaching down, she felt Jonnie's forehead.

"My dear girl, you're not at all ill." She pulled back the bedcovers, squeezed her nose in disgust, then threw them back to cover Jonnie. "Good Lord, get up out of that bed and bathe."

Quickly she walked to the window and pulled back the curtains. Sunlight spread through the room, lighting the walls, ceiling, lighting up Jessica's yellow linen suit and her floppy straw hat with its bright yellow ribbon. Life embraced the room.

"Jonnie Dash, get up out of that bed this instant. Stephan's in a state. He's sure you're contemplating suicide—exaggerating an incident over a silly dress. Maxie swears you're going through the menopause—he has such a foul mind. Gérard, our ancient rebel, is wearing out the carpet in the salon. Claire threatens to sue him for destruction of property. She's convinced you're dying of some dread disease. And I—dear Jonnie—have missed you terribly."

The last, simply stated, brought a thickening to Jonnie's throat and tears to her eyes. "Is it your son, Jonnie?" Jessica asked, her eyes searching through Jonnie's.

Jonnie glanced in the corner of her mind where Emmanuel crouched, not to be brought or thought out. How had Jessica learned about him? Gérard? "N-no, not my son. I—I guess I'm just tired, Jessica."

"Aren't we all, Jonnie? Isn't that what it's all about? Being tired . . . and keeping on?"

An ancient anguish surfaced in Jessica's face, her eyes. What did this wealthy, cultured British woman—slaver, instead of enslaved—know about a tortured existence? An existence, no, mania, that could strike out to hurt, intentionally, someone so kind, so simple as Afrique?

"I—I can't work," Jonnie answered, finding a shield big enough to hide behind. "I doubt that I shall ever work again."

"What rot," Jessica scoffed. "Gérard brought down your painting of Old Ambroise. Superb. Magic. Absolute magic!"

"You like it?" Jonnie asked.

"Like it? I must have it! Whatever bruised your mind, my dear, left you somewhat of a genius."

"It's not finished."

"One more stroke and it will be irredeemable. Now, will you get up out of that bed."

Jonnie stirred, and the smells trapped beneath the covers over the past few days rose to overwhelm her. "I stink," she said.

"I'll say," Jessica nodded, agreeing. "But don't let that add to your malaise. I've inhaled far more noxious fumes and am happy to recommend the restorative power of water."

Jessica Winthrop had restorative powers. Her yellow suit and the floppy hat with its bright ribbon had restorative powers. Jessica's hand on her brow had the healing power of a medicine man. Jonnie slipped from beneath the covers and staggered to the bathroom. But the moment she got under the invigorating shower, she felt the returning of her strength. She let the hard spray tingle her scalp, her shoulders, her back, and turning on the cold tap, she laughed, not knowing the reason for her laughter. Had she forgiven herself for her intended abuse of Afrique? Would she ever forgive herself?

Standing at the window, Jessica heard the laughter and frowned. Jonnie's fast-shifting moods were unsettling. Something terrible had happened at the beach to occasion Jonnie's three days of self-imposed solitude. Stephan had suggested that Jonnie enjoyed exaggerating. Cécile had complained that she lay in bed *"comme une folle."* Either way, they both had pointed, without knowing, to one conclusion. Jonnie Dash was a disturbed person. She might very well be mad.

After peeking into the shadowy substance of her mind that early morning, Jessica had hoped that all Jonnie needed was a bit of rest. Possibly she needed more extensive and expert care.

Emmanuel? Immaculate Conception? Whatever did she

mean? How did one find out? How did one get into Jonnie Dash's mind when every path one took one stumbled over giant boulders guarding a vault of shadows? Clearly she needed help.

Jessica looked out at the picture-perfect mountains. They put her in mind of Jonnie's chiseled face. Her face superimposed itself against them. Jessica blinked to clear the vision, then stood staring up at the lofty, indestructible creations.

Haiti. She loved the island. Slavery and imperialism had created its poverty and its glory—the enigma, the metaphor of the Americas. Here, in Haiti, where slaves had mounted the only successful slave rebellion to win their independence, all the great powers—Britain, France, Germany—had converged to prevent her progress. Even the United States, itself a newly liberated colony, adapting to the customs and mores of the existing world, on the brink of industrialization and in need of cheap labor, refused to come to the aid of the fledgling nation—fearful that the glorious independence of a Black nation would arouse the passions of its own slaves. And so, like Christ's, Haiti's glory became her cross to bear, exemplified by Charlemagne being nailed to his cross by the American marines who occupied the island from 1915 to 1934.

The Haitian dilemma had always been, and continued to be, how to lift the island, degraded by Europe's eighteenth-and nineteenth-century greed and debauchery, into the twentieth century, when greed and debauchery were endemic. The ruling circles on this insular island were prideful of their revolution and scornful of intellectual scrutiny, jealously guarding patterns of culture leftover from the long-discarded patterns of eighteenth-century Europe.

Yes, in Haiti all things remained constant—the inevitable overthrow of governments, its lofty mountains, its peasants shackled to the past in the slow movement of time.

Herein lay its charm, its mystery: the almost imperceptible movement of time—twenty-four hours taking forty-eight hours to pass—giving the illusion that one had nothing but time, to think, to plan, to dream. Intellectually, and with a shudder, one knew it had to end. But one had all that time to think and muse upon its end.

Strong fragrances, herbal perfumes, forced Jessica from her

reverie. She turned to see Jonnie standing before the mirror ap-
plying oils over her firm, muscular body. She had lost weight. Not
that it mattered. Neither Jonnie's weight nor makeup nor enticing
sheer dresses hid the beauty that lay in a shrouded mystery hinted
at by her deceptively bright eyes. An enigma—as much an enigma
as, indeed, Haiti. Their eyes met in the mirror, and an electrical
charge bristled from one to the other.

"What were you thinking, Jessica?" Jonnie asked.

"That your face looks like an African carving."

"That's because you always have Africa on your mind," Jonnie guessed.

Startled, Jessica searched through Jonnie's eyes. "I never
stop," she admitted.

"I have always wanted to go there," Jonnie said. "As a child
crowds of us listened to African nationalists talking about Africa
on street corners in Harlem. Nobody thought of going.

"Marcus Garvey had thought of it. But he had been discred-
ited and banished from the States by the government. Still, his
cause made lively conversation. Africa became our dream. It was
out there somewhere, but no one had the money to go. We were
all trapped dreaming in this hemisphere."

"You have missed a lot by not going," Jessica said.

"I know. I know. What is Africa like?"

"Africa as a continent is diverse. Its countries—some are
quite beautiful. One never goes there and wants to leave. The
people, the places are beautiful. Africa is ugly. Its ugliness is its
history—still being played out. A wound on the soul of Europe
that Europe refuses to let heal. Its history binds them together—
Africa to Europe, America—the world.

"I went after the Second World War. Germany's bombing of
London dragged me out of a sheltered and boring existence. I
went to assist with the wounded in London, and when the war was
over, I never wanted to go back to my previous life.

"I decided to visit our overseas territories—just before they
started becoming our former colonies. I first thought to settle in
Rhodesia, then found that I detested British colonials. Incredible
the intelligence—or lack of it—of those we chose to govern the
lives of others.

"So I went to French West Africa. The language, of course,

was the challenge. I adored Senegal, became infatuated with Da-
homey, and settled in Gabon to work at the Albert Schweitzer
clinic. Hard work. But I loved it."

"But he was racist," Jonnie said.

"My dear, we all were," Jessica said. "Times were different.
We didn't concern ourselves with those terms. We owned the
bloody place, don't you see. . . .

"I was working at the clinic when I attached myself to Doctor
Faye—Doctor Ibo Faye, as his assistant."

"Your lover?" Jonnie guessed.

"My fiancé. He was Senegalese but doing his practice in
Gabon. A remarkable man. The French, at that time, refused to
pay the African doctors the same salary as they paid white doctors,
even though they had done the same training in France. As a result most African doctors remained behind to practice in France,
while white doctors went to Africa, assured of rapid advancement.
Regardless of that, Doctor Ibo Faye had refused to remain in
France. Insisted that he work in Africa, though there could be no
advancement for him and his pay would never be commensurate
with that of whites. He had gone to school, done his studies for
the African people, and that's where he intended to work."

Jessica paused to look out at the mountains, allowing her
thoughts to take her back over the miles and miles traveled
through villages, forests; having to hack their way through thick
brush on a suspicion that a village, unknown, unserved, might be
found. She remembered the introduction of the first Citroën with
its suspension chassis. Ibo Faye had demanded one. It made it easier to discover lost villages.

How to tell Jonnie Dash of working so hard, of being so tired
that one simply did not feel tiredness, of realizing this only by
looking into the serious face of the person one loved?

"You have no idea what poverty is, Jonnie."

"How dare you," Jonnie bridled. "What do you know about
me?" Standing in panties and camisole, Jonnie looked young,
much younger than her years. "How do you know what I know of
poverty?" she cried.

"You cannot know, that's all," Jessica said, tired thinking of
her experiences even now. She knew that Jonnie had had a hard

life. She had no desire to trivialize a life that had left Jonnie, so lovely a person, mentally distressed.

The entire story of the slave trade has never been told. How does one tell of the damage done by the forceful removal of every strong, able-bodied person from villages leaving only babies and the old? The forest soon reclaims its own. Quickly it overruns paths that had been hacked out for roads. It creates impassible barriers, forcing the weak to forgo a future, destroying their present, locking them into a past they had long outgrown. Lost villages. The miracle babies and the old survive. Forests take care of their own.

"You may have been to Africa," Jonnie said in the way of a challenge, "but you haven't been to Harlem."

"And Haiti?" Jessica asked, to prevent what promised to become a tirade. And Jonnie fell silent.

"Jonnie, we went into villages where over ninety percent of the people were blind from diseases for which we already had the cure. Lost villages we stumbled upon. Even then, there was only one doctor who cared. Doctor Ibo Faye.

"One time we encountered an old clinic run by two nurses from Canada. No, Jonnie, don't turn away. They were white. But they had lived in the bush for years and had been forgotten by the outside world. They cared. Women from surrounding villages had heard of them and had walked miles—days and nights through forest and brush—to have their babies delivered. These women gave birth, then had to walk back the way they had come, their babies wrapped in ragged blankets used over and over again and returned. The people around the clinic also had to walk miles for water for the babies and for the two nurses to wash their hands and cook. They looked a sight when we found them, from blood spattered over their faces and aprons, which had been washed, but which had remained stained, for years.

"We saw them only once, left them the few medical supplies we had, promised to be back with more. We never went back. We tried and got lost. Oh, the work we had, the distances to travel, with one or another village needing us—because of outbreaks of this or that terrible disease."

Jonnie sat on the bed. Jessica looked at her, wondering if she had heard a word. Did she understand? Could she even begin to comprehend the cruelty of the forests, the bush? Could it have the same meaning to she who had spent her entire life working to pull herself up out of poverty? How to explain in a hundred words or less the bleakness of a land where the strong had disappeared, leaving the old enfeebled, dazed, and never understanding—and so never capable of explaining to their young the vastness of the loss from which they were still suffering? How many generations would it take to undo that which had been done? Could it ever be undone? How to tell this to Jonnie Dash and not challenge her right to be considered the poorest, the most betrayed? Indeed, how to tell that to any Haitian peasant?

Jonnie stared at Jessica with contempt, devilment twinkling hard in her eyes. "What you are saying, Jessica, is that you white mothers . . ."

Jessica stared into the vindictive eyes, then she said, "I loved him. For years we worked side by side—sometimes without speaking. I knew so well what was needed, and I was always ready—beside him, his willing nurse. I worshiped him at first, for his dedication—and then I realized that I loved him.

"One night we stayed over in a village and fell asleep in an old thatched hut. During the night, I felt his arms around me holding me—and this long, gangling woman, whom you see here before you, curled into him, and my body fitted into his short, slight build perfectly. . . .

"What poreless skin, Jonnie." Jessica broke off to gaze with hunger at Jonnie's smooth darkness. "Polished ebony. A homely man, my Ibo, a tender man. He taught me gentleness—that was his genius." Sighing, Jessica once again looked out at the mountains.

"Love and compassion were his tools—this man who spent his life studying medicine for his people. Villagers swarmed around him wherever he walked. They knelt before him. He was their god. He touched the head of a child and it was like a benediction. He smiled and the elderly were healed. They had faith.

"Nights we spent driving on the road. Days we spent in villages, giving vaccinations, performing operations, or caring for vexing diseases—blindness, eczema, yaws. Oh, the relentlessness of the tropics.

"Villagers loved him, children loved him. But no one loved

him more than I. I cannot, I shall not give that honor to anyone. No king or chief, no god has ever been loved as I loved Ibo Faye.

"I have never been considered lovely. Never have I been praised for tiny hands, well-formed feet, or perfect teeth. I have never been a woman whom men found easy to adore. Ibo Faye adored me. He loved me for my courage, for my work. I went to Africa bored, arrogant, courageous—and grew into a great human being. I am a great human being, Jonnie Dash. Because I care."

Jessica waited for Jonnie to react, agree with her challenging statement. Jonnie sat waiting. "When Ibo Faye died, he received absolution from the tears of the villagers. Babies hushed their fretting to allow parents their anguish. Everyone who had known him mourned his passing. And I, Jonnie Dash, I died with him.

"Eight years we lived together. For five of those eight, we were engaged. One day we set the wedding date—the next week he was dead.

"Yet I knew he was going to die, Jonnie. The woman I had become knew he had to die. My senses told me. The world had no space for a man so good as he, nor for happiness so great as mine. He was good, strong—and so fragile."

From across the room Jessica searched Jonnie's eyes, and still Jonnie sat, not moving. "A fragility as intangible as atmosphere, as mystical as the forests through which we had to hack our way. A fragility as persistent as the illnesses that laid to waste those forgotten bodies in their remote villages. No—the world had no place for such greatness.

"I remember one day driving back from the bush in his Citroën. His one indispensable luxury. We had to stop for a herd of goats to cross the road. After they passed, Ibo started the car just as one kid doubled back into its path. Ibo nudged it and it ran bleating back to the herd. Onlookers seeing it laughed. No harm had been done. Ibo was badly shaken; we stopped at a bar and sat for the longest time, drinking.

"Another time, again on our way back to town, a flock of birds—beautiful, silver-blue birds—flew from a nearby tree. They broke formation, some veering to the right or left, out of the car's way. One flew directly at us, hit against the windshield. Blood and feathers spattered over the glass.

"Ibo stopped and wiped the blood from the windshield. He

gathered up the feathers from the road—I have them still—beautiful silver-blue feathers. Then he pulled to the side of the road, laid his head against my breasts, and cried.

"Never have I seen such tears. Perhaps he simply had become weary. Or perhaps the overwhelming responsibilities that he had so boldly undertaken had become too heavy. Or perhaps he had just begun to understand the enormous and enduring impact caused by the enslavement of his ancestors, the poverty created for his generation and the generations yet to come. Or it might simply have been because he hated killing so lovely a bird.

"His hot tears burned into my breasts—a premonition? An omen? He died on that same road a month later. I had not gone with him. I had stayed in the town preparing for our wedding . . . but I see him now racing back to me. He loved to drive fast. It helped release his tensions, gave him respite, a bit of excitement from the monotony.

"No one saw the accident. Early the next morning, a *baron sharet*—an old man with a donkey cart—found him mangled in the wreck of the car at the root of a baobab tree."

Silence held them, and somewhere in the space between there was a reaching out—a begging. So much told, an entire life bared—a crime against generations. Pain. Heartbreak. Agony. And yet she had not told all—couldn't.

Jessica Winthrop didn't cry. She had no tears. All had been shed once upon a time when she had lost her life.

Tears came to Jonnie. How many psychiatric sessions had Jessica needed to extract her pain and to inject Doctor Ibo Faye into her bloodstream, into her brain, her pulse, her heartbeat, to canonize him within her so that she might speak his name as she had today? Tell this tale without tears?

Jonnie looked away from Jessica's agony. A tragic tale. A wounding tale. A humbling tale—and it had touched every tender part of her. Yet side by side with the tenderness, the familiar old resentment. Envy that this woman born to luxury, the aristocrat, had so moving a tale to tell about Africa, a tale to which everyone would listen, wanting to hear it. While she, Jonnie Dash, born in despair, despair framing every inch of her growth and development, had only tales that evoked shame in her and made others turn from her.

"I shall never love again," Jessica said. "I have never loved again. For that—that would encourage infringement on the most precious days of my life."

The martyr. And Stephan? The name sprang to mind and hung suspended in the air. Their eyes clashed. "And Captain Lavel?" Jonnie asked, conjuring up just the right person to lighten the atmosphere.

Jessica laughed. "Dear Jonnie, at our age we women need excitement to get along with life and living—or what's the use?"

"Our age?" Jonnie turned an indignant eye to the gray-haired woman at the window.

"Yes," Jessica said with determination. "We are around the same age. We relate to the same time frame. Somehow, Black women do stay young-looking longer—and you . . ."

"That's because Black women take much longer to really start living," Jonnie snapped.

Jessica's eyes when they met Jonnie's in the mirror were soft, friendly, probing. "Your son, Jonnie—how old is he?"

Jonnie reached for her earrings, her hands fumbling so badly she couldn't put them on. Jessica dropped another question: "And your husband—did you see him after he left your bed early that morning?"

Jonnie stared at Jessica, surprised. As Jessica had suspected, Jonnie didn't remember having spoken to her that morning.

"Now and then," Jonnie said, speaking slowly, carefully. "Sometimes at his mother's. We went to visit her. Or sometimes he called to find out about Emmanuel. I think he wanted to come back—after about a year—two. But he never did. She killed him."

"His mother?"

"No, his lady," Jonnie said.

"Oh—my dear . . ."

"Yes. We—his mother and I—went to the morgue to identify his body."

"How awful for you!"

"Funny seeing him there—on that slab of concrete. Tall man. Big. Handsome. Lying there. Prick all useless . . ."

"Devastating."

"His mother cried. 'He's so young,' she said. 'Only thirty-five. He had so much to live for.' "

"At thirty-five, he certainly did," Jessica said.

"But I told her. 'He had a great life,' I said. 'Better than mine,' I said. 'There lies a man who had everything he wanted in this life,' I told her. 'And I guess he'll get more of the same in his next,' I told her."

"You didn't."

"Didn't I? I looked at that handsome sucker with his worthless prick, lying on that slab of concrete, and I said to him, 'Baby, what you wanted most in this life was a bumping and a grinding. And you got it—enough so it lasted your lifetime.'"

"Hohoho," Jessica chortled. "Jonnie Dash, you're a wicked woman." Then they both laughed, long and hard.

BOOK
~
FOUR

1

RESURRECTION. RESTORATION. Unshackled from morbidity, intoxicated, light-hearted, happy. All because of Jessica—the magician. Jonnie moved her hips to the beat of the music, skirting the appetizing spread of the grand buffet—her frivolous white chiffon dress matching her mood, the mood of the gaily outfitted musicians, and their lively beat of the Haitian merengue. Celebration! Indeed, celebrating her return from the near-dead.

Jessica and Stephan were not among the diners. Claire and Sam were. They were sitting at the back with the rest of the expatriates. Even they did not seem so morbid, so dull in her rejuvenation. She moved toward them only to be halted on the way.

"Nonono, you don't want to do that. You don't want to go back there. Those home folks are into their Nixon thing. What you need is cheer after being so sick and all." Maxie Gardener stood before her, taking her hand, teasing, his smile expressing disbelief in her illness. "Come with me," he said. "Got this great place. Serves the best Haitian-Italian pizza. I got all dressed up to take you."

He delighted her, this new Maxie, with his hair combed and curly; his shirt wrinkled but clean, pushed into khaki-colored trousers belted beneath his massive stomach; his feet, thrust into leather thongs, had had a pedicure!

She looked into his wide brown eyes with their thick overlapping lashes. Hadn't she liked him? Why? Whatever, her mood had opened her up. She liked him, she liked everybody. She shook her head in disbelief. Laughed.

Mistaking her laughter for rejection, Maxie looked over her frilly evening dress. "Whatcha want?" he growled. "That I should put on tux or tails? Nooo way, baby. I've gone as far as I'm gonna for you. From now on you take me as is."

He walked away. She tried to think of words to stop him. But already he had made his way through a throng of new arrivals. His being insulted dimmed some of her well-being. She wanted to call him back, to talk to him—hear the familiar vernacular pounding at her ears. In a strange way, his voice, since she first heard its argumentative quality, had become background for her thoughts in the same way that the black eyes of the begging child had fastened to her consciousness, like family with whom she had never been close, yet knew they were linked.

At the back table she found that, of course, Maxie had been right. The expatriates were arguing as they usually did when they had an audience, and this time they were arguing with Claire, who had the customary two red spots burning bright in her cheeks. Major Windfield waved a cigar, which he had forgotten to light, over the table.

"To hire special investigators to investigate a sitting president is an insult to the office of the presidency and to the American people who gave him his mandate."

"Major Windfield, I will defend the president and our flag to the death," Claire said. "But I think the American people have a right to know. How can we defend his honor when he acts without honor?"

A surprise. A few days before, she had been defending the honor of the president against Maxie as though she had known all. Looking up and seeing Jonnie, she said, "Jonnie, Nixon's fired Archibald Cox. Richardson and Ruckelshaus have resigned."

"Goddamn traitors!" Major Windfield raised his voice. "Who the hell do they think they are?"

"Honest men?" Sam asked, trying to maintain humor.

"That's right," Claire cried. "By resigning, they showed the world that we, Americans, are a people of integrity."

"You goddamn pinkos." Major Windfield pointed his cold cigar at Sam. "All a son of a bitch has to do is be against our president and they're in good standing with you? What? You some goddamn liberal or something? A fucking Democrat?"

"I'm a goddamn whatever I want to be," Sam said. "One thing's for sure, I ain't no McCarthyite. I don't let no sons of bitches into my polling booth nor inside my head to pull no goddamn lever." At that the wives tittered in confused disagreement.

They were friends until they talked politics. Nowhere had Jonnie heard politics discussed so much as on this island. Yet never the politics of this island, where they had chosen to pass the rest of their lives.

Tomorrow they would be friends again, these people who now sounded like enemies. On the one side, Sam and Claire, who believed in their innate goodness, on the other, expatriates, retirees—for flag and country right or wrong—their allegiance once given, turned to stone, never to be changed, never challenged. Yet they were joined in a holy alliance, these whites who lived in a style they had never before dreamed of, on this island inhabited by poor Blacks and the mulatto elite, protected by American warships on call. One saw them together in the newspapers, at balls given by the president at the palace or at the swank homes of the elite—laughing, smoking, patting backs, regardless of day-to-day atrocities committed by the Haitian government, their soldiers and policemen—all laughing buddies.

"Makes us all look like damn fools," Archie Wilson stuttered. "*Newsweek*, *Time*—those rags distributing their garbage all over the world."

"So that the world can know that there are people among us with . . ." Claire searched for a word to better project her meaning only to wind up repeating, "integrity."

Again, Major Windfield waved his cold cigar over the table. "No president of the United States, defender of our flag, ought to be put in that position. Those catchall phrases don't make it right.

Those sons of bitches are not worthy to shine his shoes. Do you understand that? Nixon is our commander in chief, the ruler of our nation—and the world."

"With vice president Spiro Agnew second in command," Jessica said, walking up. "Or is it vice president Gerald Ford? I don't recall—but then it's so difficult keeping up with your American politics."

Hostility against the Englishwoman bound them. Backs stiffened, making of them one island in the noise-filled room. Major Windfield finally lit his cold cigar, puffed on it, then said, "I can hardly see how it concerns you, madame."

"Oh, didn't I hear someone speak of the ruler of the world?"

"Which, Madame Winthrop"—the major puffed again on his cigar—"at this moment in history happens to be the role of the United States. Although I dare say England hardly did any better in her day."

"They only ruled the waves," Archie Wilson stuttered, attempting humor, to which his wife responded with an insipid chuckle. Jessica Winthrop exposed her long teeth.

"Yes, yes. England has committed gross, barbaric deeds in her time. But she did them with such elegance." Faces closed. Once again the music took over, and they looked out at bodies on the dance floor, jerking around, wildly intent on enjoying the dance. Jessica walked from the table, Jonnie behind her. Two soldiers joined in victory.

Stephan at the entrance of the bar, seeing them walking up, said, "Well, here you are at last." He took Jonnie's hand and pulled it through his arm. "You did survive, after all. But Jonnie, why the exaggeration? Such sulking because Afrique brought you that tired little dress? He did the best he knew—and for that you decided to end it all? Ask Jess. I was so concerned. But here you are, looking in good health and more beautiful than ever."

Had he seen nothing? Had he put no meaning to what she had said? Perhaps Afrique hadn't either—for that she had to be grateful. Jonnie looked at Stephan's mouth, its determined laugh lines. She had worn his shirt to cover her nakedness back to the hotel. He had come bare-chested, his ascot around his neck blowing in the wind, laughing all the way. Did the things she did, said, merit that much laughter?

"I know," he said. "You feel guilty for tearing up that horrible dress. But banish all guilt, Jonnie my love. I took the loveliest dress back for Afrique's daughter."

"Jonnie." Jessica turned to her. "Stephan and I must dash off. We're on our way to Captain Lavel's yacht—making sure it's seaworthy, now that all the invitations have been sent."

Jonnie's surprise reflected on Stephan's face. They had not expected to be separated. Both watched as Jessica walked out the entrance. Then Stephan squeezed Jonnie's arm. "Wait for us, for me, at the bar. We won't be late." He hurried after Jessica.

Jonnie stood on the top step watching them walk toward the car. They disappeared in the darkness. She stood listening to the loud music blasting around her head, waiting, trying to hold on to the euphoria of minutes before—her sense of well-being, her intoxication. She saw the car driving toward the entrance. Without stopping it rounded the curve to the gate. All the while she stood there she kept saying, "They have made a mistake. They don't intend to leave me. They must come back for me." The car drove through the gate. They had shut her out.

Once again she plunged into the depths of despair from which she had risen—was it only today? She was still standing there, looking toward the gate, when someone whispered in her ear.

"Jonnie Dash, you must not do that again. Never make us so afraid again, do you hear?" André Bienaimé. "You are our artist—our speciality—and you must never be sick again."

She leaned back against his broad chest, smelled his mild perfume, and said with a note of despair, "*André, voulez-vous coucher avec moi ce soir?*"

He started in surprise, looked into her face, and said, "*Avec plaisir, madame.*"

It didn't matter that he might not want to go to bed. She needed him. Now. Tonight. Something might come of it. But what? In one moment of panic, she thought, I might destroy our friendship. Taken unaware like that he might never want to speak to me again!

"Dominique," she called, as they pushed their way through to the bar. "Let's have some drinks. Scotch for me. Coke for André."

Dominique looked over the counter, studied their faces,

stared at their arms around each other, then took his towel from his waist and started the wide circular wiping of the bar.

"Madame," he said, in a formal tone. "This cannot be. You see yourself, the poor boy is tired."

Anger flamed through André. His mouth turned ashen. Reaching over, he took Dominique's collar and pulled the little man off his feet. *"M'sieur, je ne suis pas pauvre. Et je ne suis pas* your boy." He set Dominique down and walked away, leaving Jonnie, leaving them both shaken by the intensity of his anger.

Jonnie made no attempt to follow. His anger appeared to have been directed at Dominique, but might it not have been caused in part by her demand?

They stood there, she and Dominique, fighting for control. Then Dominique said, "Claire say you sick. You sick still? You want that I make for you my rum punch?"

"Your rum punch makes me drunk, Dominique."

"Mais oui. Why you drink if you don't get drunk?"

"At my age, Dominique? At my age . . ."

"Mais oui, Jonnie Dash. Vous êtes toujours jeune."

They who had always had such an easy friendship were trying so hard to feel at ease with each other. "I love you, too, Dominique," she said, and another voice interrupted.

"How quaint—a love affair at the bar." Roxanne had come to stand beside Jonnie. "Sam, give us some drinks, will you?"

Jonnie merely stared at Roxanne Anderson's smiling face. A strange woman. They still never spoke. Roxanne always looked away when she saw Jonnie approaching. Now there she stood, smiling, eyes bright, shining; her face deepened to a copper tone by the sun, glowed. "What are you drinking, Jonnie?"

"Nothing," Jonnie said, moving away from her, from the counter. Roxanne held her arm.

"Jonnie, my chauffeur is taking me to a voodoo ceremony tonight. Will you come with me?"

"No, I'm not religious," Jonnie answered.

"You can hardly call voodoo a religion."

"What else?"

"A cult. Fetish—worship—a happening."

"Religion," Jonnie repeated with a shrug. She attempted to walk away. The woman still held her.

"Please, Jonnie. I need you to go along with me—I want to talk to you."

"What about?"

"This island—its mountains, its valley, the sea. Who would have thought such a place existed? I always spent my vacations skiing in the Alps or Colorado. But here it is heaven, isn't it? I am so free—since he's been gone."

The place she hated had suddenly become heaven. "If it's freedom you wanted, you ought to have tried it a long time ago," Jonnie said.

"That's easy for you to say."

"Why easy for me who has never been free?" Jonnie asked, knowing they were speaking at cross purposes.

"Spare me your ancient history of slavery and discrimination," Roxanne snarled. "I'm talking about women. Free women. Women without chains. Women like you, like Jessica. Women free to travel the world over, to play, to make love."

Ancient history? The image of a man at the window of a burning tenement, of a little girl dead of TB, peasants crouched on the other side of the flower-carpeted wall. Where did history end and current events begin? "A divorce would set you free," Jonnie said. "It's easy to come by for those with means."

And there, pressing in on her, depression—the emptiness of being closed out, with or without means. Her flesh stirred in sudden need for André Bienaimé. To be twisted into him in some grotesque position—with or without pleasure—giving vent to ancient angers, cauterizing ancient wounds.

"He's brutal," Roxanne hissed in her ear.

"Who?"

"Jonathan. He enticed my daughter Nicole into marrying his cousin because he knew that I loved him."

Nonono. No more confidences. Spare me. Spare me the bitterness, the anguish of your tears. My shoulders are miserably thin.

Roxanne let her scarf fall from her neck, exposing deep dark marks on her throat. Yes, that had to be Jonathan's type. Wealth and decadence. Aging and handsome. Insisting on virility—and so the growing obsession for young boys and hostility toward his aging wife. What else was new?

"I don't want to go back to the States with him—not now," Roxanne whispered.

"Then don't," Jonnie shrugged, trying to move away from such confidences.

"He'll not let me stay." Roxanne's face appeared flaccid. But only for an instant. "Please, you must accompany me. I do want to know you better."

"I'm waiting for Jessica and Stephan," Jonnie said.

"To get back from dinner?"

"Dinner!" But of course. Jessica had been wearing a lovely green silk dress and pearls. Obviously for dinner. She had not thought. She had seen without seeing. But why not? Why the hell not? Cousins had the right to go out to dinner together.

She left the bar and went into the ballroom to stand looking over the buffet, by now greedily consumed, the remains not worth the effort.

Listless, trying to recapture her élan of earlier, she stood listening to the band, trying to move in time with the music. She wanted to stay alert, stay awake waiting for Jessica and Stephan if for nothing else, to show them she had no hard feelings. It was all right that they had gone, had deserted her.

André stood at the door of the ballroom. She walked over to him. "So, Jonnie Dash." He spoke first to block her invitation. "Did I make you promise me that you shall never again be sick?"

There it was, the distance he had erected between them. Nevertheless she asked. "Why were you and Dominique so angry—was it because he was afraid you might be going off with me?"

"*Dominique se comporte comme une vieille fille.* An old maid who wants always to interfere."

He had bypassed her question. She looked up at him, studying his beautiful black face, searching for a flaw to his perfection through which to challenge him—a weak chin, a tremble to his lips, cunning in his eyes? No! He appeared honest, lovely. The most lovely of men. Certainly perfect enough for canvas. Still she hadn't found the level in him that pushed his beauty beyond itself. She knew it existed, waiting just beyond the borders of his eyes—waiting for her to capture.

Then, as she studied him, two teenagers walked into her peripheral vision. Without turning she said to him, "They must be looking for you."

André turned. Then white teeth flashing, he moved toward them. Jonnie put her hand on his arm to restrain him. "Is that what you really want, André?"

"Yes, I think so," he said.

"You are so young, André."

"*Oui*, Jonnie Dash. I am very young. And in this life I want to marry to have beautiful children—ten of them." He searched through her eyes, then added, "But first I must be rich, *n'est-ce pas?* Very rich to afford my children. I must live in the States, in the big house, have the big car. . . ."

"What you need is an older woman," Jonnie said, a wicked suggestion twinkling in her eyes. "One who needs and can appreciate an energetic, virile young man."

"Virile? I don't know that word."

Jonnie looked down at his crotch and grinned. "Potent," she said.

"Ahh, but Jonnie, I am young. I want to marry a young, young lady. I am a lover—not a boy. And you, Jonnie Dash. What do you want from this life?"

The unexpected turnabout startled her. Words pushed to her lips: *I have already lived my life; I don't expect anything new or different.* Words that refused to be uttered. She didn't believe them. "I have always wanted to paint and I have done that, André. . . ." What else? Why had she come here to Haiti? Why had she come to Gérard?

"*Magnifique!*" He flashed his teeth. "You are like me, Jonnie Dash. We—you and me—are the dreamers. Stardust in the eyes. Lost souls, *mon amour*, reaching, reaching out." He shrugged, rubbed his fingers together as though letting ash fall to the floor. "Yet we know that we are so tiny in space, and we are afraid. Afraid that one step this way or that and we shall fall into oblivion, *n'est-ce pas? Voilà*, the dream."

He walked from her to the girls who were waiting at the entrance, giggling. He fit his arms around them. She wanted to call out, "No, André, I have my paintings. I shall not go down to oblivion. Nor shall you. I will preserve you on canvas—when you're more than just a pretty face." He had gone, disappeared with his giggling girls. And with him her patience for music. She moved to leave, sensed eyes on her forcing her to turn, to search the room until she found herself trapped in the malevolent eyes of Charles McCellen. Panic held her motionless, formed a tight knot between her chest and stomach. At that instant Cécile rushed up to her. *"Madame, une dame veut vous parler."*

"A woman to see me? Who is she?" Cécile shook her head she didn't know. "Tell her to come in here," Jonnie said.

"I tell her already. She say she want talk in the *jardin— derrière votre chambre, madame."*

In the dark garden? How stupid to want to talk in an unlit garden. Still this was Haiti, not New York. Whom did she have to fear? Charles McCellen? His hate-filled eyes filled her mind. Had he sent someone? "Are you sure it's a woman?" she asked.

"Oui, madame."

Nevertheless, her heart pounded as she followed Cécile out of the hotel to the annex. First, however, she entered her room, put on the lights, opened up the drapes to make sure light broke through the outside darkness. Then she cautioned Cécile, "I want you to stand right outside this door and wait for me, *entendez."*

"Oui, madame," the frail girl responded—Gérard had appointed her protector.

Jonnie walked to the back and, standing in the beam of light from her window, peered into the surrounding shadows. "Hello, hello." Only the varied strumming of insects rustled the silence. Seconds passed, minutes. Then, as she turned to leave, a shadow detached itself from the rest moving toward her.

"C'est vous!" A woman hissed, spattered her with sprays of spittle. Jonnie stepped back. *"Oui, c'est vous! Vache!"* The woman loomed over her—tall, big-breasted, broad—a big woman whose face remained in the shadows. *"Vache!"* she repeated. *"Laissez mon mari, vous entendez? Il n'est pas pour vous*—he not for you," she added in heavily accented English.

Jonnie searched her mind for some husband she might have inadvertently met and forgotten, or had smiled at with the possibility of flirting. No such person came to mind. Surely the woman could not be talking about Stephan. Not Gérard—unless he had another Galatea.

The woman's hot breath gushed into Jonnie's face, forcing her to speak. She began softly, gently, *"Madame, vous vous trompez. I don't know your husband. What is his name? Qui est-il?"*

"Menteuse! Liar!" The shout gave rise to a restless stirring of insects all through the woods. The drums in the distance that had blended smoothly into the evening air seemed suddenly ominous. The heavy chest heaved and fell, heaved and fell. "Thief!" she spat out in perfect English. "Leave *mon mari, entendez?* Or I fix you."

Another spray of spit struck Jonnie's face, and suddenly her fear turned to fury. She had dragged herself from the depths of suicidal depression that morning; had thought she had gained a friend only to lose her come evening. Had thought to gain a lover, only to be denied. Had looked into a man's hate-filled eyes from across the room knowing that he intended her harm—to prevent her from doing him harm. And now out of the dark came this woman calling her a liar, a thief.

Who in the hell did she think she was, coming out of nowhere to stand before her, accusing her, threatening her, frightening her? Fool, bitch, threatening her? Did she look like her ass was made of cotton that anybody could take pleasure in kicking? This woman who knew so goddamn much, did she know that she was face-to-face with Jonnie Dash and that Jonnie Dash was a crazy woman—from New York City?

"Fix me?" Jonnie hissed back into the woman's face. "You mean you're gonna put a voodoo curse on me? Sh—it, you can't feed your kids with that goddamn voodoo. Can't put clothes on their backs. Got kids begging the streets and big white daddies trying to get into their pants. For a couple of gourdes, your tonton give them away like slaves. And you gonna fix me? Go fix your husband. Make him stay in your bed. Fix me! Go ahead, bitch! Do the best you fucking well can."

Silence. Heavy silence, except that the drums sounded louder. The woman had gone. Vanished. Jonnie leaned against the wall, waiting, listening. Then she backed out of the garden, keeping close to the wall. A touch on her shoulder made her spin around. Cécile.

"Cécile, where did she go? Where in the hell did that simple bitch go?"

"*La femme? Pas connais, madame.*"

"How come you *pas connais?* She had to go by here."

"*Non, madame.* Nobody go by here." Cécile stared hard at Jonnie, her eyes wide with fear. "*Ça va, madame? Ça va?*"

"I'm okay," Jonnie said. "I'm okay. But I want to know where she went."

"*Elle est peut-être une femme méchante,*" Cécile said.

"*C'est quoi une femme méchante?*"

"*Femme de diable. Elle a disparu.*" Cécile threw her hands wide.

"Superstition, superstition. Is that the best you can do?" Jonnie snapped. "A wicked woman? A woman devil? Nobody just disappears."

"*Oui madame—les femmes méchantes.*"

Jonnie turned from the girl, anger deserting her. Her knees buckled. Steadying herself, she walked quickly, almost ran, back to the bar to find Roxanne, determined to go anywhere to get away from the hotel.

2

JONNIE SAT BESIDE ROXANNE, staring out of the window as they drove through the darkness. Her blood still raced, nerves beat throughout her body. Anger, the liberating force of vulgarity had energized her, had blown away her depression, leaving her exhilarated, yet displeased. The exchange in the garden had spoken more of their sameness than of their differences. Theirs had been a language of poverty. Whatever they had become, poverty had been their beginnings. They understood one another. They had lashed out to hurt because they were poor, because they were women, helpless, and at the mercy of . . .

Jonnie slumped into herself, unwinding. She remembered that she'd had to check her impulse to strike out, to mix things up. The woman was big and strong but simple as hell. Messing with a crazy whether she knew it or not. Jonnie chuckled. Still, the woman had had the upper hand: she had made herself disappear.

Whatever, the encounter had forced her to leave the hotel, stopped her from waiting for Jessica and Stephan—like a good child expecting to be loved for obedience. How unbearably young she had acted! How possessive she had felt!

"You're not listening," Roxanne complained, leaning against Jonnie in the way of young girls sharing secrets, her soft body touching Jonnie's, her lips close to Jonnie's ears—an adolescent sharing a confidence. No, she hadn't been listening.

"What did you say?"

"I said that after I talked to you at the bar, I also talked to some Haitian painters at the hotel. They agree that voodoo is devil worship, and they ought to know. Isn't that exciting?"

"So we're driving to some unknown place to witness the workings of the devil? I should suppose that we're all well acquainted with his rites."

"Are we?"

"Wouldn't you say? The Middle Passage, the Holocaust, Hiroshima—whatever we witness tonight's got to be child's play in comparison."

"You're being serious."

"Weren't you?"

"We can't compare the workings of the devil with the evilness of men."

"Is there a difference?"

In the following silence, Jonnie gazed out at the dark road, the same road traveled with Stephan and Jonathan on their way to Le Renard. Transformed by night, with fires flaming under big, black pots of boiling oil for *grillo*—fried pork and green plantains—vendors crouched along the roadside, selling legumes or fruit, their candles dots of flickering lights that stretched along the unlit road, blowing up their shadows to prehistoric dimensions. In the surrounding darkness, roosters crowed, donkeys brayed—and drums beat.

Their headlights, boring through the darkness, magnified the potholes in the center of the road, making them appear bottomless craters around which traffic maneuvered with marvelous dexterity. Surely the best drivers in the entire world lived on this little island.

They drove into the drumbeats that haunted the island, a part of its rhythm, its atmosphere, its mystery. The farther they went the louder the drumming, and Jonnie, who'd had no intention of attending ceremonies, felt that in some way she had been maneuvered—against her will—by a force other than Roxanne.

Neither she nor Boysie nor Sylvie had gone to church since the day Boysie had taken them. He had been bragging about the Baptist Church being the best of all religions. But on the day they had gone, women with white dresses starched stiff and proper had taken one look at them—three kids, shoes tied with rope, clothes ragged, dirty—and barred their way.

Boysie had cried. Jonnie had never seen him cry before. He had cried and run away—stayed away for days, leaving them, her and Sylvie, alone and so afraid. Yes, religion had left her by bits and pieces through the years, and she had no desire to flirt with yet another.

"Pierre," Jonnie heard Roxanne say. "No other driver could have been so gracious as you have been to me."

"Madame's most charming," Pierre demurred.

"No, it's you who are charming. The most charming man I have ever met. Mrs. Winthrop was clairvoyant to realize that you were exactly who I needed."

"Madame, the pleasure, it is all for me."

A false note ran like a thread through their conversation, alerting Jonnie. She leaned her head back, closed her eyes, letting pieces of a puzzle drift around in her mind, fitting into each other where there seemed no obvious fit. Jean-Pierre. Maxie had mentioned that name to Jessica. Claire, too, had mentioned a Jean-Pierre—an unemployed mulatto who had been engaged to Colette. She had broken their engagement when he had become a chauffeur—a mere servant for tourists. Thinking of the two sisters, Colette and Germaine, using charm to entice dinners from American tourists, Jonnie shook her head. Jessica had sponsored

him. She had bought him two cars and he had them built into a
fleet to service all the hotels. Still, Colette had objected. Never
would she marry a mere servant.

Jonnie noticed the back of Jean-Pierre's neck, his hair curling
beneath his chauffeur's cap. A mulatto? A dark brown mulatto?
How did one tell? One didn't. One had to know.

The woman in the garden! That would be stretching to
make that piece fit. The woman had been mistaken. But for
whom had Jonnie been mistaken? Roxanne? Highly improbable. Still, peasants insisted on lumping all Americans together as
Les Blancs.

Hilarious. Funny as hell. Roxanne moved closer to Jonnie in
the dark. At the feel of Roxanne's too-soft body touching hers,
Jonnie recalled for one intense moment the flame of the woman's
breath, the woman's unreasoning anger, her intimidating fury,
and shuddered. Better it not be Roxanne. That woman was
strong—and although Roxanne Anderson might be silly, she had
no madness working for her.

3

LANTERNS AND TORCHES LIT THEIR WAY through the woods.
Torches which, pushed into the ground, added light to the already bright amphitheater. Whispers, laughter, friends greeting
friends, grabbing folding chairs and finding places to group themselves in semicircles, looking out at the ceremonial grounds—all
gave the vast arena a circuslike excitement.

Worshipers coming in offered bottles of rum as contribution,
giving them over to ushers. Workers, peasants, and some who
were definitely from the middle class, all crowded the space, and
still more kept coming. Government officials sat on the makeshift
stage looking pompous alongside the tourists—uncomfortable
and excited—they had brought as guests.

Jean-Pierre appointed himself as guide, pointing out to them the *hounfour*—a cabinlike structure in which preparations for the ceremony were being finalized. It was made up of yards of canvas stretched around well-placed poles, with the sprawling branch of a nearby tree as its roof.

An altar had been erected outside its opening on which stood the suffering figures of Jesus Christ and the Virgin Mary, her fingers draped with rosary beads.

"You see," Jean-Pierre said to Roxanne. "Here is no devil's religion. Here, too, we believe in Jesus, Mary, and the Catholic Church—although we have many gods."

Roxanne's disappointment was palpable, as was Jonnie's. They had expected more baring of flesh, shaking of hips, freedom of expression—an abandon. Instead, the women in the ever-widening circle of dancers wore white dresses, their heads wrapped in the white cotton cloth they call fulahs. The men, too, wore white shirts with dark pants. They moved in a one-step dance, first in one direction, then the other, clapping their hands, and singing in Creole—probably the same tunes heard nights from the distance, but which, close up, were robbed of the mystery that distance had given. The drums held their magic. The drummers, at the side of the *hounfour*, flying fingers, faces serious, strong; bare arms, muscled; sweating chests glowing in the lights of torches, transformed into gilded African statues.

Gérard. He had spoken about the drums: the *kata*, the *boula*, the *bébé*, each having its own particular sound from bass to high pitch. But Jonnie had no way of telling one from the other. Her body responded to the composition. Every night. This was her enchantment with Haiti.

"When do we see the sacrifices?" Roxanne asked. "The sheep, the goats, the chickens—the bloodletting?"

"This is not one of your tourist traps," Jean-Pierre reprimanded her. "You asked me to bring you to see the real Ceremony of Vaudun, and this is it." When she protested, he cut her off: *"Voilà—le houngan*, or as you will say, the priest."

Tall, broad, and handsome, even before he spoke, the *houngan's* charisma spread to capture the audience. He, too, wore a white shirt, opened to expose his strong neck. The fit of his pants invited the eyes of women—and indeed, there were many more women than men in the audience. He spoke, and his deep bass voice brought cries from his flock, energized the singers, who raised their voices with renewed energy. He began to preach, and devotees were invaded by spirits. Some fell to the ground, shaking in every limb—possessed—and had to be helped out of the arena.

"His message. What is he saying?" Jonnie demanded, and Jean-Pierre said, "He tells us that we are a great people who live in a great land, and we come from a greater land, Nan Guinea, where our fathers are kings and our ancestors sit in judgment. We will join them one day. But now we must work and share and love one another. Our gods are here with us, to help us. Damballa, the god who holds up the earth; his wife, Ouido; Shango; and he say that Erzulie, our goddess of love, will be with us tonight. She will prepare and guide us, for it is she who must lead us, when we are ready, to the gates where our ancestors await us in Nan Guinea."

The drums muted when he began, grew loud, louder, the worshipers cried out, ecstatic; the dancers became more frenzied.

Incredible. She had not understood one word, yet through his cadence, his rhythm, she got the message. He sounded like a Black Baptist preacher in the States.

"*Et voilà*," Jean-Pierre cried. "Our Goddess of love, Erzulie."

The woman who danced out to the center of the amphitheater wore a white dress sparkling with jewelry. Her long hair flowed in deep waves to her hips, and as she spun around the vast circle her jewelry caught the lights of torches, setting the night ablaze. An incredible beauty. A great dancer—such form, such grace, she held them all riveted.

"But isn't that Captain Lavel's mistress?" Roxanne whispered, grabbing Jonnie's arm.

"Monique?" So it was! Monique. With her hair loose around her she had become an entirely different person. Other dancers moved around her with conservative little steps, first to the right, then to the left, as she whirled and whirled filling the night with herself. Worshipers clapped, their faces bright with admiration. They enjoyed her, this woman abuser of the poor. They loved her, not caring that her dance had been designed for the stages of Paris or New York and had nothing to do with voodoo in the forest of Haiti. Yet she needed a stage, and she had chosen this as

her stage. She needed an audience, and she had chosen these people—her people—who, whatever she did, forgave her—their
goddess of love. Jonnie wondered if she would ever understand
the Haitians.

A tug on her arm forced Jonnie's attention to a little girl
stooping beside her. "*Viens,*" the child said. "*Tant vais parler ou.*"

"What does this child want?" Jonnie asked Pierre.

"*Allez,*" he said, shooing her away. The child went to stand
beside him. For a time they spoke, then Pierre said, "It's Madame
Thompson. She must talk to you."

"Who is Madame Thompson?"

"A Jamaican woman. A good woman. She lives near. She
takes care of orphans."

"What does she want with me?" Jonnie asked, and Pierre
shrugged. "Why me?" He shrugged again. "Ti Moune here says
she must speak with the American lady with the *cheveux frisés*—
that's you, *n'est-ce pas.* Ti Moune will take you."

The American with the kinky hair? That was she? Was she
then the only Black American woman in all of Port-au-Prince who
wore her hair natural? And so had become the butt of Haitian jok-
ers? Did everyone laugh at the lady who dared to walk through
the streets of Port-au-Prince dressed like an American but wearing her hair nappy?

"How did she know I would be here?" Jonnie demanded.
Five minutes before she left she didn't know she was coming. Did
the Haitians have a secret method of communication?

"She's a good woman," Jean-Pierre repeated to reassure her.
Jonnie looked again at the dancer. She didn't want to go. She
thought of the woman in the garden and really didn't want to go.
And because she recognized that she was indeed frightened, she
went along with the wisp of a child.

The child pulled her from the arena into the woods, the
other side from where they had entered. Here there were no
paths. Here their feet sank into dew-softened leaves. And as they
plunged deeper into the woods, slinking around trees, melting
into shadows, moving quickly through patches of moonlight,
moving as in a dream, her tension heightened.

Yet listening to the drums as she had every night since she
had come made the walk seem in the pattern of things. Then the

child's hand, so small, holding hers, gave her courage. A little surefooted girl who walked bravely through dark woods, so canny that she had been able to single Jonnie out because of her *cheveux frisés*, to take her to a place where Mrs. Thompson, a good woman, took care of orphans. That, too, had to be the way of things.

And so they walked in darkness, where insects collided with unseen leaves with a loud *ping*, where branches hit at her face, forcing her to suspend thoughts and concentrate on the vibrations of drums felt through the soles of her feet to keep hold of reality. And the wisp of a child kept hold of her hand, guiding her.

The woods echoed at the edge of a road, and when Jonnie went to cross it, the small hand held her back. They stood in the shadows of trees, looking across the road at a large sprawling house, which might once have been a mansion but now had the look of a cluster of overdecorated Christmas trees—a beacon through the dark—their destination?

Impatient and tired of the prolonged mystery, Jonnie pulled at the restraining hand, determined to cross, only to find that the wispy touch was no longer wispy but strong. At that moment, a man rose from the shadows of her mind, where he had been waiting, still not fully thought out.

A brown man stepped out of a car parked beneath the steps of the brightly lit house. The door of the car closed silently. He climbed the steps to stand in the glare of the spotlight of the porch. The pleasant-faced brown man, in his brown suit, with everybody's father's smile on his face, the big brown gun. And Jonnie remembered its brown holster with the thick belt heavy with bullets. The familiar anxiety in the presence of armed authority held her paralyzed in the shadows while laughter focused her attention on the porch. Hearty laughter, laughter shared by the brown man and a round, plump woman with a merry face.

They both stood, clearly outlined in the spotlight of the porch. She leaned against the rail, her loud laughter alerting neighbors in darkened houses along the road. Jonnie sensed them listening, sensed ears against windows, eyes peering through curtains.

Her heart thundered. She backed away, fear mounting. But the strong little hand, the protector of secrets, held her.

The brown man, with a final loud laugh and a wave of his hand, ran down the steps. With another wave he disappeared beyond the reach of the light. The woman leaned over the rail, still laughing. The lights of the car went on: two bright streaks pierced the darkness of the road. In seconds it was gone.

Still the little hand held Jonnie's. They waited. Minutes passed. The woman on the porch kept leaning over the rail. Then the motor of another car, loud in the dark, drove by without lights. They saw it outlined by the light from the porch. Then it, too, was gone. They strained, listening as the motor faded in the distance. Now the discordant tones of insects mingled with the sound of drums.

They crossed the road, went up to the porch, where Jonnie found herself clasped against the soft bosom of the big-breasted woman with the laughing face. Then she was being taken into the house. The door was bolted, and the woman stood against it, arms folded across her chest.

Jonnie looked around for her little guide, to find that the child had faded into a room of wall-to-wall children. Children blending into children, faceless, in the way of orphans. They sat or stood, staring at her, these children of different complexions— from black to dark to tan to light tan to white. They sat on the floor, on the steps leading upstairs, on chairs, on the couch. The woman with the broad face opened up her arms wide. "*Petite yo,*" she said, in mother-hen fashion. "*Pour moi.*"

"*Je ne parle pas créole,*" Jonnie said. "*Je parle seulement un peu le français, mais pas créole.*"

"*Anglais?*" the woman asked.

"Yes. That's right, you are Jamaican," Jonnie said, relieved to communicate in English. Whereupon the woman started to speak a dialect-English used in Jamaica, which Jonnie didn't understand at all. "*Je ne comprends pas.*" She shook her head, falling back on her limited French. They looked at each other distressed. Then the woman said, "*Garçon?*"

"Boy?" Jonnie nodded. And so they had decided that with a word here and another there in imperfect French, Creole, and English they might communicate.

"*Garçon ou.*" The woman pointed to Jonnie. "*Ici.*" She pointed to the ceiling. "*Caille—moin . . .*"

Jonnie shook her head no, she had no son. *"Pas de garçon,"* she said, but the woman nodded, still smiling. She called the wisp of a girl, who once again disentangled herself from the rest to reemerge as a distinct little being. The woman spoke to her. The child nodded and went up the steps, weaving through the dozens of other children, sitting on the steps or hanging over the banister, looking down at Jonnie.

They waited, and while they waited, the woman kept smiling, her arms around her ample stomach, her face squinched into a smile. Jonnie kept looking around at the children, at the house—a large, generous house, with two stories—but it took a small miracle to fit so many children into it. Yet they all were clean, clothes well-patched; some even wore shoes. They were of all ages. Babies, taken care of by the older ones, and going up to fifteen. The one white girl might have been eighteen. They sat together, she and a crippled boy, whose legs were crushed beneath him. Born a cripple, with the pained look of an old man.

"Cette fille," Jonnie said, pointing to the blond, recognizing the spaced-out look in her eyes. *"Elle n'est pas haïtienne."*

"Non," Mrs. Thompson replied. *"Americaine. Elle est à moi . . ."* She cradled her arms to show that the girl, like the others, also belonged to her. *"Moi—embrasse toutes . . ."* She spread out her arms to include the entire room or house filled with children; all were a part of her grand embrace.

A movement on the stairs signaled the return of her little guide. She came down the stairs, pulling a boy behind her. She brought him to Mrs. Thompson, who in turn pushed the child to Jonnie. *"Ton enfant,"* the woman said.

"No, he's not mine!" Jonnie cried. *"Pas pour moi."*

"Oui, oui. Il dit il est pou ou," Mrs. Thompson said, as though once the child had spoken, they had no choice but to believe him.

"Je ne le connais pas!" Jonnie cried in desperation. "I don't know him."

Not true. Not for one moment since Chez Renard had he been out of her mind. Never had those black eyes—angry when he looked at Renard, terrified when he looked at the brown man, ashamed when he looked at her—been out of her mind. No more than the hatred that registered in Charles McCellen's eyes earlier when he looked across the room at her.

It suited his image of her: the Black American revolutionary anxious to challenge authority. Wild—forcing a pattern where none existed. Wild. The boy had run away. He held her responsible.

"Lucknair," the woman said, pushing the boy toward her. And Lucknair pleaded with her; his black eyes, their whites eaten up by their pupils, sent a shaft of pain through her. *"M'sieur Constant—tonton Constant. Viens ici. Pour le . . ."* So the brown man was *tonton*—probably *macoute*.

How? Why? She had not come to this place, Haiti, to be dragged into intrigue—not with the *tonton macoute*, not with the American Embassy.

She did not know the boy. She had given him a dollar once, by chance. She had been in a house where he had been brought—again by chance. He was not her responsibility. He was Haiti's responsibility, Gérard's responsibility. *"M'sieur Constant, il revient—pour le. . . ."*

"Je suis desolée, madame. Mais je ne le connais pas. Je ne sais pas. What do you want from me?" she cried in English, and backed away from the woman's smiling, imprisoning face, backed away from the children gaping at her. She pushed past the woman to the door, fumbled with the bolt, then, afraid they might all converge on her to prevent her from leaving, she flung the door open and ran across the road and into the woods in terror.

She ran in one direction, got lost, ran in another, and still lost she heard: "Madame?" The little voice came out of the dark, the little hands sought her out, plucked her from the surrounding darkness, led her up to the clearing, and then she was gone.

4

THEY HAD GONE. Roxanne and Jean-Pierre. The drums had ceased, the air was still, the last of the worshipers, their torches like fireflies, were disappearing through the woods. Jonnie had to run to catch up, only to find, when she reached the road, that the place where Jean-Pierre had parked the car, empty. Gone? Left her? How dare they bring her to this strange place where she knew no one, then simply drive off?

Had Jean-Pierre arranged to send her off deliberately to be alone with Roxanne? Had Roxanne agreed?

Jonnie stared down the road along which they had come. The long road stretched long in the candlelight flickering on crates behind which vendors sat selling their tired legumes, withered fruits, waiting for the lone customer driving up from the south or for the *grand homme*, after an evening of leisure, leaving the home of his concubine. An island that never sleeps. An island that can't afford to.

Jonnie listened for the car without lights, the car that followed the car of the brown man in brown clothes. A faceless somebody searching for the woman with *les cheveux frisés*.

Stupid. Who had seen her? How had the little girl, Mrs. Thompson, come by that description? If the men drove up on her—if even by accident—she did not want to be out here alone. That fear sent her across to the nearest flickering candle.

She waited until her presence awakened the dozing woman, then asked, *"Pardon, madame. Il y a un homme haïtien avec une femme américaine—blonde, dans une grande voiture noire."* She pointed to the space emptied of parked cars.

"Ils sont partis," the woman said, pointing with her chin toward the south.

"Madame Thompson?" Jonnie asked, expecting that name to be known. The woman nodded. Jonnie wanted to say more, to ask more, to find out exactly how, where. But a long, detailed, dragged-out conversation in either Creole or French would serve neither of them.

Walk back to the hotel? she asked herself, pondering the long road. How? Put one foot out, the other is bound to follow, fool. Her attempt at humor calmed her. She headed in the opposite direction—because Mrs. Thompson's round dimpled face had been a good face, deeply good. She would have no part of schemes thought up by Jean-Pierre.

Perhaps Jean-Pierre had driven south to get to Mrs. Thompson's house on the other side of the woods, expecting to find her there or on her way back to the amphitheater? That probability calmed her further.

Slowly she walked, moving south, along the moonlit road,

and the bright light of the moon also reassured her. Strange walking down a road, in a place she didn't know, a road darkened by woods on each side, without feeling threatened by muggers, indeed, feeling so safe. So different from her experience in the States, where to step out onto a dark street alerted a network of tensions. Perhaps because vendors, in the shadows of their crates, drifted off to sleep to dream without violence. Their shield against muggers. Poverty their shield against muggers or men in brown suits. The still night, with its jumble of sounds—frogs and crickets and grasshoppers—reinforcing their security. What men would gain by adding misery to their aching poverty?

The moon, big, round, bathed the road and filtered through the dense woods, giving to Jonnie a sense of well-being. She pushed aside her anger, her sense of aloneness, to enjoy the silence, the safety of the seductive night.

Strange country. Walking in the light of the full moon, thoughts of evil slipping away, leaving her calm.

Strange night and a long, strange day. She had sprung back from days of fasting with remarkable fortitude. She had been dumped by friends, perhaps with reason; threatened by a strange, perhaps mad, woman; upset by the dancing of someone called the goddess Erzulie, perhaps a voodoo witch; had been summoned to an unknown woman, Mrs. Thompson; and had seen the boy—the boy. She had run—in fright? She hated that she had run from him in fright.

Now, walking in soft moonlight, she wondered about the peasants, the poor. This deep calm. A calm so deep it anesthetized the soul . . . made it easy to accept the pain of poverty, of abuse, leaving in the hands of God, or gods, the means of just punishment.

Coming to a fork in the road, Jonnie hesitated. She wanted to keep on along the soothing moonlit road but knew the darker more thickly forested road logically led to Mrs. Thompson's.

She had gone only a short distance along the dirt road when she saw a woman, a tray on her head, lantern in hand, walking toward her. "*Bonsoir,*" Jonnie greeted her when they came abreast.

"*Bonsoir, madame,*" the woman responded in that lilting voice that charmed Jonnie.

"*Mamzelle, je cherche une grande voiture*"—Jonnie spread her arms wide to indicate the length of the limousine Jean-Pierre drove—*"avec un homme haïtien et une femme américaine."*

"Moi, madame?" The woman looked at her, eyes bright, stretched wide with humor. *"Il faut demander les femmes que vien là . . ."* She indicated two women farther down the road walking toward them. They, too, carried large baskets of foodstuff on their heads.

Jonnie walked on until coming abreast the women, again asking, *"Mesdames, je cherche une voiture noire avec un monsieur haïtien et une femme américaine—blonde. Les avez-vous vus?"*

"Nous, madame?" Laughter rippled beneath the surface of their eyes. *"Il faut demander à la jeune fille là."* They pointed down to where a girl stood beside a flickering lantern using a long stick to dislodge fruit from the high branch of a tree. Indeed, the full moon allowed no sleep, even to children, who kept the food chain flowing.

"Ti fille," Jonnie said. *"Est-ce que vous avez vu une grande voiture avec un homnme noir et une dame blanche?"*

"Moi, madame?" came the answer, which because of repetition had become questionable. This girl's eyes, alive with mischief, glanced across the road, then away. *"Madame, il faut demander . . ."*

Jonnie had looked across the road. She too had seen a splash of brightness through the trees, metal glittering in the moonlight, and thought: In Haiti, someone always tells. Surely she had been told—in a most charming way. No one was guilty.

She walked across the road, stepped over a low wired fence to maneuver through a grove of trees and into a cleared section awash in moonlight. Calm had forced her mind to an accepted blankness, an ease forbidding thought. She wanted no secrets to share—not with Roxanne, certainly not with Jean-Pierre—no more than she wanted to know where little boys were hiding or why a woman in the garden had raged at her, accusing her. She wanted only to remain deeply calm, ignorant. Nevertheless, her feet kept moving on toward the object glittering through the trees.

This was, of course, a lover's nook—woods dotted with trysting places. The atmosphere demanded it. The sultry breezes blowing from the sea made it inevitable. The scent of ripening fruits, the smell of green, of grass—the moon. . . .

The bush through which she moved caught and pulled at threads of her frivolous dress, yet she kept walking. Stepping into the clearing, walking boldly up to the lump of blackness, the glittering metal. No one heard her, nor did they sense her presence. From where she stood, she looked into the empty front seats of the car. Groans alerted her to the back. She moved to the side to see better.

There they were—Roxanne on her back, legs spread apart, feet touching the roof of the car; Jean-Pierre wedged between her thighs—both locked into themselves.

Moonlight had robbed the countryside of color, and them of nuance. No gold glints or brown tones softened their act to make them picturesque. Stark moonlight had reduced them to negatives—a portrait in black-and-white writhing into each other.

Voyeur, voyeur! Jonnie shouted to herself, yet she stood, silent, calm, waiting until she heard Roxanne cry, "Jean-Pierre, Jean-Pierre, I'm coming. Yes, yes, yes. I'm coming. I beg you. Come into me, now, now, now. . . ."

And Jean-Pierre's hoarse reply: "*Oui, je te penêtre, je te penêtre, bon dieu—bon dieu, je viens. . . .*" Only then did she turn away.

Jonnie fought to keep her mind empty, tried to hold on to the calm keeping her safe, insulated from emotional chaos waiting to once again tear her apart.

Oh, she had reason for rage. She had been used! Then abandoned! Oh, she had reason to shout, to scream out here with no one to hear, or care, except vendors to awaken, perhaps to rage at her for disturbing their sleep. She ought to shout and yell and awaken them! Let them shout and yell, create madness out here on this moonlit night.

Walking in anger, Jonnie stumbled into potholes, wetting her sandals. When they became wet, slippery, she took them off, walked barefoot—stepping on sharp stones, fit punishment for allowing herself to be brought out here, to be so duped. Thinking of the women she had encountered. Their bright eyes. The sense of bubbling laughter. Insolence! "*Moi, madame?*" They knew! They all knew about the Black Haitian with the blond American in the black car. They had seen, and those who had not seen had been told.

The woman in the garden—did she know, too? Had that assault on her been the woman's way of sending her message? Had she, too, used Jonnie—as a messenger!

A tightening of her head, a ring of anger, spinning pure gold in the moonlight. A halo ringing her head—marking her out as a woman of remarkable stupidity. Silly. Dangerous to be so maddened. She kept reaching for calm again. Standing in the middle of the road, struggling against anger, she heard music. A flute being played in these woods? Its notes floated toward her through trees. Familiar the tune. She knew it. She moved from the road to the trees at its side, pushing away clumps of brush in her way.

In the clearing, sitting on the ground, his back against a tall, wide tree, she saw him: a youth playing. The moon—big, round, fading as day approached—showered its light on his face, his shoulders.

Quietly, she approached to stand staring down at this dark boy with his golden flute shining in the moonlight, its notes sweet, clear, recalling to her mind another time. His eyes were closed, full lips curled down to his flute, like Boysie—lips she had wanted to kiss, to nibble on, to bring him back from the far-off places to which he traveled away from her when he played. She had never kissed him—never had the courage because he had once said she smelled like fish.

But she didn't smell like fish. Never. Not since the day she had read Sylvie's porno book. She had washed and washed; every time she went to a lavatory she had washed. And she had bought perfume from the five-and-ten and had rubbed perfume all over and she didn't smell like fish. Still she had never gained the courage to kiss those soft, full lips when he blew his golden flute.

"Even after Sylvie died," she whispered, sitting next to the youth. Whispering not to disturb him. Whispering so that she could lean against the tree and look at the notes dancing through its leaves. "Even when the synagogue's cold restless soul, its shadows, its laughter—Sylvie's laughter—frightened us, pushed us more and more out into the streets, we sat on the cold sidewalk, he, his eyes closed—frog eyes some said—his back to the lamppost, its light shining down on him, and I squatted down beside him listening, needing the feel of his arms around me to comfort me. I wanted so much, so very much to kiss those full lips. He was all I had, you see. Yet I never dared. He hated kissing. "Nothing," he said, "ever stopped girls from smelling like fish."

"Still he wanted me with him, needed me next to him on that cold street. . . .

"God, how young we were. How tender. Before Sylvie's death we had often gone separate ways: he to play, and I to sell my drawings. After Sylvie's death we were never apart—stuck together, glued by loss.

"Boysie always played sitting, like you are now, beneath the lamppost in front of Mr. Katz's record shop. He liked to listen to and sometimes practice new recordings. Next door to Mr. Katz's music store, in the beauty parlor, customers listened and on their way out tipped him. After Sylvie died he played long after the parlor was closed, long after Mr. Katz's store was locked, just sitting there playing with the light from the lamppost shining down on him just as the moon is shining down on you." Sitting beside the youth, talking softly, watching as the fading moon moved the shadows over his face. Watching his closed eyes, listening to the melody drifting, drifting, blending with the whispers of the trees before seeping out to the road. . . .

"And then one night the police came. Just like that they came—driving up in their green-and-white car, jumping out, standing over us—big, red-faced, angry. 'Where you swipe that flute, boy?' one said.

" 'Ain't none of your business,' Boysie said. 'It's mine.'

" 'Leave dem kids alone,' one old gray-haired wino sitting on the curb, listening, said, 'He ain't done nothin.'

" 'We want to know where this li'l nigger got a gold flute.'

" 'It's his,' the old man said. 'He been have dat dere gold thing.'

" 'We heard different. Gold is it? Let me see that thing.'

" 'It's his,' I told them. 'His uncle sent it from France.' We were always afraid of the police. They were so big. And they used to chase the kids, arrest them. Sometimes we never saw those kids again. So we never tangled with the police, no sir. We stayed away from anywhere we even thought they might be.

"But I knew Boysie. And he wouldn't let them have his flute. Boysie never let anybody touch his flute, not even me or Sylvie. Even though we looked over it with our lives.

"Boysie held it to his chest—tight. 'I don't have to let you see nothing,' he said. 'I ain't stole it. It's mine.'

"One officer grabbed it. But he thought wrong if he thought he could just take it. Boysie was strong. He never messed with folks and folks never messed with him.

"So there he sat clutching on to his flute, when the other officer brought down his billy on Boysie's head. *Wop!*

"Strange the sound of a head cracking. Boysie fell—fell holding tight to that flute. And when the cop raised his billy again, I jumped at him. 'Leave him,' I shout, keep shouting. 'He ain't done nothing. That flute is his, his uncle sent it to him from Paris.'

"That big cop picked me up and threw me against the stoop of Katz's music shop. My back hit against the wrought iron top step. Boysie looks up. He sees me and tries to get up.

"*Wop!* The cop hit him again, picks him up by the back of his jacket, pulls him along the sidewalk, throws him into his green-and-white cop car. From the stoop I see him in the car, clutching his golden flute to his chest. I shout with my mind: Don't let them have it! I see blood gushing, thick, pulpy from his head. I open my mouth. I can't speak. But we are close, Boysie and me. I know he hears my mind shouting: Don't let them have it, Boysie. I know he hears me. His big eyes—frog eyes—staring, staring. They drive away with him. . . ."

SHOUTS FROM THE DRIVERS of the tap-taps coming out of side streets, alerting early morning riders, brought Jonnie to full awareness. She had been walking a long time. The moon had disappeared. Wisps of pink colored the sky. Dawn. She walked in the center of the road and must have tripped into every open pothole from the look of the mud all over her dress. Barefoot, her shoes clasped to her chest. A tap-tap—its brightly painted name, *La Vierge Marie*—pulled up beside her. "*Amenez-moi à Old Hotel,*" she said.

"*Sais tu dire vingt-cinq gourdes,*" the driver said.

"Okay, okay," Jonnie said. A ten-cent ride for five dollars, a swindle. That's the way they did Americans. She climbed in. Sitting in the back among the early morning riders, she knew that everyone had seen her muddy feet, her dress, black with dirt and torn. Yet all said good morning, then carefully looked away. For this discretion she was grateful.

The tap-tap pulled up at the gate. Dominique, instead of the gateman, opened the door. He paid the driver. "*Mais tu es un bandit,*" he growled to the man. But she had promised.

"What happen to you?" he asked. "You in a accident?"

"What are you doing at the gate?" she answered with her question.

"Jonnie Dash, it's M'sieur Anderson. He come back from Santo Domingo. He ask for Madame."

"Why tell me?"

"I tell M'sieur that Madame, she go with you."

"But as you see, she's not with me," Jonnie said.

"I tell him she is in good hands," Dominique said.

"He didn't believe you? Isn't she out with your friend Jean-Pierre? She's in good hands."

"But he is there." Dominique pointed to the hotel's entrance, upset, excited. "M'sieur Anderson."

"So?"

"Jonnie Dasah, *soit gentille.* You go with her, *n'est-ce pas?*"

"Dominique, look at me." Jonnie pushed her tattered slippers in his hand and, in doing so, noticed a wooden flute stuck in one. She took it back, examined it.

"Does it seem that I was with anybody? Didn't you just have to pay the man in that tap-tap five gourdes?"

"M'sieur Anderson, he didn't see you. If you go now, he think I don't tell him the truth."

"You have problems," Jonnie said. "You worry about everybody, Dominique: André, Roxanne, Jean-Pierre. What about me?"

"Please, Jonnie, will you not wait with me until Madame come?"

So, they had not yet arrived? How long had she been walking that perilous road? She kept looking at the flute. A wooden flute? A beautifully made wooden flute. She weighed it in her hands. Where had she found it? She shook her head. "I don't give a damn about M'sieur Anderson, and I give less than a damn about his wife."

If she was by nature a gossip, she would go directly to Claire, awaken her, tell all about her guest and the chauffeur. But she wanted more than anything to get into her room to think about the flute.

"Please, Jonnie Dash ..." Dominique caught her hands, pleading. Jonnie snatched them away from him.

"Why don't you show the same concern for me, Dominique? Is it because I don't call you Sam?" The bitter edge of her voice surprised her, but Dominique didn't hear. To him, American slurs were American jokes, never insults.

"But you are my friend," he pleaded. "We are friends, *n'est-ce pas*, Jonnie Dash? Are you not Claire's friend—and Sam? Can you not see the unhappiness this can cause them—the business. Is it necessary?"

"Look at me, Dominique. My dress—the way I had to come back here. What does that do to business?"

Nevertheless Jonnie waited. Jean-Pierre drove the limousine up to the gate. She got in and sat beside Roxanne in the back. Jean-Pierre drove around, let Roxanne out at the entrance. And there stood Jonathan Anderson, face expressionless. "He's brutal," Roxanne had said. Jonnie believed it.

Getting out of the car, Roxanne went up the steps to stand beside him. Jonnie closed and locked the car door. "Miss Dash," Jonathan called out to her. "May I ask where you took my wife?"

"Mr. Anderson, I took her out to have a ball. And I think she did just that—had a natural ball."

SHE PLACED THE FLUTE on the dresser and lay down facing it. Tired. Had she ever been so tired? She closed her eyes about to drift off when she heard a whispered name. "Mrs. Mealy." Jonnie turned trying not to hear, but she heard again, "Mrs. Mealy." With the repetition of that name she looked at the wall, at the profile of the woman formed there. A handsome woman, Mrs. Mealy—smooth brown skin with a bronze tinge that spoke of Black being crossed with Indian somewhere along the line.

Mrs. Mealy. How had she ever forgotten the woman who had, on that Monday, found her sitting in her hardened feces on the stoop of Mr. Katz's music shop, next door to her hairdressing parlor?

How dare she not have thought of or spoken of this woman who had taken her home and scrubbed shit from her backside,

scrubbed so hard she had scrubbed off skin along with it. This
woman who had reached out to her and on whose bed she had
lain, barely conscious, watching the blood from Boysie's head
thick and clotted dripping down the walls, every night. Unable to
speak, hearing the squeaking boards as they tiptoed—Mrs. Mealy
and her old mother—around her all those weeks.

What had brought Mrs. Mealy to mind now? This morning—when her tired bones needed only rest? Mrs. Thompson?
She didn't know. On such a strange night with all that had happened, how to know?

Mrs. Mealy had cared. She had put up with her surly manner,
her hate-filled looks. She hadn't hated the woman. Just resented
her. Yet she had loved her old mother—the dear lady who never
went out into the streets but sat at her window to see her world
changing. She remembered now the sound of the old woman in
her soft slippers going around, her mumbling, mumbling about
she knew not what. She remembered the pots of lungs (called lites)
and hearts the old woman cooked. She used to steal the lites. And
she remembered hearing Mrs. Mealy complaining: "Mama, seems
to me I don't never get to eat lites no more," and the old lady answering, "If you want to eat more lites, I reckon you got to buy
more lites, that's all." And so Jonnie had more lites to steal, never
asking, only stealing and eating. It became a big joke with them.
They never reproached her.

Why then had she washed them so completely from her
mind? They had cared. No, it had been things said that had affected her, things that she'd had no words to answer, and so she
had become evil, silent. "Come to the shop and let me do something to that nappy hair of yours," Mrs. Mealy used to say. Jonnie
never went. Nor was it because of the job Mrs. Mealy had found
for her. Her factory job to make her self-sufficient, which had
kept her imprisoned for so many years. She had understood that
Mrs. Mealy had a mother to care for and so didn't need a girl from
the streets adding to her burden. No, it was something else—
something said that she had held deep in her subconscious as she
lay in that bed recuperating. Mrs. Mealy had repeated them the
day she had married: "Thank the Lord," Mrs. Mealy had said.
"She done made it—got hold of Agnes's boy to marry. Handsome
boy. Who'd have thought it. Used to get me so mad seeing that

pretty li'l old gal out there in the streets drawing them nasty pictures and messing around with that ugly Black boy. . . ."

Jonnie stared hard at the flute taking form in the dwindling darkness as Mrs. Mealy's words came back to her: "But we fixed that, didn't we? Sure did. Ain't seen him no more. And she ain't drawn one nasty picture since she's been with me. Praise the Lord. Got herself a good paying job, saved her money, and Lord, Lord, Lord, done got herself married to Agnes Dash's pretty boy."

Jonnie lay still, staring at the face of the handsome woman, waiting for it to fade away from the wall, fade out of her mind.

5

"HEY, PRETTY LADY, when you gonna give me some?" He spoke loud to awaken her, but she kept her eyes closed, against the sunlight and against him, wanting to be alone with her thoughts. She had come out with the sun to be alone but had fallen asleep. It was late morning. She squinted an eye open, saw a foot at one side of her, turned her head to find a foot on the other side.

"Don't you lie there pretending you sleep." The deliberate street vernacular prodded her, forced Jonnie's gaze upward. Slowly she studied the thick legs straddling her, their smooth skin disappearing into orange latex swimming trunks, the full crotch in which a heavy penis bobbed. The soft belly folding down over its waistband, the sparsely haired chest, the recently trimmed beard around the full mouth. She closed her eyes.

"I know you hearing me," Maxwell Gardener said. "You got to be feeling these vibes same as me." He bent down to whisper, "Lady, I can say things the way you like 'em said. Do things the way you dig. Now—that's a promise.

"I been wanting you since the first day I seen you—and you

been wanting me, too. So don't lie there playing them games, pretending nothin' ain't happenin'."

Because he said it, it happened. Desire—thousands of nymphlike fingers massaging her, her stomach. Her heartbeat quickened. The thinness of her nostrils distended. The tiles beneath her towel suddenly hard.

"Okay, if that's the way you want it." Maxie waited, then after a few seconds: "But you missing out, baby. Time's running out."

She wanted him to go, leave her alone. He did, simply by lifting one foot from one side and walking away. She had wanted him to stay. Still she lay, eyes closed, refusing to expose the riotous emotions he had triggered. Her nerves quivered in agony. She imagined him walking to his chaise, sitting back, adjusting his dirty captain's cap over his eyes, moving his long fingers to caress the hairs covering his chest and stomach. She had studied those movements many times.

To block that image, Jonnie tried to focus on voices rising from the pool, jumbled words without meaning. Only he had meaning. She wanted him.

Yet sex with Stephan had been too precious to duplicate. Its very intensity had sprung from her death wish, the invitation of the sea so calm, contrasting with her turbulent, unstructured life. Intensity opened her to a full being, grateful to be nurtured by sun and rain, stretched to exquisite agony.

Had orgasms like that happened in her youth, might she have been more womanly? More generous? Full-blown like Mrs. Ilma, with a bigness that reached beyond the ordinary, beyond petty sensibilities? Would they have nourished the intelligence? She'd had to make do with clitoral orgasms to take her from one time to another, creating an emotional vacuum.

Ahh, but vaginal orgasms came with the territory. One had to afford the luxury to love and be loved to share the force of life, the futility of death. Poverty was such a curse. The anxieties, the day-to-day energy to survive, the bending of the will to others—their biological urges, the heavy hand on the head, hot bullshit tears: "My dear, it is wrong . . ."

"Stop! Stop! Don't you touch that woman!"

Jonnie sat up in terror, looked around, not knowing what to expect. Policemen? M'sieur Constant? On the terrace, around the pool, swimmers, waiters were likewise looking around, standing in different postures of paralysis. Then she looked at Maxie Gardener, where he sat looking at her, smirking.

He frowned when their eyes met. "Now, that's better," he said. "Come here."

She obeyed. Walked slowly to stand staring down at him. "What the hell's the matter with you, scaring folks out of their wits?"

"Matter with me?" he cried. "Matter with you! Who the hell do you think you are lying there wanting me like a goddamn bitch in heat, pretending that you're holier than the Virgin daughter of the Virgin Mary. Sh—i-i—it, you fuck. You know you fuck. And you know that you and me, we gonna get it on. So why put on airs. And why put it off?" Hands beneath his head, he wiggled his hips. His fat belly shook.

Wonderful vulgarity. It repelled her, and yet she loved it. It tied her to him in language, tone, and emphasis. Inheritance of the Black street scene. She wanted to answer him. Wanted to say: "Yeah, I'm with you. Come on. Let's get it on."

Continuation of games played too far beyond puberty. No, now she needed truth as real and as comprehensible as the truth she had pierced floating at sea—the truth of her madness.

She gazed down, studying his thick, uncombed, curly hair that prevented his cap from fitting, his full mouth, his fleshy chest, the heavy thighs, the protruding crotch. He moved his penis deliberately to entice her.

"If we were in the States, you wouldn't even look at me," she accused.

"Oh? Good as you look, and you got complexes? Baby, I ain't one of those. My old lady's a Black, nappy-headed woman just like you. And I'm crazy about her."

"That why you took to the sea?"

"Because of my ma. She the reason it took me so long to split. Anyway, I didn't run. Just dropped out."

"From school?"

"Society."

"I take it you like society here better?"

"Are you for real? I hate little islands, provincial towns. I hate what they do to people. Islands like this, could have been the oasis of equality for all. Instead they opt out—become extensions of the mainland, ruled by puppets who pretend they're the real power, when all they do is line their pockets to help keep poor folks poor, a source of low wages and cheap paradise. Them guys are insecure, dangerous."

"Haiti's not a puppet island," Jonnie defended. "Haiti's independent. These rulers wouldn't give up their people's hard-won independence to become puppets."

"My future woman," Maxie's big voice boomed. "Haiti was born to die!"

His loudly spoken words sent fear slithering through the listeners. Eyes turned from them and remained turned: guests disassociating themselves from the loud-talking, unkempt sailor.

"You're mad," Jonnie hissed, lowering her tone.

But Maxie kept on in a loud voice: "Do you know the greatest mystery in this world today? It's that Haiti still exists. Every great European power from the nineteenth into the twentieth century tried to blow her out of existence, singly and collectively.

"The only reason they haven't is because on this island time goes so goddamn slow. Every peasant knows that with each passing day Haiti's time gets shorter. Since the Yankee marines nailed Charlemagne to the cross, they been waiting for him—or Jesus Christ—to come back to deliver them. Damballa answers their prayers by holding the sun in the sky longer than he got the right to, so Charlemagne and Christ think they got nothing but time. But whatever they think, the sun always got to rest. Jonnie Dash, you ever ask yourself how, in this century, a country with ninety-five percent illiteracy manages to survive?"

"Men don't die as quickly as you will have them, Maxie Gardener."

"But they do die, Jonnie! People don't live in poverty and ignorance, they die in poverty and ignorance! The old sages knew that. That's why Napoleon kidnapped Toussaint and jailed him in France rather than build the schools Toussaint wanted. That's why the United States didn't rush to send teachers to help build schools here—even though Haiti was its sister in revolution. They wanted all these ex-slaves dead, killed off—a grand lesson to their own slave population if they talked of freedom. They just didn't know how slowly time passes in Haiti. And so they're still waiting.

"Dreamers die, Jonnie Dash. Black dreamers die. Toussaint had to die, just as King had to die, as Malcolm had to die. Patrice Lumumba, Charlemagne, Jesus Christ all dreamers. All dead. Yes, the peasants still live—in ignorance. But for how long, in this world of reduced ozone layers, polluted soil, air, and mercury in the fish swimming the waters, with them not knowing a damn thing about it, nor what to do if they did know. It's all about power and money, Jonnie Dash."

"You make everything sound so brutal and the people so ordinary."

His eloquence reminded her of Gérard in Miss Ilma's living room. Except that Gérard had always spoken with hope for the masses: their inevitable rising, taking power, overthrowing tyrants.

"Even educated people are ordinary, baby—and ignorant people got the worst of it. Ignorant people are afraid to know. And nothing can save a mother's child who is scared. They're bound to die!

"Don't look at me like that, baby. I'm a revolutionary—not a dreamer. I was once. I followed Malcolm and Martin—been to jail, a part of the Black Revolution. Yes. Me. Dropped out of school to join—but made it back in. You are talking to a doctor of philosophy, Harvard grad. I and lots of my Black Power friends. Graduated and started making those big bucks—we were in demand then. Until I found that those bucks were big enough to keep my buddies from thinking. They got to like being ordinary. Yeah, keep me quiet as long as I make that loot. Easy to become joiners instead of doers—a new Black elite. That's why the ghettos of yesterday are the inner cities of today."

"Ordinary I ain't. I cut out."

"What do you call yourself now?" Jonnie asked. "A drifter? A beachcomber?"

"Hell no. I'm a hemispheric man, goddamn it. I lay claim to this whole hemisphere. I travel up and down its coasts, talking to all who want to listen. Am a free man."

"Even free men need money."

"Got it. Enough for me. I sail the sea—from Canada to Peru. Brazil's the place I aim to settle."

"Brazil? Blacks are oppressed in Brazil."

"Baby, everybody's oppressed everywhere—Blacks, whites, and all those in between. Some just don't know it."

"Everybody knows Brazilian leaders are corrupt, lining their pockets with money meant for the people."

"Coming from the States, you can talk? Trouble is, you ain't been reading up on your history. Corruption's the accepted rule of this hemisphere. Only difference—Brazil ain't had their revolution—yet. That's what I'm searching for. Revolution. The only way for a revolution to succeed is to be there to grab the chance. Keep it what it started out to be.

"Brazil's up for grabs right now. When they get it all together, that's gonna be the richest, freest country in this hemisphere—or the most screwed up. But then they'll only be joining the world—know what I mean?"

Jonnie shook her head no, she didn't know what he meant.

"Look, since the fifteenth century, Europe's been plundering this hemisphere to build Europe. They used the Natives, then Africans, then Indians, then Chinese. Everybody came here—Syrians, Jews, Lebanese—they would have made it all white, all European, but they got to mixing and matching so that their roots got all tangled and they still tripping over them.

"Look, my great-grandfather came from Africa and landed in Brazil. His brother landed here in Haiti. The youngest brothers were taken to the States. Baby, folks in this hemisphere got to screwing and carrying on so that we don't look African no mo. We look American. Sure those in power try to hang on to outdated aristocracy—Spanish, Portuguese, British. But they can't tell their kids one from another. From the U.S. on down, masters tried to make an elite class from their bastard kids, just in case. They figured if not them, then their grandkids would take over—rule this hemisphere. See what shit they're doing in Haiti? But come the revolution, Brazil's gonna be the greatest, most egalitarian place on earth."

"Spoken like a true romantic," Jonnie applauded. "I hope you live long enough to see it."

"Trouble with you is you don't have the faith. But I promise you I ain't 'bout to grow old. It ain't gonna take no hundred years." He caught her hand and pulled her down beside him, pushed his fingers through the thicket of her hair, pulled her head back. "Come with me, Jonnie Dash. Sail with me. Let's have a ball." His lips hovered over hers, his breath gushed into her open mouth.

Oh, to be so young, so committed, and still have rage, to have that spirit of adventure while all of life still lay in the future. To be a revolutionary, to spit in the eye of fortune, and to set sail on a boat without doubts, and never, never look back. Jonnie's eyes shone. She felt them shining. She tasted the salt of the sea, felt warm breezes brushing her face. To dare. To be young enough to dare.

"How old are you?" she asked, then wanted to unsay it. She wanted to push those words back, far back out of her mind, out of memory.

"Thirty-three, if that makes a difference," he said.

Thirty-three! Younger than Emmanuel! The bright glow of possibilities dimmed. Mentally, she distanced herself from him, tried to disentangle her fumbling desires, her rampaging fantasies.

"Doesn't it make a difference?" she asked, a cold, polite smile on her face. "What was it that I heard you say about my going through the change?"

"That goddamn Jessica," Maxie groaned.

"There is that to consider, isn't it? Children—that sort of thing."

"I intend to have children," Maxie said.

"Is that why you carry this?" She joked, patting his protruding stomach. "A built-in incubator? Have you actually thought of forgoing the use of women?"

What unbelievable torture. What flippancy. Uncivilized. Why not simply tell him calmly I'm past the age of childbearing—more in the age of grandmotherhood. Instead, she kept up her mockery. "They'll certainly not be entering this world through me," she said, and felt tears stinging the back of eyelids as she spoke.

"Do they have to?" Maxie chided, his brown eyes actively serious. "After all, people who love love, *n'est-ce pas?* Intelligent folks decide the kind of world they want and work to make it that way. I want children, whichever way."

"To school in your fishing boat?"

"Yes, to school them at sea. Where better? What better to learn than how much fish is in the sea, how fish act, react one with the other. No hypocrisy there. No lies. No betrayals. Yes, I want my kids to learn at sea—boys, girls, I want them with me, holding them to me. Why you think I got these"—he touched his fat chest—"bosoms?"

Surprising words from the mouth of a man so young. They opened up possibilities not yet thought of. Her plans had always been so ordinary, landlocked, limited by blinders of religion, shackled to poverty. He did remind her of the young Gérard.

"You must have been a very bright child." Jonnie's cheeks burned, hearing her patronizing words.

"A brain," he admitted. "Graduated at twenty-two."

"That's not so long ago."

"You got to be kidding. At least a hundred years."

"Your father a Southerner? Are you one of the Black elite?"

"My father was a Jew."

"Yet you claim African ancestry."

"Lady, you ain't been listening good," he scolded. "I told you my old lady's a Black nappy-headed lady who does not know, nor could she ever fit into, your Black bourgeoisie. No more than the Haitian peasant fit into this island's mulatto elite.

"My father was Russian. A Jew. A communist hounded to death because he was a Jewish communist—a professor married to a Black American. They left the States once, to get away from the stigma. They went to Trinidad, where he taught at the University of the West Indies. My mother's life there was pure hell. My father was invited everywhere, to everything. My mother had to sit at home, ignored. They didn't accept her, baby. Blacks not accepting Blacks. I know these islands, this hemisphere. They changed a bit since the Black Revolution in the States—but lady, they ain't changed half enough.

"When my parents went back to the States, my old man died. A massive heart attack. That left me a single-parent kid out there. An Afro-American boy. I needs no validation."

"I hate the way you twist things!" Jonnie cried.

She had not intended to challenge him. She had no right. She who had no credentials to even research her lineage. She, a Catholic in a Baptist world with roots buried so deep beneath the sidewalks of New York that a bulldozer and the most powerful lens ever invented couldn't unearth them.

"Is your mother still alive?" she asked.

"Still alive and still fighting causes. She's one hell of a woman."

How old . . . But she didn't want to know his mother's age—didn't even want to think about it. "You're so very young," she said instead.

"Goddamn right I'm young." He measured her with streetwise eyes. "Younger than that blue-eyed son of a bitch you been giving it up to."

"Stephan . . ." They heard the name loud between them and looked up at the terrace. Jessica had called the name. Stephan came strolling out onto the terrace.

"You don't like Stephan?" Jonnie asked.

"Got nothing against the dude—except he's too easy to read." Maxie lay back, pulled his dirty captain's cap down to cover his eyes.

Jonnie looked out at the swimmers in the pool—aliens making the world over for their pleasure—the pool, the swimming, the days of luxury that she had so recently joined. "What do you read in Stephan except that he's a young man who—"

"Young! That cat's bending the hell out of middle age. He don't show it. Why should he? He's born into one of the wealthiest circles in the world; his folks been living from the rotted, dying flesh of the poor all their lives. Vampires! Keeps them young. Look at him acting the playboy."

"He is Jessica's paid companion."

"Paid, is he? When a guy's got so much tradition to break, he can't help looking like a flapper."

"Maxie, you're jealous."

"Damn right, I'm jealous. He might have rights to the heavens and most of the earth, but he ain't got no right to you."

"Jessica's the lucky one. He's devoted to her."

"She can afford him."

"He's her friend—and cousin."

"Then that makes dozens."

"Street."

"The accepted word is vulgar," Maxie grinned. "Learn to use them wisely, words." Jonnie moved to get up, but Maxie caught her hand. "Got everything from me you wanted?" He leered.

"Yeah, they're cousins—too much alike to be just friends. But what you want with that turkey—babies?"

"I'm going through my change, remember?"

"All the more reason to come away with me. We never have to worry about making babies—they'll come."

Jonnie looked up at the terrace. Seeing Jessica and Stephan had dampened her desire. She had been upset, jealous when they had left her the night before. Still she had never expressed interest in Jessica's cruise—which seemed to be the center of Jessica's thinking. "I doubt that I'm the one you really want, Maxie."

"You are, you are," he insisted. "I don't give one good god-damn about your menopause. I need you—your company, the world we can build. Come, let's glide away from disaster, sail away to love. . . ."

"This may surprise you, Maxie, but the world has all been discovered. The same people rule it all. Wherever we sail, we'll be meeting up with them, those with money, the power—and the diseases they spread."

"You don't believe that, Jonnie Dash, or why would you be here? Why are you in the mountains painting? Why is art impor-tant to you? Because you believe in something. You know there are worlds to discover. You're searching—just like me." He pulled her to him, touched her cheeks with soft lips. And so she didn't tell him that she painted because that was all she knew to do, all she had wanted to do. "We're a different breed, destined to dis-cover the new in the old.

"Why is it that of all the Black people in the United States, the world, that we—you and me—had to meet here?"

Jonnie thought of Gérard and smiled. "You're mad," she said.

"And you?" He startled her by asking, by searching for an an-swer through her eyes. What did he see? What did he know about her? "What do you want, Jonnie Dash? To break up an ongoing twosome, become a permanent threesome? It won't work. Mr. Blue Eyes is an Old World man in a New World setting out at a precarious age. He needs more than a piece of pussy, and you say you can't go beyond that?"

"And you?" Jonnie challenged, anger mounting. "A piece of pussy is enough for you?"

"No. I'm young. I want the world. Young enough to expect

to change it. I'm not Old World. I'm Mr. New World Hemisphere. My heirs—heirs who will know all about fish and tides and time, and how to bring about changes—are its future. I'm your man, Jonnie Dash.

"Picture us, Jonnie, on the stormy sea, the rough sea, the pure and truthful sea, the no-fooling-around sea, the calm, seductive, loving sea.

"We'll wake up every morning and make love. Then we'll have coffee and make love. We'll catch a mess of sardines for lunch and make more love. We'll tangle together and let the boat rock us to sleep. We'll hold on to each other when it heaves, and when the waves are high and there's nothing else to do, we'll batten down the hatches, curl into each other, and make more love." His arms pulled her, held her against his chest where she rested, feeling its softness, listening to his heart thud, thud, thud.

"All those days and nights eating fish and making love?"

"Only with a madwoman. The sea would spit us out if we weren't mad. Only the mad can live in its loneliness, its loveliness, its vastness, its grandness, its madness."

"There has to be more to life than eating fish and making love," she said, her voice skeptical. She had to break this closeness. Important to break the closeness. Why? Why end this romantic moment with someone she felt at ease with and wanted to be with?

Because of the two on the terrace? Did she want to inspire them with pity for her—the lonely little girl, the orphan they had deserted?

Maxie sensed her wavering and pushed her away. "What else is important?" He stared at her. "Yeah, yeah, you want to be precious, thought of as great, the greatest-on-earth artist. Like them who wants to be the world's greatest writer or actor or grand dame, European-style: the professional Black.

"The busy people. Busy-as-cockroaches people, busybusy-busy-like-bees people, concocting their brand of lies, propagandizing how crushed they are to live in a racist society, and getting rich doing it. They who put cats like Nixon in office to make the lie look like the truth.

"How much do they pay for a painting, lovely lady? How much did they pay you to come down to this poor island to strut your arrogant Black self? What promise did they make to blind you, to bind you to keep the faith? What inducement did they offer for you to stretch those gorgeous limbs in the sun and to look the other way while they stiffen the pricks of these Black sons of bitches with guns to keep the docile docile."

"You don't know me!" Jonnie cried, terrified by his abrupt change of attitude. "What do you know about me? My suffering? How dare you lie there accusing me! Expecting me to apologize for my life—my work!"

"Talk about betrayal," Maxie roared on, relentless, refusing her indignation. "Our Black leaders all killed, our boys sent abroad, made into killers in the East, the Middle East, in Africa, to drain what's left of the wealth of Brown and Black peoples—and the sons of bitches writhe and groan because one motherfucking clown burglarized a hotel—Watergate. While your son—"

"You know nothing about my son!"

"You got one you gave a name to. . . ." He had to say it! He had to go where he was forbidden. Jonnie shrank inside herself to shield the name knocking around inside her head—clunk, clunk, clunk. She couldn't bear it!

And the clouds had been waiting for her to call his name: Emmanuel, Emmanuel, Emmanuel. She refused to call it and the sky darkened. And the sun had been waiting for her to speak his name, and when she refused, it hid behind the darkening clouds, and now the clouds clashed, thunder roared, streaks of lightning flashed across the clouds.

Maxie stood up, shaking his fists at the cloud. "What did the White Power Establishment give him for his silence?" he shouted. "The same as they gave to me? The same they offered my Black Power buddies—a Judas bag of gold, sixty-thousand-a-year bags of gold. Or did they dim his wits with drugs? Did they throw him in jail to keep him silent, to keep him from ever, ever, ever—Do you hear me?—ever knowing how his habit keeps the rich rich, while he keeps himself, keeps us, forever slaves.

"I'm thirty-three years old and I've seen it all. I am the product of Black Slavery and McCarthyism, bold enough to march behind Martin Luther from Selma to Montgomery and unlucky enough to be thrown in jail and given jolts of electricity in my ass for the sole reason that some ignorant white bastards with cattle prods in their hands and nothing in their heads got jealous—because Black brothers professed intelligence after they had spent centuries trying to make retards of them.

"And while the fuckers in Washington spoke of Christian values, we all watched on TV while innocent women and children ran down the street thousands of miles away, their flesh burning, while Christians laughed and prayed for their death so that their killers would come home—and be cleansed of their sins.

"You talk about madness! Be glad to be mad. Be glad you're not the mother who prayed, Kill, kill, kill! Madness keeps us from hearing the applause, the cheers over the death of the world's colored people. It keeps us from being upset and shaking our heads in horror because a son of a bitch in the White House is accused of having a safe burglarized.

"I went to school to make my dead father proud and my living mother proud, and because I was proud to be living in the greatest country on earth and proud to be struggling for equality—which everybody ought to have already had if honesty and integrity had meaning. But those back-slapping motherfuckers were orchestrating our lives! They killed those of us who fought for decency and gave those of us who looked away sixty grand a year, asking us to discover what they had long known: what makes poor folks poor and what makes poor folks violent. Sixty grand a year and the betrayed became the betrayer."

Rain fell suddenly. It beat down on the pool emptied of swimmers; it blew onto the terrace emptied of diners. It beat down on the heads of Jonnie Dash and Maxie Gardener standing at poolside—a young man challenging the world, his fist upraised, gazing into his future, and a woman who refused to age, eyes wet with rain and tears she refused to shed, looking back into a life through which his words echoed.

As quickly as it had begun, the brief shower stopped, the sky cleared, the sun came out, and Maxie Gardener, water pouring from his captain's cap, down to his shoulders, his chest, ended his sermon.

"I said all that to say, Yes, that's what life's about to me—eating fish and making love and looking around for revolution."

6

L IKE A CHILD playing at the game "May I," she kept taking down her suitcases according to the commands of the partially paralyzed brain: "Yes you may," then putting them back on the shelves when the command concluded, "No, you may not." So it took more than money to do what one wished. It took will.

Threatened because she had given one dollar to a child, being accosted by a woman in the garden whom she didn't know. Nor did she understand how she came by the flute now in her possession—all giving off a sense of impending ill. Now came the threat of entanglement in the wild dreams of the too-young man, his dreams of revolution pushing her back in time to all the anxieties she had been struggling against. Trapped. Danger approaching from all sides. She had to pack, had to get away. Yet she lacked the will.

Even those things she had grown used to came hard. She dressed for swimming, then instead of heading for the pool, went to the bar to stand looking down at the deserted pool, at listless waiters walking or sitting at tables waiting for improbable guests—most had flown the hotel for the cooler breezes of beaches.

In the heat fronds of coconut palms drooped, flowers wilted. The pool looked the same—serene, inviting. She longed for its soothing coolness, wanted to be absorbed into its depths, but ruled by a sense of impending danger, she brooded.

"Why hasn't Maxie been around?" she cried to Dominique, who stood beside her.

She hadn't meant to ask, didn't want to know where the too-young boy with his cushioned stomach and soft, full lips had gone. Young, so young, yet his arms around her had been strong. She had leaned against him and felt safe. She longed to lean against him once again. Such a longing.

"Maxie?" Dominique said. *"Il a disparu comme toujours."*

Disappeared? Like always? How dared he? How dared he push himself into the crevices of her mind, then simply disappear? She bit her lips and stared out at the still water of the pool, the drooping palms, the waiters, spotless and restless in their clean white shirts, their bow ties.

"Hélas," Dominique said, after moments of silence. "Rain is coming sure."

"Why doesn't it come now?" Jonnie blurted in anguish. "This heat is too much to bear." The heat, too, had become a part of the conspiracy created by the too-young man, keeping her from taking the next step, getting on with her life.

"Sacré, Jonnie Dash." Dominique made a rapid sign of the cross. "Don't pray for rain. Don't do that. Is coming."

Surprised. She had never thought of him as religious. She studied his face. Its seriousness forced her to change the subject. "Seen Madame Winthrop today?" she asked.

"Madame Winthrop? She gone."

"That cruise—takes up all of her time," Jonnie complained.

"No," Dominique said. "She go to Red Cross. Somebody tell her they take peasant blood to send to the States. Hah, Madame fly out—like a hawk."

Jonnie imagined Jessica, her seven-league stride, her missionary zeal. Busybusybusy like cockroaches, missionaries, rushing to keep peasants from scrambling over each other to give blood for dollars—honest money that Jessica in full indignation would deprive them of. Why? The government allowed it. The Church allowed it. Sell, sell, sell, sell blood, sell lungs or kidneys or heart—just give your soul to Me.

A surge of restlessness pushed her from the window to the bar, then back to the window. She had not done enough to help Jessica. Why criticize? She had cared nothing about the cruise. But she had wanted to help out at the hospital. She hadn't. Couldn't. Gérard had taken her to places where she had seen children running around naked, seen ragged women attempting to hold their lives together as they did their ragged dresses, with empty hands. Some had pushed their babies into her arms in the vain hope that she could take them out of poverty.

White American, they considered her. But she was Black American, as powerless as they. That gesture—handing her a baby—had shown her. It had had the effect of scratching up scabs from old sores to be picked until they bled, oozed puss.

Jonnie shook away the vision, thinking of herself and Maxie bleeding into each other in the rain, and the nightmares suffered while lying in bed, watching herself running, running through woods, running from the large, staring eyes of a child who called her friend. . . .

Afraid? Yes. She had always been afraid. Fear had dogged her through her life—intangible, her best-held secret. Nothing she had ever done in life had not been accompanied by fear.

Half a million dollars had not given her courage, except to come to Haiti. The strong Black woman, she had never been. Perhaps that strength came with being Baptist. She had always been a hard-working Catholic—and vulnerable.

Going back to her room, she pulled on white linen slacks with the intention of staying in that cool air until evening, but she found herself back at the hotel. She reentered the bar as Dominique stood near the entrance talking to a stranger. Settling in her corner she saw the young man glance at her, then quickly look away.

Instant apprehension. Paranoia. Uneasy currents tingled her nerve ends. The man—tall, brown skin, a good-looking Haitian in a light brown short-sleeved cotton suit. She had seen him before. But not here at the bar. Very few ordinary Haitians frequented the bar of Old Hotel. Wealthy Haitians sometimes, businessmen frequently—and artists. Rarely one who wore clothes of such simplicity.

His was an evasive alertness—eyes that pretended they did not see when in fact they saw everything. He did not look back at her, yet she knew he held her in his peripheral vision. For some reason she had become the object of his interest, and that caused her heart unrest. Did his presence have to do with the wooden flute sitting in full view on her dresser?

"Who is he?" she asked Dominique when, unable to interest the man in a drink, he came over to her. Dominique shrugged.

"Maybe he wait for somebody. And you, Jonnie Dash, you want that I make you a *citron pressé?*"

"No, a rum punch," she said.

"*Mais non*—is too hot." He shook his head in all seriousness.

"You're always bragging about your rum punch. Now when I want one, you give me a story."

"*Oui, c'est une boisson exceptionnelle.* But in this heat, *c'est pour les imbeciles.*"

"*Comme moi en ce moment.*" She laughed. But she needed a boost to fuel the machinery, shake her mental paralysis, force alertness. Where had she seen the man before?

Guests were slowly trickling back. The young man standing at the entrance studied each in turn. None held his attention for long.

"Jonnie." Stephan had come into the bar through the back door. Standing behind her, he held her shoulders and turned her to face him. "You have been avoiding me," he said.

"No, I'm here," she said. "It's you who have been busy—you and Jessica. How are her plans for the cruise going?"

"I really can't say." He laughed. "All that money being spent and I can't say. It's this ghastly weather. Everything ought to take a backseat until the weather makes up its mind. Of that I can't convince her. She's a woman obsessed . . . but never mind. Let's you and I take a drive out to the shack and spend what's left of the day." Jonnie shook her head no. "I promise there won't be a repeat performance of the last time," he pleaded. "Jonnie, I shall take care. I shall remove your clothes myself, fold them, tuck them neatly away from the tide and the sand. You have nothing to fear."

Then, as Jonnie kept shaking her head, he asked, "I have done something to upset you?"

Still she shook her head. Even remembering their being together, the beauty of it, the never-to-be-forgotten fullness of their lovemaking, she kept shaking her head. "It's over," she said.

Dominique set her rum punch down before her. She took a sip, then another, before she managed to look into Stephan's face.

"What's over?" he asked.

"We are."

"What have I done?" Jonnie took another sip of Dominique's strong punch. But that did nothing to help her say what she wanted to: When I had the best of sex with you, when I was in your arms, you said to me, "I love Jessica." Jealous? Yes. Jealous, jealous . . . In every affair she foolishly expected to be loved with a forever-after love. Theirs hadn't even started out that way.

She didn't hold him responsible. She had walked into what Maxie had called an ongoing twosome. So who was to blame if he didn't love her—enough? No one had ever loved her enough. Not her husband, not her Aunt Olga. Why did she think of Aunt Olga now? Aunt Olga, whose hatred she had always accepted? Aunt Olga, whom she had never seen again since leaving for school that long-ago morning.

She had seen her cousin Daphne once. A few weeks after she had sold her now famous painting, a few days after the review of the works had appeared in the *New York Times*, she had seen Daphne, a saleslady in a department store. A saleslady? She had expected her cousin to be a grand concert pianist. Daphne had not recognized her. But she had known Daphne immediately. Her cousin, full-grown and plump with an aristocratic set to her face, selling panties.

Nor had Daphne read about her success. Daphne didn't read the *New York Times*. "How's Aunt Olga?" she had asked,

"Mother is dead," Daphne had replied. "She's been dead ten years now."

Aunt Olga dead? Aunt Olga dead! In an instant everything she had ever accomplished lost significance. The woman whom she hated more than anyone on earth—dead! Aunt Olga had not been on this earth to realize that every evilness she had or could have ever thought up had not been enough to destroy Jonnie Dash. How crushed she had been. Only after weeks of depression did she realize that she had been fighting against evil, that hatred of her aunt had been a driving force in her life. She had worked so hard to "show her." But the woman had been dead! She had made up her life from a fairy tale and when it had become meaningless, she had reached into her mind to pull out the smoldering long, lost love for Gérard, which she had dashed to Haiti to rekindle.

But Gérard had never loved her. No more than her husband—even the Muslim. Yet she had clung to them begging. Even her friend Harry, who had lived in the loft above hers.

She and Harry had fought the landlord together in court after the *Times* had discovered the poor artists and their ingenuity in finding wonderful, abandoned lofts in which to work and had written them up. That article had sent hordes of middle-class, wealthy buyers to their dingy buildings, which they transformed into fabulous duplexes, pushing the poor artists into the streets. She and Harry had fought for their space in court and had won. For years they had worked in their silent, dedicated way, counseling each other, always envisioning a wealthy future while expecting to be forever poor. They were, she had thought, friends for life. Yet when she sold her painting and had told him her happy news of a half-million-dollar sale, he had said, "You're full of shit." He had gone back into his space. They never spoke again.

"I saw you with Maxie," Stephan said. "Is he the reason?" Jonnie took another sip of the strong punch.

"Maxie's a child," she said.

"No, Maxie's no child," he contradicted, then waited. She sipped her rum silently, feeling the loosening of her limbs, the pleasure of being drunk—or almost. Then, "It's the bloody heat," he said. "Nothing's over between us, Jonnie Dash. I shall not let it be."

He walked away from her and Jonnie watched him go. She watched him walk by the young man near the entrance to the bar, and as he disappeared out the door, she felt the stirring of dread again, wanting him back, the bulwark between herself and the unpleasant something about to happen.

"*Mais, qu'est-ce que c'est?*" Dominique said, reaching out to hold her hand. "My Jonnie, she does not look so happy." Jonnie laughed then and wondered about the business of laughter—that window dressing to hide fear, cowardice, confusion.

"Give me another rum punch," she said, enjoying her easing from paralysis, pleased with her rum-soaked philosophy.

"*Mais dis-donc,*" Dominique said, protesting against a second drink. Nevertheless he took her glass to refresh it as Roxanne came into the bar, upset.

"I have been looking all over for you," Roxanne said. "Jonathan has dashed off to Santo Domingo again. He's threatened to take me to the States when he gets back. I told him that we—you and I—had made other plans."

"No you didn't," Jonnie snapped. Even in her near-drunken state she refused to forgive Roxanne. She never expected to forgive—or forget—being abandoned in a strange place where men with pistols in their holsters roamed, anywhere and everywhere, perhaps looking for her.

"I'm not going back with him."

"Why tell me?"

"You have to help me." Disheveled, on the verge of hysteria, Roxanne appeared young, reaching for pity.

"Roxanne, you're a grown woman—well over fifty, lovely, rich as hell—now what do you think I can do for you?"

"Jonnie, you're angry with me."

Jonnie grew impatient. At the same time she sensed the young man at the end of the bar, listening, hearing them while pretending not to. She remembered him. He was one of the men who had shoved the little boy into the room at Chez Renard! Her heartbeat shook her body even as she lowered her voice.

"No, Roxanne, not angry, just indifferent. Never in your life think that I shall run interference between you and your husband, ever."

"Because of the other night? You're not all that pure," Roxanne sneered.

"I'll suffer the consequences of my impurity," Jonnie answered.

"It is because of the other night," Roxanne said. "I thought that you'd understand."

"What's to understand?"

"You're my friend, Jonnie." She appeared almost innocent saying that. Amber eyes burned feverishly from sunburned face, adding to her attraction.

"We might be many things, Roxanne. Friends we ain't."

"I like you, Jonnie."

Jonnie sipped punch. A rush of sweat poured from her, adding to her body heat. Such heat. She was a damn fool to drink strong stuff on such a day. She glanced at the entrance. The young man had gone. Her knees buckled in relief. She leaned against the bar for support, forcing her breath to flow evenly.

"I never had a Black friend before," Roxanne said. "I never even had a Black maid."

Jonnie let the words turn over and over in her ears and still didn't believe she had heard them. Impossible for someone to live in the fractured racial edifice from which they both had been formed and not even develop a dialogue to bridge the gap to common courtesy.

"You don't have a Black friend now," she said, standing up. Dominique reached over the bar to hold Jonnie's hand.

"Give your compatriot a break," he pleaded. "She's trying."

"You must be in love with her." Jonnie snatched her hand away, suspicious of his innocence, this merchant seaman who claimed to have traveled the world and seemed to have learned nothing.

"*Mais*—she is beautiful, *n'est-ce pas?*" He grinned, his wise-owl eyes gazing at Roxanne, admiring her.

"And me? Am I not beautiful?" A low blow. He did not see beauty in her. Wonderful, talented, good to talk to, nice-looking enough perhaps to make love to. Beautiful? "Who influences whom around here, Dominique," Jonnie snarled. "Does André influence you, or is it the other way around?"

His doggie smile vanished. Out came the bar-wiping towel. Jonnie turned from him to Roxanne. "Never, never—do you hear me—call on me as a friend. If you need help, ask Jessica. Jonathan has all kinds of respect for her."

"That bitch," Roxanne said.

"What has Jessica ever done to you?"

"You ask me that? You have seen how she behaves around that young captain."

"So?"

"It's monstrous. He's half her age. The woman has absolutely no shame." The image of Roxanne's legs wrapped around Jean-Pierre's black body flashed through Jonnie's mind. Did Roxanne then have a scale of morality that she applied only to the deeds of others?

"Her Imperial Majesty," Roxanne jeered. "The way she tries to order him around. Doesn't she know that Captain Lavel's no ordinary sailor? His father happens to have been Commodore Lavel. Someone ought to inform Jessica Winthrop that America won the War of Independence. We no longer have to jump to attention when the British command."

"I'd rather you not speak to me about Jessica Winthrop," Jonnie said quietly, trying to control her intoxication.

"Why? Because she allows you to be a part of her entourage?"

Jonnie slapped Roxanne hard across her face, then realized that Dominique's holding her arm had prevented her from throwing her drink. The rum punch. She'd had it. She jerked her arm away from Dominique and turned to Roxanne. But Cécile came up.

"Madame, somebody want speak to you." Jonnie turned her anger to the unseen person. So she had come again? What for this time? Jonnie stilled the urge to grab Roxanne and pull her along, give to the woman the one responsible for her rage. Instead she stumbled behind Cécile, surprised indeed that she had so little control over her feet.

Squaring her shoulders, she made a determined effort to stand tall, to march right to the back garden. But Cécile stopped her at the door. "My room?" she asked. How dare she come into my room? She pushed past Cécile into her room, then stood, gazing around, the coolness from the air conditioner adding an instant chill to her sweltering body. "Where is she?" Jonnie asked, going to the curtains, which had been pulled, forcing the room into darkness.

"*Il est là, madame.*" Cécile went to the closet, opened the door, and pulled someone from its dark interior. "*C'est lui qui veut vous parler.*"

It was he! Jonnie looked down into wide black eyes, black, black eyes, that overwhelmed their whites. Instantly she sobered.

"What's he doing here?" Her mouth had gone dry. She saw again the young man standing at the entrance of the bar and knew that the two connected. "I said, what's he doing here?"

"*Il a demandé d'après vous, madame.*" Cécile, putting her hand over her mouth, forced her words out softly, timidly.

"Get him out of here," Jonnie said. "Get him out—now."

Madness. When she thought of him she felt guilt for having run from him; when she saw him she felt only fear. She fought against the desire to tear at her clothes, to run naked out into the yard. She looked around, expecting to find a broom, a stick, something to mount, to ride away on—or barring that, to lose consciousness instantly, to regain it at some future date in an entirely other experience. She waited, expecting something to happen. But the longer she waited, the more sober and focused she became.

This was actually happening. The child only meant trouble for her. From the minute she had laid eyes on him, she had known. She had been waiting for something to happen and here it was. The two stood looking at her—two children really. He and Cécile.

"But, madame, where he go?" Cécile asked.

"How do I know? What do you know about him? Who is he? What does he want from me?"

"Madame," Cécile said, shaking her head. "I don't know the boy. He say he stay with the Jamaican. He say, *l'homme méchant* look for him so he come to you, madame."

"Why me? He doesn't know me."

"He say you his friend." The frail girl squared her shoulders, pulling herself into a confrontational stance. Against whom? The United States authority on this island? The *tonton macoute?* Certainly not her.

"Take him to your patron, M'sieur Gérard. He's Haitian. He'll know what to do. I'm a stranger here."

"*Mais, madame*, the boy want to go *aux Etats-Unis.*"

So he thought he had choices? The young man at the bar sent to look for him, the big man on the steps talking to Mrs. Thompson. And Charles McCellen! She remembered the look of pure hatred in the eyes of Charles McCellan, looking at her, letting her know he hated her—because of this child. Everybody after his Black butt and he thought all he had to do was come to her and she would make his dream real for him.

"But I'm not going back to the States!" Jonnie cried, knowing then that from the moment she had left the States, she'd had no intention of ever going back. "I'm never going back." Never had those words been formed into a sentence, even into a thought. But saying them, she knew she had spoken the truth.

"But madame," the boy said. "You my friend . . ."

Jonnie turned from the plea in those eyes—eyes that had been hounding her. Eyes that had driven Charles McCellen mad. This child whose image had already been painted across her mind—this poem of a child whom she would preserve on canvas, one day, but for whom she had no friendship to give. It came to her quietly, in that part of the mind where such creations are formed; she could draw from him, even now, what she hoped to find one day in André Bienaimé.

She turned from him. He expected bravery from she who had never been brave—no braver than that little girl sitting on the iron stoop of Mr. Katz's music shop mired in shit.

Jonnie stared at Cécile, who stood staring back, awaiting orders. What to do? What did they dare do? She put her hands to her temples to shut out the rumble of thunder. Behind the heaviness, the heat, to the north and the south, the rumble of thunder, the threat of thunder—and no Maxie.

She left them there in the room with their questions to which she had no answers. She walked back to the hotel slowly.

She thought again of Mrs. Mealy, in whose house she had lain for months not speaking, not wanting to talk again.

Shock, they called it. Old people. Old-fashioned people who didn't believe in hospitals, who had nursed her. No, she couldn't turn away from him. What now? What now?

Whole periods of her life were closed. Deliberately? She remembered the factory, her years of anguish that Mrs. Mealy said were making a good woman out of her. Years of being trapped without thoughts or being able to think of her art, the one thing she loved. And so, in turn, she had closed Mrs. Mealy out—completely.

Jonnie walked into Claire's office and stood startled. The blond girl who had been at Mrs. Thompson's was sitting with her.

"What's she doing here?" Jonnie demanded, her voice hoarse.

"Oh, you know Alice-in-Wonderland?" Claire asked. Jonnie stared at the girl. She still had the spaced-out look. "No, how would I?" she asked.

"She's from the orphanage," Claire said. "We call her Alice, Alice-in-Wonderland, or just plain Jane Doe. I hear that soldiers went into the orphanage last night and wrecked the place—totaled it. Seems they were looking for someone. I don't know why. But they didn't find him, so they totaled the place. All the kids slept in the woods last night. Alice came to me this morning."

"Haitian soldiers?" Jonnie asked.

"Who else? I suppose they were looking for someone Mrs. Thompson was hiding. They didn't find whoever it was. But did they have to wreck the place?"

The man had to be mad! She had guessed the depth of Charles McCellen's feeling at Chez Renard, then his near madness when looking at her. "They might have been mistaken," Jonnie offered. But this—this was more than an obsession.

"Someone told them," Claire said. Or why be so excessive? Claire's doll-like face held a gentle, pained expression. "One must be ever so careful in Haiti," she whispered. "The Haitians are the world's most gentle people—but if there's a secret, someone always finds out—and always tells."

Jonnie's eyes snapped to the girl sitting next to Claire, searching her eyes. They had been blank when she first saw her. They were blank now. Alice or Jane Doe or whoever—did she remember her? Spaced-out kids sometimes snapped back. They sometimes came and went, came and went. Had she heard talk about *l'Américaine aux cheveux frisés*, whom the wisp of a child went through the woods to find? The eyes remained vacant.

Leaving the office, Jonnie walked quickly through the lounge, through the dining room, then to the bar. She looked around for the young man in the light brown cotton suit. Not there. Still, she sensed his presence. Close. But where?

She left the grounds, walked out of the gate, then to the corner, and turned, stopping to lean against the bricks of the bare wall. She waited. The young man had not followed. She walked on alongside the wall, where the sleepers had not yet begun to congregate. Every few steps she stopped, looking around, waited. When no young man appeared, she kept on walking but with a new determination. Walked to where the bougainvillea at the walls no longer grew and the branches of trees from the woods jutted out—some reaching the center of the road. Shading branches that she hoped hid her from eyes of the curious. Where the wall ended, the woods kept on until it came to an asphalted cross street, which separated the woods from a group of dwellings.

Jonnie stopped, then turning, walked into the woods, expecting the wall to guide her back to the hotel. Instead, the haphazard growth of overlapping roots kept forcing her into the center of dense woods and darkness, where, unable to see, she had to use her hands to ward off branches hitting her face and shuffle her feet to find walking space or roots, which she clambered over. Confused, tired, forced to realize that she was not as young as she sometimes believed, she wanted to turn back, but a strange determination forced her on.

It wasn't far. She had walked only a half mile, possibly a mile from the hotel. But a half mile through dense woods with thick underbrush had its own meter. Soon she lost all sense of direction, and time. It had been daylight when she left, but in the woods it might have been midnight. More, humidity caused by the recent shower made it difficult to breathe. After a time she leaned against the trunk of a tree to demand of herself: "What the hell are you doing here, Jonnie Dash?" Then it came to her that if she simply stopped, refused to go on, it might not even matter. What difference would it make? She had to admit to being tired—of life, of everything. Then she heard the drums.

Twilight? Already? Soon even the sense of daylight would be gone and she would be left to plod in darkness, if she chose. She had never feared the dark—only people. The story of her life had been one of walking in darkness, plodding, plodding, with an occasional flash here and there to reassure her. Gérard had been one such flash: knowing him had brought her to this island with its drums. Its beat pushed her. Leaving the tree, she once again groped in darkness.

She had taken the plunge into the woods with an agenda, unknown to her at the time. But a thought had been planted and had kept growing, steadily, if for no other reason than to disprove Cécile's belief in the devil or in the *femme méchante* and her evil powers.

And so she, Jonnie, kept on tripping over vines, climbing over roots. Thorns tore at her clothes while gnats and other insects mistook her ankles for food.

Then suddenly she was there. She had come to a fretwork of branches through which shone the lingering light of day. Another step and she had made the clearing where trees had been sheared away as with a magic scythe. She stood behind the back garden, seeing the outline of her room, where the curtains at the windows had been securely drawn.

Cécile opened the door to her knock, then went to sit in a chair near the dresser, folding her hands in her lap like an old woman, and looked at Jonnie with suspicion. And Jonnie, seeing herself in the mirror, her clothes stained, her hair messed up, her face shining from sweat, the look of madness about her, shrugged.

"*Les soldats*—they will come here—soon," she warned.

"*Pourquoi?*" Cécile demanded. "How you know . . ."

"*Parce que*," Jonnie answered. Indeed, because—because of the stifling heat, the hot sticky air that brought out the ugliness in people. Because men in passion can be small, evil—and because men in power were the smallest, most evil men of all. And because a tall young man in a brown cotton suit with slippery eyes, an ordinary man, was searching for the ways to get into power. "Where's Lucknair?"

Cécile shrugged and only looked on with disdain as Jonnie searched the closet and did not find him. She went to the door but did not open it. Would he have come here to her, calling her friend, then slipped out without giving her a chance? To go where?

He didn't trust her. He had reason. He had reached out to her and she had run—indeed she had been running since she had first seen him. From him? From herself? Sitting opposite her, Jonnie took Cécile's hand.

"Cécile, do you know that they wrecked Mrs. Thompson's orphanage? They didn't find him. They will wreck here. They intend to find him. They don't care where they wreck. We must get him away."

Cécile sat for a time, her hands clasped, her body moving back and forth like an old woman's. Then, having satisfied herself that Jonnie meant the boy no harm, she went to the bed and, kneeling, whispered: "*Lucknair, viens.*"

Lucknair crawled from beneath the bed and, seeing Jonnie, went to sit at her feet, looking so very much the orphan.

How terrible he hadn't been able to stay at Mrs. Thompson's for a year, two—until he was just a bit older, less vulnerable. Like she had done with Mrs. Mealy. The crinkly faced Mrs. Thompson with her massive breasts and love enough to take care of a million Lucknairs. But here, as Claire had said, someone always tells.

That was easy to believe from the manner in which she had been led directly to Jean-Pierre's car in the woods with only two words asked in all innocence: *"Moi, madame . . . ?"* Innocence!

Jonnie gazed down at the boy at her feet. How different he looked from the beggar at Exposition or the little ragged prisoner dragged into Le Renard's living room. His hair had been cut, and it became him. His shirt, dirty and torn, was made of silk and fitted well, as did his pants. A magic wand had transformed the beggar into a prince.

"Why did he run away from his patron?" Jonnie asked.

"He didn't like his patron," answered Cécile.

"Why not? He did well by him. Isn't it better for him to live in a nice house and be well cared for, instead of begging on streets or having to hide?"

Jonnie wanted to say more. She wanted to say that it was better for him to be in the care of someone who loved him. Certainly she had never seen such tenderness in the face and manner of anyone as she had seen in the face of Charles McCellen that day. Yet she hesitated.

"Madame." Cécile stood tall. The shielding hand dropped from over her mouth. The exposed brown rotten teeth robbed her of her look of gentle fragility. *"Il déteste son patron. Son patron, c'est un homme méchant. Nous, nous sommes des Haitiens. Nous ne sommes pas des pédérastes."*

Jonnie saw again the snake-eyed man pushing the boy into the room at Chez Renard, and thought of all those orphans forced to sleep in the woods. The pure savagery of it. That act gave the lie to Charles McCellen's tenderness.

Going to the window, she drew back the curtains and stood brooding, staring out at the dense woods. Tired, drained, uncomfortable from the sweat on her body cooling from the air conditioner, the itching from insect bites, her clothes torn from thorns and brambles. Indeed as much as she could bear. Yet she kept standing, staring out at the monster woods. But then the silence behind her lost its combativeness and she said, "Cécile, do you remember the woman who disappeared from the garden the other night?"

"*Oui, madame.*"

"You still don't know how she did it?"

"*Non, madame.*"

"Well, I'll tell you how. It's easy."

A SIMPLE PLAN. One doomed to failure. *Pourquoi? Parce que.* Because her matchstick plans were always doomed to fail, hatched as they were in that corner of her mind where happy-ever-after was the constant, like her trip to Haiti. But unlike her trip to Gérard, which had not been based on reality, this plan—a closed secret between her, Cécile, and Lucknair—had been well thought out. Lucknair's freedom depended on it.

(1) Cécile had to leave without being seen; (2) Cécile had to find her way through the woods to the cross street; (3) she had to get a taxi to take her to Gérard's; (4) she had to get the key to the cabin and convince Gérard that Jonnie needed something that she, and she alone, could bring; (5) by that time it would be black night; Cécile had to take a flashlight from the cabin then come back for Lucknair, take him through the woods to the cross street, where (6) Jonnie had to have a car and a driver—one she could trust—waiting to take them up into the mountains to the cabin. There Lucknair had to remain until Jonnie made arrangements for him to get out—in some way not yet imagined—to safety.

And Jonnie? Jonnie had to be where she could be seen at all times—necessary since the young man with the slippery eyes had probably been stationed at the hotel to keep an eye on her. Also, she had to get a car and a driver who could be trusted. Dominique's Volkswagen beetle was always parked nearby with its key. But whom did she trust?

André? Could he be pried away from his teenagers long enough? He might turn the escapade into a story to make his teenagers giggle. Claire? Jonnie let her mind rest on Claire for a moment. She thought of Sam. Perhaps as a last resort. She didn't want to put Sam and Claire and their business at risk. Stephan? He had gone to the beach. Jessica? She thought long on Jessica before finally shaking her head. No, not Jessica. Never Jessica. She believed too firmly in all her noble literature. The thought of Jessica going to Charles McCellen to openly confront him, demanding from him the reason for, the meaning of . . . made Jonnie shudder. Jean-Pierre? She knew about him—all about him. Black-mail? Why not? Why the hell not?

Jonnie waited until Cécile disappeared into the woods. She waited minutes, looking around, making sure no one had seen, that no one would follow. Her strange paralysis had lifted. Success or failure, she had sprung to life. She was, after all—although it took some time getting used to—a wealthy woman, an artist, she had a mission. And so changing her clothes, she set out.

She wanted to ask Dominique for Jean-Pierre. But André and Dominique were having an argument, shouting at each other. She stood waiting, anxious, impatient. The plan, once set in motion, had to proceed like clockwork. They had timed the entire operation to take two and a half hours, three the most. She had to get a driver.

"Dominique," Jonnie tried to intervene. But Dominique was wiping the bar with a vengeance. Nor did she understand one word, for they were arguing quickly, intensely, in Creole.

Finally, Jonnie went out on the terrace and, seeing Maurice coming up from poolside, asked, "Maurice, have you seen Maxie?"

"Pas depuis quelques jours, madame. Il est parti . . ."

"Isn't it time that he came back?"

Maurice gazed at her in amazement. *"Mais non, madame.* Any time is Maxie time."

Of course Maxie was the one needed. The Black Revolutionary, outgunned, outmoneyed, but not outclassed. The thought of joining forces with him in this enterprise made her shiver with excitement.

Leaving the terrace, she raced through the bar out to the entrance. But seeing the slippery-eyed man standing on the top step studying each guest as they walked by, she stopped. He turned, saw her, and his eyes turned blank, looking through her, sending a message that made her scurry back into the bar.

André stalked by, not seeing her. And Dominique kept wiping the bar with his wide circular stokes. The counter shone like glass. She sat down and looked at Dominique. He refused to look back. Would her simple plan remain just that—a mere plan? Disaster. What was new? She thought she had switched stations, found a new and stronger frequency, but somehow the dial was being switched back. Nevertheless her back twitched in anticipation and she forced herself to ask, "Dominique, where do I find Jean-Pierre?"

"How I know?" Dominique grumbled. *"Ils sont partis."*

They left? Did he mean that Jean-Pierre had taken Roxanne out? For the evening?

"What you want I get for you, Jonnie Dash?"

"Rum punch." It had worked earlier. It ought to work now. But her first sip heightened her nervousness. The glass in her hands shook. She looked around in exasperation. A driver, a driver. If they'd had time, they might have found someone they could trust. Someone who wouldn't tell . . . in Haiti?

She sipped her drink, kept sipping. The wealthy, famous Jonnie Dash did have something to fear: her elastic imagination, the habit of stretching things beyond logic—the way of orphans. So she had stretched a raid on the orphanage into a plan, bringing her face to face with intrigue, like Lucknair attempting to stretch a one-dollar contribution into a trip to the United States.

"Dominique, scotch and soda." The voice from the end of the bar caused Jonnie's face to twitch. It kept twitching. Sensing her new-found courage slipping away, she finished her drink, then demanded another by banging her glass on the bar.

Dominique brought Charles McCellan his drink, and when he brought hers, in a desperate attempt at bravado, Jonnie turned toward McCellen, raising her glass in a toast.

A damn fool thing to do. Hostility hard in his eyes, he jerked his head, looked over his shoulder, suspicious. He looked back, studying the space around her, searching for her reason. Did he think that by toasting him she had challenged him? To do what? Find the boy? No, she had intended no such thing. Just nerves, nerves.

They had never spoken. Their thing—their American thing— had to do with symbols, murky ideas of one another. A mutually accepted nonunderstanding that made their battle furious, if futile. They were separated by pride, prejudice, and poverty, keeping them at far ends of their great divide. So why else would she toast him, except to challenge him?

And if not, why not? If the poem of a boy stashed beneath her bed was the prize? That's why not—because Lucknair was the prize. Oh shit, shit, shit. Not only had she involved herself in intrigue, she had now committed herself to it.

And so she sat. No driver. The heat and humidity reached into the bar to question her resolve. Night darkened. The doomed plan had fallen to pieces as she had from the first imagined it might. Cécile had been gone almost two hours. It felt like four. Jonnie wanted to get up but was afraid to move.

"Another rum punch, Dominique."

"Another scotch and soda."

The dark outside, the silence inside, tied them together, each pretending the other invisible, both waiting. He, suspicious of her intentions, held her there. He had no intention of leaving. If he left, she might disappear. And if he left, she intended to do just that, disappear. She knew about his man outside. Understood her situation. She had a plan of which he had no knowledge, only vague suspicions. He had no plan—or had he? If she left, however, if she disappeared, it would point a finger, confirm his suspicions.

"Another rum punch, Dominique."

"Another scotch and soda."

She desperately wanted it to be tomorrow, to have gone to sleep and awakened when everything that might have happened this night was over and done with. But when had time ever rushed forward on this island?

They came—the soldiers. Suddenly in the silent hotel, they appeared, rifles drawn. Soldiers, marching through the dining room, the terrace, the pool area. Marching around the hotel guests who looked at them with frozen indifference—as though having come to this island, with its history of dictators and *tonton macoute*, they had expected nothing less. Jonnie, too, kept a demeanor of frozen indifference, although they had surprised her, frightened her. She now knew that the man with whom she was playing over the bar also had a plan—and had held her to the bar. So who had won?

"Another rum punch, Dominique."

"Scotch and soda—please."

Jonnie now looked squarely at Charles McCellan, trying to penetrate the skull of this man, who wasn't even an ambassador but had so much power. This ordinary, slightly built young man who had the means to engage—at American taxpayers' expense— mercenaries to tear the heart out of a poor, weak country and to enslave a poor Black orphan child. Madness? Frustration? Lust? Love? Whatever. That was power!

She looked at him while apprehension kept her ears tuned to the sound of marching feet, their direction, their numbers, toward the cabins, toward her dark room, past her spirit standing a sentinel outside her door, preventing their entry.

It was how she had watched over Emmanuel, days when she had to work and leave him alone, keys around his neck. It was how she willed harm away from him. So long as her spirit hovered over him, preventing evil from moving past it and to him, the child was safe.

Now she sat, a spectator watching players moving around the entrance to the bar. Time was no longer on her side. She had lost. The loss was compounded by the searing pain of witnessing this independent Black country's soldiers, proud Gérard Auguste's country's soldiers, doing the bidding of this ordinary-looking bastard and appearing dedicated doing it—as dedicated as those white cops beating on the head of another little Black boy on a New York City street because he was the proud possessor of a golden flute.

"Dominique, rum punch, *s'il vous plaît.*"

But Dominique, incensed at this intrusion, had rushed out from the bar to stand, challenging the soldiers. *"Mais qu'est-ce qui se passe? Non, non,* no Haitian hide here. No Haitian hide here. This bar American." No one listened.

Sam and Claire had come down. They grouped together outside the bar, speaking to a brown man wearing a brown suit, a pistol in a brown leather holster. The pleasant-faced man with the pleasant smile: everybody's father, everybody's uncle. Constant was his name. Tonton Constant.

Charles McCellen sat stone-faced. And Jonnie sat frozen. She didn't want to draw attention to herself; she tried to concentrate on her spirit standing sentinel outside her door.

She had not done well. Cécile had done what she had been asked, while she had just sat at the bar, drinking rum.

"I am outdone." Jessica Winthrop strode grandly into the bar. Tall, square-shouldered, in her trademark yellow knit suit and white floppy hat with its yellow ribbon. "Dominique, I say, have you seen Captain Lavel today?"

Dominique turned from the group to stare at her, baffled at her simple question when his world was crashing around him. Jessica turned her attention to Charles McCellan.

"Sir, I have been wanting to talk to you about your compatriot, Captain Gilbert. He is a rogue and a thief." Her gray eyes stared out of her face in anger. "Yes, a thief. He has stolen money from me—yes, I said stolen. And he's gone. Where is he, Counselor? I demand to know where I might find your Captain Lavel."

"I have no idea where to find Captain Lavel, Mrs. Winthrop. Nor am I aware of any money transaction you might or might not have with him."

"Then I shall tell you, Counselor. I entrusted a very large sum . . ."

Charles McCellen, not wanting to know of or be involved in the much-discussed transaction between his countryman and the Englishwoman, and angered because she had broken the hold he had over his now-drunken opponent, left his seat to stand with the group outside. And Jessica Winthrop, now really outdone, demanded: "Will someone please tell me what's going on here? What are soldiers doing on these premises."

"The soldiers are looking for an escapee, Mrs. Winthrop." Charles McCellen said, his eyes on Jonnie.

"An escapee?"

"A boy, Mrs. Winthrop. A dirty sneaking little thief." He turned from them to Claire and Sam and—Jonnie was sure—directed M'sieur Constant's attention to her.

"Here?" Jessica said. "At this hotel?"

"In my room beneath my bed," Jonnie muttered under her breath. She laughed drunkenly.

"But I say"—Jessica went to join the group outside the bar—"isn't that the province of the police?" she asked. "My God, I had my hands full with the police today at the Red Cross. Now the army here? This is an invasion of an American establishment."

"America has no establishment in Haiti, madame," M'sieur Constant informed her. "In Haiti, Americans are our guests."

"That's good to know," Jessica said. "At any rate, Claire, Sam—Mr. McCellan, here is your representative. I'd register my protest with him." She walked out the way she had come in—grandly.

"JONNIE, JONNIE, ARE YOU IN THERE?" Jonnie's eyes squinted open, then closed. "Jonnie . . ." She waited until the pounding in her head softened before opening them again. The pounding grew louder. "For God's sake Jonnie, open this door!"

Getting out of bed, Jonnie swayed and was forced to sit, her head in her hands. "Jon-nie." Claire's voice calling through the door brought her once again to her feet.

"Coming," she called. Her voice was hoarse. Her body ached. She staggered to the door and opened it for Claire, who came in dressed for town.

"Dominique ought to be jailed for serving that shit he calls punch," Jonnie groaned.

"The entire supply is not intended to be consumed all in one night, Jonnie," Claire said. "But you certainly tried. What did you want to prove? It was lucky that nice M'sieur Constant was here. He helped me get you to bed."

The words hit her brain scattershot. She sat on the bed, and looked around the room, her mind a blank. "Who did you say?"

"Mr. Constant. He was here for information on the where-abouts of a boy, and there you were, drinking rum punch and falling off the bar stool. There was nothing else to do but get you in here. He helped."

"Put me to bed?"

"I put you to bed, Jonnie. He just helped me get you in here."

"Did he find anything?" Jonnie asked, trying to focus on the wooden flute on the dresser.

"What's to find? Cécile takes good care of you and your things."

Yes, Cécile did her part. The plan. She had done nothing but pass out. She didn't remember passing out or leaving the bar or getting to bed. And Lucknair? What about Lucknair?

"Have you seen Cécile this morning?" she asked.

"No, I haven't seen Cécile. I searched for her last night so that she could look after you. But then the hotel staff were all in shock with the army coming around. I couldn't find anybody. But I haven't seen her this morning either. Listen, some of us are driv-ing out to Mrs. Thompson's. She needs help. I thought you might want to come along."

"I want to," Jonnie said. "Did they find who they were look-ing for? I mean the army."

"Not that I know. Why would they look here? Hurry if you're coming. We must be back by lunchtime."

Maurice and Jacques were still packing food and clothes into the already overflowing trunk of the car when Jonnie came out. Claire sat at the wheel. In minutes Claire was driving along the now too-familiar rue Jean-Jacques Dessalines. On this road, women with wise, smiling eyes had pointed the way to the limou-sine in the moonlight. It was as if eyes sent messages that the mouth dared not speak lest the words put lives in danger. And Cé-cile? Where was Cécile? Had eyes seen her slipping out of the dark woods? Before? After? God, what a fool to get drunk and not to know. Jonnie recognized the fork in the road. They turned and were pulling up at what had been the magnificent old house, where she had seen again the gentle-faced man in brown who had put her to bed last night when she was drunk.

She was still drunk, she realized when she stumbled out of the car to look at the once marvelous structure now totally demol-ished. It looked as though a bulldozer had been used to ram it through. Destruction intended to intimidate. Instead, people were out in vast numbers, helping. Men, women, and children, even toddlers. The clergy, housewives, ordinary folk from all walks of life determined to rebuild the house to show support for the "good woman," as they called Mrs. Thompson.

They had organized themselves in remarkably efficient groups: those actually building the house; those bringing planks, wood, nails, screws; even bare-bottomed toddlers bringing nails and screws or just being around to give a hand when some small part fell and had to be picked up. Others were handing out food to the hungry.

All worked seriously. People coming and going in shifts—all determined that the orphans would not sleep in the woods come night. Still, there was a carnival aspect about the work—laughing, talking, the laying out of food and drinks. Women stopping with hands on hips to talk about *"les fous,"* and the men, laughing but never allowing themselves to be drawn into the discussion, just working.

Mrs. Thompson came out to them when they drove up.

She embraced Claire but pretended she didn't know, had never seen Jonnie before. She did, however, send the message with her eyes that Jonnie's coming might not have been the wisest thing.

And indeed Jonnie's mind remained unfocused, unable to find a place to fit in. She didn't know what to do. Even after Maurice and Jacques and Claire were busy passing out clothes and food, she stood looking around in a drugged haze until she saw a woman giving out nails to small children, who ran gleefully to pass them to men working on ladders. She joined them, handing out nails, too.

Yet she sensed danger in her being there. Obviously Mrs. Thompson felt endangered by her presence, knowing that Lucknair had come to her. A dilemma. She wanted to be gone, but how to make the move? Then she saw Jessica.

Taller than most, Jessica stood out with her face blackened and her suit—the one she had worn the night before—grimy with dirt. She was carrying a plank of wood, which she handed to a man on a ladder, then immediately returned to a pile of planks and grabbed another. Jonnie went over and took an end of the plank, and for a time they worked silently, bringing planks to the builders.

They drove back together, she and Jessica, barely speaking a word. Jonnie remembered seeing Jessica the night before at the bar and didn't remember much else. She kept looking at Jessica's strong, dirty hands on the wheel of Dominique's blue Volkswagen, not really knowing what to say. Then Jessica said, "Now, Jonnie Dash, will you tell me to what bit of undercover work I have lent my talents?"

"What's to tell?" Jonnie asked.

"What?" Jessica cried. "You have me dashing out in the night . . ."

"I—had you . . . how?"

"By saying 'beneath my bed.' "

Had she performed her part after all? "Did you, Jessica? Did it work? Did you understand, from that . . . ?"

"Of course, I'm a dunce," Jessica said. "I walk into the hotel to find the army. I go to the bar, and there you are, drinking Dominique's horrible concoction, shrinking inside yourself, eyes wild, out of focus. There are Sam and Claire, all excited, speaking to the remarkably devious M'sieur Constant—and you slurring about under your bed. Why wouldn't I make it a point to understand?"

"Did he get away, Jessica? Did you get him up to the mountains?" Jessica was concentrating on the crowded road. "He's good at running away, you know," Jonnie added.

Jessica remained silent—the silence of a conspirator. Suddenly her face lit up. "Bit of an actor, wouldn't you say, Jonnie," she preened. "Oh, I put on a good show. Brilliant."

Jonnie collapsed in the seat from relief. "So all's well?"

"Your girl had just come back from Gérard's when I got to your room. Oh yes, that was a beauty she fetched from beneath your bed." She paused to give a roguish grin. "Cécile told me the plan. So there I had to go—stealing Dominique's car to pick them up at the crossroads—*et là voilà*. . . .

"The things you ask of me, Jonnie Dash," Jessica mused. "I haven't driven in years; then I had to drive on that narrow mountain road in the pitch black night without one light to guide me. I can't say with any certainty how I got there. That Cécile, a lovely girl. She directed me going. But how I got back is anyone's guess. She stayed up there with the boy. But I had to get back to bring word to Mrs. Thompson—the boy demanded it of me. So, Jonnie Dash, fill me in on our cloak-and-dagger operation and just what it's supposed to have achieved."

Jonnie stared out at the road. What had she achieved? She did not want to tell Jessica about Charles McCellen and risk direct confrontation. What would she accuse McCellen of? All that had happened had been between eyes and mind, without words. She had not even had a chance to talk to the boy about it.

So what had she achieved? She had a simple plan and her simple plan had worked. She had given Lucknair a place to hide. She had given him time. Now it had to be a Haitian affair. Gérard's affair. He who had scolded her for being upset by boys begging. It had to be up to him. . . .

"I say, Jonnie," Jessica said, "that boy is a beauty but frightfully young. How do you manage?"

"Very badly," Jonnie answered, and decided to change the subject. "How did things go at the hospital yesterday?"

Jessica weighed whether or not she wanted to change the subject. She shrugged. "I can tell you I didn't make many friends."

"Had you gone expecting to?"

"No—I suppose it was pretty much a lost cause from the start."

"Then why did you go?"

"Trying to prevent the poor and hungry from selling their blood to the rich, which I have made my raison d'être."

"Even though it's a lost cause?"

"It's my statement."

"I don't believe in fighting lost causes," Jonnie said.

"I know."

"Just what's that supposed to mean?"

Their eyes met in the mirror, then veered away. "That's something we might discuss at another time," Jessica said. Jonnie nodded. She didn't want to know what Jessica meant. Didn't want it to matter.

"What happened at your dinner date?" she asked to change the subject.

"Dinner? Date?" Jessica asked, puzzled.

"Yes—with Captain Lavel. A few nights ago."

The deepening lines at the side of Jessica's mouth, the nerves quivering in her cheeks sent a rush of anguish through Jonnie. She was being vindictive and didn't like herself, her cheap cruelty.

"There was no dinner," Jessica said, her voice hoarse. "Captain was not on his yacht. Nor has anyone seen him since. He seems to have disappeared—simply vanished."

They had just driven past the place where Jean-Pierre had been parked the night of the ceremony, and Jonnie saw the image of Monique sparking the night with her brilliance, and knew. Captain Lavel hadn't disappeared; he had been very close. Probably had been looking at Jessica—laughing.

"Call off the cruise, Jessica," she advised.

"I shall not!" Jessica's face clenched beneath its layers of dirt. "I most assuredly shall not! I have given thirty thousand American dollars to that young man for a weekend cruise to Jamaica. And I intend to have a weekend cruise to Jamaica!"

Thirty thousand dollars. Jonnie had never held more than five thousand dollars at any one time in her life until she had sold her painting. She still found it hard to adjust to her new wealth and impossible to think of such extravagance. Thirty thousand dollars for any one thing—particularly a cruise from this island, where peasants sold their blood in order to live another day.

"A contradiction?" Jessica asked of Jonnie's silence. "I have them. But I'm not mad, Jonnie."

Jonnie stared out at the jostling roadside scene. Uncanny how Jessica followed every twist of her mind. "I have money," Jessica said. "I have always had money and so I have never felt the need to worship it. Nor do I suffer any agony in spending it. I do what I can here—without stuffing the pockets of the corrupt. I'd rather pay for things I enjoy."

"What about what he enjoys—needs, Jessica?" Jonnie asked, thinking of Captain Lavel, his bright playful eyes, the weak smile at the corners of his mouth. So obviously an addict.

"He likes and needs money. I need excitement. I pay the price for my excitement—in pain, in sentiment. But then I'm a silly old woman. But as silly as I am, I shall not be cheated. It is, after all, a question of honor—of integrity."

Jonnie kept her eyes on the teeming road, her face still. Who was she to question this woman? This woman who had dashed off to face whatever had to be faced because a drunken friend sitting at a bar had slurred one sentence: He's beneath my bed. "Is there anything I can do, Jessica?"

"There must be," Jessica said, raising her hand from the wheel and clawing the air in a futile gesture. "But I just can't think what."

Embarrassment. The crumbling of her kingdom, the twittering of knaves, the snickering of underlings waiting in the wings for her downfall.

"I'm here, Jessica—whatever you want," Jonnie said.

"Of course you are, my dear. Of course you are."

A clap of thunder caused her to grip the wheel tighter. Another clap, even louder, shook the earth so that clusters of people on the road made signs of the cross.

"Not to worry," Jessica said. "Everything will be—perfect."

They drove on, listening to the thunder rolling, grumbling in the distance—a beast, hungry, insatiate. And Jessica said, "Perhaps it's the coming storm. Things happen in Haiti when the atmosphere gets so dense, dense enough to defy logic and nature. Imag-ine—soldiers making a shambles of the orphanage of that magnif-icent woman. Yes, yes, it must be the oncoming storm."

7

THE AIR HEAVY with the threat of things to come hung over them, sealed them in a sort of gloom, keeping them silent. A big question mark hung over each. What next? What next? They turned into the drive at Old Hotel, and there stood Cécile, wait-ing. *"Madame, mon patron.* He wait for you."

Cécile's face showed strain. Her bravery the night before spoke of secrets held from Gérard. Without intending to do so, she had lied to him and expected Jonnie to make things right. Jon-nie left Jessica to park the car and went to make things right.

"Why are you still here?" Gérard rushed to Jonnie as she came through the door of the lounge. "Cécile, she came last night, took your key, and told me you are going to the house. Today, early, I went there. And it's she who was there. What are you do-ing here?"

Jonnie looked around, thankful that Jacques and Maurice were away. She hoped that Gérard had not been carrying on a high-pitched argument with Cécile within hearing of others.

"I went to help out at Mrs. Thompson's—the Jamaican woman. You heard what happened out there?"

"They tell me that soldiers came here last night. And that man, Constant. He looks nice, you know. But you must be careful with him. He's dangerous. What did he want?" He looked around the empty lounge, unsure of his next move, of himself. Jonnie squeezed his hand to reassure him. Then, unable to suppress her sly wickedness: "He put me to bed last night."

"What!" His hands shook, his lips became dry.

"Let's talk about that on the way up to the house, Gérard,"

she said. "I'm joking." She paused and grinned to make things easier for both of them.

The tension in his face lessened. "So long as you're not in danger, *ma chérie.*" He held both of her hands to his lips. "Jonnie, *mon amour*, I am the happiest man now that you say you are coming back."

Jonnie took her hands from his. Words did change meaning from one lifetime to another, but she wasn't sure what the few they had just shared really signified. She had only begun to realize how farfetched her reason was for coming to this island, to this man for whom she had not existed for thirty years. If her fairy-tale fantasy of what might have been ever had any reality, that time had passed.

Still, as they drove through the city toward the mountains, he held to the tone he had set. "You have so much for which to forgive me, Jonnie *chérie*. I know I did cause you pain. No, I did not think of it before, but since you have come, I . . ."

But since she had come that dialogue had ended. She had shown him by not seeing him, by refusing his messages, grateful for the lack of telephones that had made separation easy. After all these years, now he had decided to take his betrayal seriously. But it was over and they had other things to discuss, namely, what to do about Lucknair.

"I'm a brute," he kept on. "A vagabond. I remember back in New York, before I left, I wanted to tell all, explain my life—my family. I had no courage."

"Gérard, please." She refused to let him flog himself for his past deeds. Life had flogged him enough. He had paid with his years in jail, his self-imposed solitude in his own homeland. Slinking into shadows, with his books, their once powerful themes branded only into his brain—and with his retarded son.

"*Oui*, these days since I have seen you," he insisted, "I think, how she did suffer because of me—this extraordinary woman, this talented woman—still so young, so beautiful, who loves me enough to travel across the ocean. . . .

"I should have offered you marriage—at once," Gérard kept on. "But, *chérie*, how did I know? Even when I read your letter to say you are coming. It had been thirty years. And to find you so—*vivante.*"

In fascination, Jonnie studied Gérard's lips, upturned at the corner in self-congratulatory sadness. She noticed his hands on the wheel—expressive hands, long, thin fingers. He'd always had expressive hands. "You said from the first I had talent, Gérard."

"I had the confidence—the courage. When no one else believed, I believed." He pointed a slender finger over the wheel.

"Did it take that much courage, Gérard?" Jonnie laughed.

"I said to them, 'That bright-eyed Black girl with so much talent can be molded, and I, Gérard Auguste, will prove it to you. I shall show you and the world what can be done with our Black potential.' Yes, yes, that's what I said to them. *Et là, voilà*—you are the proof, *n'est-ce pas?*"

Did the man hear what he had been saying? Thirty years she had believed that he had loved her and that he was coming back to her, even though he never even came for a visit. Ahh yes, the sow's ear.

His words shafted deep into her. The little Black girl with potential. The wisp of a girl . . . and all the children sleeping in the woods, those little girls with round bottoms and distended bellies, red hair, bare feet, all those Black children with potential, he had looked over them all to find her in the richest city in the world.

"And so," Gérard kept on, "I am offering marriage, *ma chérie*. No, no, take your time. It's all right. Now we have the time."

"Somebody's in the house, Gérard." She spoke to cut him off, to highjack the conversation.

"Somebody—in my house? In your place? No, no. No one is there. I went earlier. . . ."

"There is someone there, in your house in the mountains."

"But who?"

"A boy."

"What boy?"

"A wonderful child, a lonely child, an orphan with the making of a true revolutionary—like you used to be. I think he's in danger. He's the one the soldiers and Mister Constant are looking for."

"Aaark . . ." The car veered, wobbled at the edge of the steep cliff. Jonnie grabbed the wheel, turned hard to keep it from plunging over the edge. It swerved into the path of a *camionette* hurtling down toward them. The driver of the *camionette* turned his vehicle to avoid them and plunged into the ditch on the opposite side of the narrow road.

Market women crammed into the *camionette* started to shout: "*Mais, il est fou oui. Il va nous tuer.*" They kept shouting, shaking the *camionette* with an outpouring of rage. Gérard sat frozen at the wheel of his car. Jonnie shook him. He simply sat. She jumped out, rushed to the other side, opened the door, shoved him over, got in beside him and started up the car. Driving up the mountain she saw peasants emerge from the sides of the road, converging on the disabled *camionette* to help the driver while the quarrelsome market women, without giving up their places, kept shouting in fury. Gérard sat motionless, his face a pale gray, his eyes glazed.

A mistake. A mistake. His time in jail had turned his revolutionary zeal into flab—flab of the soul. What they had to do, she and Lucknair, they had to do without him. Why had she taken this old fool into her confidence? Now they were all in jeopardy.

But what to expect from this mother's child who had filled her head with simple-ass nonsense, then run off leaving her—for thirty goddamn years—and then added insult to injury by saying he had created her! Just like that other motherfucker shedding hot tears on her, not because he had molested her—a nine-year-old— but because he had been scared shitless that he'd burn in the fires of hell! Whores! Every last one of them. Whores!

Simple old bastard gloating over her pain, talking shit, and believing that she was willing to listen to it for an eternity—even though he was dried up and ready for the grave. Forgive? Forgive hell. Forgive a son of a bitch who had puffed up his ego at her expense, and her son's expense, leaving them floating and fantasizing in a maze of bullshit!

Sweat pushed out of Jonnie's pores. The roar of thunder, loud in her ears, brought a swelling, a ready-to-burst feeling into her head. She longed to tear at her clothes, let cool mountain air calm her, put her back in control.

They reached the house. The car stopped with an ear-splitting screech. She jumped out, rushed to the door, fumbled in her pants for the key, and opened the door, stalking into the house shouting, "Lucknair, Lucknair, Lucknair!"

Stupid, stupid, stupid. She tried to stop. Those living around would hear and rush to tell. She fought for control, but she was beyond control. She rushed from one room to the next searching closets and beneath the bed, then stood simmering in rage, waiting for Gérard, who came inching into the house slowly, slowly— an old man—holding on to the door frame for support.

"So," she heard him say, "this is the boy for whom all of Haiti is searching?"

Jonnie spun around. Lucknair stood behind her, his fingers interlocking, wide eyes watching her anger-distorted face. At the same time she heard the chant outside: *"Volé, volé."*

Jonnie rushed out the door, saw the skeleton of a man with his high-flying balloons and blown-up brown paper bags flopping in the air around his head walking by, his rags flapping around his thin, black frame, hair matted on his head and neck, bare-chested, ragged pants revealing his naked behind and long testicles hanging to his knees.

> *Ou volé tè*
> *Ou volé fruit boi'm*
> *Ou volé*

"Old fool." Jonnie ran behind him screeching. "They already stewed up your goddamn brains, they got your trees, your fruit, your forests, every breath in your kids' lungs belongs to them. *Attendez!*"

Running, running, dozens of arms reaching out to her, hands holding her, forcing her back, back. This time she fought, spit foamed in her mouth, veins pushed from her neck. She fought.

"They got all you ever had to give, you poor son of a bitch. They took from you like they took from me—work gone up your nostrils, little mother's child, in your veins, you twisted asshole . . . you lip-sucking Immaculate Conception, you goddamn son of a bitch with your goddamn hot tears, burning, burning, burning my fucking brains. . . ."

THE CURTAIN OF DARKNESS LIFTED, revealing faces looking down, down. Eyes, wary eyes, frightened eyes, staring. Where was she?

Who were these people? She lowered her lashes and reached for one familiar point on her road back. Did Boysie make it? Had Boysie made it? Had he gone back to the stoop to find her gone? Had he gone to the old synagogue to find it had been turned into a Father Divine kitchen? And had he waited in despair, thinking he would never see her again?

Jonnie moved her arms—or tried to—and found them tied across her chest. Straitjacketed. She chuckled. Opened her eyes, stared up at the ceiling, and then she heard the drums. Already the drums? Her eyes moved to the window. Night. Night and here she lay robbed of will. Straitjacketed into submission. She chuckled again.

She had been in a straitjacket before—she remembered coming out of a dark space and looking at the window to see streaks of sunlight beaming through. That time it had been daylight.

She remembered it clearly. She remembered everything clearly. A male nurse had come to stand by her cot. "Mrs. Dash," he had asked, "how do you feel?"

"Feel fine," she had answered. "I have to get back to work. I am finishing a very important painting."

"You're looking better," he said. "You have been out of it for a long time—almost a month. Your doctor ought to be here soon."

She didn't know how she happened to be there, nor did she ask. Unlike today, when finding herself once again in a straitjacket, everything had suddenly become clear.

Emmanuel. They had been so close—then suddenly they were not. It's hard to give up a child to the streets. It had been the night of her first one-woman show. She had sold a few paintings and had made five thousand dollars—the first time she ever had that much money. They had celebrated. But later one of her checks had bounced. She had cried. Because she had paid up all her bills and thought that she was ahead, only to find that she was now deeper in debt.

Emmanuel had comforted her—he always comforted her. They were so very close. They fell asleep that evening. They often fell asleep together. During the night he held her. His penis grew hard against her, kept getting harder. Suddenly they were both wide awake. "Time for you to get to your bed," she joked.

"Yeah," he agreed. "Time for me to stay in my bed."

After that night they were never so close. After that night he started staying out nights, grew to be a hard to control teenager. Still later, her paintings would be missing. Then having to go to court, he was caught stealing—and then prison.

He blamed her. Confused, angry with himself, he accused her of betraying his father, of sending his father to the other woman and his death.

Drugs? But there had always been drugs. Not when she and Boysie were out there, but certainly when Emmanuel was a kid. He had decided against taking drugs. Survival for them had been her painting—until he decided he didn't want to survive. And yes, he took drugs. But that wasn't it. No more than it is for many of the kids out there with their hidden agendas—dreams they can hardly even guess at.

She remembered the knock at the door, remembered the two policemen.

"Mrs. Dash, we're here about your son."

"In jail again," she had said, anxious for them to be gone. Anxious to get back to her work.

"No, ma'am. He got caught stealing the silver chalice at Saint Paul's. The priest caught him. He shot the priest. Killed him. Then he got shot trying to run from the scene, ma'am. Your son's dead."

Yes, she had been in a straitjacket a long time now. How long? Who can tell? One lifetime runs into another and another. How strange she had not rid herself of madness by knowing she was mad. Was she rid of it now?

"Lucknair?" she called out. They came. Both of them. They came to stand in the bedroom and stood together, a distance from the bed. Lucknair stretched out a thin arm and touched her.

Lovely child, poem of a child, he had lived with madness and so wasn't afraid. But Gérard was still pale, ashen, eyes uncomprehending.

So you see, you didn't save this girl from the street. You didn't remake her in your likeness, street urchin that she was. You might have, if you had loved her. But who's to say? You're sad. Sad because as Pygmalion you failed? Because at politics you failed? Look at it this way, my love. We were both doomed to fail.

Our lives are only about trying hard and celebrating our failures. And here we are—you old and I mad. Only I shall be sane. I shall be sane.

"Gérard," she said. "Come get me out of this contraption. I'm all right now. I ought to be getting back to the hotel."

BOOK
~
FIVE

1

HER LIFE HAD OPENED UP to be evaluated as never before. But not now. The problem now had to be Lucknair. How to save him. Whatever manner he had come into her life, responsibility for him—his freedom, maybe his life—rested with her. All her fault she had sent him to the cabin.

Gérard. She had no way of knowing how Gérard's time in jail had crushed him. Seeing his cowardice had infuriated her. Not fair. Why be so angered by his terror when she had not been able to bring herself to confront Charles McCellen, intimidated by his power and the authority he represented.

But Gérard, when she had first met him, had been strong, bright, ambitious, ready to take on the presidents. To think of him then and to compare him with the trembling, frightened old man caused Jonnie's heart to shudder.

Horrible! But that, too, had to await evaluation.

On her return to Old Hotel, Jonnie found Claire in the pool, forced there by the sweltering heat. "Claire, when will Maxie be back?" Jonnie stood looking down at Claire floating on her back in the corner of the pool out of the way of the guests.

"I suppose he's trying to get as much fishing done as he can before the storm. That's his livelihood, you know."

"Does he usually stay out this long?"

"Sometimes longer. And if he finds himself in the path of the storm, he might berth down wherever he is to keep out of its way. One never knows. This storm might be a bad one."

"I wish it would hurry and be over with," Jonnie said. "However bad it is, it can't be any worse than this heat."

They studied the sky as though expecting clear signals. The hesitant sun sent heavy rays through layers of haze, coloring each layer with orange-gray tones.

"It might shift—head out to sea and spare us."

"I must see Maxie," Jonnie said. "Is there some way to get word to him?"

"Is something the matter?" Claire asked. "Perhaps I can get someone else who could help you."

"No, no one else will do," Jonnie said.

Claire's eyes quickened. She held on to the side of the pool and, looking up, tried to probe Jonnie's eyes. "Maxie is a wonderful friend—an adorable puppy, but . . ." She let her words trail off significantly.

Quips that she might have used yesterday, the day before, last week, ran through Jonnie's mind. But the time for that had passed. There comes a time when laughter dies—or is stilled by the force of events. Laughter had always helped her spit in the face of the gods, something she no longer cared to do. She had balled up her laughter in a makeshift straitjacket back at the cottage.

Emmanuel, the baby, gurgled and pushed his fingers into her mouth. She thrust his image out of her mind to recall, instead, Gérard: the look of terror in his haggard eyes as he drove her down from the mountains. Poor Gérard, he had come to her offering marriage, thinking that her perennial youth might give him strength, only to find himself tangled in a web of madness. She thought of Jessica, of her Doctor Faye, and sighed. Everything in life had already happened. They were in a sense just hanging on.

Jonnie turned to walk away just as Stephan and the girl Alice walked up. He put his hand on Jonnie's shoulder while speaking to Claire. "Claire, Jessica said that you're tired and so she elected me to take Alice to town shopping. I'm not sure that I can make it."

"In that poor child's state I'm sure anybody can do as well as I," Claire said. "Thank Jessica for me. I am tired. These have been some of the most trying days of my life. Can you imagine—soldiers!"

It had been a strain on all of them. Some guests had left because of the invasion, while the entire staff bristled with intrigue.

"Can I get you to join us?" Stephan asked as they walked to the bar. Jonnie shook her head. He held her hand. "Do you know how very much I like you, Jonnie Dash?"

Jonnie nodded. She knew. Would not forget.

The doors of the bar were open at both ends to coax cross ventilation. Fans whirred above the guests, mostly men, standing four deep at the counter. Sweat sticking shirts to chests and backs, loud talking, louder laughter, and continual drinking attempted to transform the misery of the heat to good times. "Beer, Dominique," she called. Then when it came she settled into her corner, rounding her shoulders over her glass: the witch protecting her brew, gazing down into the amber-colored liquid, wishing for Maxie. Without question he had the answer to their problems—hers and Lucknair's.

"Miss Dash." She looked around to find the man, Stanley, behind her. "They tell me you have a place in the mountains," he said. "I just thought I'd tell you that the reason you haven't seen us around is that we now have a little chalet up there over the clouds."

She hadn't really missed him—or his companion—had not really thought about them. "I hope you're enjoying it," she said.

"Oh, it's so wonderful—to be up there at the top of the world, to see the sunsets. Have you ever seen such sunsets in your life, Miss Dash?"

Remembering the big ball of red dipping behind the mountain range in the evenings, her throat tightened. "No, I never have, Stanley, never before—it is magnificent."

And then she heard Maxie's voice, rich like a baritone's, rising over the babble at the bar. "Now I ask you, how is this for a crustacean specimen?" His voice, that of a true revolutionary, refusing challenge. "Just look at it!" he cried. "I ask you, look at it."

There he stood in the middle of their silence while men grouped around, admiring the giant lobster he held. It had to be five feet long and almost as wide, and in the hands of this six-foot-three-inch giant with his dirty shirt and dirty captains' cap, with his beatific smile exposing teeth that could stand a good scrubbing—it indeed made a beautiful poster. "If this isn't the most exquisite specimen you've ever seen, without disagreement I'll take it and put it back where I found it. Tell me . . . tell me."

Proud, laughing, bragging, and happy. His thick uncombed hair had grown to double its length since she last saw him. He walked to one end of the barroom and back.

"Lucked up on this monster off the coast of Cuba," he said. "Biggest sucker I ever caught." He looked around, expecting admiration and getting it. Then over the heads of his admirers he saw her. Immediately he called, "Jacques! Jacques!" And when Jacques appeared, he handed him the lobster. *"C'est pour Madame Claire*—from the barefoot captain," he said, then made his way to her.

"Hey, lady, I want to talk to you," he said.

"I wished you here," Jonnie answered.

"What for?" he asked.

"You first. What did you want to talk to me about?"

"But you already know what," he said, grinning. "I wants me this finest woman of the hour."

"Of the hour or for the hour?" Jonnie teased. Surprised herself that she felt young enough, happy enough. Laughter unraveled the tightness in her chest. But perhaps this signaled the return of madness, this rapid shift in mood, from tragedy to levity.

She did love his voice, its tones, its New York street accents. "Stop being so hard on yourself, baby."

"I ain't hard on myself, feller. You hard on me."

"Sho am. Aim to get harder." He pushed up against her, his penis hardening against her thighs.

"It sure can't get no harder," she said, grinning and thinking, *I am no longer mad.* But isn't this madness—this sense of being happy when nothing has changed? Or had it? Didn't his just being there change things?

"Bet," he said. "Bet it can get ten times harder."

"Bet's on," she joked.

"But first, milady, I'll let you buy me a drink. Dominique," he called.

"If you need a drink to get a hard-on, then I already win," Jonnie said.

"That drink is to celebrate you being glad to see me."

"Dominique!" Jonnie cried. "Give this man a drink."

"Champagne!" Maxie shouted. "A bottle."

"Madame?" Dominique asked her.

"The man wants a bottle of champagne; the man must have a bottle of champagne."

"What did I do to deserve this?" Maxie asked.

"You won." Jonnie grinned.

"If I get this much just for the asking, what have I been waiting for?" He pulled Jonnie from the stool. "Come on, baby. Come on."

"I missed you, too," Jonnie said, sitting back down. "But we must get serious. I have something I must ask of you."

"Do tell."

Jonnie sat, her arms at his waist, pulling him to her, feeling his softness, his hardness, wanting to sink into it, into him. Had she ever felt so at home, so together, with anyone before?

"*Voilà.*" Dominique came to them and slammed two drinks down on the bar, one beer and one rum punch.

"Man, this ain't what I ordered," Maxie protested.

"The lady buying," Dominique said with authority. "You drink my rum punch."

"Dominique, you the hardest man I know," Maxie groaned. "You been working here so long you think you own the joint."

"*Non,*" Dominique said, shaking his head. "I work here so long I know I run the joint."

"Okay, okay already," Maxie said, picking up the glass. But Jonnie held the glass, keeping him from drinking.

"Dominique, this man asked for champagne; this man must have champagne." And it was the first time that she had ever shown the authority of her newfound wealth.

"Lady," Maxie said, "something must be troubling you."

"Yes, we must talk."

But three girls, teenagers, pushed their way between them to the counter. "Are you Dominique?" they asked, and to Dominique's angry look: "Where do we find André Bienaimé?"

"Don't know . . . ," Dominique mumbled. Then to them: "Everybody, everybody want André, André. I don't want them here—no more. That André, he make me crazy." He put his finger to his temple and turned it, then took out the ever-present towel to wipe down the bar.

"That stud better get his rest if he wants to keep that fine frame and good looks," Maxie cracked.

"Rest," Dominique scoffed. "In his grave he rest. When that thing don't work no more, he carving a stick to keep them coming. Hear what I say?" He pulled the skin down beneath an eye.

Jonnie stood up. "The champagne, Dominique."

At her impatience, Maxie asked, "You sure now?"

"Sure of what?"

"Sure it's me you want? I got the feeling you were looking for a great white swashbuckling knight in armor. But if it's me you want, here I is." Of course he was still talking sex—always sex.

Like a cape blown off by a blustery wind, her sense of contentment evaporated. She had hoped they were bound more closely in thoughts. She pushed her way through the customers who were standing behind her, and as Maxie followed she said, "Maxie, your lips are full and soft to the touch. Your chin's young and firm. But your mouth is big and filled of recycled shit."

"Can't have everything," he said, grinning.

Then Claire came up. "Maxie, that is the greatest lobster I have ever seen. How do I thank you?"

"Invite me to dinner," Maxie answered.

"If you promise to wear shoes." Claire laughed.

"Promise."

"Done."

"Maxie," Claire said, getting serious. "Have you heard anything about Captain Lavel?"

"No, he never invites me."

"You must have heard something around the sea lanes. Jess is going out of her mind."

"She knows where the sucker's yacht is anchored. Anyway, he's got to get out before the storm. What's she worried about—

thirty thou? That's a lot of bread for poh me, but to Jess and Gil, that amount might pinch, but it don't puncture."

"There's a principle involved, Maxie," Claire said.

"What goddamn principle?" Maxie growled. "The only principle that gets lost around here is Monique."

"Yes, yes . . ." Claire moved her hands in a helpless gesture.

"What about Monique?" Jonnie asked.

"I don't believe you, Jonnie Dash," Maxie said, angry with her. "Monique, in case you haven't seen her, is tall, dark, beautiful—everybody's dream girl." Somehow he had distanced himself from her and that upset Jonnie. Because of course she had seen Monique. She was not to be missed. She had decided not to consider her. Because she didn't like her or because she was so beautiful? She had hated the way she had acted with the waiters. Had resented her way of dancing at the voodoo ceremony. No business of hers.

"Claire," Maxie said. "You're going to have to hold that invite until I get back. I got to get my yacht away from these shores."

"Maxie, you know as well as I do, frozen lobsters are worse than none at all."

"So—be my guest," Maxie said. "There will be another catch. Got to go. From the way that storm's brewing I ought to have been gone. But that's love for you. I had to come just to give my baby here a shout."

He grabbed Jonnie, held her, kissed her long and hard on her lips. "Baby," he said, "we'll have that talk when I get back—and I'll collect on that bet."

"Dominique, champagne, champagne." Reaching over the heads of customers, he grabbed the bottle out of Dominique's hand and rushed from the bar.

CAPTAIN GILBERT LAVEL ALSO MADE an appearance that night. He and the lovely Monique came in at dinnertime. Unfortunately, Claire had decided to celebrate the biggest lobster ever to be served at Old Hotel by having a dinner party. And Gilbert Lavel insisted on sitting beside Jessica.

"Jessica," he started off the conversation, "I've been hearing every step of the way that you have put out a dragnet for me. So I have humbly come to put my head in your hands and submit myself to your mercy."

Claire attempted to neutralize the rage evident in Jessica's straight back and bristling demeanor with a little decorum. "We expected you to surface soon," she joked. "With all this work you and Jess have to do for the cruise. But aren't you pushing it mighty close, Gil? The storm's due to hit anytime now."

"Oh, the storm, the storm. The *White Swan* can withstand the best of them." He appeared happy, bright; his eyes gleamed.

"Well, there's that to celebrate," Sam said, and held a bottle of champagne up for Jacques to open. "We had been thinking that you made yourself scarce because the old tub wasn't fit. But here you are, ready to honor your obligation to Jess and do justice to Maxie Gardener's contribution to the evening." Sipping champagne, laughing too often at jokes that weren't funny, loudly praising the size of the lobster and the excellence of the cook, they tried hard to cloak the disquiet simmering below the surface.

Monique's superb tranquillity at the center of the oncoming tempest fascinated Jonnie. The air was charged with rage in addition to the heat, the rumbling thunder, the noise of the whirling fans. Monique sat calm, silent, magnificently in control, as she broke lobster claws, daintily putting the flesh to her lips where it disappeared into her mouth with exquisite elegance.

Jessica sat stern, waiting, pulled up to her full height in her chair. They all knew she waited, and when the theatrics had come to an end, when every light remark that could be said had been said, she turned to the miscreant and spoke in a hoarse voice: "Captain Lavel, we had appointments that you have not kept. I have sent messages that you have not answered. If the funds that we had agreed upon were not sufficient, then you had the obligation to inform me. Or hadn't it occurred to you that one doesn't simply hand over thirty thousand dollars to a mere stranger?"

"Stranger? Oh come, Jess. Need we discuss this matter here?" He smiled, deliberately provocative.

"The cruise is still on if you want, Jessica. I simply need more money. You must understand, Jess, my crew has to be paid. The ship must be made seaworthy . . . expenses, my dear Jessica, expenses."

"Unfortunately, it's you who must understand, Captain

Lavel," Jessica said. "Whatever the color of my drawers, I expect that yacht to be sailing to Jamaica—shortly after the storm—with all the amenities for which I paid: captain, crew, and caterers."

"Sorry, Jess." Her handsome, dark-haired lover, his face unlined—young, younger than his years—leaned back friendly, confident. "Without money it can't be done."

"Yes, it can and it will." Stephan spoke then, quietly, forcefully, from his chair across the table.

"Begging your pardon, Mr. Winthrop—I mean, Mr. Henshaw—this happens to be a private matter between Jess and me."

Stephan reached across the table, snatched him by the collar, and smashed a fist into his face. Bedlam. Waiters, guests, running, screaming. Claire pulled at Stephan, but he vaulted over the table, held Gilbert Lavel down where he had fallen, knee into his chest. Sam and the waiters rushed over to pull him away. It all had happened suddenly, too suddenly. It left them all shaken.

As quickly as it had begun it ended. "Come," Sam said. "Let's go to the office to discuss this. We're all friends. Why make scenes in public?"

"There's nothing to discuss," the captain said, wiping his bleeding nose with a napkin. "The goddamn cruise is off."

"Don't hand me that," Sam said. "Whatever you do is your own affair. But I negotiated the deal between you and Jessica. I handed you that money. And that has got to be settled. Now, what's your problem?"

"My problem is that I have no money."

"Then you'd better blooming well get some," Stephan said. "Or I'll split your arse wide open and use your shit to bury you!"

The common sailor transcended the proper English gentleman. No more window dressing. Jessica loved this man—companion, lover, protector, her most treasured possession. And she should have known. The sudden insight cut Jonnie away from the table, forced her to sit, an observer viewing the scene as from a great distance.

Nothing was to be settled, of course. Captain Lavel's glistening eyes attested to that. Drugs had been responsible for his unceasing arrogance—as they had been responsible for the lies he told, the theft of Jessica's money. Drugs had created his need for money. And nobody ever had that much money to give.

"Above all, I value integrity," Jessica said. "I paid for a trip, and I intend to have that trip." Impressive, regal, managing to stake her claim in that impossible atmosphere. Monique broke open a claw, deftly pushing the meat into her mouth. There will be no cruise to Jamaica.

A flash of lighting. Eyes turned to the garish light in the window. Thunder rolling, then fading, fading.

A voice beside her, reflecting her pain, pulled Jonnie's thoughts to the table. "Please—Sam—Claire, where Jean-Pierre is? Where is my friend Jean-Pierre? Did you not see him? I need him. I need him."

Short, round, his face with eyes tiny and red behind thick silver-rimmed glasses. "*Oh, mon Dieu!*" Dominique cried, "Jonnie Dash, Claire, Madame Winthrop, I need somebody. My boy— André—he is dead."

2

HUNCHED OVER THE WHEEL of the Volkswagen beetle, Dominique's pain filled the entire car. Pain beat against its windows, pushed at the roof, spilled out to overwhelm the formerly overwhelming darkness.

Lightning stalked them. From time to time, its flashes separated them from the bare tops of mountains, the scrubby plains, but when extinguished left them again bound and formless, staring out at the twin beams of headlights in which insects danced while the car sped in and out of craters on the dusty road.

How long had it been since she and Stephan had traveled this road to spend their day at the beach? One hundred years? One hundred years since floating on her back at sea, since she looked inward and had discovered madness, made her pact with death, rediscovered the joy of living, and sounded the depths of her hypocrisy.

The road stretched alongside the devastation of eroded

mountains and plains. Ghosts haunted those dried-out plains. Ghosts of children hiding behind the hardwood trees. Tiny messengers who once scurried, whispering, moving urgently, sending or bringing messages from one end of the island to the other. Ghosts of children who had risked death to secure for themselves and their future something called independence. Children betrayed. Now their heirs roamed the streets begging on this island that Maxie said had been born to die.

Like she and Sylvie and Boysie had been meant to die. Like Emmanuel had been born to die. Like André had been born to die. And Lucknair?

Those girls who had brought news of André's death— teenagers, heirs of the rich and powerful. They brought the news of this most recent death, this tragedy. This greater-than-they-would-ever-know disaster! Had they given a thought to what role they had played in his death? Did they care? Were they any more concerned than their fathers and grandfathers and great-grandfathers that their pleasures destroyed the lives of so many?

A smell from the sulfur pits permeated the car. They were nearing the sea with its mangroves—the place where she had seen a graceful egret perched on the back of a wide-hipped horse, picking ticks from its hide. Soon they would be driving past Jessica's shack, concealed by the strip of scrub brush. But as they passed, the lightning flashed more intensely, the thunder roared with increased velocity, branding that place, and Afrique, more securely into Jonnie's memory. And Afrique. And Afrique . . .

A few miles farther on, lights appeared in the road. They drove into them, lanterns held by a group of peasants, men who spoke to Dominique in somber tones. With heads bowed in the shadows of flickering lights, the men explained what had happened sadly—in the poetic cadence of Creole.

Jonnie and Dominique were led down an incline beneath a stretch of mangroves to a strip of sand: a secret cove, one of the many scattered along the coastline, favorite haunts of lovers or lone swimmers. And there he lay, ringed by torches. André Bienaimé—the Black Pearl—so young, so beautiful, so still.

But the sea raged. It pounded against the dwindling shore, demanding payment for the outrage of André Bienaimé's death. Even those born to die deserve something grand.

Had his young teenagers loved him as she had loved him, bound as they were by a nameless longing that had been set like stone in their souls from birth? Had any loved him enough to write a poem about his black-as-a-raven smooth body—its pure lines? Or would they keep the excitement of him, his smoothness, a secret to be tucked away with the memories of youth as they settled into their moralistic and materialistic adulthood?

What a sin on her soul that she had not seen a way to paint him. Had not thought him secure enough, stable enough to have been preserved on canvas. Who was she to judge?

Jonnie studied his eyes, which reflected agony; his face, which bore a grimace resembling a smile; his chest, which seemed to be breathing still—up down, up down. . . .

Did you come? Did you share your semen among the three women? Or had the semen remained caught in the passage of that long prick, never to give its final satisfaction?

Would that smooth, black chest continue to rise and fall, rise and fall, throughout all eternity? Will your cries, your moans of passion, forever echo, haunting this stretch of beach, the road above? And would strangers driving by puzzle over the heavy, lusty breathing coming from down near the mangroves? And would drivers filled with fear press down on their pedals to race by this spot where once upon a time a great lover died unfulfilled, never knowing that the sound they heard was his writhing in final agony?

The crashing of angry waves beat against the beach, devouring it. Gusts of wind beat against her ears, lashed her legs, her arms, the back of her head. She stood stoically, wondering: each time he had brought his girls here, had he made them listen to the waves while he spoke poetically as Haitians do, the way of lovers who believe they have mastered the universe when in truth they had mastered only style?

Gazing at the elegant nude in his father's arms, listening to the father's harsh, dry sobs—the sobs of a man whose very life had been wrung from too many long hours of too-hard work for money needed to sustain his son's life, robbed of both his time and his love.

God, how hard a penalty. How hard. She threw herself to her knees beside Dominique, giving in to the ancient act of contrition.

She stretched her arms around his shoulders. *"Oui, Dominique, nos fils sont morts.* Our sons are dead." His sobs, the raging waves, forced the silent men in the background to hum a dirge.

The doctor arrived to tell them what they already knew, that Dominique's son, André Bienaimé, was dead. Claire and Jessica had come, too. "I am so sorry," Claire said, crying. She had been crying since she had heard.

"I, too," Jessica said. "Dear friend—what to do?"

What more? André Bienaimé, beloved by women, held in the arms of the man who bled for him, who repeated what had been a secret to some but was now apparent to all: "My son, my son, my son."

Dominique refused Jonnie's offer to accompany him back. *"Madame, je vous en prie,* but allow me this last time to be with him alone."

They all helped. They wrapped the corpse in a sheet and placed it beside Dominique in the little Volkswagen. Then they stood watching as Dominique drove off, until his taillights had been swallowed up in darkness.

Jessica and Jonnie sat in the back of Claire's limousine. Claire sat in front beside the driver, Paul. A small procession: Dominique's Volkswagen far ahead, then the limousine, and bringing up the rear, the doctor's car—a Ford. They drove slowly on the dark, dark road.

"Claire, did you know that André was Dominique's son?" Jonnie asked.

"Yes, Sam's André's godfather."

"And the mother?"

"A Frenchwoman—I never met her."

"White?"

"Yes."

"André's incredibly black."

"Yes—the Black Pearl. There are many very black mulattoes. But it seems the mother could never come to grips with his blackness. She had expected a fair mulatto. She ran away—left the little boy with Dominique's sister—never came back. . . .

"As small as he was—I think he was only two years old—he seems to have remembered her. He never accepted the woman who cared for him as his aunt—nor Dominique as his father. God only knows what myth he invented in order to survive."

"Didn't Dominique have it out with him?"

"At first, but when André rejected him, he felt it was for the best."

Jonnie shook her head. Whatever tale André had woven, he knew Dominique was his father. The intensity of their love-hate relationship. André had blackmailed his father—forced his life-style on him, making him pay for what he considered a betrayal. It could not have been a secret, their relationship. In Haiti someone always knows—and tells. . . .

They drove for minutes in silence, then Jessica sighed. "That poor boy—he literally fucked himself to death, wouldn't you say?" Her words instantly lightened the atmosphere in the somber car.

In the future, tales would be told of the life of André Bien-aimé: the way he had lived it, the manner in which he had died. A Haitian fable told by old men to exaggerate the prowess of Haitian manhood. André would become the stuff of legends.

THE RAINS CAME. Big raindrops spattered the windshield, then became sheets of water as wind whipped the rain into blizzard-like intensity.

"Paul"—Claire expressed their fears—"*c'est trop fort. Il faut s'arrêter.*" Yes, the storm was too strong, but where to stop on this long barren road that had no houses or huts for miles? How to escape the vast ocean?

"*Nous allons jusqu'à la station d'essence, madame.*"

The gas station! The only gas station stood at the edge of town. Impossible. Of the three cars that had set out, only the Volkswagen had a sealed bottom to protect its engine. The other two, the Cadillac limousine and the Ford, would get wet—and stall—long before reaching the station. In the mind of each passenger were the often repeated tales of cars stalling in tropical downpours and their occupants drowning.

Jonnie and Jessica maintained a respectful silence, enjoying the storm's fury with a fatalism inspired by their life experiences. A sort of grim satisfaction that with all of man's pretensions, there were forces beyond his scope.

In flashes of lightning, Jonnie thought she glimpsed the

ghosts of children jumping, laughing, whispering, pointing to the lonely car struggling to maintain its dignity in the overpowering assault of the storm. Their eerie chant seeped into the car along with the whistle of the wind.

> *Volé, volé*
> *Tu vol fruit moi . . .*

"*Voilà la station.*" Paul heaved a sigh of relief. His knowledge of the route, his experience, had served him well. The others peered out into the darkness for minutes before finally seeing the string of lights getting closer. Then they pulled into the familiar-looking gas station, with its three pumps, built of reinforced concrete at the intersection where the road ran into town, built on an incline. Water from the cross street swirled around its base, forming whirlpools before emptying into the sea. They drove into its shelter, and the car shuddered briefly as its engine died.

Physically spent, they sat in meditative silence for minutes, giving thanks for their safe arrival, before looking around for the Volkswagen and the Ford that had been following them. Two cars had pulled into the station before them—not the Volkswagen. The doctor, they surmised, must have turned back. But what about Dominique?

They sat staring out at the rain, waiting, not daring to think, as they gazed at the flow, a virtual waterfall down the cross street, emptying into the sea. Suddenly Paul said, "*Là, voilà Dominique!*" They saw the car, the Volkswagen, floundering on a wave, its wheels spinning. As they watched, they heard a roar, deafening, paralyzing, a powerful rush of water racing down the cross street.

It came—a giant wall, an avalanche, cascading down the opening, carrying with it trees, cars, animals, people, everything in its path. It picked up the Volkswagen—Dominique hunched over its wheel, the unyielding body at his side—and carried it, too, out to sea.

IT WAS EARLY MORNING, when the rain had slacked off, that a crane picked them up from the station and drove them to Old Hotel. The brunt of the storm seemed to have bypassed it, although enough rain had fallen to flood the grounds and the cabinlike rooms of the annex, forcing guests to herd together in the ball-room, where chairs and tables had been pulled together as makeshift beds. Some passed the night at the bar drinking them-selves into a stupor. The staff—maids, waiters, cooks, grounds-keepers, and gatekeepers—had scrounged around for space in which to bed down unobtrusively.

Sam, who had been moving among the guests, tired, bewil-dered, seeing new arrivals deposited at the entrance, rushed to greet them. "God, what a night! Why did all this have to happen on a night when Dominique wasn't here? God, I need Dom-inique. I need that man."

He walked from them without registering their silence or the look on their faces—delayed shock from watching the Volkswa-gen swept away, never to be seen again. Sam walked off and they let him go. They were unable to speak to him of Dominique or André. They had yet to convince themselves of what they had seen. To speak of it might turn their nightmare into reality. This they did not want. And this need to keep reality at bay bound them together, anchoring them in the midst of chaos.

Wet and muddy, they stood at the glass doors, gazing over the terrace into the rising water beneath which the pool had vanished.

"Well, one thing's for sure," a man looking out at the rain jested, "it has got to let up some time." These words proved to be a challenge to the gods, for the storm then turned its full fury against them. It slammed into the hotel, shaking it to its founda-tions. The sleeping guests wakened and huddled together, need-ing bodies to touch, to hold on to, a bulwark against the unknown. Wind and rain blew at hurricane force, beating against the glass doors, tearing tables and chairs from the terrace, uprooting trees and smashing against the wavering structure. The building shook. From upstairs came the sounds of shattering windows, bringing more guests down to the crowded room.

And then a sound, almost sickening in its softness. The col-lapse of the bougainvillea-covered walls, their disintegration ac-companied by the shouts and cries of the homeless who had been clinging to the other side for shelter and now came rushing over the grounds, up the steps to the terrace, hammering against the glass walls of the ballroom, demanding to be let in.

When Claire rolled back the panel they were blown into the room. Claire tried to close the panel. It fell from its track. Jonnie and Jessica rushed to help, pulling, pushing, lifting; waiters emerged from hiding places to give a hand. And as they worked to adjust the panel on track, the wind blew in, whipping sand and grit around like a funnel, sand that cut like pinpoints of glass.

Outside, the water rose steadily, high waves resembling an angry sea, while the wind kept blowing, blowing. Finally, the panel restored to its track and rolled back in place, the three women stood, their backs to the glass, looking at one another, hardly recognizing one another plastered as they were with mud and sand. They looked around the room filled with survivors, then turned to stare out at the hard-hitting rain that threatened to shake the panel off its track again.

Jonnie gazed around at the scene—a tableau—bodies wedged together, bodies curving into bodies, rich, poor, guests, workers, beggars, hair, clothes, faces, all covered with masks of mud and sand blown in by the rain, indistinguishable one from the other. A tableau to be done in bronze—awesome.

"Jonnie? Jonnie, is that you?"

Jonnie saw the woman peering into her face. "Jonnie?" Roxanne, starkly different from those around her, in a lovely white robe, a clean face.

"Yes."

"Thank God you're alive. And that you're here." Roxanne hugged Jonnie, transferring dirt from her clothes to the lovely robe. "We heard the storm had washed away roads. We heard people had drowned. I was so afraid." The scent of perfume stifled. Jonnie pulled away, but even as she did, she felt warm tears. Roxanne? Crying over her?

"Dominique. Where's Dominique?" Jean-Pierre had come to stand beside Roxanne. He, too, offended with his clean, refreshed appearance. "They tell me André's dead," Jean-Pierre said. "They say Dominique, he look for me, and I was not here. Where's Dominique? Where's my friend?" He spoke earnestly, tearfully. He cared. He really did care. And because he did care and dared to look clean, well rested, Jonnie answered, speaking brutally.

"Dominique's dead." The words, once spoken, had the effect of concreting the nightmare.

"Sam, Sam," Claire cried, pushing through in the direction Sam had gone.

"Stephan," Jessica said, looking around.

"Has anyone seen Stephan?" Jonnie thought about Lucknair. Had the storm reached the mountains yet? Had it destroyed the little cabin? And Maxie? What about Maxie out there in this devastating storm?

"*Nonononnon,*" Jean-Pierre cried in anguish. "It is not true. It cannot be true. Tell me, tell me . . ."

"Well, now," Jessica said, still looking around. "Everyone looks a sight—a disaster. Come, Jonnie, let the storm do what it will. I think I might have something upstairs that will fit you."

They did look a wreck, worse than the rest, wet and caked in sand and mud from head to foot. Jonnie followed Jessica.

On the steps they found the chambermaids huddled together, Cécile among them. Cécile stood up and went to Jonnie. They stood for a moment looking at each other. They had nothing to say. Their silence meant their secret remained their secret. Nature had taken decision out of their hands for the moment. But it had also taken decisions out of the hands of their enemies. For the moment, everything had to remain as is. Jonnie touched Cécile's face and smiled, then went on.

"Drink first, or a shower?" Jessica asked when they entered her suite.

"Drink—please." Jonnie pulled back the drapes to look out at the rain. Next she went to the mirror, where in the dim light, seeing herself and Jessica, she laughed. "The wretched of the earth," she said. "Make it a brandy." She shivered.

Jessica took a decanter from a cabinet and poured Jonnie a drink. Then she poured herself water from another bottle. "Well, Jonnie, that's another one we aren't likely to forget." Handing Jonnie her glass, she said, "Tell me, Jonnie, were you afraid at any time out on the road?"

Jonnie shook her head no. She sipped the brandy, staring out at the storm. "I think I was beyond fear." How could it have been otherwise, André dead. "So much has happened, Jessica. My mind's not prepared to understand—or accept."

"Precisely," Jessica agreed. "I have had so many experiences—caught in air raids, forest fires, lost in the desert knowing the sun was about to have the final say. I have been confined to remote villages during epidemics. So you see, I am sort of a chronologist of disasters. Yet last night—last night . . .

"But I say"—Jessica pulled herself together—"that Claire, she held up quite well, wouldn't you say? Remarkable control. And she's really quite young, much younger than we . . ."

"We?" Jonnie cried, her anger rising. Then, suddenly aware of the vain reason for her anger, she laughed. How mediocre, her insecurity in the face of the storm. She laughed louder. Bending over, she held her stomach to ease the pain of laughter—then realized she was laughing alone.

Jessica had gone. She went looking for her and found her at the bedroom door, standing silent, motionless. Going to stand beside her, she looked, too. She saw Stephan on the bed, his suntanned body thrusting, plunging, thrusting, plunging. The girl beneath, Alice, her long thin legs wrapped around his hips, her toes curling. . . .

The rain beat harder at the terrace door, thunder hammered down on the roof. Lightning streaked through the room, yet they stood, the two of them—spies, voyeurs—staring at the bodies as they had stared out the window of the car on the road, helpless observers of the anguish, the torment, the passion of the merciless, uncaring elements. Then Jessica said, "I say there, Stephan—isn't it a bit early?"

3

DAWN. A BIRD CHIRPED. A chorus of birds joined in. Clear, alert, they celebrated the miracle. Survival. The sun, unrepentant for the devastation its absence had caused, rose in an incredible blue sky. Its rays shining through the glass partitions met over the heads of those who had gone to sleep believing themselves doomed. They, too, raised their heads in wonder. Those accustomed to living in its warmth rushed out onto the terrace shouting, "*La pluie est finie, la pluie est finie. Voilà le soleil, le soleil,*" while guests proclaimed their relief: "Well, can you top that? The sun's out." Joy radiated from every face as the survivors staggered out to survey the devastation and, suspending religious differences, bowed their heads in silent acceptance of the sun as the mighty healer.

Cranes and bulldozers moved piles of mud heavy with the cadavers of animals and trees, clearing roads. Plants trampled to the ground in the heavy downpour shook themselves upright with amazing vigor. Peasants and vendors searched through the devastation for fallen fruit and legumes to be salvaged.

The atmosphere challenged the right to grieve. It demanded forgetfulness, forgiveness of the god who had brought such havoc. Bodies were found at the bottom of the pool when the water receded—those homeless who had mistaken the pool for solid ground in the wild dash to escape the punishing storm. Their bodies were silently removed and they, along with others who had lost lives, limbs, or property, took a backseat to the glory of the island's survival.

In the ballroom of Old Hotel, gratitude at having survived manifested itself in a universal benevolence. Neighbors embraced neighbors. Water receded, and guests returned to rooms abandoned during the storm to find themselves ankle-deep in mud and silt. Benevolence turned to borderline hysteria. Demands were made on Sam, Claire, the maids, for an accounting of items lost or destroyed in the rains.

Small things reasserted importance: a silk tie, a scarf, a slipper, luggage. Hysteria grew with talk of more rain. What if another storm broke? It's possible. Everything is possible. *But we were promised good weather.* Paradise lost. One hell of a place to get stuck in a storm—Haiti, the goddamn poorest island in the entire hemisphere.

Haitian workers, remarkable for their efficiency, restored the grounds in days. Dozens of eager hands grateful to hold extra gourdes, were recruited. Clothes were washed and ironed, along

with curtains. Floors and walls were scrubbed, windows washed
and rubbed to brilliance.

All around the countryside it was the same—mud shoveled
from streets and put into mounds, with some being carted off for
rebuilding huts; fallen trees stacked high, some to be burned into
charcoal. Wide leaves used for roofs of huts, roads trampled back
to smoothness by bare feet and shovels. In forty-eight hours of
day-into-night work, the countryside reassumed a semblance of
normalcy. The roads to the airport were cleared.

But news of more rains turned guest against guest. Smiles became snarls, congratulatory remarks turned accusatory as each demanded the right to be the first on planes leaving the island.

Sam and Claire, at their amazing best, took charge, imposing
order on the threatening chaos. The exodus began. Jonathan Anderson arrived on the first flight out of Santo Domingo, and Jessica decided to have a celebration.

Only with the restoration of order to the city did rumors
from the mountains filter down. The storm had hit the mountains
after leaving the town. Houses were said to have crumbled; some
had slid down hillsides. One *camionette* overloaded with passen-
gers had slid from the road during the downpour and had
plummeted down the slippery embankment into the gorge.
Ambulances and the police were even then attempting to get
through the debris-blocked road to climb down the mountainside
in search of survivors.

Jonnie had been waiting in her room for word from the
mountains when someone knocked. She opened the door to find
Jean-Pierre standing outside. "Madame, I must talk to you,"
he said.

"To me? What about?"

"About Madame Anderson."

"I'm not the right person for you to talk about Madame Anderson," Jonnie answered. She hadn't seen Jean-Pierre since the
day of the storm. Nor had she thought about him. But now that
he stood before her, she remembered how clean, how uninvolved
he had appeared before she had told him of Dominique's death.
And she remembered that he had been the one Dominique had
wanted to be with when his son had died.

"Madame Anderson wants to take me back to the States with her."

"So?"

"I cannot go," he said.

"I suggest you tell her," Jonnie answered.

"I don't want her," Jean-Pierre said, and Jonnie's face burned in embarrassment for Roxanne and because he dared take her in his confidence.

"Why did you fuck her if you didn't want her?" Jonnie said. As she spoke she noticed his clothes were muddy, dirty from his efforts to help restore order in town. But tomorrow, the day after, when his cars could move again, he would once more be the handsome, immaculate man whom Jessica had set up in business and whom women like Roxanne found irresistible.

"But, madame—that's the way life is . . ." He preened.

She hated his arrogance. Hated that he had salvaged something from the horror of the past few days to preserve his ego. "If that's the way life is, then that's the way you must live it," Jonnie conceded. "Just spare me." She tried to close the door, but his foot remained on the sill.

"Madame," he pleaded. "You are her friend. Talk to her. I beg you."

Tagging along with them to a voodoo ceremony and running interference with a suspicious husband was no basis for allegiance. Still, Roxanne's embrace, her tears—real tears—the morning of her return had touched her.

"Why don't you discuss this with Mr. Anderson, Jean-Pierre? Perhaps he doesn't need the services of a chauffeur in the States."

But sarcasm was lost on him. He smiled, brushed up his mustache. "Madame cannot be so naive. But then you Black Americans cannot understand *la subtilité*. You were mere slaves."

Jonnie's scalp tingled. "And you"—she spoke softly—"were you not slaves?"

"Madame, we fought for our independence—and won."

"I see, I see. Well, as you say, I am naive, Jean-Pierre, so I cannot possibly be the person suited to discuss your problems."

"But Madame Anderson has said that she's going to my wife." He pleaded. "I have no intention of leaving Haiti—my wife, my children."

Jonnie laughed. "You're taking yourself too seriously, Jean-Pierre. I'm sure if you speak to Madame Anderson you'll find she has no intentions of leaving her husband."

She closed the door, stood with her back against it, thought of the angry woman in the garden, thought of Roxanne—soft, vulnerable Roxanne, and shuddered.

BOOK

SIX

1

IT SUITED JESSICA'S STYLE TO CELEBRATE. And having made the announcement for her grand gala, she adjusted her seven-league boots, leaving the arrangements in the hands of management and staff, and dashed off to charitable pursuits.

Waiters, cooks, maids, and the remaining guests threw themselves into its preparation with unbelievable zest—a sort of hysteria—banishing the tragedy of flood and storm from their minds. And Jonnie decided that the time for her departure had come.

Frenzied banging, hanging, and decorating had exasperated her, finally forcing her out of the hotel. Taking a taxi to town— to replace suitcases destroyed in the flood—she found herself trapped in bumper-to-bumper traffic on streets narrowed by mounds of mud banked on their sides.

Jonnie didn't want to celebrate. She wanted only to grieve. She needed to grieve for André, for Dominique, for the homeless found dead at the bottom of the pool. Yes, she wanted to grieve for them and for all those forced to live in poverty, on whom the gods seemed to take such pleasure lavishing punishment.

And, too, she wanted to grieve with Jessica for their unnameable loss. She hadn't seen Jessica since the storm. She didn't want to, and Jessica didn't want to see her either. What to say? What sense to meet and grieve over a loss that neither acknowledged?

Entering the commercial center of the city, Jonnie realized why she hated it with such a passion: The place had been stripped of all beauty to accommodate the greed and avarice of the colonial rulers. Trees had been ruthlessly cleared, denying shade. At high noon pedestrians were forced to walk in the merciless glare of the sun. Shops and warehouses had been built close together, almost touching, to secure as much profit as a square inch allowed, thus blocking the circulation of cooling breezes blowing in from the sea a short distance away. From 1804 to 1973 it had been so. Perhaps the internecine struggles between the two groups had used up so much of their energies that no one—neither mulattoes nor blacks—in the 169 years since independence had devoted thought or effort to the possibility it could be changed.

The taxi dropped Jonnie off in front of a luggage store, where upon entering she was greeted by a lovely girl. "Madame?"

"*Je veux—j'ai besoin . . .*"

"You're American?" the girl said.

"Yes," Jonnie answered, relieved. She had no desire to be fumbling with languages. Now that she had decided to leave, she needed energy to plan. She no longer wanted to struggle to belong. She no longer wanted to want to belong. She simply wanted to be gone.

She grieved the loss of madness. She missed it. Madness had fed a terrifying need. Its absence created a void: rootlessness. Loneliness, like a disease, invaded her. "I want to see some luggage," Jonnie responded. "A train case, an overnight bag . . ."

The young woman walked to the back of the shop and returned with two samples of suitcases—one goatskin, product of the country; the other leather, imported. "I'll take the goatskin," Jonnie said. "Match it the best that you can. My luggage was ruined in the flood."

"Ahh, such a storm. It was awful," the girl said with a deep sigh. "But what to do? It happens that way sometimes."

"Killer storms? It's horrible," Jonnie agreed.

"Are you from New York?" the girl asked.

"Yes."

"I love New York." Her eyes sparkled. Jonnie liked her, liked her eyes, their brightness, their intelligence.

"Did you go to school in the States?" Jonnie asked.

"No, I went to school here, in Haiti—and in France. But I learned my English in New York. I have family in New York."

"Why don't you live in New York?" Jonnie asked.

"And leave Haiti? Never." Her eyes widened in amazement. "Madame, Haiti's my home. I love Haiti."

Jonnie followed the girl's gaze through the door, over the heads of people skirting the mud pushed high at the curb, to the mountains, shining green jewels in the sunlight. She, too, loved the mountains, the drums—drums that had been silent since the storm. Would she ever hear them again? Before she left? Listen to them as she fell off to sleep? Or stand in the softness of twilight, warm breezes caressing her arms while softly in the distance the beat went on and on far into the night—deep within her.

"You can make more money in New York," Jonnie said.

"Yes."

"That doesn't tempt you?"

"And I can go to the theater, Lincoln Center, Broadway. It's exciting—and dangerous."

Remembering walking along the moonlit road, the vendors nodding as their candlelight dimmed, without apprehension, without fear, Jonnie's gaze lingered on the mud piled high weighing danger against danger. "Yes, New York is dangerous," she agreed.

"But fun," the girl laughed, then shivered. "And cold." She looked out at the storm-ravaged street. "My country, it is poor. But we cannot all leave. Some must stay—and see if we can help in what happens next. . . ."

Leaving the luggage store, Jonnie walked over to the nearby café and ordered *jus de corosol*. The proprietor stood next to her while she drank. "Our *jus de corosol*, is it not good?"

"Best juice in all the world," Jonnie agreed.

"You see"—he spoke as though they had been having a long argument—"our Haiti has much to offer, beside storms and death, *n'est-ce pas?*"

"*N'est-ce pas,*" Jonnie repeated, and went out.

At the travel bureau Jonnie stood, leafing through brochures, when Stanley came in. "Jonnie Dash!" he said, overjoyed to see her. "What are you doing here?"

"Trying to decide my next destination," Jonnie joked.

"You're leaving, too? So are we. Our place has been broken into."

"The lovely place in the mountains that you spoke about? You were robbed?"

"No. But someone broke the shutters with a stone. Robbing is the next logical step, isn't it?" He, too, studied brochures. "I think we'll try Saint Martin."

"Is there any place on earth safer than Haiti?" Jonnie asked, then laughed. "Except for its torrential rains. How did you make out in the storm?"

"Wonderful," Stanley said, his round face lit with a beatific smile. "What an adventure. Simply divine. We were never really threatened. We have a good, solid house. What a grand feeling to look out the windows at the elements gone wild. For two entire days we had the whole world to ourselves. . . ."

"At least someone found something to love in the killer storm," Jonnie said, stilling a disquieting stir of anger. "What about that horrible accident? Were you able to help? Did you see where the *camionette* went over the side?"

"We heard about it. Lots of commotion. But then one expects such things in underdeveloped countries, right?"

Jonnie shuddered, watching his round, smiling face. Grotesque, selfish. The face of privilege. The face of Charles McCellen, Jonathan Anderson—those who cared only that their needs were met.

"At any rate, the storm did keep those horrible creatures from your door," she quipped.

"Creatures?" Stanley asked, his eyes widening in fear.

"People with stones," Jonnie said in jest.

"It certainly did," Stanley answered primly. "I lived in constant dread that that horrible fellow might take it into his head to visit."

"What fellow?"

"The one to whom you were speaking at the bar—the fat man."

"Maxie?" Jonnie asked, not believing him. Maxie with his big mouth and gentle soul? Maxie with his nonviolent violence and revolutionary rhetoric? Maxie, the guy who talked loud so that no one listened? The man thought him violent?

Her extraordinary insight into Maxie confounded her. How had she scaled all his self-imposed barriers to his inner being? Maxie. She longed for him. Why hadn't he been born when she was born? Why had such a man not existed when she was young? Or did it take generations and revolutions to mold a Maxie Gardener?

"Well," she said, still in a jesting tone. "Let's hope that your next place will be your Shangri-la." She turned, but he caught and held her hand.

"Jonnie Dash, there is such a place, isn't there? There must be such a place, mustn't there?" Searching, intent, his eyes held hers, begged her to pull from her bag of tricks the answer he wanted. What right did a man so small in deeds and thoughts have to ask so much in life?

"If there is, Stanley, I'm sure you'll find it," she sneered. "When you do, drop me a line so that I can head in the opposite direction." She pulled her hand from his and walked to the door. But guilt forced her to turn back. "There might be such a place, Stanley," she said gently. "There certainly ought to be."

Out on the street, just as Jonnie hailed a taxi, Claire drove up. "Going back to the hotel, Jonnie?"

"Don't think so, Claire. I'm going to Biscentnaire. Isn't that where Maxie's yacht is tied up?"

"He's not back yet."

"How do you know?"

"He'll wait until the water gets more settled—another day or two."

"A day or two?" Jonnie cried in despair. On this island where it took forty-eight hours to make one day? How could she bear it? True, she'd had no word from Lucknair. But he was up there—up in the mountains still needing help, her plans, the possibilities she developed. "He must get back before I leave!"

"Leave?" Spots reddened Claire's cheeks. "You're not leaving, Jonnie Dash. How can you think of leaving at a time like this?"

"Everything that can happen to me in this place has happened. It's time to go."

"It's all been so sad," Claire said. "But Haiti's a wonderful place. You'll understand and appreciate it, given time." She searched her purse for a tissue.

"It's hard, Jonnie," she said. "Sam cries. When we're alone, he just cries. I have no words with which to comfort him. Dominique was his dearest friend." She blew her nose. "We were always so happy. So safe. We were always laughing, always had something to laugh about . . .

"Jonnie, we laughed at André, teased him about his good looks, his exploits. Jonnie, isn't it awful that we laughed at Dominique's son?"

Jonnie saw again the long, black body stretched on the sand, the waves whipping themselves into a fury charging against the shore—the heavens opening up and the rain pouring down its terrible, unjust punishment on the heads of a long-suffering people. Who had allowed one so lovely to go his way bearing the burden of the name Bienaimé?

"I can't bear the thought of your going, Jonnie," Claire sobbed. "I depend on you—your just being here—on this island. Gérard—he'll miss you. He's in love with you, you know." She waited for a response, then cried again. "Don't go, Jonnie, please—please, at least wait. Wait until after Jessica's gala celebration." Then she added in a tone of despair, "It's madness, the way she goes about it. So determined, without joy. No good can come of it, Jonnie. There's been too much sorrow, too much sadness. Jonnie, talk to her. Tell her . . ."

"I suppose the cruise is definitely off?" Jonnie asked.

"Yes," Claire answered. "Jess gave in. The weather took her choice away. But she still insists on getting her money back. She's brutal on that score. Oh, I wish we were over this time and that everything were back to normal."

Jonnie looked out the window, then up at the blue sky, thinking of cadavers at the bottom of the pool. But of course Claire meant back to normal when suffering the shame of Watergate took up their leisure time. Then the American contingent could remember the past saying, "What about that storm—some humdinger, huh?"

Jonnie shrugged. "Maybe the best thing Jessica can do, after all, is have a celebration."

GÉRARD STOOD AT THE ENTRANCE, WAITING, when they drove up. "Jonnie," he said, rushing to the car. "We must talk."

Jonnie sat in the car studying him. His face, ashen, agitated, frightened her. She had hoped that after their last meeting, he would take things into his own hands. Hoped that despite his fear and because of his understanding of the place, he would find a solution. He hadn't. She knew now he hadn't. It was still all up to her.

"Wait in the lounge for me, Gérard, I'll be right there."

Taking her luggage and leaving him at the car with Claire, she walked to her room, keeping alert for any trace of disturbances.

The work crew was still cleaning up, replanting, pruning, raking mud. The blinds of her room were drawn. She hesitated, looked around, and moved cautiously toward her door. As she approached, she saw it crack open. Then Cécile slid through the crack.

"Your patron—did you see him?" Jonnie asked, and Cécile put her hands to her mouth.

"*Oui,*" she whispered.

"What does he want?" Jonnie lowered her voice. Cécile shrugged her shoulders. "Is it about Lucknair?"

"*Lucknair? Mais-il est là.*" She pointed her chin to the room.

"Does your patron know?"

"*Non.*" She spoke secretively, shaking her head. "I say nothing—to nobody."

Leaving the luggage with Cécile, Jonnie walked back to Old Hotel. It had to be serious. More than she imagined. Cécile had never kept secrets from Gérard even when Jonnie demanded it—except for that one time helping Lucknair. What had happened now?

Gérard and Claire had not gone into the lounge. Instead, they were sitting at the bar. "I ordered two brandies for you," Claire said, getting up when Jonnie appeared. "Gérard seems to need one. And—well . . ." She left. Jonnie shook her head. Claire, always the romantic.

Gérard waited until the tall, gaunt man, Nicholas, who had

replaced Dominique, had served them and was out of earshot, before he said, "Jonnie, the boy—he is gone. I think the *tonton macoute* or the police took him."

Cautious, go slow. . . . "You—think? Why would you think that?"

"They come. M'sieur Ambroise—the peasants, they see them. They were at the house. They break up the house—my house. I'm responsible . . ."

"If you'd only start at the beginning, Gérard." She wanted to tell him, to assure him that the boy had arrived safely. But Cécile's warning checked her.

"Jonnie, I liked the boy so much. Believe me. He liked me, too. It's you who said the army came here, to this hotel, looking for him. Why, Jonnie? Who is the one man, or woman, so powerful to have the army, the *tonton*, looking for him? The president? His wife? I don't understand this. Forgive me. The child is poor. He has no home. He cannot go on hiding. I know that. They will catch him, wherever he goes on this island. It's a small island. He tells me he wants to go to the States. I told him that I have a friend at the American Consulate."

Jonnie's heart contracted. She forced expression from her eyes, her face. "And you spoke to this friend of the boy?"

"Yes."

"But, Gérard, we weren't supposed to say anything to anybody."

"But this is my friend—a good man. A gentle man. I told him the boy had trouble with the law. And that you—my friend— asked me to look after him. And that he wants to go to the States."

"You didn't!"

"I was afraid for the boy, Jonnie. They will find him. He can't hide forever. Since the time you are there the peasants all know he is there. This is Haiti; somebody always tells. . . ."

"How right you are!" Jonnie shook her head at the irony of it. Of course she had focused attention on that lonely house when she had showed her madness on the road.

"I told Lucknair to wait for me. Then I went to my friend, who promised to help me. But then the storm broke and I couldn't get back to Lucknair. The roads were blocked. Then the accident.

When I got there, the boy—he was gone. The place is all broken up. They'll be coming for me. To question me . . ."

"Why?"

"I don't know. I don't know why they want him. But he was in my house. I'm responsible—for the boy—for you . . ." He tapped the bar with nervous fingers. "If they take me away, what's to become of my son?"

"Maybe they didn't catch him." Jonnie spoke to calm his fears. She wanted to say Lucknair is safe. Instead she said, "If they did he will run away. The *tonton* won't give you trouble. Just tell your friend at the embassy that Lucknair ran away. He'll understand. Lucknair always runs away. He's a strange boy, Lucknair, fearless, not wild. A careful dreamer. They might never catch him."

"But you're his friend," Gérard said, taking hope. "He loves you. If he gets away and comes to you, what will you do? Take him back with you to the States? He will have a good life with you."

"Never," Jonnie smiled. "I'm never going back to the States. Isn't it you who said in the States young boys put knives to the throat? Don't you remember how in the States young Blacks are abused? Didn't we use to talk about the police killing our Black American children? They still do, Gérard."

"But they were poor children. You are rich now—a fine woman, an artist—a genius."

She smiled, listening, hearing. No talk of love here. He had seen her madness and wanted her gone. Take your troubles and go. So much for her trip and happily-ever-after. She shrugged. "It doesn't matter. In the States the police can't tell the difference between a poor Black boy and a rich Black boy. There's no life on the streets for a fearless Black boy. And your friend at the consulate—did you say his name?"

"Charles. Everyone calls him M'sieur Charles. His other name is McCellen."

2

L ONG AFTER GÉRARD HAD GONE, Jonnie sat at the bar wishing
she could share this new development with Jessica. But they
weren't talking. Not true. They simply had avoided speaking. It
was up to her now—only to her. First to undeceive Lucknair. Tell
him that his dreams did not lie in the States but elsewhere. Where?
That, too, was for them to determine—Lucknair and Maxie.

She drank the last of her cognac, looked at Nicholas, gawky
and gangling in the background, smiling without nuance. Beside
him she saw Dominique, short, round—his impish face, his cherubic smile, the forceful wiping of the bar. The haunted bar. How
good to be gone from it forever. How good to be free of this little
island crippled by the excesses of the entire hemisphere—its prejudices, its thirst for vengeance, its greed, its hunger for power, its
questionable morality—never great enough to absolve the wrongs
that had been done.

Roxanne, an apparition walking toward her, forced Jonnie to
stand. Enough of ghosts. She had to go to Lucknair.

"Jonnie," the ghost Roxanne called. Jonnie walked toward her, expecting to walk through her, if not halted by her flesh.

"You must talk to Jonathan. He's being beastly. He's trying to force me to go back to the States with him. I won't go back—now. I told him so. 'Jonathan,' I said to him, 'I'm a grown woman, and I shall not go.' He laughed, Jonnie. He laughed at me. 'Get your things packed,' he said."

A different Roxanne stood before her. A Roxanne with dark circles beneath her eyes. A tic beat in her cheeks. Her face frightened, haggard, almost old.

"What do you think I can say to Jonathan? I hardly know him."

"He likes you."

Jonnie shook her head. Jonathan didn't like her—or anyone. He had stopped liking people, except those he could use, those who could justify his existence, a long time ago.

"Madame?" The smiling Nicholas spoke to Roxanne. She replied, "Bourbon." Then to Jonnie: "He says you're a strong woman. He likes strong people."

"I have nothing to do with Jonathan—or with you, for that matter."

"Jonnie, I'm in love with Jean-Pierre," Roxanne said.

"How does Jean-Pierre feel about you, Roxanne?"

A customer came to sit at the end of the bar, and Nicholas moved toward him, his loose limbs fumbling. Jonnie looked around, shivering. She wanted to get away, go to Lucknair, tell him that he was no longer alone, talk to him before all the time they had slipped away.

"He adores me," Roxanne said.

"Who?"

"Jean-Pierre—he told me."

"In French, of course," Jonnie said, and caught her lips between her teeth. She hadn't meant sarcasm. "What about his wife?"

"His concubine," Roxanne corrected her.

"Are his children concubines, too?"

Roxanne shook her head, shrugged her shoulders. "He does love me—I know. I need to stay here to convince him. He has nothing to fear. The children will be taken care of."

"You're planning on taking them to the States?"

"No! Of course not. They can hardly come into my home. Four children?"

"But Jean-Pierre can? He'll be living with you and Jonathan?"

"There's a lovely apartment over the garage that can be furnished. . . ."

"Roxanne, you're not suggesting that Jean-Pierre will be your chauffeur?"

"He is a chauffeur, Jonnie."

"No, that's not what Jean-Pierre is, Roxanne. He's the proud owner of a fleet of cars."

"In Haiti. What does that mean in terms of money?"

"Maybe not in the way that you and Jonathan know money, but in Haiti that means he's on the way to being a *grand homme* with a future to give his children. Do you think he'll leave them? Go off to the States to a room above a garage? Is there enough money in all the world . . . ?"

"Don't make it sound impossible, Jonnie. What can I do?"

"Go back home with your husband. Give yourself time. Think things over. You'll be doing all concerned a favor. You'll be unhappy if you stay."

"What do you know about unhappiness!" Roxanne cried. "My husband is a pervert. To make love to me he has to tear off my clothes, then he rides my back, kicking my flanks as though I'm a horse, then enters me only after he forces me to say I'm a whore. I'm not a whore, Jonnie.

"My daughter's a tramp who married the man I love."

Jonnie laughed. "A soap opera—a real tearjerker."

"God, Jonnie, you're hard." Roxanne rubbed her arms, her thighs, bent over to massage her calves. Her poise shattered.

Jonnie shook her head. "No, Roxanne, I'm not hard. That storm was hard. It showed what hardness can be. It destroyed self-pity, chased away and replaced fear with clarity, exposing the shallowness of our thoughts, the futility of emotions, the hopelessness of dreams. . . .

"That storm fused our lives into one, erased the differences, robbed us of identity, joined us together with water, earth, and sand. It numbed our wills and kept us waiting for the inevitable—and there was nothing we could do about it. Just think if it had gone on one more week, two weeks. . . .

"Roxanne, if you're unhappy with Jonathan, divorce him. Stay on in Haiti and take your chances."

"Divorce Jonathan? You are mad! I admire Jonathan Anderson. I have most of my life. I spent my childhood dreaming of him; my adolescence, grooming myself to become Mrs. Jonathan Anderson. I am the respected Mrs. Jonathan Anderson. I shall die Mrs. Jonathan Anderson!"

"Then you are happy," Jonnie said.

"Is that all you have to say?"

"Yes. In years to come you'll have grandchildren. People like Jean-Pierre—like me—will be the proverbial skeletons in your closet that you can display or keep locked away at your discretion. Isn't that the way of attractive, wealthy women?"

"What the hell do you know about wealthy women?" Roxanne cried. "Who are you to pretend to be giving advice? You're only an observer in our lives. If it wasn't for this unnatural hotel situation, do you think you would be tolerated?"

Jonnie walked away from Roxanne quickly, filled with an overpowering need to get to her room and to set the plans for the oncoming days. No! One was not strong if one always stood alone. She did not want Lucknair to think no one cared.

Roxanne ran behind her and grabbed her arm. "Don't go, Jonnie. I didn't mean it."

Jonnie pulled her arm away. Yet she held Roxanne's hand to show she had no resentment. She understood Roxanne's weakness. "You can't help it, Roxanne. You're American. And what's more—you're rich, white, and American, with access to power. It takes time and strength to begin to see through that shit. And, Roxanne, you don't have that much time—nor that kind of strength."

"Jonnie, I beg you. Help me."

"You're not listening, Roxanne. I'm too old to play baby-sitting games. Go on home. Think things over. You might be grateful you took this time out in Haiti, in this unnatural hotel situation."

LUCKNAIR'S EYES WERE STARING at her from behind the high-backed chair when she entered the room. They were magnets pulling her past the waiting Cécile to the chair. She sat. He came to her. Silent as a whisper, light as the air, to sit at her feet. Mud still soft on his clothes, leaves sticking to his hair—a damp kitten. How hard it must have been: the walk down from the mountains, the hiding, the waiting, and that forest, huge obstacle, all to reach her.

And yet, looking into his eyes, their endless blackness, she saw an alertness, felt in his limbs impatience, a need to be gone—a gazelle ready to bolt at the first sign of danger. Such energy.

"Lucknair, I know you want to go to the States. But there's no place for you there."

"*Pourquoi?*" he asked. "*Les Etats-Unis*—it is big—there is much money."

"Not just lying around to be picked up. It takes hard work to make much money." She brushed leaves from his damp hair, feeling as she did so the rapidly beating pulse in his temple.

"I shall work—hard," he promised.

"You are too young. They will not let you in."

"I am going with you," he said.

"But I am not going to the United States," she said bluntly. "I don't know where I'm going when I leave here. But it certainly will not be there."

"But what he do?" Cécile asked. They had, it seemed, decided his fate between them.

"I promise you, he will get away from here."

"Where to, madame?" Cécile asked.

"*Sais pas, Cécile.*"

Cécile showed clearly her disappointment. If not Jonnie, who? Jonnie had been her only hope when Lucknair had told her of her patron's visit to the consulate.

"*Madame, le patron—qu'est-ce qu'il a fait?*" she asked.

"*Rien,*" Jonnie answered. "I did not tell him the boy is here."

"*Et madame, qu'est-ce que vous faites?*"

"I'm waiting for Captain Maxie. You know him?"

Cécile nodded. "*Le gros?*" she asked.

Patiently Jonnie explained that they had to keep Lucknair hidden, a task made easier since so many guests had gone, leaving rooms empty.

"Maxie will be back soon," she said. "You have to keep on the lookout for him. He's our one hope, Cécile."

"*Et vous, madame?*"

"Madame is a big girl now, Cécile. It's Lucknair we must look out for." Maxie had to be there for them— for her. If not? Why not? But one step at a time . . .

Cécile sat on the floor looking down at her hands. She did not know Maxie well enough to trust him. But then she had trusted Gérard Auguste with her life, and he had betrayed them. After a few minutes she shrugged, smiled. "*Il a de la chance, Lucknair.*"

Indeed Lucknair had luck. More luck than natural. He had fantastic survival instincts, darting through the cracks of people's good and bad intentions, escaping lairs, traps, gathering languages as he went, using them—a life force.

Jonnie gazed at the wooden flute on the dresser. She thought of Boysie. He, too, had had a life force. But he had been so young, too young to have had so much baggage: her and Sylvie.

"*Oui, Lucknair, il a de la chance,*" she said, then added, "Cécile, Boysie didn't make it, you know? Boysie never made it, *comprends?*"

"*Oui, madame.*" Cécile nodded her head obediently. She turned away not understanding. It didn't matter. Most times she found the behavior of Americans very strange.

3

THE NIGHT OF JESSICA'S GRAND CELEBRATION, and still no word from Maxie. For hours Jonnie debated whether to go or not. Staying close to Lucknair, listening to every sound, every movement in or around the grounds near the annex, sniffing out any possibility of danger to the boy. Waiting for news of Maxie's return had become Jonnie's one reason for staying. Leaving her room, being too far from the boy, seemed to be asking for trouble. Still, Jessica always gave more than she asked, and she had asked Jonnie to attend.

Dressed for evening, Jonnie stepped from her room and remembered why she had never worn that gown. Its narrow hem made it difficult to walk. She paused, debating whether or not to change. She decided to go, stay a short time, then leave. It was a ridiculous celebration. Celebrating what? The further erosion of the lives and the land of a people?

Slowly Jonnie walked to the main building, her too-narrow skirt hampering her stride, and with every small step she took, her anxiety at having left the boy mounted.

She entered the ballroom, and the musicians struck up a chord, the tango, announcing her arrival. She had been the last of the expected guests to arrive, and when she came in, a cheer greeted her.

Candles had been lit on tables pulled together to accommodate Jessica's friends and Claire's few remaining guests, their flickering shadows playing over the ceilings, reviving the sense of ghosts at play. Crystal glasses sparkled, awaiting the pouring of the assorted whiskeys on rolling carts, champagne in buckets at every few seats. Waiters stood at attention, awaiting the command to pour.

Everyone had already been seated and every eye followed her mincing steps as she moved to the table. Maurice met her and escorted her the rest of the way to the seat with her nameplate. Beside her, the other unoccupied place at the table carried the nameplate of Captain Gilbert Lavel.

Jessica sat at the head of the table, Jonnie to her left, and Stephan to her right. Next to him Alice-in-Wonderland. Next to Captain Lavel's empty chair, Roxanne sat with Sam beside her and Jonathan across from her. At the far end of the table Claire sat among the last of her hotel guests.

The disconcerting silence at the table, in what was supposed to be The Grand Celebration, forced Jonnie to signal Maurice for a drink. He took that as a cue to pour drinks all around. Jessica, for her part, sat, hands clasped beneath her chin, eyes closed. Not at all her brilliant best. Indeed, she had the aspect of one deep in prayer.

The first drink elevated Jonnie's spirit. She drank quickly, and not wanting to flag, called for another. The strains of the tango had already touched her. Now, her spirit elevated, she felt a deep stirring of sentiment. She wanted to dance. But with whom?

Not Stephan. Never again with Stephan. This was the first day seeing him since the day of the storm.

She glanced across the table, noticed how tense he appeared speaking to his Jane Doe. And she, Alice-in-Wonderland, answered him, her eyes lucid. The first time Jonnie had seen them so.

Jessica's eyes remained closed. Jonnie gave a sign and Maurice poured another drink. And as she drank the strains of the tango sounded sweeter. She wanted to dance. Where in the hell was Maxie, any goddamn how?

"So, Jonathan." Sam broke the uncomfortable silence. "Running out on us, are you? Just when the deal with Le Renard was going through."

Jonathan shrugged. "Haiti's too big an order, even for me, Sam. The land on which I was supposed to build has turned into a quagmire."

"Come off it." Sam laughed. "You knew what to expect here—or in any developing country. That's why we, from developed countries, come to make a killing. Your engineers come with their know-how, and *voilà* . . ."

"Haitians are a strange breed," Jonathan said, but he leveled his loaded gaze at Roxanne. "All this poverty. This island needs everything. Everyone needs work. Yet workers aren't all that easy to come by. There's a phobia called American. Some Haitians are too proud to work for Americans. Hell, I never knew we'd invaded this island in 1933 . . ."

"1915," Sam corrected him. "We left in 1934."

"So what?" Jonathan snapped. "Countries are always invading other countries. They call that history."

"It wasn't the invasion," Sam answered. "It's what we did during the invasion that made our name mud."

"Like what?"

"Like trying to reintroduce slavery to this island. That's a real sore spot to Blacks, wherever in the world you meet them, in or out of the States. Whether true or not, Americans have a habit of thinking they shouldn't treat Blacks as equals—and they show it. Both mulattoes and Blacks resent it.

"Let's face it, this is the country where both the present exploiters and the exploited were slaves. They all fought for their freedom. That fellow, Charlemagne, who took up arms against the marines, was a mulatto, and Blacks made up most of his army. People here have long memories—and enough time to play with them."

"Ignorance," Jonathan snorted. "Time marches on. Look at the Japs. Look at what we did to them. You don't see them holding grudges. Look at Korea—and it will be the same with Vietnam. Someone ought to tell these fools that no people can live in the past and survive."

"Do we have to wait for Gilbert before we start serving?" Claire called from the other end of the table. "We're starving. Why can't we eat now?"

At that Jessica opened her eyes. She reached for a bottle on the rolling bar. Maurice hurried over to pour her drink. She raised her glass in a toast: "Hear, hear . . . we're here to mourn the passing of our dearly beloved Dominique—and his dear son André Bienaimé . . . to celebrate the fact that they lived. Dominique was my dear, dear friend." Her words slurred, eyes glazed, she looked around the table. "Dominique was kind, loyal—faithful—," she stammered. "He was the best of us . . ."

Jessica, drunk! But Jessica didn't drink! Jonnie stared at Jessica and realized that her own drinking had affected her focus. "Didn't I say keep the table heavy with whiskey?" Jessica lisped. "Jacques—food! This is, after all, a *grande fête*—a celebration."

In relief, waiters rushed away, coming back in seconds with platters laden with squabs, roast pig, mushrooms, blackened rice, white rice, beans, bananas, plantains . . . The *fête*, the feast, the grand celebration was about to begin. "Maurice, whiskey."

Maurice looked over at Claire for approval. Jessica obviously showed the effect of her drinking. Claire shrugged helplessly, and Jessica, seeing them, cried, "I—am—drunk. Damned right I'm drunk. And I have lots more to drink before I eat. You know me, Claire; you can trust me. I am the one person at this table who can be fully trusted. I take care of myself."

She looked over her shoulder to Maurice standing by with the whiskey. "Fill 'er up, Maurice."

"Jess, stop this!" Stephan laid a hand over Jessica's.

"Did you hear me, Maurice? I want a drink."

Stephan looked at Jonnie, a plea in his eyes. Jonnie, seeing him, laughed. Pleading for her to save Jessica's soul? She raised her own glass for a refill.

"Hear, hear," Jessica shouted joyously, hitting her glass against Jonnie's. Their whiskey spilled over on the table and they giggled. Jessica handed over her glass to be filled again. This time, Stephan spoke in a stern voice. "That is enough. Do you hear me, Jessica. . . ."

"That, my dear Stephan, is disrespectful," Jessica protested. "No respect at all." She turned to Jonnie, pushed her head up to hers, and winked. Jonnie giggled, glad to join in.

Celebration. They had come to celebrate—to get drunk, to forget the storm, death, and lovers who didn't measure up. And why not? Why the hell not?

"As for that—that . . ." Jessica pointed to Captain Lavel's empty chair. "That . . ."

"Motherfucker," Jonnie supplied.

"Tha-at's right. Motherfucker." Jessica bared long discolored teeth. "No decency."

"Right," Jonnie lisped. "Dirty mother, you know it." Down their throats went the whiskey, until Claire stood up. "That is enough. Please, Jess . . ."

"Please?" Jessica snarled. "Please what? Please whom? I'm the world's greatest pleaser. Am I not, Stephan? Am I not, Alice? I ask you, Jonnie. Am I not the world's greatest pleaser?"

Jonathan, to change the subject, held up his glass. "I want to drink to my wife, Roxanne. For the great time we have enjoyed as your guest, Claire. And hoping we'll be back—"

"I . . . am . . . speaking." Jessica refused him his moment. "Don't you hear me speaking?" she cried. "What am I? Don't I deserve your respect, Jonathan?"

She raised her glass to him. "To respect, Jonathan." She looked over to Sam. "Your respect, Sam." Then she raised her glass to Alice. "Your respect." Alice squirmed. She tried to push herself back into her habitual haze. But she had allowed herself to step too far into their world. Now she remained in it—their victim. She stared at Jessica, in terror.

Stephan dropped his hand below the table to cover hers, and Jessica roared, "Don't you dare!" Quickly Stephan replaced his hand on the table.

"I asked a question"—Jessica stared into Alice's faded blue eyes—"and I want an answer now!"

Not waiting for an answer, she reached over the table, grabbed Alice by her neck, and shook her. Alice's head flopped around like that of a Raggedy Ann doll. "Answer me, I say." Jessica kept shaking the neck; the head, its eyes popping out, kept flopping from side to side. Then Jessica jumped to her feet, pulling the girl over the table. Glasses and bottles went crashing to the floor; food spilled everywhere. Jessica, disoriented, her glazed gray eyes probing the girl's face, kept squeezing the fragile neck. "Do you hear me, slut? Answer me, answer me. . . ."

Jacques, the first to react, got to them, attempted to pry Jessica's strong hands loose. Sam jumped up, rushed over, releasing the rest of them from paralysis. Soon the two were surrounded, and Roxanne kept wailing, "Will somebody tell me what's going on around here?"

Sam lowered the girl, unconscious now, to the floor, while Claire, hysterical, kept shouting, "Do something—please, somebody do something!"

Everything in the room contracted, moved in slow motion. Claire realized that she was the one with the experience to help and rushed to give Alice mouth-to-mouth resuscitation. Stephan prevented her. He picked the unconscious girl up from the floor and walked out of the room. Sam and Claire followed. Jonathan pulled Roxanne from her chair, led her out of the room. The musicians had stopped playing. They stood, staring, poised but puzzled. Confusion had rendered them and their music unimportant. Jessica picked up two bottles from the rolling bar, put one under each arm, and stalked from the room. Jonnie jumped up, tried to run after Jessica, but trapped in her narrow skirt, fell. She scrambled to her feet, tripped again.

On hands and knees, she crawled to the table, reached up, took a knife, cut the seam of her dress, opening it from ankle to thigh, staggered to her feet, and wove an unsteady path to the door. By the time she got to the steps Jessica had vanished.

THE TAXI DROPPED HER OFF in front of a streetlight, the only streetlight on the darkened stretch—the jetty, where a group of men had gathered. Jessica had come here. The gateman at Old

Hotel had told her. He had laughed and called Jessica *"la vieille, l'Anglaise-là."*

Jonnie had resented that he had called Jessica old. Jessica wasn't old. Jessica was drunk and needed her. Approaching the men sitting around in the glare of the lone streetlight, she attempted speaking in Creole, *"M'voule palé-ou."* She smiled and added, *"S'il vous plaît, moim cherche ami-moim."* Her smile slipped and staggered over her face, her voice slurred, her eyes felt dangerously close to crossing.

The men looked at her, puzzled. She tried again. *"Moin cherche ami-moin . . ."* Then she chanced: *"Une vieille—l'Anglaise—là . . ."*

"Oho, la vieille avec les bouteilles." They laughed. One pretended to be holding invisible bottles in his armpits. She hated that they laughed at Jessica and hated the way they looked at her, kept looking her over, her dress torn almost to her navel, and dirty.

She tried to summon dignity. From the tips of her toes she pulled herself tall. *"Oui, oui, c'est elle. Ou est-t'elle?"*

"Elle est partie-là." They pointed with their chins over the dark water. *"A bateau Lavel là."*

Jonnie looked out into darkness. She saw no yacht, no boat, only black water. Nevertheless, she pointed to herself. *"Moi, je vais aller au bateau Lavel là."*

Hard to speak English, impossible to speak Creole, but the men—the wonderful men—understood. But more, they made themselves understood. *"Le voilier, il va venir bientôt . . ."*

And so she waited until finally the little skiff came back to touch the jetty. Then, on hands and knees, she managed to crawl in. Sitting hunched down on the cross seat, she found herself being rowed out over pitch black water—water so black it refused to reflect the lonely light they were leaving. She couldn't see the little man, could barely make out his form where he stood at the front of the skiff. But she imagined his muscle-knotted arms and calves, short pants, old felt hat. She listened to his paddle skimming the surface of the water barely making a sound.

In the silence, Jonnie asked herself, "What am I doing out here drunk instead of in bed guarding over my poem of a child. I am responsible." She closed her eyes, trying to cover the distance between them and Old Hotel, the annex where her little charge slept—projecting her thoughts to act as the sentinel.

His voice awakened her. *"Madame, nous sommes là."*

Jonnie opened her eyes to see the hulking shadow beside which they had pulled. She had fallen asleep, and for a time she didn't know where they were or why. "I think I drank too much," she said to herself.

"Oui, madame." He hadn't known what she said, and only answered to assure her they had indeed arrived. In a daze Jonnie gazed up the side of the shadowy hulk to a light shining at its top. It reminded her of standing on the sidewalk and looking up at the Empire State Building.

Why had she come? For Jessica? What for? What could she, Jonnie Dash, do about anything that Jessica might get herself into? Did it matter? Jessica had helped her out without asking why when she needed her. Jessica needed her now.

Even in her half-drugged condition, Jonnie knew that attempting to help a drunk Jessica had to be trouble. She fought the desire to go back. The little man had already taken her hand to guide her to the aluminum ladder that hung down the side of the yacht. "Well, here I go," she joked to the silent man, who obviously didn't see anything crazy in whatever Americans chose to do.

Kicking off her sandals, she grabbed hold of the fragile handrails, hoisted herself upward, and climbed a few rungs before looking back to shout, *"Attends moi, comprends?"* He didn't answer, but she kept on climbing.

Drunk enough for courage, too drunk for balance, she clung with desperation to the unstable aluminum handrails. She kept looking up because looking down would be to court disaster. She kept thinking of Lucknair. What about him? What am I doing up here, about to kill myself, leaving him on his own? Thank God I told Cécile about Maxie.

"Worm." Jonnie heard Jessica's voice, looked down and saw only darkness, then scrambled to the top plank and on to the deck. "I've paid the price to be here," Jessica said.

"Miss Winthrop, I told you once, I will not tell you again— leave this boat." The tone, the threat in the voice, raised her concern for Jessica.

Padding on bare feet, she moved toward the light, came to a glass enclosure, an empty sitting room through which the light reflected. Walking around that room, she came suddenly upon the three standing before the open door of a stateroom. Jessica stood in obvious confrontation with Gilbert and Monique, except that she held two whiskey bottles, one under each arm.

The two had been in bed when Jessica had surprised them. Gilbert wore only the shorts of a striped pajama. Monique, her long hair flowing to her hips, wore a pink satin-and-lace teddy. Jessica, dear Jessica, so dirty and muddy, even her hair. Her clothes were in tatters and yet she hugged those two bottles of whiskey beneath her arms.

"I am not going anywhere—and what do you intend to do about it?"

"I'm going to throw you off." Gilbert spoke from thin, angry lips. He moved toward Jessica and she stood tall, firm, on her long bare feet. She swayed as though held to the floor by suction.

"Throw me off? No, I'll throw you off. I paid for this bloody barge. It belongs to me and I'll stay so long as it pleases me."

"No, you won't." Gilbert lunged toward Jessica. Jonnie stepped into their line of vision.

"Jess," she said. "I've come to get you."

"Another one?" Monique cried from her post at the stateroom door. Gilbert whirled around and stared at Jonnie as though at a ghost.

"Damn good thing," he said. "Yes, get her out of here or so help me—over the side she goes."

Jonnie approached Jessica, dimly aware that she was drunk and that under the best of conditions she'd have a hell of a time getting Jessica down that fragile ladder. So going up to Jessica, she took hold of one of the bottles. But it felt like pulling at something stuck in cement.

Had Jessica heard her? She gave no sign of recognition. Her glazed eyes had fastened total attention on Gilbert Lavel. He alone existed to her. Monique laughed, and Jonnie turned to her, begging her with her eyes.

Monique looked through Jonnie as though she did not exist. Monique's interest at the moment lay in the drama being played

out between Gilbert and Jessica. Jonnie went to Jessica, put a hand
on her shoulder.

Jessica never felt her touch. Monique laughed. And the sound
of her high, piercing laughter pierced through Jonnie, her heart,
her head. She saw them—herself and Jessica—as Monique had to,
as the men at the jetty had, as the gatekeeper had: Two old
women, drunk, dirty, looking as though they belonged on the
Bowery or its British equivalent. She lunged at Monique, caught
her by her hair, and banged her head against the door.

Tall, graceful, frail-looking, and strong. Monique came back
at Jonnie, held her head, and brought her knee to her stomach.
The wind knocked out of her, Jonnie held her stomach, waited to
breathe again before rushing the younger woman. She grabbed a
handful of hair and pulled, trying to bring her head back against
the door. Monique pushed her hard. Jonnie stumbled backward,
caught a glimpse of Jessica lifting a bottle, bringing it down on
Gilbert's head, saw blood spurt.

By then Monique was leaning over her, hitting, punching her
in her chest, her stomach. A goddess? No goddess had a right to
be that goddamn strong. Jonnie stumbled to her feet. She reached
for Monique's hair again. But from somewhere inside her head—
deep—she heard a splash, saw Gilbert walking toward them,
blood running down his face. She looked for Jessica. No Jessica.

Jonnie ran to the side of the yacht, looked down into the
darkness, ran back. But Monique and Gilbert had disappeared.
The stateroom door was closed. Locked.

Jonnie rushed to the ladder and started climbing down looking for signs. Not even the sound of a ripple disturbed the black
sea below. How long did it take someone to drown? One
minute—two? She had only climbed down halfway when she let
go of the handrail and dove. Breaking through the wet darkness,
she sank down, down, down before remembering to lift her arms
to resurface. Then down again, and still blind in the water,
searched until her hand contacted with the hull of the ship. Using
it as a guide she swam until she felt the chain—the anchor—then
surfacing again, called: "Jessica . . . Jessica . . ."

"I'm drunk," she told herself. "Still drunk." No reason to give
up. "Jessica . . . Jessica . . ."

Although she had spent much of her life on the street, she

was never in a street brawl. She had waited until she was damn near wealthy and respectable to have a drunken brawl.

Anger and shame didn't prevent her from being grateful that the water was tepid, and that, except for the darkness, she felt relieved in being away from the yacht where she came damned near to being killed. Of that she was sure.

"Jessica . . . Jessica . . ."

"A—looo, a—loooo." A faraway voice. The boat man? Oh please, let it be he. Let it be he. She stopped swimming to listen. "Help! Help! Help!"

"Alloo . . . alooo . . . alooo . . ."

"Here. I'm here," she called back, hearing oars skimming the water, hearing them draw near, nearer. . . .

A beam of light hit the water and she swam to it. The canoe came up.

"You're two simple mother's children, I hope you know that! You broads can pick the goddamnest places in the world to get drunk and go acting the fool."

"Maxie? Maxie!" She held on to the canoe. "Maxie, Jessica's out here—somewhere. . . ."

"Got her," Maxie growled. "She's on the dock out cold. She could have made it a lot damn easier if she had let go of those goddamn bottles she got stuck under her arms."

HOT WATER—WHATEVER ROUTE IT TOOK to get to the pipes, faucets of bathrooms—had to be the world's greatest invention. Letting the scalding shower loosen the mud from her matted hair, melt dirt from her body, and beat against the lumps and bruises, watching the grime and grit rush down the drain, she felt childish in her happiness. Maxie had come back. He had deposited her at her door. She had crawled into the bathroom to bring life back into her body—and had found hot water.

Drunken bums, Maxie had called them. But Jonnie had been sober by then. Maxie had thought her drunk because she had rambled on about him being her savior. She had done a lot of talking about what had happened and how she had changed and how she had missed him. But when she had wanted to tell him about Lucknair, he had stopped her. "Will you shut up," he had said. Wet and dirty and feeling like hell, she had postponed the telling until the morning.

She turned off the shower and heard drums. That, too, surprised her, like the hot water. They had ceased since the storm. Their resumption meant that life and living had prevailed against the odds—against all odds.

Lying across the bed, eyes closed, she tuned her hearing to movements outside. But the room began to spin. Upset, she sat up. "I'm not supposed to be drunk," she muttered, "it's just that goddamn alcohol." She lay back on the pillow and listened only to the drums. . . .

The pounding of the drums in her head grew loud, louder; it became a rapping on the door, the window. She kept dreaming of a voice calling her. It kept calling! "Jonnie, Jonnie—I demand that you open the door."

Then she sat up, struggling to stand, to walk. "Jonnie, do you hear me? Open the door this instant." Dazed, Jonnie looked around, saw her robe at the foot of the bed, struggled into it, and moved to open the door.

Stephan pushed into the room, then stood staring at her, his eyes lit with anger. "You wanted her dead!" he accused.

"No!" Jonnie cried out in anguish. How long had dinner been? Days? Weeks? This horrible night with its bizarre twists and turns, its nightmarish qualities—drunkenness. No, this same night, from a dinner show to a hot shower—and still more to come?

"How could I want her dead?" Jonnie asked. "An orphan. A poor deserted child. How could I want her dead?"

"I should have held a mirror up to your face!" Stephan cried. "You're evil, Jonnie Dash. I saw her death wish on your face."

"But I wasn't the one doing the killing," she shouted. "Jessica was."

She had said those words and wanted to unsay them. Guilty, guilty, guilty. She did share Jessica's guilt. But guilt of what?

"Jessica was drunk," Stephan said.

Accusing her? Jessica was allergic to the stuff. Everybody knew that. But she? She had her madness to blame. Had he taken that into account?

No! She had left her madness in the Haitian countryside. She no longer had madness to hide behind. "I wanted you dead!" Jonnie cried. "You had abused her—that poor orphan. . . ."

So now she had become a liar, a hypocrite, an ordinary woman, upset because it had been so easy for him to find another.

"I made love to her," Stephan said.

"A child. A mindless child!"

"She's not nine," Stephan said, and the drums in the distance heightened their beat, attacking Jonnie's temples.

"She's sick," Jonnie said, putting her hands to her temples.

"Young," Stephan corrected her, and that word hung between them, blazed between them. "Young—and she can bear children. I'm taking her away—to the States—tomorrow. And Jonnie, I expect to spend the rest of my life making her well again."

He walked to the door, and in anger Jonnie leaped to bar his way. He pushed her. She reached out, raking her fingernails into his face, then stood back to watch the blood slowly come.

He caught and held her wrists.

"And me?" she mocked. "This one who's not so young? And Jessica? Doesn't she need looking after? Are we two old dears—one to feed the belly, the other to feed the ego, the need for the exotic?"

How good to be angry. Anger stronger than madness. A healthy anger—anger in defense of a thing called dignity. Anger just as much against herself as at him—perhaps more so. Because in her madness she had seen him as a gallant knight, a hero undaunted by the quirks and prejudices of ordinary mortals. More of Jessica's literature? In her eyes he now had been reduced to this cat who needed to fuck someone who might bear him a child—a Henshaw. And that was so goddamn ordinary.

4

URGENCY. SHE FELT THE NEED TO GET OUT. She had to see what had happened, was happening, a crisis that was affecting her. She had to get to the door, through the door. But her attack on Stephan had taken the last of her strength. She lay back on the bed and fell asleep in layers. Down, down she went, with one layer easing anxiety, another layer folding over her, comforting her. With pleasure she gave into the luxury of sleep, and then . . .

"Jonnie, Jonnie, are you in there?" She hugged her comfort, trying not to hear. "Jonnie, Jonnie, wake up. Do you hear me?"

One thought: Lucknair. She jerked herself awake. Sat up in bed, her heart pounding. The banging kept up at the door. She opened it for Claire.

"Jonnie, Jessica is in the hospital. I just came back from there. Her head's been fractured."

Still drugged from whiskey and sleep, Jonnie washed her face in cold water to see, to hear Claire. After Maxie had dropped her off at her door she had thought, if indeed she had that ability, he had taken Jessica to her room.

"Maxie brought her home and put her to bed after he dropped you at your door. God knows what the two of you were doing—at the jetty. Then he noticed her face. She had been so badly beaten. Jonnie, I don't know if she's going to make it. . . ."

JESSICA'S FACE WAS SWOLLEN beyond recognition. Her head swathed in bandages had assumed frightening proportions. Her tall frame stretched out on the single bed—long, still, deathlike. Looking down at her, Jonnie clutched her chest at the pain shafting through her, ravaging her, holding her to the side of the bed, helpless. Pain at seeing this strong woman—fallen.

Then she put her lips to her ear and whispered, "Hey, girl, didn't I tell you knights in shining armor ain't no more." She stared at the thick bandaged head, the waxen face, waiting for a reaction: a hint of a smile around the lips, a quiver of a muscle in the cheek, the beating of a vein. No movement. No life.

"Yeah, but these mother's children—that took their places calling themselves men—ain't nothing but crippled maggots playing in shit. They can't do us in. We won't let them—will we?"

"I don't think she can hear you," the doctor standing behind her said. A Haitian doctor with an American accent—tall, slim, intelligent-looking. "Is she in a coma?" Jonnie asked.

"She's been unconscious since she was brought in. We took X rays. But we don't have modern facilities. We must wait to know the extent of the damage." Silently he looked down at the still woman. "What if she doesn't recover? Such a good woman." He spoke with a sense of helplessness. "Whoever did this deserves to be stoned. I love her," he said. Jonnie looked up at the tall, handsome Black man, his tears.

"It is bad, then, doctor?"

"We all loved her," he said, speaking in the past tense. "She loved her work. She gave us strength, money—her heart. There will never be another like her. We love her so much. . . ." He sobbed, then controlled himself to answer Jonnie's question. "We don't know. We don't know. . . ." He walked away.

Watching the prone figure, Jonnie thought of Jessica's seven-league stride, her yellow-ribbon hat flopping—belonging, a woman who belonged everywhere and looked at home wherever.

How proud she had been to know this woman whom she had

never asked one favor, but who had done a great one without having to know the whats, the whys, even if it had meant her life.

Proud of this white woman of whom she had been jealous. Jealous? Yes. Jealous because their lives had been so different. Jealous because from birth Jessica had had the means that prepared her to face life fearlessly—truthfully. She had despised her for being at home in Haiti, while she, Jonnie Dash, had expected history and race to be her entry, only to find herself an outsider— *la blanche aux cheveux frisés.*

Deeper yet her envy because Jessica knew Africa well—knew the continent that had forged her identity along with that of all Haitians—linking them. Africa, which she, Jonnie Dash, might yet know, but which most Haitians never would.

Yet Jessica had lived there and had loved there and had suffered there, while all their suffering had been done in the harshness, the ugliness, the nightmare of greed as Jessica's people plundered this hemisphere—their "New World."

Yes, why not jealousy when Jessica had had the means while she was still young. The means to have made of her life an adventure. While she, Jonnie Dash, had been thrown into the streets. Boysie was her adventure—fighting to survive, hiding in the shadows of half-truths, downright lies, lies carrying over into Emmanuel's life, poverty forming the curve of her soul. Poverty preparing her for the struggle of survival, her duel with madness.

They had known each other such a short time. Four weeks—days overlapping days—making of the slow movement of time on this island four years. Here they were. The miracle of Jessica Winthrop could not end on this bed, beaten to death by a junkie.

Jonnie laid her cheek against the bandaged head, whispered, "Jessica, Jessica—this time, too, will pass. Dear, dear Jessica, you shall not leave me. You must not leave me. I cannot bear the thought. Not now. Not now. . . ."

Surely if Jessica were going to die, it should have been in Africa with the death of her Doctor Faye and her hopelessness at ever finding another in the entire world to replace him.

"I died with him," she had said. And in that great expanse she called soul, she had curled up, joined him, indeed, had dedicated her physical life, her grief, to him. Yes, that long time ago she would have died and they would never have become friends. "And she cannot, will not die at the hands of a junkie."

CLAIRE ACCOMPANIED JONNIE to the lounge, where the American contingent had assembled to hear Captain Gilbert Lavel's charges against her and Jessica. They had intruded on his property and attacked his person and that of his companion. Archibald Wilson, Major Windfield, and Admiral Clarke—judges and juries of crimes done to, or by, American citizens—were already seated at a hastily pulled together conference table. Charles McCellen sat with them. That startled Jonnie.

Of course he knew that she was the so-called fiancée, of whom Gérard had spoken. He knew that she had been responsible for Lucknair being at Gérard's mountain cabin—and he held her responsible for his loss.

Claire's determined innocence had kept Jonnie from confiding to her that her freckled baby-faced counselor, his behind-the-scenes intriguing with army and *tonton macoute* and perhaps the police, had been responsible for the invasion of the hotel, the wrecking of the orphanage, creating hardship for Mrs. Thompson and the orphans, and the hounding almost to death of one poor little boy.

Jonnie sat facing the men, waiting for their questions to begin. And as she waited, it was again like waiting for her first brush with justice—American justice—in the New York City court system. Emmanuel had been accused of stealing. She had waited through the case of a white boy whose parents had pleaded that it was the first time their child had done wrong—shoplifting. They promised he'd never do it again. The judge let him go.

Then it had been her turn. Emmanuel had been accused of stealing a woman's pocketbook. He claimed he had found it. The woman said he had snatched it. Jonnie, too, had pleaded that it had been his first offense; she, too, had promised he would never do it again. "Spare jail and help the child," she had pleaded. But the judge had snarled at her, "That's the trouble with you people—always blaming the cure for the crime. If you mothers would . . . Remand him."

"Mrs. Dash." Jonnie realized that Major Windfield had been

speaking. "We understand that you, too, were an unwelcome visitor to Captain Lavel's yacht last evening?" Sun-bronzed, indolent, hairy chest exposed. He leaned back, smiling that familiar I-know-you-so-well smile. But he didn't know her well. He never would know her well even if given one hundred years. "Mrs. Dash . . . ?

"I wasn't welcome . . . ?" Jonnie hedged. What had Gilbert Level meant in calling this investigation when Jessica was lying close to death? And why had they involved Charles McCellen?

"You did go aboard Captain Lavel's yacht—with Miss Winthrop—I understand."

"Is this a case against Mrs. Winthrop?" Jonnie asked.

"I don't recall saying this is a case against anyone, Mrs. Dash. There's no reason to be hostile."

"I wasn't aware of my hostility," Jonnie said. "I am being questioned, and I can only answer questions that concern me." Charles McCellen kept staring at her, his hatred of her burning through her cheek.

"It's a simple enough question, Mrs. Dash. Did you go to Captain Lavel's yacht the night before last with Miss Winthrop?"

"Yes, I did go to Captain Lavel's yacht. No, I did not go with Miss Winthrop."

"Whom did you go with?"

"I went alone."

"Alone—uninvited?"

"Yes."

"May I ask why?"

Jonnie blinked, thinking hard. Why indeed? What had she thought to accomplish out there on that black, black sea? She hadn't thought. She had no answer to why. She must have gone to save Jessica. From what? She hadn't thought that out.

Drunk, drunk, drunk. Jonnie sighed, shook her head, stilling an urge to laugh. And she might have laughed if Jessica wasn't lying in bed, beaten up. How to start explaining that Gilbert had grabbed Jessica, had pulled her away, without telling of Jessica's attack with the bottle? How to tell she hadn't seen Gilbert actually hit Jessica? She had been too busy fighting. Yet she knew Gilbert Lavel had beaten Jessica before throwing her overboard.

"Why?" she repeated. "You see, I had never been on Captain Lavel's yacht before—I was never invited."

"Are you telling me . . . ?"

"Major," Claire said, interrupting him. "With all due respect for this line of questioning, something very serious has happened. We can't let Gilbert Lavel get away with what he did. This is a charade."

"Claire, my dear," Archibald Wilson said, injecting fatherly caution. "You were not there."

"Whether she was or not"—Sam came charging into the lounge—"I was about to bring a charge of swindling against Gilbert Lavel. But now it's sounding more like a case of murder!"

The word hung in the air, hovered over their heads.

Jonnie stood up, looked around the table, and walked from the lounge. Leaving the main building, Jonnie went to the room where Lucknair was hiding. He and Cécile were sitting on the floor playing a game with stones. *"Viens avec moi,"* she commanded. Taking his hand, she pulled him along to the main building, into the lounge, and up to the table.

By the time she returned, drinks had been ordered in an obvious intention to change the atmosphere. "Oh, come now, Sam," Archibald Wilson was saying with it's-a-man's-world attitude. "We can't let the faint heart of a dowdy, disillusioned British dowager turn into capital offense against one of our boys."

"That dowdy British dowager happens to be the woman I love," Sam answered.

These powerful authorities called together to disembowel one woman had their weapons blunted by Sam's honesty.

"Gentlemen, I take it that your inquiry is over? I'm sure you no longer have need for my assistance," Jonnie said. "I'm glad. I'm getting ready to leave this island and there are things I must take care of before I go."

They all looked at her. She kept her eyes on Major Wilson, but saw Charles McCellen where he sat, his glass half raised, his lips dry, his eyes staring, the thinness of his nostrils, chalk white, flaring. His face red, reddening. She felt Lucknair start, try to pull away from her, ready to run. She held on to his shoulders with a firm grip. Smiling, polite. She had learned the way of the diplomat.

"A fine-looking boy you have there, Mrs. Dash," Admiral Clarke said. "He's Haitian, isn't he? Planning to adopt him?"

"Yes, Admiral. I have already adopted him. He's an orphan. His name is Lucknair. He's absolutely captured my heart."

"Wonderful. Wonderful. There are so many poor and homeless children here on this island. We're always trying to encourage Americans of means . . . Americans who care—to try that route. Adoption. It's good for the country—and for U.S.-Haitian relations. I'm sure the embassy will give you all the assistance necessary—right, Charles?"

"Wonderful," Jonnie said, waited for Charles to answer, then she repeated, "Wonderful." She turned and looked into Charles McCellen's eyes. They had never spoken. They didn't speak now. They simply stared at each other. His eyes hard with hatred.

No, she sent him back her message. You shall not have this child. He shall never be yours to have.

What could he do—now—this minute? Challenge her? She wished he would. Send in the army? The *tonton macoute?* No. She had claimed her victory right in the center of his—their—great power morality.

Taking Lucknair's hand, she walked from the lounge with long strides, back to where Cécile waited at the door, suspicious, fearful.

"Bonne Cécile," she said. "Now you can take Lucknair to Captain Maxie."

An exquisite sense of elation overpowered her. She had challenged authority and had not been swept into tongue-tied oblivion. It had been so simple after all. She laughed, kept laughing, and then remembered: she had not yet talked to Maxie about Lucknair. . . .

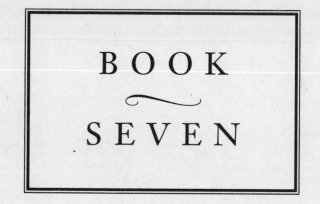

BOOK

SEVEN

EVERYTHING HAD HAPPENED SO QUICKLY in this place where slow motion had been the rule. Tomorrow and tomorrow and tomorrow collided. There was nothing left to do but leave. She had sent Lucknair to Maxie. She didn't doubt that Maxie would keep him safe or that Lucknair would be content. So he wasn't going to the States. He had to understand that he needed time. He needed to grow more before he made up his mind. She had no doubt he would get there—if he kept wanting to.

While waiting for Cécile to return, she began to pack. She packed with the door open, waiting for the men to finish their talk in the lounge and leave. Such a weight had fallen from her shoulders. She no longer had to fear spies, the army, or M'sieur Constant. Charles McCellen, still drinking in the lounge with the American contingent, was probably contemplating his next move. Whatever retaliation he might try—and he was a vindictive man— he dared not move against Lucknair. Only against her. Jonnie shrugged. She had done everything she knew how to gain what she wanted most. Now let him do his worst. She had come to a graceful state—she no longer had fears.

Then she thought of Maxie. She had not really seen him. Through her haze of whiskey and water she thought she had heard his voice, and heard that he had saved her life—hers and Jessica's. What if it hadn't been him? What if Cécile came back with the bad news that Maxie had gone again. Maxie had changed the berth for his boat. Maxie had said no. To Lucknair? Impossible.

Jonnie stepped outside as shadows deepened around newly planted hedges to settle softly on the grassy island separating the annex from the main building. She surveyed the forestlike trees that stretched out, belligerently defending the back gardens, the hotel. Jonnie felt a sadness overcome her.

She had, it seemed, lived many lives since coming to Haiti. She had confronted her madness and now had challenged Charles McCellen. She had come a long way. Now, as shadows gave way to gloom, she sensed an approaching emptiness. That emptiness, which upon hearing of Aunt Olga's death, had driven her to this island in search of Gérard—chasing thirty-year-old dreams—weak straws in a brutal wind—ghosts of times past—dreams turned to dust, turned to ash.

She thought of Stephan, remembered clearly the passion spent, yet felt no pain in his loss, not even a twinge of jealousy.

This must be the way men feel after the pleasure of ejaculating between the soft thighs of an unloved woman, then walking away. But lasting tenderness came with bosoms, with ovaries—things like that. Maxie. She had to get to Maxie.

The cars of the American contingent raced around the curve, leaving the grounds, and Cécile still hadn't returned. Gloom turned to dark. Nothing could happen—or could it? Cécile would take Lucknair to Biscentnaire, to the wharf where Maxie moored his boat, and tell him of the boy's plight. Then Maxie would take him away. Or would he? Of course she had to go to him—explain. She had money. She could always get some to him—if he accepted—or would he?

Jonnie went into her room, closed her valise, then saw the wooden flute on the dresser. She had intended to give it to Lucknair. She picked it up—weighed it in her hand. How had she come upon it? She didn't know. Did she want to know? A mystery. Another happening on that moonlit night. Pushing it to the bottom of her valise, she closed the lid.

THE LOUNGE AND THE BAR WERE EMPTY except for the waiters preparing tables or sitting out on the terrace, laughing, talking, not expecting many guests for dinner.

She looked around for Claire and Sam, and not seeing them, went into the bar.

"There you are, Jonnie Dash." Jonathan Anderson sat at the bar. "I was hoping to have a chance to say good-bye. Roxanne and I are leaving tomorrow morning," he said. "We were set to go today, but then we heard about Jessica. . . ."

Jonnie nodded. Actually she had nothing to say to him. She no longer disliked him. Nor did she like him. "Jess is in a bad way," she said.

"Yes," he sighed. "I'm sorry. However, I wanted to thank you for looking after Roxanne during my many absences." His smile barely touched his eyes. "I guess you and I shall be meeting again—perhaps in the States. We'll have lunch. . . . I'm looking forward to it."

Of course he expected no such thing. Only on this little island, living in this hotel, had they chanced to meet and move together. But of course, for Jonathan Anderson, all possibilities remained open. He would beat his wife, ride her back, make love to women, boys, girls, the world over. Perhaps they might meet again.

She liked that he had remembered her name the day when going to Chez Renard. She liked that he pretended that she had done him important favors. The secret of his power—his success. He wedged himself in people's memories, making it difficult to forget him.

Nicholas approached with a bourbon for Jonathan and, for a moment, she saw again Dominique's cherub smiling face and thought of the world he had tried to structure around the bar, the crazy-quilt patterns of hopes, dreams, of better tomorrows.

"Jonathan, do me a favor, will you?" Jonnie studied his handsome, smiling face. "Tell Roxanne for me—be happy."

Jonnie hailed a taxi for Biscentnaire. And as it made its way toward the pier, she hunched in the darkest corner of the seat and

kept her mind hovering over Jessica. Over Lucknair. Not actually
thinking, keeping them safe, keeping them alive. As she had kept
Emmanuel. It had worked. Only when her thoughts had shifted to
other things, her factory work, bills, and finally her paintings, dis-
tracting her, did trouble overtake them—the inevitable knock on
the door. . . .

So now she kept her head in the shadows, her mind, hovering
over the unconscious Jessica and the restless Lucknair.

The taxi stopped. Shouts, excited voices reached her in the
corner. *"Qu'est-ce qui se passe?"* Jonnie demanded.

"Il y a un incendie, madame."

Fire! Jonnie peered out the window and saw people milling
around the car, preventing traffic from moving. She heard whispers, excited exchanges of people not wanting to be heard or
quoted, yet nevertheless they were heard and quoted—like prayers
repeated by multitudes. *"C'est le palais . . . Le palais, oui . . ."*

Fire at the palace? The honking of car horns from cars
wedged in by crowds—*camionettes*, tap-taps, donkey carts, private
cars, taxis. Gridlocked. Loud sirens of fire engines, a glow in the
skies. Indeed a great fire. Jonnie pushed against the weight of bodies to get the car door open. Then she had to work through the
crowd: hundreds of people, their faces glowing red as the fire
brightened. Young boys climbing over gridlocked traffic, over the
roofs of stalled cars, to better see tongues of orange red flames
leaping toward the sky.

New York rush hour subway experience helped her push her
way through the throngs—waiting, the slight turn, the intake of
breath, pushing, shoving, gaining inch by hard-won inch, moving
from the center of traffic along the corniche to the sidewalk, then
pushing forward to the dirt of unpaved road beneath her feet.

Here, the crowd grew thinner, although still pushing in from
the countryside, to join those already in the center of town.

Crowds joining crowds, blanketing the road, moving against
Jonnie, pushing in the opposite direction.

Then she was no longer pushing. Arms had gone around her.
Someone whispered in her ear. "Knew it had to be you. That
white suit's a dead giveaway." Maxie! He had come out to join
those looking up at the brightening sky, his face as inscrutable as
the surrounding onlookers'.

"They say it's the palace," Jonnie whispered. "What do you think?"

"Don't start me to lying," Maxie answered.

"Who could have started it?" Jonnie asked.

"Who said anybody started it?" Maxie answered.

"Someone had to."

"You working for the CIA, the *tonton macoute*, or some such?" He spoke, still looking to the sky. "Jonnie, give me a break. Let's just say it must have been a massive voodoo concentration, or that someone's dreams came true. Nobody's going to start a fire like that unless they have something to back it up. Folks here have started to dig the basics of modern life. The guy with the gun wins."

"Is it that simple?" Jonnie asked, not wanting to continue. They hadn't said hello, and here they were, already into politics.

"Believe me, believe me, it was forever thus," Maxie said. "The ones who made up the lie about right winning over might— all have been sacrificed for the common good. It's not even a question of who wins. We know that might makes right. Once upon a time it was said that the pen is mightier than the sword. That was before TV. Now everybody knows it's about guns. When the mighty gods say War, little mindless bastards get ready. It's that simple."

"No, life's not that simple, Maxie," Jonnie protested.

"Go ahead and complicate it," Maxie said, and pulled her deeper into his soft embrace. "Go on, Jonnie Dash, complicate my life. For example—tell me why you came to Haiti if not to meet and make love to me."

Jonnie laughed in relief. Her sexual response to him sprang to life. His arms around her, his words—even spoken in jest— shattered her recent calm. She tried to remind herself once again of the years between them—years that stretched around curves, over ravines, through seemingly insurmountable barriers.

"I wanted to belong somewhere," she answered, wanting to add: "and to somebody."

"Go on, Jonnie Dash. Admit it. You came here to get out from under the gun and found yourself down its muzzle—no space to run. And talking about muzzle, what about that brat you sent here to me?"

"Lucknair? So they made it?" Her throat tightened with tears. Relief. Not until that moment had she accepted that they might have reached safety, despite the confidence she had in Cécile. "Where is he?"

"Sleeping." Maxie gave a jerk of his head toward the sea.

"What did you do? Give the kid drugs?" Jonnie joked.

"No. I guess he's tired of running and hiding," Maxie replied.

"He must be happy that he's here with you," she said.

"Are you joking?" Maxie cried. "He tried to get away from your girl. Said you had sold him out. He ran off for a while. But she found him, brought him back, and told me to hold on to him until you came. I held him. He went to sleep."

"You're joking, Maxie."

"Yeah, said that he trusted you and that you took him to the very man he had been running from. Who is this M'sieur Charles, anyhow?"

Jonnie looked away from him. No use telling Maxie about his American counselor and risk starting an international incident. She intended to do something about M'sieur Charles—write to the State Department, to the President, when this was all over. But not before, and not until Lucknair was safely on his way.

"I gave him his freedom, Maxie. I sent him to you."

"To me? I'm no big-time baby-sitter."

"You said you wanted children—so I gave you a child." Jonnie spoke in a light tone to give her self-confidence. Maxie could not turn away from her, from them.

"Yeah, but I'm not ready to settle down with pots and pans and such," Maxie said. "I want to start off with diapers."

"I depended on you," Jonnie said, her voice cracking with tears.

"Hey, don't." Maxie pulled her closer. "You sent him. I'm keeping him. What's to cry about? I'm getting out of here with the morning tide. Just waiting for the tide. Take him anywhere he wants to go—Florida, Cuba, Jamaica—he'll be old enough to choose by the time we leave Brazil. But first it's Brazil. He's safe, baby. He is safe."

"What about scallops?"

"On the way. I'm leaving with the morning tide. Got to stop off in Cuba to close a deal, then away. Got boat, will travel."

"You were going without saying good-bye?"

"I never say good-bye. I don't believe in it."

"So, I just caught you in time?"

"Jonnie, that storm did something to me. I believe in the order of nature. And nature is saying something to us, Jonnie. It's saying we're not doing enough fast enough." He laughed. "A revolutionary got to take time out to think. I'm glad about the kid. He gives me reason to think—and the chance to see you again."

"At any rate, Lucknair will be glad to be with you."

"Not the way he tells it. He accused me of being like you. Hah." Maxie's belly shook with laughter. "I told him no—that I was his Black American brother," and he said, *"Aime pas les Américains."*

Tears clogged Jonnie's throat. How had she, of all people, become the ugly Black American? Sobs shook her body.

"Hey!" Maxie cried, and led her from the road down the path to the rickety wooden wharf where his boat was moored. "He didn't really mean it. He was scared—poor kid."

Jonnie kept on crying, and Maxie said, "I know, I know. You had a hard time. It's not every night you get fished out of the water, drunk. Then you had to go through this trauma—getting rid of an ungrateful kid."

He spoke in a tone designed to make her laugh. She did. "He's a wise kid," she said. "I suppose he did have reasons to doubt me." Yet she knew she had not failed him.

But she had needed tears. More than being fished out of the water, the storm had been hard, harsh. Oversensitive, she knew now that there were not tears enough in the entire world to make up for her failure with Lucknair, her lifetime with Emmanuel.

"Feel better?" Maxie asked, as they stepped from the wharf into his boat. A yacht. A small one, compact. Not at all the tub Jonnie had imagined. Over fifty feet, it was made of wood, its deck gleamed, its cabinets were highly polished and sturdy. Starboard, which had been specially constructed for fishing, was well kept—organized. Obviously Maxie took better care of his yacht than of himself.

"She's got four bunks and sleeps eight," Maxie bragged. "She can go around the world four times and folks never bump into each other. Whatever old Jess said, I can give one hell of a cruise."

He took her into the stateroom, where she found herself

looking at something so familiar that it caught at her heartstrings: her first sketch of M'sieur Ambroise.

"How did you get that?" she asked.

"The boy brought it."

"Lucknair."

"Yeah, he had it stashed when he left the house. That's where he went when he ran away from Cécile. When she had to go looking for him, I knew you had sent me trouble. And then he brought this."

"He liked it. . . ." Gratitude to him for having liked something she had done. For having risked himself. The peasants hadn't liked it. They laughed at it. But he—he knew.

Maxie took her into the cramped cabin with the squeezed-together bunk beds. On one Lucknair lay, curled up in sleep. Looking down at him she noticed that, again, he had leaves in his hair. The skin of his face, his long legs curled now beneath him, were ashy. Cécile had cared for him in the annex, not she. In their times of meeting and parting she had never even combed his hair or hugged him close—little things that said I care. Yet she did care, very much.

She rubbed his head, wanting him to open his eyes, wanting once again to see life in his dark face, feel the excitement in those wide, black eyes, with their sliver of white, their intenseness.

"You like him," Maxie said. He had been watching her, reading her expression.

"He's a poem," Jonnie answered.

"I'm not talking about his looks."

"Yes, I love him—he's a child that people love. He refuses to be pushed in places he doesn't like—he has no place to be pushed into—your kind of child."

Back on deck, Jonnie sat holding her knees to her chest, cradled by the motion of the boat, straining to hear the reactions of those on the road. Maxie brought drinks from the cabin, sat beside her, and together they gazed up at the reflections of the fire in the sky.

A nostalgia, a remembrance of once-upon-a-time, when she and Gérard and Emmanuel had been together and had loved each other, that moment in time when she had felt safe.

That time had been doomed to end, just as this night, too,

had to end. Tomorrow, Lucknair and Maxie would sail away with the tide, possibly never to be seen again.

Pain shafted her at the thought. "I have money," she said. "Wherever you go, whatever you need, write. Write to me in care of Claire at Old Hotel. I don't know where I'll be, but I will keep in touch. She'll know where I can be reached."

He played with the tips of her fingers, his cheek against her head. "I expected you to come with your things all packed ready to go. You are my woman, you know. I didn't think you could resist me."

It had been hard. She had thought of bringing her valise. But Cécile hadn't come back. And she had found herself playing the game: May I? No, you may not. May I? Yes, you may. And so she had come without it.

They sat on the deck, hands laced, waiting for the fire to die, for the excited voices to hush and be gone from the road. Those voices now raised, and still rising, keeping them attuned—wedded to the fragile universe, adding dimensions to the importance of their being together.

"See what you've been missing, milady?" he said. "I got all this to offer. Instead, you go messing around that hotel with a bunch of crazies. . . ."

Like youth, he aimed for the big picture. Streetwise, he had come away with snapshots.

"I was the crazy on that scene, Maxie. I came to this island crazy—mad." How did one explain to him who was so young? So sane?

"But there's that about Haiti, Maxie; it peels layers away, bit by bit, exposes one, forces one to see right down to the bare bones."

"That's because it's such a goddamn poor country," Maxie said.

"Yes, yes," Jonnie said, snatching at his words with hope. He understood. "Poverty is hell, Maxie. In the States or here in Haiti, or anywhere. But in the States, in all of the countries in this hemisphere, north and south, where the heirs of Africa live and were promised rewards for hard work, only to be denied the rewards— we become dreamers. We shout loud over our puny successes, then blame ourselves for our failures. Dreamers don't make for a better people—having to struggle on inner city streets, or with the dead or dying earth only makes for hunger and frustration and ultimately abuse.

"My son, Emmanuel, was so beautiful. Never have I loved someone more. Yet, all I had to offer him was the street full of dreams—lies really. What madness to think dreams can survive on the cracked sidewalks of slums. Madness to think one can protect the young by blowing balloons and floating them in the air. That's madness, Maxie—madness."

Side by side on the listing boat, toes playing with toes, the sound of the sea constant, dozens of people at the water's edge, whispering, excited, intense, she remembered suddenly she hadn't heard the chant of that old man—not since the storm.

"Methinks that thee came to me because thee wants to fuck," Maxie said to change the subject. And pulling away from the cradling comfort of his arms, she answered, "Hush your mouth. Fuck's a dirty word."

"Only for those too young or too crazy," he chided. "Now that your young Stephan went off with his Lady Godiva, what you need is a good fuck."

"My, but you do keep up with the life and times of Old Hotel," Jonnie joked.

"There's always someone who tells. Lucky, too, or else you and Jessica would have been out there in the ocean and never known what killed you. Loose talk brought Sir Maxie to the rescue."

"Jessica—has to make it, doesn't she, Maxie?"

"Jessica and her death wish," Maxie said. "And you got caught up in it."

"You blame Jessica?"

"Who else? Jessica is an intelligent woman, Jonnie. She has eyes that can spot suckers like Gilbert Lavel and Jean-Pierre—except when she wants to be blind."

"You blame her because she likes excitement? Because she likes young men?"

"No. Because Jessica is wise and understands the difference between excitement and adventure. . . ."

"And me? What about me sitting here next to you with my toes curling with desire. Is this excitement or adventure?"

"It's love. We have this thing going for each other."

"Stop it. My son was older than you."

"But I have no age, Jonnie. And you'll never grow old. Where are you going when you leave Haiti? Back to the States?"

"I haven't decided yet—certainly not to the States."

"Then it's on to Brazil."

How she wished it. How she wished that they had been around the same age, that they had fought through the Black Revolution, that she had shouted "Power to the people!" marching side by side with him. And that they could sail side by side, understanding as they did now, the kind of consciousness that made people strive, not as victims, but as people, demanding control of their lives.

"Yes, yes, Jonnie Dash, say yes and we'll shove off this minute. I won't even wait for the tide. We won't care. It doesn't matter if the sea's calm or stormy. We'll have us a ball, Jonnie Dash."

Brazil? Why not Brazil? Where to, if not Brazil? Why not sail the sea with this intensely free, this intensely sexy, lovable young man and her poem of a boy? She laughed. Her happy-ever-after dream come true?

What was she thinking? Had she changed her mind because he had cupped her breasts, because he had kissed her with soft, full lips? Because he handled her so possessively? Had she decided because his tongue searched through her mouth, because he had pulled her head against his damp chest? Here, after all, was where she wanted to be. Where she longed to be. Or was this another shift of mind, proof of instability? Was she still mad?

She did love him. They were a part of some grand design—they had the same emotional pattern, except that he had held on to sanity. What difference their years? Something profound within him told her. His caressing hands told her he might joke but he did understand well her troubled past; he bled for her—and wanted to share with her. The sea? Why not the sea to fill that emptiness, that terrible emptiness waiting to engulf her?

Enfolded in his embrace, pressed into his soft bigness, his breasts—a mother's breasts against her cheeks—waves of tenderness washed up from her curling toes to tingle her body, spreading through her, spreading through her. . . .

She had come wanting this moment. She had come wanting to feel his nakedness next to hers. To have their smooth flesh rubbing one against the other, to have him enter her, penetrate her with his thick, hard prick right to the core of her.

And it had to do with life, the orgasm that spun her, kept her spinning out out into the starless smoke-filled night. It had to do with life. . . .

"So," he whispered. "Thought you were leaving—getting away from me, were you?"

"Never," she whispered. "I never want to leave you. Never ever want to get away from you. Do you hear? Never—ever."

"Then it's on to Brazil?"

"On to Brazil," Jonnie laughed. "On to Brazil."

FROM A PROFOUND SLEEP, she woke sensing danger. Jonnie lay still. Beside her, Maxie slept, breathing heavily. She lay in the crook of his cushioning arm, listening. Whispers from the road had stopped. A breeze had blown, was blowing smoke into wisps of chiffon. Night sounds—the croaking of frogs, the distant crowing of roosters—countryside in full somnolence. Snuggling closer to Maxie, Jonnie matched his breathing, letting sleep once again pull her under.

It happened again. She opened her eyes. This time she came to full consciousness. She looked up, around. The smoke had dissipated. An early morning pink tinted the air. Overhead a pride of flamingos, as pink as the sky, winged southward. Had they awakened her?

Closing her eyes, Jonnie lay, silent, until another wave hit the hull of the listing boat, sending sprays splashing over its sides. Water rushed over the deck, flowed beneath her, wetting her back, then emptied back into the sea. Again and again it happened. Waves hitting the sides of the boat, water splashing over its sides, rushing, covering the deck, wetting her back, her hair, racing back into the sea.

Jonnie jumped to her feet, snatched up her clothes that had been scattered around the deck. Holding them to her, she climbed out of the boat to the wharf, ran its length, stopped by the roadside to pull on her wet things, and running to the boulevard, hailed a taxi.

Getting into the car, she gave the driver her destination, sitting at the edge of the seat, her heart beating hard, breath coming in spurts, urging the driver on, needing distance between herself and the sleeping Maxie. Staring out into the early morning, the smell of smoke stinging her nostrils, she could only see bold headlines in the *New York Times:* BLACK ARTIST DIES OF PNEUMONIA. ILLNESS DUE TO EXPOSURE AT HAITIAN PORT.

Driving through streets deserted except for soldiers stopping an occasional car, Jonnie wrung her hands in desperation, relaxing only when Old Hotel came into view.

Then a paroxysm of laughter convulsed her. Uncontrolled laughter forced her to bend over, holding her stomach. The taxi driver looked over his shoulder, his eyes wide and round with terror. He kept darting terrified glances in the rearview mirror, as he hunched over the wheel, pressed hard on the gas, racing through the streets. Jonnie laughed even harder.

She longed to talk to Jessica. She wanted to say to her: "Never did I know I had taken my fame so seriously. There I lay in the arms of the man I wanted most to be with. And what do I do?" She heard Jessica's response: "My dear, you know, at our age . . ."

Yes, she knew. Her action hadn't been as spontaneous as it appeared. She hadn't brought her valise.

Since her confrontation with madness, she had rid herself of fear, of anxieties. Her habitual inner turmoil, the turbulence, her driving force—which had brought her from there to here. The constant grief, the tears, the wall of pain on which she had beaten her life, and which had held her to her madness, existed no more. Such agony belonged to the young—and she was no longer so young.

She had assuaged her guilt. Lucknair had called her "friend" and she had run from him. Since then she had changed deeply. She had been a good friend, faced her responsibility, she had brought Lucknair to the man she most loved and trusted. And hell, after all, had she not confronted the devious, placid-faced diplomat, representative of the power on this island and of the world? It pleased her to accept that as her *raison d'être.*

Still smiling when the taxi drew up at the gate, Jonnie paid the driver, tipping him extra for his speed and his terror. On her way to the annex she noticed the lights on in the main building and went there instead.

But as she walked up the steps humor deserted her. Going through the entrance, past the darkened bar, a sense of doom assailed her. At the doorway of the well-lit lounge, she stopped to observe what appeared to her to be a staged scene.

Characters walked around in pantomime in search of their parts. Beneath the chandelier a group of servants had clustered. Cécile, upon seeing Jonnie, walked up to her. Claire and Sam, in their bathrobes, looked bewildered. Jonathan Anderson sat in a stuffed chair, waiting it seemed, for a cue. Guests in their night-clothes stood together in tight, frightened groups.

Claire, seeing Jonnie, came to her. "Jonnie, I'm so glad you're back. We need you. I need you."

"Jessica?" Jonnie said, a sense of loss overwhelming her, guilt weighing her down. She had intended to go to Jessica from the boat, but had stayed to make love.

"No, Jonnie, it's Roxanne. Roxanne's dead."

In Jonnie's world of fantasies Roxanne's death had to be the most bizarre. The golden lady lay on the king-size bed, golden eyes wide open—surprised. Death had surprised her. It had come unexpectedly. Her face reflected no agony, no torment—only surprise, which gave her the look of youth regained—and peace.

Peace impossible for her alive. She had been too aware of her loveliness, her wealth, too spoiled by a life made complacent by symbols. Death she had not recognized, except perhaps in the final instant.

Jonnie grieved. She gazed down at the golden woman, who by walking into a room commanded attention. She grieved for the woman who'd had everything to make her happy, yet had not been happy. Jonnie grieved because, despite all, Roxanne had been her friend, and she, Roxanne's. Somehow beneath the cultural veneer superimposed by their nation, they had reached out and touched each other.

Did it matter? To what end? Born-and-bred Americans—under different circumstances, they had been formed by its bigotry, its intolerance, its poverty—a poverty branded so deep into their psyche that upon meeting they immediately recognized themselves in each other.

Jonathan, suddenly an old man, grieved. Red eyes, gray stubble the color of his face. He looked nothing like the Jonathan Anderson to whom she had said good-bye earlier. Death had struck him at the same time as Roxanne—as surely as Dominique's death had been decreed at the moment of André's.

Mr. and Mrs. Anderson: an interdependence that both abused, but from which neither wanted to be free. A rich man, Roxanne had been his most cherished possession. Her pride had been necessary to his lifestyle. Her extravagance had been the other half of his self-indulgence, his narcissism. Her death had left him defenseless, vulnerable. Seeing Jonathan sitting there, an old man, staring down at his shaking hands, she thought of Maxie Gardener, so alive, even as he slept on the deck of his little yacht. The tide was rising. Soon he would awaken, see that she had gone, hoist his sails, Lucknair at his side. They were both so young, so very young. Looking down at Jonathan Anderson, so suddenly old, she had a terrifying need to be with Maxie, with Lucknair.

Yet, her sympathy tied her to Jonathan. It was right that she grieve with him for Roxanne. As she grieved for Jessica, for Dominique, all those of Old Hotel who had met in the path of a storm during their search for outrageous happiness.

"We quarreled," Jonathan kept repeating. "We kept quarreling. She wanted to stay, you see. She threatened to stay without my permission. I could never permit that. She fought me. Never before had she fought so hard. I shouted at her. 'Roxanne,' I shouted. 'Shut your goddamn mouth and let me sleep.'" His spine once so straight, now curved to the back of the chair; his head shook as though from palsy. "We turned from each other—to sleep, I thought. . . . God, if I had known it meant so much, of course I would have allowed her—as long as she damn pleased."

"They did quarrel," one guest agreed. "Made such a racket. We heard him say, 'Shut your goddamn mouth.' We were asleep when we heard him scream. Such a scream—I tell you . . ."

"I touched her," Jonathan explained. "I turned to her, put my arm around her . . ."

Death walked among them—a quiet presence. Servants clustered, silently waiting. And through the silence, Sam's cry.

"In all my life never before have I lived through such a year." He covered his face with his hands. Tears spilled through his fingers. "The storm—that goddamn storm. Dominique, Dominique, Dominique . . ." The rest of them silently bowed their heads.

The sun had already risen high in the sky when the police finally arrived. "A fire at the palace: ammunition exploding," the captain apologized. "Disturbances in the street, road blocks everywhere—everything to hold us up."

They went to look at Roxanne, and the captain said, "Strange that so beautiful, so healthy-looking a woman can just go to bed and die," gazing around like a sleuth in a murder mystery.

Then Jonathan said, "We quarreled," wanting to accept full blame for Roxanne's death, wanting to place himself in the hands of the law. "I upset her and she—just lay down and died." In relief the captain stepped back. "I see. That makes it a matter for your embassy."

"*C'est la femme,*" Cécile whispered to Jonnie.

"*Laquelle?*" Jonnie asked.

"*Dans le jardin.*"

"Oh, Cécile, please. *C'est la vie.* It's life." It was she whom the woman in the garden had accosted. How had Cécile decided that the assault had been on Roxanne? She would never in her life understand the Haitians. She turned from the maid to agree with the captain that it was better out of Haitian hands, the red tape, the formality—and the gossip.

Roxanne's death had devastated them all, paralyzed them. Sam and Claire, who should have been responsible for making arrangements, just stood over Jonathan, as bewildered, as crushed as he.

Jonnie remained in the room after they all left, looking down into Roxanne's golden eyes. How did one prepare a body for death? How did one bury a corpse—one that looked so alive? It offended her to think of Roxanne buried, the end of a life, the end of a saga.

And she was still standing next to the bed, looking down into Roxanne's eyes, when Jessica came into the room with the young doctor from the hospital and with Jean-Pierre. Jessica's head was still bandaged, her face deathly white—more so than Roxanne's. Behind them came Claire, Cécile, and the waiters.

With Jessica's taking over, restraint had lifted, paralysis had gone. Everyone awaited her instructions. Jessica noticed. "Well, I am glad Jean-Pierre showed courage and came to tell me what happened. You must have known of my concern. Yet, only Jean-Pierre showed courage."

Courage? Courage to go to a sick, dying woman and get her

out of bed for support? Courage to bring her to yet another tragedy? All that courage, yet Jean-Pierre refused to even enter the room, refused to look at the body. Terror held him in the doorway, the same terror holding Cécile there—both with faces taut and staring.

The doctor examined Roxanne's eyes; then Jessica closed them. That released Jonnie. She and Claire went down to wait while Jessica and the doctor looked over the body. They all waited, standing around Jonathan in the lounge—a silent, haunted group, giving him, by their presence, support.

Enough had happened on that little island in the last weeks to cause the devil to weep.

"Did your wife suffer from hypertension?" the doctor asked when he came down. Jonathan shook his head. "Was she under any undue pressure—a high-strung woman . . ."

"Rather a controlled sort," Jessica offered.

"I would say she suffered a massive coronary," the doctor said. "That sometimes happens to vacationers. They sometimes lose control. . . ."

"A matter for the embassy," the captain insisted.

"Precisely," Jessica said. "Any autopsy on Roxanne ought to be done in the States." Then, using a high-backed chair as a throne, Jessica proceeded to issue directives that grateful underlings were happy to carry out: Sam and Claire to make arrangements for the casket and transport of the body to the States. Jonnie to alert Roxanne's family. The maids had to pack and assist Jonathan. And waiters and cooks to get to work rejuvenating Old Hotel for business as usual.

By late afternoon the body had been removed. Sam and Claire had accompanied Jonathan to the airport. Then Jessica collapsed and had to be put to bed. Jonnie sat beside her until darkness fell and the drumming began.

Only when the drumming started did Jessica open her eyes.

"Where am I?" she asked.

"Where ridiculous women who will not take care usually end up—in bed." She had planned her reply and used it in relief at Jessica's first sign of life.

Tragedies piling one on the other ought to have become commonplace to her. But when with the removal of Roxanne's body, the mattress on her bed had been turned over and the sheets changed—when Old Hotel, actually did spring back to life as before—Jonnie thought it indecent, unforgivable. Roxanne, Dominique, André, whatever their shortcomings, had been so alive, so wonderful in their flaws. That life should go on as before without them seemed the ultimate betrayal. And so she sat beside Jessica, holding on to her, believing that her presence had to make a difference.

The miracle of Jessica's survival, her strength in leaving her own deathbed and appearing the angel of mercy at Roxanne's had been overwhelming. To see her sit in that chair and give orders, making Roxanne's death acceptable to most, had been awesome. So Jonnie sat with her now. Jessica's tragedy had already occurred—and she had survived.

"That was dumb, you know," Jonnie said. "Leaving a comfortable bed, with that handsome young doctor looking over you, to come back to this bed."

Jessica's face twisted in a grimace. "Come now, Jonnie, I'm too old to be afraid of dying."

"Now she admits it," Jonnie scoffed, pleased to hear the returning strength in Jessica's voice.

"That's more than you have done," Jessica said, trying to affect her vagabond smile. "If I died today I still wouldn't know exactly how old you are."

"That's because you haven't been around lately. I've been shouting my age all over the countryside."

"That I shall never believe," Jessica said, and closed her eyes. She lay perfectly still, and Jonnie waited in a long, long silence. Finally Jessica squinted an eye open. "Not to worry, Jonnie love." She affected a cockney accent. "You have time. I'll be pulling through. . . ."

Again silence stretched between them, broken only by the distant drums, then from outside the chant:

"Volé, Volé . . .
Ou volé tè . . ."

Ahh, tomorrow everything would be as it ever was, except a fat young man and a little boy—how far were they now?—had started out on a journey, with dreams of perhaps one day changing the world.

"Jonnie." Jessica's voice was so low. Jonnie leaned forward to hear. "Jonnie, I heard you. I was going, don't you know. Slipping away. I wanted to. I wanted to get away. There seemed no sense in being around, don't you see. After all, I have been around a long time—sixty-eight years. And it seemed so easy—so easy to just let go.

"Then I heard you—your voice coming to me from somewhere. I stopped and listened—oh yes. I had gone that far. But I stopped to listen. I knew it was you, Jonnie. So I decided to come back. I want you to know that I wouldn't have wanted to make it—nor could I have—if I didn't know that you were waiting on the other side of the veil."

Tears sprang to Jonnie's eyes. Too many, rolling and spilling, so she had to wipe them with her shoulders, with her hand, then unable to control them, she stood up, leaned over, pretending to smooth out Jessica's pillow while reaching for a tissue. A tear fell to Jessica's face.

Jessica opened her eyes and seeing the tears said, "Jonnie Dash, you're a bitch."

"After my years of practice I'd be a mad sister if you hadn't noticed." Jonnie blew her nose. Again a long silence lengthened in the dimly lit room as each grappled with her own thoughts. Then Jessica said, breaking the silence, "He's really a good sort, you know."

"Yes, he is. Claire called him and told him about Roxanne—and what happened to you. He's putting her—Alice—up in a hotel to wait, until he can take you home." Another long silence, then: "Jessica, there's one question I have to ask, and I want an answer. What the hell were you trying to do to that poor little Alice?"

"I don't know. I can't really say." Jessica attempted her familiar smile—her leer? "I think I must have been trying to shake the youth out of her."

"And what about your going to Gilbert Lavel's yacht?"

"Did I? Really? Him, too, I guess. The lot of them who think they can put one over. Don't you see? They believe that gray hair makes a woman weak—gives them a passport to exploit. And you, did I dream you went after Monique?"

"Yeah, trying to pull all her hair out."

"It would only grow back."

Laughter sparked the air between them. Laughter that had to wait for another time when translating tragedies into comedies wouldn't affect Jessica's health. Then Jessica asked, "Jonnie, did you find what you were searching for in Haiti?"

"Yes—and no," Jonnie answered.

"Did you think you might settle here?"

"Did you?" Jonnie countered. All those dreams she had been chasing, all the confusion, the anxiety before she had broken through. And then the storm.

"Oh yes, I wanted to, don't you know. But then my reasons were selfish." Jessica's tired, rasping voice came—a confession. "In my little mind I thought of creating a dynasty, don't you know? My island. A place to do my work, to plan, to dream. Dreams of empire die hard. . . .

"I have never been lovely. But I was wealthy. I had had the ideal love. When my Doctor Faye died, somewhere in my boozed-up mind, I gave birth to that silly dream. But, my dear— no one can make of Haiti their dynasty."

Then she asked, "And you? What will you do now, Jonnie?"

"Work," Jonnie said. "I think now I truly have a masterpiece to create. Then there is the matter of my son. He's dead, you know. His death brought on a long period of confusion for me. I am going back to the States, find out where he's interred, and give him a decent burial.

"Oh, not because I'm superstitious, nothing like that. But, Jessica, he was the wealth of my life. I won't have him flushed down the drain of that city and forgotten, like Boysie and Sylvie.

"The world must know that Emmanuel Dash passed through— well loved, if poorly understood, by his mother. I shall have a monument erected over his remains, a headstone that reads: HERE LIES THE IMMACULATE EMANNUEL—THE INNOCENT AND THE DAMNED— SON OF JONNIE DASH, BLACK AMERICAN ARTIST.

Jonnie looked inside herself, envisioning that picture, and nodded her head, pleased. "Then I shall leave the States and go somewhere—another country, in this hemisphere. Sit down and complete my masterpiece. I have the most incredible idea for a bronze that I shall call *The Storm.*"

"Brazil . . . ," Jessica suggested with a spurt of delight in her voice. "Why not Brazil? A champion idea. Jonnie, what say I go home, get this head cleared up, and after your rites for your boy, we hook up in Brazil?"

"Jessica," Jonnie said, groaning. "Do you think that Brazil can stand the two of us?"

"At any rate, my dear Jonnie, after us Brazil will never be the same."

ⓟ PLUME **DUTTON**

Contemporary Fiction for Your Enjoyment

☐ **ABENG by Michelle Cliff.** This book is a kind of prequel to the author's highly acclaimed novel *No Telephone to Heaven* and is a small masterpiece in its own right. Here Clare Savage is twelve years old, the light-skinned daughter of a middle-class family, growing up in Jamaica among the complex contradictions of class versus color, blood versus history, harsh reality versus delusion. "The beauty and authority of her writing are coupled with profound insight."—Toni Morrison (274834—$10.95)

☐ **ANNIE JOHN by Jamaica Kincaid.** The island of Antigua is a magical place; growing up there should be a sojourn in paradise for young Annie John. But as in the basket of green figs carried on her mother's head, there is a snake hidden somewhere within. "Penetrating, relentless . . . Women especially will learn much about their childhood through this eloquent, profound story."—*San Francisco Chronicle* (263565—$9.95)

☐ **OXHERDING TALE by Charles Johnson.** One night in the antebellum South, a slaveowner and his African-American butler stay up to all hours drinking and playing cards. Finally, too besotted to face their respective wives, they drunkenly decide to switch places in each other's beds. The result is a hilarious imbroglio *and* an offspring. "Memorable . . . a daring, extravagant novel."—*The New Yorker* (275032—$11.95)

☐ **MIDDLE PASSAGE by Charles Johnson. Winner of the National Book Award.** "A story of slavery . . . a tale of travel and tragedy, yearning and history . . . brilliant, riveting."—*San Francisco Chronicle* (266386—$10.95)

☐ **COPPER CROWN by Lane von Herzen.** The story of two young women—one white, one black—sharing a friendship amidst the divisive and violent racism of rural 1913 Texas. "A fresh, poetically evocative and down-to-earth novel."—*The Washington Post* (269164—$10.95)

Prices slightly higher in Canada.

LITERARY FICTION

☐ **UNDER THE FEET OF JESUS by Helena María Viramontes.** This exquisitely sensitive novel has at its center Estrella, a girl about to cross over the perilous border to womanhood. What she knows of life comes from her mother, who has survived abandonment by her husband in a land where she is both an illegal alien and a farmworker. It captures the conflict of cultures, the bitterness of want, the sweetness of love, the power of pride, and the landscape of the human heart.   (939490—$18.95)

☐ **WHEN THE RAINBOW GODDESS WEPT by Cecilia Manguerra Brainard.** Set against the backdrop of the Japanese invasion of the Philippines in 1941, this brilliant novel weaves myth and legend together with the suffering and tragedies of the Filipino people. It shows us the Philippines through an insider's eyes and brings to American audiences an unusual reading experience about a world that is utterly foreign and a child who is touchingly universal.
(938214—$19.95)

☐ **THE UNFASTENED HEART by Lane von Herzen.** Anna de la Senda possesses an extraordinary empathy that draws to her a marvelous collection of lovelorn souls, who form a mischievous chorus and play matchmaker between Anna and a lonely widower. While Anna is rediscovering passion, her daughter Mariela in encountering it for the first time. Anna wishes to protect her from all worldly disappointments, but she cannot. "Evocative . . . a story of love and longing in a near-fantasy setting."—*Boston Globe*   (272904—$10.95)

☐ **ENTERTAINING ANGELS by Marita van der Vyver.** Griet Swart's life is not exactly a fairy tale. Her once marvelous marriage has ended in divorce. She has lost her husband, her home, and her baby in yet another miscarriage. But late one night an angel appears on her doorstep and breaks her spell of sadness with a joyful sexual adventure. A modern-day fairy tale that is outrageously witty, unblushingly candid, and magically moving. "A real rarity . . . wry . . . hard to resist."—*New York Times Book Review*   (273390—$10.95)